Francesca,
Merry Christmas!
Hope you enjoy
the book — a
gift from
your daughter Di.
Best,
Gayle Crosby

THE SEDUCTION
OF THE GREEN VALLEY

Gold, Greed, & Grapes

Gayle Crosby

DEDICATION

THE SEDUCTION OF THE GREEN VALLEY, Gold, Greed & Grapes
is lovingly dedicated to my family; each one a beautiful, vital and central
part of my life.

New York/Baltimore Family
John Hagan Smith
Michael Hagan Smith
Brooke Hagan Smith

Texas Family
Christina Trevino

California Family
Floyd Crosby/McDowell
Lois Crosby
Tom Crosby
Russ Crosby
Don Scheibe

ACKNOWLEGEMENTS

Looking back on my journey from the 'idea' of THE SEDUCTION OF THE GREEN VALLEY, Gold, Greed & Grapes to its 'actualization', I marvel at the love and support given to me by so many in just the right way and at just the right time. The following is a chronology of events and the people to whom much credit is given for making this book a reality. I appreciate each one of you and offer my heartfelt thanks!

The Idea of Writing a Screenplay

Producer Ron Witte, Witte Productions, is responsible for the idea of writing the 'screenplay' based on a story I had in mind about The Green Valley; Redlands, Yucaipa and Oak Glen where we both live. On July 4th, 2017 Ron and I were at a party together and I shared the story with him. He suggested I write a synopsis for a thirteen-episode, made for TV series. I laughed and said, 'yea right!' Ron pursued the idea saying, "it's a great story, and I think you should do it!". While I had written articles for sixteen years, I'd never even considered writing a book, much less a screenplay. "Just do it Gayle", was Ron's final push off the cliff. So, I tried, but not without the aid of a real screen writer, journalist, and dear friend, **Laura Paull.** The result of our collaborative effort was the synopsis for the screenplay, THE SEDUCTION OF THE GREEN VALLEY which received great attention and continues to simmer on the stove.

The Idea of Writing the Book

The idea of writing the book was a natural consequence of writing the screenplay, but as I'd never done it before, I needed encouragement and support from people I respected and trusted. **Don Scheibe,** my 'significant other' and my dear friend **Gerow Smiley,** are both common sense men who will tell you the truth in the kindest way possible. So, with their firm insistence, I jumped off the cliff a second time.

Encouragement Needed to Keep Going

My trusted friend, avid reader, and book club member Mary Mook, was the first to read the manuscript and pronounced it – "Wonderful! A compelling read, a page turner and a roller coaster ride, terror, empathy, unexpected outcomes and more! WOW!" While I had not been hailed as a literary genius, I felt good about my first efforts and thanks to Mary, continued down the path.

Was the Book Any Good?

There was only one person who could answer this question and that was my mother, **Lois Crosby**. Most people can count on family to tell them what they want to hear to spare their feelings, but my mother loves me too much to let me publish a marginal book, much less an awful one. For years she has been my trustworthy article editor, who has no problem wielding a red pencil. I gave her the book and held my breath. A week later, I arrived on her doorstep awaiting her critique. To my great surprise she answered the door sobbing; "Mother, what's wrong"! I cried, thinking something horrible had happened. She had difficulty gaining her composure but finally blurted out, "she died!", referring to a character in the book. I hugged her, there could be no greater compliment from **Lois Crosby**, my truest critic. Her desire to 'want more' and the fact she put her red pencil down 'just to enjoy the book', told me everything I needed to know.

I Forgot You Had to Edit, Again & Again & Again...

Climbing the editing mountain of a nearly three-hundred-page book, when spelling and punctuation are not ones forte, requires a 'Book Coach' who feeds you dark chocolate, fills your wine glass and cooks dinner because the 'author' has a headache. That Book Coach is my dearest Donny

Scheibe. We've known each other since the first grade, where we attended, Yucaipa Elementary School, and remained close friends all through high school and college. After going our separate ways for nearly thirty years, we reconnected again just five years ago. Having Donny's love, continued friendship and endless support, means everything to me!

Characters Came to Life

Alycia Bromar, award winning photographer, artist and my 'sister' friend is not only talented, but one of the most courageous, loyal and dedicated people I know. Alycia is responsible for the brilliant illustrations seen on the cover, and if you love these, wait until you see her entire body of work! I don't know how she does it… melding her mind with mine and seeing the characters as I do. We both know when it's 'perfect', capturing the essence of the person inside. The Hartland Victorian home on the book cover is also her stunning creation offering an ideal setting for the Hart Family Saga to unfold.

Finding Little Jonathan

Ewing Dyerly came to my book booth at the Yucaipa Music & Arts Festival several months ago along with his two sisters and grandmother - another great friend. The sketch of Jonathan as an adult, Alycia had captured perfectly, but Jonathan as a child continued to elude us. When Ewing walked in, I knew immediately I'd found him… 'little Jonathan'. Ewing is a blond, and Jonathan has dark hair, but that was an easy fix. It was the face, the eyes and well…just look at the front cover and you can see why every mother and little girl will fall in love! Sorry Ewing.

Making Me Look Good

I was told over and over again not to publish anything without having it professionally edited.

My BookBaby Editor is on a short list of people who have quite literally saved me from myself.

With total professionalism, deep insight into my characters and showing great care for the story, you, dear Editor, have done what I could not…make it readable.

Holding My Hand Through the Publishing Process

Christina Ramirez, Publishing Specialist at BookBaby is a saint! Who wants to work with a former Disneyland marketing, advertising, corporate sales and public relations person? No one! I'm fun and kind, but details and 'out of the box' requests come with the territory. Christina consistently rose to the task with gracious-professionalism to every request, question, and third and fourth explanations. Christina has made this mysterious and confusing process of book publishing clear, enjoyable and worth doing again and again. "Prepare yourself Christina dear… I'm on chapter five of our second of eight books together; THE INNOCENCE OF THE GREEN VALLEY, Vessels, Virgins & Vines to be published with your aid in early 2019.

"Hello? Christina are you there? Hello? Hello?"

Characters

YUCAIPAT INDIAN
TRIBE 1800's
White Wolf
Adoeete
Nizhoni
Antinanco
Napyshni/Red Eye
Aiyana
Flying Eagle
Honana
Odakota
Hototo
Teetonka
Cha'tiam
Swift Arrow
Sky Wolf
Kitchi

OUTLAWS
Rig
Thornton
Clem

HART FAMILY
JD
John
Katherine
Jonathan
Merritt
Emily
Alexander
Earl
Selma
Victoria
Honey

THOMAS FAMILY
George
Lucy
Georgia
Caroline

EDWARDS FAMILY
Rutherford
Eleanor
Merritt

MORLEY FAMILY
Harold Morley
Jameson Morley

HALL FAMILY
Bella
Amelia
Linda

MEDINA FAMILY
Don Jose
Alberto
Mia
Roberto
Cesar

VEGA FAMILY
Don Carlos
Hector
Isabella
Paolo
Jose

AIRES FAMILY
Landon
Kip

SMILEY FAMILY
Albert
Alfred
Edward

THE BIEL BOYS
Sam
Jeff
Martin
Danny

YUCAIPA FOLK
Dr. Crawley - Doc
Jim Rawley – Sherriff
Watson Hargrove
  – Sherriff

OTHERS
Andrew Townsend – Lawyer
Tess McDowell – Developer
Don- Realtor
Matt – Director of the Library
Kevin – Archivist
Remey – Assistant
Mason, Noah & Alex - 'The Boys'
Mr. Thomas – Vineyard Hand
Maria Luego – Housekeeper/Nanny
Mrs. Duncan – Librarian
Officer McCabe – Policeman
Grant- Mohonk Bellman
Tom- Mohonk General Manager
Maxwell – Hotel Consulting Firm
Jenny – Nurse
Melissa – airline passenger
Connie – Kopper Kettle Kafe
Tammy Grove- Roc n Fondue
Fariad - Artist

Yucaipat Indian Family

White Wolf
&
Sanana

Adoeete
&
Nizhoni

Antinanco
&
Wyanet

Napyshini / Red Eye

Alyana
&
Flying Eagle

Jonathan David
White
(Adopted Son)

The Hart Family

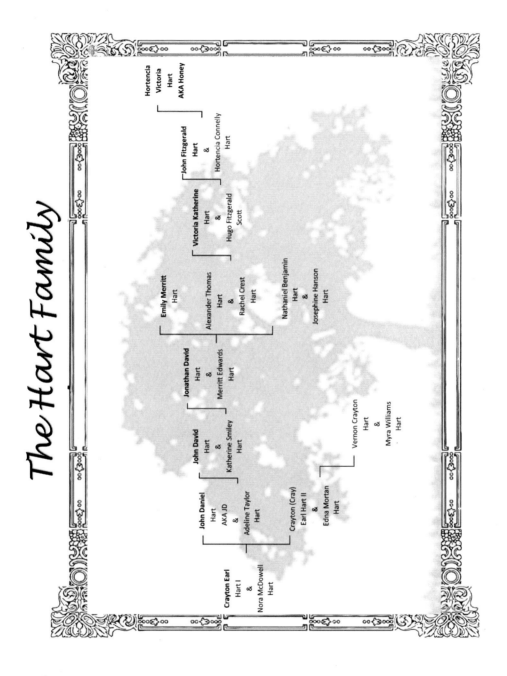

Crayton Earl
Hart I
&
Nora McDowell
Hart

John Daniel
Hart
AKA JD
&
Adeline Taylor
Hart

Crayton (Cray)
Earl Hart II
&
Edna Mortan
Hart

Vernon Crayton
Hart
&
Myra Williams
Hart

John David
Hart
&
Katherine Smiley
Hart

Jonathan David
Hart
&
Merritt Edwards
Hart

Emily Merritt
Hart

Alexander Thomas
Hart
&
Rachel Crest
Hart

Nathaniel Benjamin
Hart
&
Josephine Hanson
Hart

Victoria Katherine
Hart
&
Hugo Fitzgerald
Scott

John Fitzgerald
Hart
&
Hortencia Connelly
Hart

Hortencia
Victoria
Hart
AKA Honey

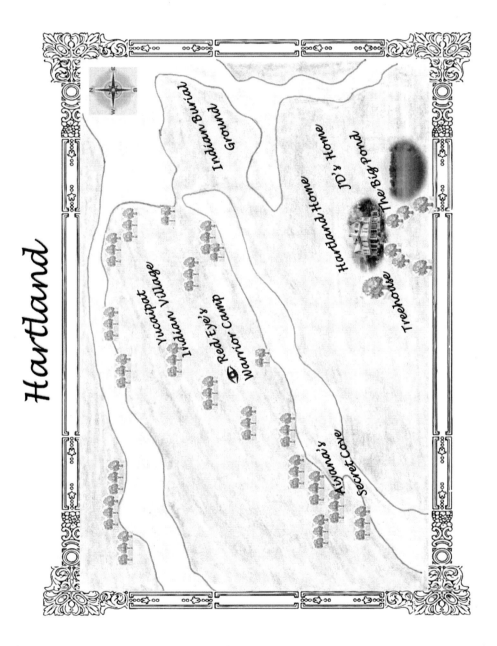

Hartland

Indian Burial Ground

Hartland Home

JD's Home

The Big Pond

Treehouse

Yucaipat Indian Village

Red Eye's Warrior Camp

Auyanai's Secret Cove

TABLE OF CONTENTS

CHAPTER ONE

AN UNCERTAIN FUTURE

New York City, April, 2018

There was no escaping now! The panicked young woman was strapped in her seat aboard a Boeing 747 with a one-way ticket from New York to California. The heat from the tarmac created mirages as the captain gunned the fiery engines into full throttle—the mighty brake alone holding back the powerful force. The crew and passengers all waited in suspense for the tower's signal at which point the jetliner would gather speed and then haul its massive weight into the air and stay there -- hopefully--bolstered by the prayers of its travelers.

Suddenly Honey was overcome with the gravity of the moment. There was no turning back now. Life had decided for her and left no other choice than to step into a world both old and new, known and unknown. Suddenly the aircraft, released from its restraints, let go. The plane flung Honey into the air. Was she being hurtled forward by an unpleasant fate, or propelled into a space made especially for her, carved by simple destiny? *This is meant to be*, she assured herself, fortifying the affirmation with her grandmother's motto. There's no such thing as chance.

Hortencia Victoria Hart, aka Honey, was the twenty-eight-year-old granddaughter of the late Victoria Katherine Hart, a woman of great beauty and wealth. Upon her grandmother's recent death, Honey became the owner of the thousand-acre ancestral estate called Hartland in Yucaipa, California. Its first inhabitants were the ancient Yucaipat Indians followed by the Europeans, Spaniards, and Mexicans, and then immigrants from all over the world. Every day for the past two hundred years, human ideas, thoughts, desires, and actions had molded and shaped the Green Valley and Hartland, the effects of which Honey would be immersed in when she arrived. Her grandmother Victoria had understood that for Honey to understand the present, create a flourishing future for herself and the land, she must unravel the mysteries of the past.

Honey fingered the large pearl, held beautifully by a circle of diamonds and hung on a silver chain around her neck. *Do I*, Honey pondered, *a modern woman educated in the finest schools, well on my way to a fulfilling career in the world of hotel management, really want to step into the past?*

Only time would tell.

CHAPTER TWO

HARTLAND IN
THE BALANCE

New York City, January, 2018

The pearl had been fashioned, admired, bought, given, gifted, and loved. Later it had been protected, stolen, burned, demanded, repaired, and bequeathed. Its beauty and great value the very cause of its long and tumultuous journey. And now it graced the delicate neck of eighty-five-year-old Victoria Katherine Hart who dearly needed the ancestral strength with which it had been imbued.

Victoria absently touched the family heirloom, a sterling silver necklace from which hung a large, rare, natural pearl, nested like a flower in an array of tiny diamond leaves and vines. If the necklace could speak, her tale would reveal many mysteries and the reasons its array of owners found themselves in their circumstances of life. The strong, unbroken chain mirrored the unbroken chain of events—of hopes fulfilled and dreams lost—that was the ongoing saga of the Hart family. Despite joy and tragedy, justice and injustice, genius and ignorance, good intentions made good or gone dangerously awry, the linked chain gave assurance that all had reason, meaning, and purpose. The power of the pearl necklace lay in its experiences while attached, as it were, to Grayson, Katherine, Merritt, Rachel, and Victoria, the succession of women having each imbued the pearl with her own unique strength, courage, and tenacity through the generations. In turn, the pearl served as a storehouse of power in times of trouble as it symbolized the value of the difficulties in life, and of the wisdom hidden in all things.

Today, Victoria was in need. Her large, soft, blue eyes stared out the window of her penthouse apartment, the view presenting an iconic picture of high-rises both new and old, tracing the skyline of Manhattan. Far below, swaths of green trees and foliage embodied the last vestiges of the once-upon-a-time densely forested New York, now contained in the passionately protected and treasured Central Park.

The pale blue of her floor-length, brocade dressing gown suited the Victorian side of her. The modern cut of her pure white hair created a glamorous sweeping effect in contrast to the essence of who she was, which was expressed in her taste of classic clothing and European antiques. Victoria, like her environment, was a mixture of intricate detail and utter simplicity, the marriage of which created an appealing balance. Like her predecessors, who knew their strengths, knew their weaknesses, and protected what was theirs—be it cattle, kids, or kin—Victoria believed every life, bequeathed the honor of living, was meant for doing something purposeful and worthwhile.

"I'll not be a lifeless twig," she announced to the small gray bird who'd landed on the windowsill. "I'll be damned if I allow myself to become old, sick, and die," fumed Victoria, "not when I have a granddaughter to care for, Edward to love, and my philanthropy work!" Victoria was delivering through the bird a message to that menacing new presence, that ghostly hand that had slipped inside her body last week. Its fingers had at first touched her heart, then pressed, grabbed, and finally squeezed so hard she thought the fragile organ would burst.

Lilly, her housekeeper for over twenty-five years, brought in the morning tea along with a package from the Children's Assistance Foundation, mercifully rescuing Victoria from her runaway thoughts. Inside the plain, brown box was a small, silver tray engraved with her name. A token of appreciation for her generous donation. Accompanying the gift was an embossed envelope and card, glued shut. Victoria realized that every task these days took her twice as long, but old age, with its own vital lessons, never promised it would be easy. Finally opened, the handwritten, heartfelt note and sweet pictures of the children softened her shoulders and warmed her to appreciate the unnecessary silver extravagance. In turn, she thanked the divine providence that had enabled her the wealth that she could contribute to assisting those in need. While her father had found success on Wall Street and the import and export trade, it was the success of Hartland in Southern California, and its highly profitable vineyard and wine industry, that had provided the Hart family a foundation for its wealth.

The heroic efforts of her grandfather, Jonathan Hart, in the late 1800s had caused the magnificent flourishing of Hartland. Not only of its wine grapes, but also olives, acorns, berries, sheep and their wool products. Against all odds, Jonathan and his wife Merritt, along with the Europeans, Spaniards, and Indians, had worked tirelessly to create a close-knit community made up of Yucaipa, Oak Glen, and Redlands—the Green Valley, as they lovingly called it. The surrounding mountains created a perfect Mediterranean climate, which allowed the flourishing valley with its wide river and meandering creeks to grow nearly anything and everything. This fertility became the very essence and identity of the place. The bounty of the Green Valley brought visitors from far and wide to enjoy the grapes and wine of Hartland, the apples and pies of Oak Glen, and the oranges and marmalades of Redlands. The Hartland Victorian home, with its beautiful grounds, riding trails, and sunlit ponds, stood at the center of this prosperity, for a time culturally and economically magnificent, welcoming the community for festivals and time-honored events. It was an idyllic era, but it was not to last.

Like most families, the lineage of the Hart family had its share of heroes, workers, drifters, and a few lifeless twigs. Fifty years ago, Hartland had fallen into the hands of drifters, Earl and Selma Hart and their two sullen and lazy daughters. Their lack of hard work and interest in the community and their place in it had been consumed by a greater passion for gambling, drugs, jewelry, expensive cars, and European travel. Their seemingly endless wealth spent at breakneck speed, the legal indiscretions, bad decisions, and neglect of the vineyard and winery business caused great suffering for the people of Yucaipa, as one by one, they lost their jobs and were forced to find work outside the community. The once thriving historic uptown with its hotel, movie theater, restaurants, and booming business dried up for lack of income and workday people. Eventually Earl and Selma died, and the daughters squandered the remaining inheritance. In 2018, news of the For Sale sign at Hartland struck the very heart of the Yucaipa community, and a few brave citizens wanted to do something about it.

Victoria remembered the precise day she'd received a cry for help from the Yucaipa group, The Hartland Foundation. The Yucaipa Valley Historical Society had somehow located her, and sent her this plea:

Dear Mrs. Victoria Hart,

The Hartland Foundation is a group of passionate Yucaipa citizens who care deeply about the thousand acres called Hartland, which has been a vital part of our community since the late 1800s. The property is for sale and in need of investors to aid in bringing about the regeneration of this beautiful and flourishing land, once home to vineyards and the Hartland Winery. The Project will begin by returning to the Yucaipa community the historic 1800s Victorian Mansion at the center of Yucaipa's rich history through a Foundation. Unseen for nearly 100 years, Hartland will now be home to artists, musicians, vineyards and winemakers, farmers, ecologists, botanists, equestrians, hikers, visitors, and agriculture-based businesses, restaurants, nature-based technologies, and a small housing community. She will harvest her bounty of olive groves and replant the giant oak trees with their array of acorn products. Preservation and the reintroduction of native plants, animals, creeks and open space will offer sanctuary for both man and nature, the goal being the reciprocal nour-ishment and growth of all.

In times past the great Yucaipat Indian tribe inhabited Hartland and the surrounding land

and by these same principles, caused it to flourish with an abundance and variety of crops whose verdant expression inspired them to name it Yucaipa, meaning "Green Valley." Building upon these ideals, The Hartland Foundation seeks to take root at Hartland on Oak Glen Road and from there grow, once again embracing Oak Glen and her apples, Redlands and her oranges, historic Uptown Yucaipa and Historic State Street and her mansions in Redlands, inviting visitors to enjoy "One Destination, One Family, One Heart... Many Unique Experiences."

This land, while still for sale, is being vied for by housing developers. We need your help now *to save it and through the heroic and passionate efforts of our Partners, we can plant, nourish, and grow the seed of potential embedded both in the people of the Green Valley and in a place called Hartland to the incalculable benefit of all.*

Sincerely,

The Hartland Foundation

Victoria read the letter three times before she picked up the phone and called her lawyer, Alfred Townsend. Unfortunately, he was on vacation and would not return for three weeks. While disappointed by the delay, Victoria thought the opportunity to keep the land in the family was miraculous. The iron-minded, eighty-five-year-old woman was not about to let Hartland out of her hands, and she would see Alfred Townsend at 10:00 a.m. on February 23rd to make all the arrangements.

"I must call Edward immediately," she said aloud, speed-dialing the familiar number. Edward was eighty-five-year-old Edward Smiley of the

Mohawk Mountain House Resort in New York. Their history began as many years back as Victoria could remember. Her family had summered at Mohawk. As a child of nine, she considered Mohawk hers. But really it was his—Edward Smiley's.

At their first meeting, she discovered he was the ten-year-old heir to Mohawk, and when the discussion of ownership arose, he reasonably and rightfully claimed, "You have to be a Smiley to call it yours." The young and tenderhearted Victoria had cried, the beautiful illusion torn asunder. But Edward, not liking to see the pretty girl cry, magnanimously decided it could be hers too. Her beaming smile and swift kiss on the cheek assured Edward he'd made the right decision, and ever since, the two had been inextricably and permanently bonded.

As children, they were a playfully naughty duo forever pushing the limits, whether on horseback, diving in the Mohawk lake, or terrorizing the kitchen staff in search of cookies baked expressly for the guests. Their teenage years led to more captivating and dangerous explorations of lips, skin, amorous feelings, and blossoming urges. It was then they discovered the magic of Port wine and the delicious effects of silky lips in front of warm fires at the place Victoria called Edward's Castle, the massive structure built on a rocky cliff. The correction was always immediate, however, as Edward dutifully towed the family line, countering, "My dear Victoria, Mohawk is simply a very large mountain house."

Maturity with its appendages of jobs, responsibilities, relationships, and duties, like the tide, could neither keep them together nor keep them apart. Those were difficult times.

Now, occasionally Victoria mused that finally in their old age it would be fun to create mischief and pursue the audacious with no one to tell them "no." But separation, protocol, responsibilities, and the effects time has on the body, made these musings simply a lovely dream.

Victoria smiled, remembering one evening months ago, how Edward had called. He'd asked her to pour a glass of Port and have a drink with him over the phone. It was lovely hearing his voice. After each poured a second small glass, they laughed and reminisced about their times together. At last, Edward sighed, confessing, "Victoria, I'd give anything to just sleep next to you tonight." The sentiment had stayed with her for days, and even now it warmed her heart.

As expected, Edward was thrilled with having Hartland back in proper family hands and he'd pried Victoria with questions, none of which could be answered until her lawyer returned. Nonetheless, Edward made her read the letter twice and then, over a better part of an hour, the two imagined what wonderful things could be done to the land and for the Green Valley.

While the Smiley family had for generations wintered in Redlands, California, just twenty minutes from Hartland, it had been ages since Victoria had been there —been home. She was in her twenties when the heartbreaking news that Hartland had unscrupulously fallen into the hands of her cousins Earl and Selma Hart. Their new ownership shocked and deeply concerned all.

Victoria's parents, Alexander and Rachel Hart succeeded Jonathan and Merritt as owners and lovers of Hartland and the Green Valley. They preserved what their parents had done and added to the magnificence of the place. At the same time, they gave philanthropically to Yucaipa, Oak Glen and Redlands, encouraging other families of wealth to do so as well. But in trying to mend the chasm and bring peace between the two branches of the Hart family, Alexander and Rachel opened themselves and the Green Valley to pillagers. Expecting the best from their cousins, they instead got the worst.

The chasm between the Harts that were flourishers, and the Harts that were pillagers, began in the early 1800s with the marriage of Clayton Hart to Nora McDowell. Nora, a Scotswoman, was a direct descendant of the first King of Scotland, King Fergus, whose wife Elizabeth was the daughter of William the Conqueror. Godfearing people of strength, dignity, a love of family and land, created the essence of who they were. This blood ran with great force in Nora, JD, John, Jonathan, Alexander, Victoria, and Honey Hart, making up the first branch.

Clayton Hart, likewise of Scottish decent, was born of traitors, anxious to take the Fergus throne that did not belong to them. After many tumultuous years of manipulation and intrigue the Harts were finally defeated. They were obliged to return to their place in the order of things as merchants and crafters of garments. The green blood of jealousy, discontent, and false entitlement, flowed with equal strength in the veins of Clayton, Cray, Vernon, Griffin, Neville, Earl and Blakley Hart.

Despite their wealth, Earl and Selma lacked greatly in character. Edward had known them all too well for all too long—especially during the cold months when he escaped the chilling New York winters to enjoy the nearly constant warmth and sunshine of Redlands.

At first the two had cozied up to Edward, the wealth and respected name of the Redlands Smileys with their donation of the magnificent Smiley Library and parklands to the City of Redlands had been useful for the Harts in terms of name-dropping. But Edward's regular visits to the Hartland Estate and his not-so-subtle suggestions to put the declining vineyard and winery in more professional hands had become tiresome to the uninterested and alcohol-prone Earl and Selma. Edward's visits were no longer encouraged. As time went by, he feared picking up the Redlands newspaper, dreading another piece about the deteriorating effects the couple's lack of stewardship was having on Hartland, or a mention of another consequence of their scandalous nature. Their irresponsibility affected the entire Green Valley, and it bothered Edward more than he could say. He'd be glad to see Hartland back in Victoria's trustworthy hands.

The morning of February 23rd found Victoria in Alfred Townsend's law office promptly at 9:55 a.m. "I don't care what it costs, Alfred. I want our land back," said Victoria, handing Townsend a copy of the letter. Marching orders given, she left confident that soon the deed would be in her hands. She'd only been home an hour when the call came.

"Victoria, this is Alfred. I'm sorry to say, I just learned Hartland went under contract last week. A housing developer. They're closing escrow late March."

Victoria was stunned. Hartland *not* being hers had never crossed her mind. "Is there anything we can do, Alfred?" Victoria asked.

"We can put in a backup offer," Alfred replied, "but unless Tess McDowell, the buyer, pulls out before her ninety-day due-diligence period, there's nothing we can do."

Victoria sighed. "Well, then, put in the backup offer, and we'll just have to pray."

Real estate developer Tess McDowell was tough. A woman among men. The profession she'd chosen was a difficult one. A successful developer needed vision, intelligence, courage, and the ability to singlehandedly roll massive boulders up steep mountains. Great effort and patience were essential qualities for any successful developer, and Tess had heaps of both. Beyond that, Tess was special. She rose above her counterparts whose chief aim was return on investment. Instead, her goal was to cultivate the art of a beautiful life. She was a lover of beauty and expressed this love through the art of building homes. The beauty in her homes came from the principle of wholeness. That meant from beginning to end, each facet of the concept, design, construction, and landscaping harmonized with the next and together they made a complete whole. The pattern of the overall design could be seen repeated in even the smallest detail. Owners of her homes couldn't put into words why they were so appealing, but Tess had indeed found the missing key.

Finding buyers for her home developments was never a problem. She would usually sell them all before they were built. Her problem was finding comparably beautiful land. When she learned of the magnificent Hartland up for sale, she immediately put it under contract. Tess barely slept for two nights, her brain whirling with visions of what she could make in such a gorgeous space, enamored with the final picture her mind had painted. It would be a masterpiece!

Tess had not explored the thousand acres on foot or in her all-terrain vehicle yet, but her engineers were there laying out the groundwork. She'd driven past the property plenty of times, and this was the most beautiful land she'd seen in all of San Bernardino County.

Since the news hit the Yucaipa *News Mirror* that Tess McDowell had Hartland under contract, her phone had been ringing off the hook with Yucaipa's version of the disgruntled and outraged folks that every community had . . . before they could see her vision come to life. Once her homes were built, these same people would be begging to buy them. Tess was not without heart or political sense, however, and she knew the old historic house must be preserved. She planned to put its care into a foundation and open it up to the community. But that was where the peace in her soul ended and the inner conflict began.

Tess the businesswoman, pragmatist, wage earner, and Building Industry Award Winner, lined up against Tess the visionary, artist, idealist, and respecter of divine forces greater than her own. The trick was to find the middle ground between the two extremes that comprised Tess McDowell. It was not about one side of herself or the other winning, nor was it about compromise. Rather, she sought whole, unfettered resolution for her inner conflicts, another key principle to her success.

Yucaipa zoning ordinance already allowed the building of one home per acre, and she could—give or take the river and some ravines—probably create eight hundred homes at a minimum. Tess was thrilled the property was on scenic Oak Glen Road where just around the bend lay the charming Village of Oak Glen. It attracted tourists by the thousands during apple season, eager for the quaint authenticity of the countryside orchards.

Tess grew up in Redlands. Since childhood she'd visited Oak Glen every year during apple season. As a kid she'd picked apples, and then ate apple pie and ice cream. There was always a visit to the candy store and the glories of the curio shop where she'd buy something wonderful to add to her Native American collection. Tess and her husband Tom had taken their own kids there, introduced them to the apple farms, helped them press cider the old-fashioned way, and rode on the hay wagons. Her housing development would offer lots of families the ability to live near this special place. Yes, this would be lucrative and popular with the Orange County folks who could afford the million-dollar gated community. Tess prayed it would all come together.

⚬⟋⟍⚬

Victoria continued the weeklong discussion about Hartland with her Maker. The whole thing had vexed her to no end, and she was heartsick about the potential loss. She'd even picked up the phone and called Tess McDowell herself to make a plea. Tess had listened politely, said the house would be put in a foundation for the community, and then ended the conversation with a polite, "But I appreciate your calling, Mrs. Hart." Victoria had hardly hung up the phone when the familiar touch of those dangerous fingers stroked her heart. Fear struck, triggering panic, and the fingers pressed harder until the whole hand grabbed her chest and her body writhed in pain, causing the Hartland Foundation letter to fall from her lap onto the floor. But just as suddenly as the cold, grabbing hand had come, it left.

Shaking, Victoria took the delicately monogrammed hanky from her sleeve, wiped away the tears caused by the excruciating pain, and allowed the chair to support her exhausted body. She was grateful it had not done its worst—this time.

⚬⟋⟍⚬

Tess McDowell hung up the phone, surprised by the call from New York and the woman on the other end. She felt a twinge of guilt that someone in the Hart family wanted to return the place to its former glory, but she could see that her housing development would be glorious too, and with the development's plan, more than just one family could enjoy it.

She'd listened to the folks from The Hartland Foundation and could see their hopes for the place. She decided to incorporate some of their ideas into her plans by calling it The Preserve at Hartland. The marketing campaign would include: "An orange, apple, and oak tree for every home." She would be a shoe-in for the next Building Industry Association Award, of which she held five. The incoming call ringtone interrupted the vision of her cover photo on *Architectural Digest*. A request from her chief engineer to "come to Hartland right away" made the situation sound serious.

An hour later, Tess met up with the engineer and his team, and they drove along the makeshift dirt road called Hart Lane, which meandered through Hartland. On one side of the river lay a vast sea of rotted grape stocks, and on the other side lay golden wheat fields as far as the eye could see. Coyotes, flocks of birds, quail, and even a fox were spotted as they traveled across the land. Though she didn't see any, Tess knew bear and bobcats roamed the higher elevations of the mountains that surrounded them.

Referring to the tract map, Tess saw they were approaching the tip of an elevated ten-acre parcel that looked like an arrowhead, the point created by a fork in the river. When the vehicle came to a stop, she stepped out to see a magnificent view of the Green Valley below. The engineer turned Tess's attention to the unusual rock formation that appeared to create a giant circle around this section of land. "There are gaps now, as you can see," said the engineer, "but at one time, the rocks were connected. The mounds of earth in the center follow other Native American burial grounds I've seen. I think that's what we got on our hands, Tess."

She'd pulled out of a deal in Palm Springs when they came across the same issue. But the Palm Springs property was only fifty acres. With a thousand acres here, she could probably work around it. "Let's see what we've got here," Tess said to one of the engineer's assistants, pointing to the shovel in the truck. "But be careful."

The confirmation of the burial ground and the immediate loss of ten of the best housing sites was quickly confirmed.

Back at her office, Tess was running the figures, calculating the loss of revenue this would cost her when the phone rang.

"Ms. McDowell," came the gentlemanly voice, "this is Edward Smiley."

The name Smiley was well known to her, having grown up in Redlands. The Smiley Library was central to her growing-up years. Over time she'd graduated from the children's library to the adult bookshelves and finally the research wing. It was behind the Smiley Library's brimming bookshelves where her childhood friend Billy Solder had stolen his first kiss. As kids, she and Billy had gotten in trouble several times for climbing on the old bronze statues of Albert and Alfred Smiley, revered benefactors of the library. But who was this Smiley?

"Excuse me," responded Tess, "have we met?"

Edward patiently repeated his name again and added, "of the Mohawk Mountain House in New York, and of course a great-nephew of my uncles Alfred and Albert of the Redlands Smiley Library."

Tess was stunned. "Yes, of course," she said, delighted to learn there was another Smiley she had not yet met. "I've spent many a happy afternoon at your great uncles' library. It's a beautiful building! So how can I help you?"

"Well," began Edward, "I've been associated with the East Coast Hart family for a very long time as well as the West Coast Harts, having myself wintered in Redlands for nearly sixty years. I've been trying to watch out for Hartland as best I could, but when it went to ruin under Earl and Selma Hart, I could do nothing. Victoria Hart, whom I'm very fond of, is the granddaughter of Jonathan Hart, who bought and built the Victorian mansion of Hartland in the late 1800s. Victoria has for decades desperately wanted to return it to its former glory as a vineyard and winery, but Earl and Selma would not hear of selling it, despite their own lack of interest in the place. You know they moved out nearly fifty years ago to live in L.A., and only a skeleton crew of caretakers had managed the place in their absence."

"This is all very interesting, Mr. Smiley," responded Tess. "What is it I can do to help you?"

Edward laughed, admiring her polite encouragement to get straight to the point. "Well, for starters you can back out of your offer and allow the Hart family, under Victoria's care, to reclaim and regenerate it again."

Tess laughed. "Well, Edward, I'd love to, but you see, I can't. I already spoke to Mrs. Victoria Hart on the phone who made the same request. It's not personal, you know. Strictly business. And my business is building beautiful homes on beautiful land."

"I understand," Edward said. "We all have to do what we think is right. I had to try. I appreciate your hearing me out."

Edward hesitated. "Oh, by the way, I have a rare collection of journals written from 1840 to the late 1800s by a woman named Maria Luego who lived at Hartland. They are quite intriguing and a wealth of information. Extremely valuable for someone like yourself, wanting to develop the land. They are historically priceless, so we keep them locked up in the Smiley Library Heritage Room." Edward chuckled. "Our archivist, Kevin, barely allows them to be touched, must less read, but if you're interested, and if you don't mind wearing white gloves, I'll see that he makes them available to you."

Tess was floored. Not had only the old man let her off the hook without a whimper, but he was offering her the one thing she couldn't resist—access to a resource usually kept under lock and key about the land that would soon be hers. "That is very kind of you, Mr. Smiley," Tess said with all sincerity. "I'd consider it an honor."

"I'm very glad to do it," said Edward. "I have your number and will pass it along to Kevin. He can make arrangements as your schedule permits."

Edward hung up the phone and immediately called Smiley Library, explaining to Kevin that only Maria's third journal should be provided to a Ms. Tess McDowell and that he should arrange quickly for her to read it.

That time came much earlier than either had expected as the curious Tess McDowell, seated for the first time in the heritage room, carefully put on the white gloves. Kevin explained, "The author of the journal, Maria

Luego, while a Spaniard by birth, was brought by her father, a Spanish explorer, to San Diego, California in 1840. There was a great deal of scandal surrounding her arrival in the company of a young handsome priest, Father Nicholas Casablanca, but you can read the story in the second journal another time."

Anxious to get started, Tess thanked Kevin, put on her red rimmed glasses, and moved the leather-bound book in front of her.

My Life At Hartland

Maria Luego

Monday, June 1880 - *Emilita is five today. From her Papa she received a brand-new pair of boots. Señora Merritt and I can't get them off the child—she insists on sleeping with both the new boots and the kitten. She is muy bonita, the same, like Señora Merritt—both so beautiful.*

Wednesday, June 1880 - *I hear Emilita singing on the front porch and talking to the kitten about her new boots. Que adorable, she's so proud. Oh – she is a naughty one, pulling Señor Thomas from his winery duties to rock her on the porch. How she loves rocking and hearing the man sing. Oh my! His voice! I need to go down to the kitchen, pies must be baked.*

Amelia, she disgusts me! The way she holds the baby Alexander, as if she were his mother. I don't trust that woman who has lust in her heart for Señor Jonathan! It is not proper. Dismiss her now Señora Merritt - you must! The activities of Amelia are troubling, she is not right in her mind. If Señora dismissed her the first day, there would be no statue of La Muerta, there would be no suffering - ah me - the Señora's blind! El Dios give me strength!

Friday, June 1880 –*Emilita fell – pobrecita –my poor little girl. Her boots are scuffed. Until I polish them, her tears won't stop. The cake is almost done – she can help me ice it.*

Monday, June 1880 - *Holy Mother it is not possible! These words are so difficult to write – my hand is shaking. Gone, how can she be? How did this happen? Our little Emilita - drowned! In the big pond, Señor Jonathan found only one little boot, the other must still be in there. How can any of us go on? The school bell ringing and ringing, I can never forget. It called to all to hurry to come search for the child. And they came but all the time she was in the pond. No one could see her. Ah me! Poor Señor Jonathan! Poor Señora Merritt – poor all! So hard is life to bear. So very difficult. Holy Father, why our sweet Emilita, why?*

The archivist observed as Tess, lost in the reading, absently wiped a tear away, soiling the gloved hand. Kevin knew the words by heart, having read them a hundred times and likewise had shed his own tears. He wouldn't reproach the woman.

Monday, July 1880 – *Señora Merritt – her soul be blessed, is trying to be brave. The funeral was upsetting. The box that held our little niña so small. Señor Jonathan carved it himself. Carried it himself followed by Señora Merritt and baby Alexander to the grave site. I am sick. My heart, it will never mend.*

Friday, July 1880 - *It is the fourth day Señora Merritt is again in bed. Getting worse. Dr. Crawley doesn't know why. Wish we knew. I light candles and pray every day.*

Monday, July 1880 – *I'm very worried now. It is Amelia who puts Dr. Crawley's medicine in her tea. It is not working.*

Mother Mary – hear my prayer, do good by our beautiful Señora Merritt. We cannot lose her! We cannot lose her too!

Tuesday, July 1880 *– Two times the tea-cups crashed! Both times I saw it - no one touched them! They flew off the table by the bed as Señora Merritt reached to drink her tea. Señora, her mother, Amelia, and I, we all saw it! Nothing like this have I ever seen. She refused any more tea – but Amelia kept begging. Then I saw Emilita. As God is my witness the child was there, then disappeared. Then shards of broken china flew through the air and landed in the face of Amelia– her neck and arms too. I knew then what she had done.*

Wednesday, August 1880 *– Finally Señora Merritt is out of bed and walking in the gardens.*

Enthralled, Tess continued to read for another hour until her phone vibrated and several texts pinged, demanding her attention. *Sorry boss need to meet you at Hartland ASAP.*

As Tess drove up Hart Lane to the Victorian house, she saw the place differently. As she walked toward the porch she could visualize the little girl with her new boots talking to the kitten. Suddenly Tess could feel the sorrow and intrigue that had been part of this house, and she'd only read one of the thirteen journals. She'd go back to read more. She must.

"Boss," said the chief engineer, "The Hartland Foundation has been here again. They asked me to give you their impact report. They claim regenerating the land into a vineyard, winery, and festival grounds along with agri-tourism will bring economic development to the region. And one of our men found something in the big pond."

"Hey, Sam!" yelled the engineer. "Bring that thing over here."

Sam handed Tess the remnants of a small child's boot. "Found it over there in the big pond. Course there's no water in it now. Kicked over a couple of old boards, and there it was."

While obviously old, Sam wanted to get a closer feel for the boot's true age. He'd found pictures on Google that dated it to the late 1800s. Showing Tess the images, he said, "The Yucaipa Historical Society will love this! I wonder how it got in the pond."

⌒◠

Victoria endured a sleepless night. The hot tea Lilly brought at dawn tasted wonderful. She was not herself this morning. Her thoughts returned again and again to Hartland and then floated randomly here and there to images of the past, her childhood, her times with Edward, and the day Hortencia Victoria Hart, or Honey as they called her, came to live with her. On that fateful day, her granddaughter was only a child. Now she was twenty-eight, an Independent Hotel Consultant, and a woman of great creativity and professionalism. Victoria had hoped Honey would take over Hartland one day and bring it to life again. But there was no hope of that now.

Hearing the distinct footsteps of quickly approaching high-heeled shoes, Victoria forced herself to straighten and put on a practiced smile, awaiting the entrance of Honey, who had been walking into this very room every morning since she was ten.

Victoria's mind flashed back, remembering that day as though it were yesterday, when the beautiful and exceptionally bright child walked into the room. Then, little Honey's eyes were swollen and blank after a sorrowful and restless night. That morning so long ago, she had just stood there, bereft and silent, in her pink silk nightgown and robe. The antique china doll, only allowed to come out and play when she spent the night at Nanny's, was perilously close to the floor as Honey held it in a daze by its tiny, fragile boot.

Victoria recalled the sound of the uniformed officer's voice who had come the day before, bringing the news that would forever change their lives.

"Ms. Hart, the New York Police Department is very sorry for your loss," repeating verbatim from the Police Officer's Manual. Seeing the excruciating pain in the woman's eyes, Officer McCabe let down his guard and, defying protocol, added the more tender words, "It's really tough losing both your son and daughter-in-law, ma'am. This kind of crash landing is so rare. I heard everyone was caught unaware by the torrent of rain and the sudden winds . . . and the fire . . . well, that was just—"

"Fire?" Victoria moaned the question.

McCabe chastised himself. "Well, ma'am," he continued as per the manual, "the airlines will be contacting you with details and instructions in terms of . . . uh . . . connecting with . . . uh . . . your loved ones."

He shifted uncomfortably as he remembered the little girl who opened the door. "I understand there's a child involved. A daughter. Was that her? The one you sent to her room?"

Victoria tried to speak the word *yes*, but all she could do was point in the direction of the bedrooms and nod. McCabe lowered his head, hating this part of his job. As no words were left to say, he simply stood, bowed stiffly, and saw himself out.

Victoria's mind returned once again to little Honey in her pink nightgown and robe, feeling the discomfort, the awkwardness, and, worse, the necessity of their new relationship. Victoria could hear the thoughts the child's eyes conveyed. *You're not supposed to replace my Mama and Daddy, and this isn't supposed to be my home.*

What had been a fun and a wonderful place to visit—Nanny's marvelous New York apartment—and the adventure of sleeping in the giant bed and playing with daddy's old toys were now gone. "I was only supposed to stay a few days while Mommy and Daddy went to Chicago for a wedding. This isn't meant to be my home. My home is in Millbrook, New York, with my parents, my friends, Elm Drive Elementary School, the corner drugstore where we get ice cream on Sunday afternoons, and the Thorne Building lawn where every year the circus comes to town."

As the present moment flooded back, Victoria regained her composure just in time as the woman, no longer a child, walked into the room. With her, Honey carried a suitcase in one hand, a purse thrown over her shoulder, and a beautiful smile, happy to see her grandmother. Victoria returned the smile and said, "There you are, darling girl. All packed and ready for business at Mohawk Resort, I see. You look lovely! Tell old Edward Smiley to take good care of my granddaughter, and to stop filling her head with stories about ghosts and gold in California."

Honey laughed, put down her suitcase, and bent to give her grandmother a kiss. "Better come and tell him yourself, Nanny."

"He'd like that, I'm sure!" Victoria winked. "Man always had an eye for a beautiful woman and a fine Port." Pointing to the credenza where a twenty-year-old bottle of vintage Port sat tied up in a red bow, Victoria said, "Take this to him, will you, my dear? And with my love."

Standing in the doorway with her apron on, Lilly interrupted, "Excuse me, Ms. Victoria, can I borrow Ms. Honey for a moment in the kitchen? I want to trade her a nice to-go cup of coffee for her trip in exchange for opening this stubborn jar of applesauce."

Honey laughed. "One lid remover coming up. Let me just put this Port in my handbag, and I'll be right with you."

Alone again, unexpectedly Victoria's mind drew down words she'd always felt but never said aloud, and even now, they streamed only as silent thoughts. *You've always been remarkable, darling girl. Not because of your inherited outward beauty and grace, but because you're alive, filled with a passion for life. You truly care for me and those in your world. Rare is this genuine kindness, which makes you all the dearer to me. Even as a child you were remarkable, enduring with courage the death of your parents and allowing a new life with me, here in New York, to take hold and bloom. Now look at you! All dressed in winter white and that long, beautiful, chestnut hair! That men have always flocked to you is understandable, of course. By twenty-eight I had hoped you'd have found 'the one.'*

Oh, never mind, she thought, *women today get married much later than we did. She was wise to wait.* Victoria closed her eyes; a prophetic picture arose in her mind. There was Honey arm-in-arm with a handsome man. Together they stood on the porch of Hartland; she and her lands resplendent.

"Honey!" she called, anxious for the child to return from her errand of mercy in the kitchen.

The applesauce finally free and the hot coffee creamed and sugared, Lilly turned to look into Honey's eyes. "I'm worried about her," the housekeeper simply stated. "She's not herself. More faraway than usual, and I've caught her grimacing and wiping away tears. I mentioned calling Dr. Krantz, just for an annual checkup, but she won't see him."

Honey gave Lilly a hug. "You take such good care of her. Thank you, Lilly." Honey thought a moment, then said, "Let's do this . . . you make an appointment with Dr. Krantz for Thursday, and I'll take her myself. I'll only be at Mohawk for three days."

Both feeling guilty for the conspiracy despite its honorable intentions, they glanced at the doorway half expecting Victoria to be standing there with her hands on her hips demanding to know what they were up to.

"I'd better get back before we're found out," teased Honey. Lilly nodded knowingly.

Returning to the room, Honey bent down, searching her grandmother's eyes. Not assured, she stroked her cheek. She reached for one of the many antique footstools, finely needlepointed and laying around like lap dogs waiting to be of comfort. From a foot above the floor, Honey looked up at Victoria, taking her hands. Both knew the familiar dance was about to begin. Who led depended on who was worried about whom. This time Honey led, stepping forward with a question about how Victoria was feeling. Victoria stepped back with a casual reply, the gist of which was always something to do about the fiddle being fit. She'd mastered the art of the twirl, saying, "I'm fine, dear." Convincing Honey of her good health was only a matter of ignoring her concerns and ending the dance when she could, sending her beloved granddaughter out the door, to where her real and meaningful life, outside their apartment, was calling for her.

Honey gave up, but only because the doorman buzzed to announce her car and driver were ready. The dance over, Victoria gave Honey her marching orders.

"Have your phone? Have your handbag? Have a hanky? Okay, girl, forward march."

Honey automatically responded with her familiar half salute, which stopped midway, her fingers instead touching her lips and forming a kiss that she blew in the general direction of her grandmother. With that, Honey lifted the handle to her rolling suitcase, grabbed her purse, received the coffee from Lilly's outstretched hand, and gently closed the front door behind her. A wave of tenderness for the woman who was everything to her threatened to bring tears as Honey boarded the elevator, selecting the lobby floor. She'd be home in a few days' time and take Victoria Katherine Hart in tow. She simply would allow nothing to happen to her. Honey sighed as several worried tears escaped.

The doorman earned his keep, having signaled with a flourish the driver of the black sedan into position under the portico. With polish and skill, he opened the apartment building door, the car door, and assisted Ms. Hart in becoming comfortably seated with her luggage secured. When all met with his approval, he closed the door, signaling the driver to move along. There was an art to being a good doorman and fulfilling his goal of making the residents of their home, Par Le Parc, feel valuable and cared for. It was his service to the world, and he liked it. Yes, he liked it very much!

❧

At Mohawk, Grant, the blond-haired, blue-eyed, well-muscled bell-man who worked out every day but Sunday and greatly appreciated (at nineteen years of age) older women, commanded the bell desk. Having heard *she* was coming, Grant was the first to welcome Honey, rushing to open her car door, take her bags, and escort her inside.

"Happy to have you back, Ms. Honey," he blushed.

"Happy to be back, Grant. Hey, you owe me a dollar! My Tommy Boy and the Patriots won

the Super Bowl again!"

"Hoped you'd forgotten, Ms. Honey."

"Well, I didn't," said Honey. "Pay up, sport!"

Grant happily forfeited his dollar, honored she included him in the fun. Walking through the hotel lobby, Honey silently collected one-dollar bills from the Guest Services Manager, the Front Desk Manager, the Lobby Maintenance Staff, and the General Manager, Tom.

"No, Honey," said a playfully disgruntled Tom, "I refuse to wear the Patriots jersey you sent as a reminder that my Pittsburg Steelers lost!"

Honey leaned over, kissed his cheek, and whispered sanctimoniously, "Poor sport!"

Edward Smiley, son of Francis Smiley, grandson of David Smiley who owned, ran, and was the benevolent but ruling force behind the magnificent Mohawk Mountain House Resort in upstate New York, was waiting patiently in a corner for his turn to be with Honey. Seeing this, and not wanting to keep the master of the castle waiting any longer, Tom directed Honey's gaze to Edward. "Seems someone's eager to see you!"

At eighty-five, Edward was a tall, handsome man. They didn't make men more refined, intelligent, and kind. He had a way about him nearly everyone found comforting, and his quick wit entertained those fortunate to pass their time with the older gentleman. Honey smiled broadly and waved, the bottle of Port heavy in her handbag. His relationship with her grandmother was somewhat of a mystery. Often, she'd tried to wriggle it out of them, but like two conspirators, they just laughed and kept the secret to themselves. But the fondness in their eyes and caring words for one another evidenced a great and mutual love and respect.

Edward walked slowly over, offering a small bow and his arm to Honey. "Shall we, my dear?"

Honey took his arm. "Victoria would not be happy to see us together. You know how jealous she gets," Honey warned teasingly.

Edward shook his head, blushing. "Dear sweet woman—your grand-mother. I hope there's a bottle of Port in your bag from her. She always knew the way to this old heart."

"There sure is," assured Honey, pulling out one of the finest Ports Edward had seen. "And she sends it with her love."

"Now this one's a beauty!" exclaimed Edward. "The only thing better would be to have Victoria here to share it with me." Edward shook his head, dearly wishing.

Arms locked, Honey and Edward strolled off on their ritual tour and talk. The first stop always the enormous framed map of Southern California, or the area called The Green Valley, made up of Redlands, Yucaipa, and Oak Glen. The immensity of the map covered an entire wall. It was impossible to miss. It was here Honey had received, over the years, her history lessons, tales of her ancestors who had migrated from Europe to the East Coast, on to Texas, then California, and back to the East Coast again in the form of Victoria and Honey. They were called history lessons, but in truth, they were much more. Edward's incredible mind was simultaneously philosophic, scientific, and artistic. It could leap to the ideal, abstract, and mystical as easily as it could to the practical and mundane. His studies knew no bounds, nor did his passion for the subjects he devoted himself to. He was very wise. Honey learned, much later in life, that the stories he told, while mostly historically correct, were also creative masterpieces, mental reflections of life in story form, meant to lovingly and unobtrusively aid his dearest Honey on her own journey through life. After all, she was the adopted granddaughter of his heart, and these bits of wisdom were his most precious heirlooms.

Honey's lessons began in earnest at the age of twenty. Graduating first in her class from Cornell with a degree in Hotel Management, Honey had landed her first job with the prestigious Maxwell Commons, Independent Hotel Consulting Firm in New York. Her choice of profession had been a natural one, given that she'd been practically raised at Mohawk and Victoria had seen to it that she'd traveled extensively, staying in many kinds of hotels around the world. Underneath that worldly interest in hospitality, however, lay a little girl's desire to create a home big and beautiful and warm enough for everyone to call home.

Upon arriving for her first day of work in a brand-new navy business suit, Honey had been met by Mr. Common's Executive Secretary, Jacqueline Dubois, who greeted her, showed Honey to her small office, and then explained that once she got settled, Mr. Commons would see her.

There was nothing really to settle except for her coat and purse and to pull out the only thing she had in her new leather briefcase—a blank pad of paper and a sterling silver pen with her initials on it, a graduation gift from Edward. She took a moment to gaze around her very own office, soaking in the feeling of finally being an adult, with responsibilities of her own. While she was grateful and appreciative of her generous grandmother and Edward, who were so much a part of her life, finally the apron strings had been cut. There would be nothing more handed to her on a silver platter, or helpful contacts to give her a leg up. No, from this day forward, Honey would pull herself up by her own bootstraps and take the falls and lessons that came with them. With that, Honey straightened her jacket, took a deep breath, and marched with confidence to her first meeting with the legend that was Maxwell Commons.

Jacqueline announced Honey, ushered her into the enormous office, smiled knowingly, and gently closed the door behind her.

"Welcome, my dear, to your first day at Maxwell Common," greeted the groomed, manly perfumed, silver-haired Maxwell.

"Thank you, sir," responded Honey, "delighted to be here, and thank you for the opportunity."

"Well, we're delighted to have you. Adding a member to our team who has graduated first in her class at such a university is certainly a feather in our cap," replied Maxwell. "Now, in terms of your first assignment, there's already a request for your consulting services."

"Really?" Honey said, thrilled by the compliment, but surprised that any independent hotel would know she existed, much less request her consulting services.

"Yes!" Maxwell said. "Edward Smiley with Mohawk Mountain House Resort has a project he would like your help with. It will likely take a month, and he is, of course, willing to pay our required fee."

Honey's face fell, and she could feel the heat of embarrassment and frustration rising in her cheeks. This was a betrayal in the highest degree of her intelligence and her ability to be her own woman in the workforce without help. How could Edward and her grandmother do this to her!

Maxwell, expecting the reaction and keeping the smile to himself, was impressed with the pride, determination, and need for the young woman to make her own way. Now he would see if she could control her emotions and be the professional he demanded of his staff. "Mohawk," he continued, "is a very important client to this firm, and we have worked hard to maintain that level of trust over the many years in our work as consultants."

Honey took a deep breath, coaching herself not to blow it. "I'm happy to be of service wherever our firm is needed."

Bulls-eye! cheered Maxwell inwardly, *a brilliant response and now I'll let the poor girl off the hook—almost.*

"Unfortunately," said Maxwell, "the Mohawk account, due to the complexity of the project, will be best served by putting one of our senior consultants on the project. I hope you understand."

Honey's smile briefly lit up the room, then appropriately dimmed to take on a more professional demeanor.

"You will, however, be on assignment for six months assisting one of our smaller clients at the Del Marco Hotel on Fifth Street. We are confident this assignment will provide you with the necessary experience to move on to other clients, perhaps even Mohawk one day."

Honey had gone off happily to the Del Marco Hotel, an unsuspecting sheep headed for Deana Del Marco's consultant slaughterhouse.

Honey, like every new Maxwell Common's consultant before her, was broken in by having been given the same tortuous assignment all were made to endure. For the next six months, Honey tried to please the merciless, irrational, and eccentric hotel owner, Deana Del Marco. The firm figured if a new hire could survive the Del Marco Hotel gauntlet, she could consult for anyone.

The day Edward rescued Honey, allowing her to gain the real experience she needed as a professional, was the day Honey's mind was open to learn. So, on that day, he'd readied his first lesson, had the kitchen prepare an English Tea for Honey's meeting with the General Manager, after which, he'd hurl her to the Mohawk marketing wolves.

"This is a map of San Bernardino County, located between Los Angeles and Palm Springs in Southern California," Edward said to the twenty-year-old Honey, whose rapt attention he now had. Pointing to the bold name *Redlands*, Edward explained, "Here, for generations, my family wintered in the Jewel of the Inland Empire, the City of Redlands. It was and still is a paradise for all of us. There's nothing like the warmth, the miles of orange trees, the smell of their fragrant blossoms, the elegant Victorian mansions and perfectly maintained cottages that line the streets. Main Street is utterly delightful, at once prestigious and homey, and the whole place as the newspaper once wrote, and I quote, is 'a charming, small community of cultured and gentrified people.' That my great-grandfather and uncles contributed to its value is a pleasure for me to recount. They cared deeply for this idyllic place and its people, so much so that Alfred Smiley borrowed money to purchase thirty acres of Redlands land, later known as Smiley Heights, in order to provide a park and the space to build the much-needed public library, which promptly was given to the city. The architecture is Moorish you know. Quite amazing. The library contains a marvelous collection of books, some very rare, in which I've spent many delightful winter months exploring. My ancestors were generous people and truly self-sacrificing, caring deeply for the community that was their second home. They encouraged many of their wealthy East Coast friends to join them in creating a warm winter paradise."

For the next ten years Edward had magically woven together for Honey the tales of the positive and constructive, as well as the negative and destructive, relationships among the many cultures and races that made up The Green Valley. Honey knew the legends surrounding the peaceful and loving Yucaipat Indians led by Chiefs White Wolf, Adoeete, and Aiyana, and the chaos and tragedy the vicious Red Eye endlessly conjured. She'd heard the story of her great-great-grandfather Jonathan Hart and how, as a child, he'd come to live among the Indians. Many of Edward's stories seemed far-fetched, like the one about the teenaged Maria Luego, daughter of a Spanish explorer, hidden away at one of the missions. He told of her affair with a priest and later, after killing the padre, fleeing for her life into the safety of Hartland and JD Hart. Stories of gold and greed, the larger-than-life characters of arrogant Harold Morley and his son Jameson and the disreputable Lester Kane must have a foundation in truth as Honey knew Edward Smiley may embellish to make a point, but he would never intentionally lie.

Honey gathered all he said into her mind and heart, holding them like precious gems. The absence of her parents, and with her grandmother being the only blood relative she knew, left an empty space. She had a deep need to belong to a close community, a family with roots and a history, and Edward filled that need with his stories.

As a young woman, she was grateful. As a twenty-eight year old, Honey was even more so. The morning's history lesson centered on the historical character of a woman named Amelia Hall, the housekeeper at Hartland in the late 1800s. The woman was obsessed with Honey's great-great-grandfather Jonathan David Hart, from the moment she met him. In her attempt to seduce him, ancient Mexican dark arts were used to marry the already married man. These stories could be corroborated. In the heritage room at the Smiley Library, Edward had locked in his safe Maria

Luego's thirteen journals, which included rare firsthand accounts of life at Hartland and of her perceptions of Amelia and the rest of the community. The journals also contained facts that directly related to Honey and her future, which Edward would reveal when the time was right.

"History doesn't have to go far to repeat itself," Edward remarked.

"What do you mean?" asked Honey.

"You may be surprised to learn that Amelia's great-great-grand-daughter Linda Hall is currently a librarian at Smiley Library. She recently sent me copies of Amelia's letters and diaries. Interesting how very differently Maria and Amelia viewed the same events and situations. One of them is most certainly lying or seeing it askew."

Honey and Edward made their way to an already prepared English tea, now part of the tradition for years. Edward seated Honey, then himself. Three cups were poured as Tom, the General Manager, joined them. Stirring in two lumps of sugar, Tom said, "Shall we get down to business?"

"Yes, indeed," answered Honey, taking a sip of tea before launching into her research. "The yearly occupancy report you sent, Tom, shows it's been an excellent year. According to the National Tourism Board, we can expect another one next year."

Tom welcomed the good news with a toast of teacups.

Honey continued, "I do think, however, we have some work to do on the off-season months, and I have a few ideas I wanted to run by you." Honey's phone vibrated, but she ignored it.

Tom added, "My new Sales Manager, Laura, would appreciate spending some time with you to discuss a couple of good ideas she has."

"Sure enough," Honey replied, her phone vibrating again and then again, the caller not giving up.

"Please excuse me, gentlemen," apologized Honey. "Seems somewhere the sky is falling and Chicken Little is in a panic." The two men chuckled, and stretched their legs while Honey turned to answer the offensive intruder. *This better be important.*

"Hello, this is Honey." The color drained from her face as she listened to the voice on the other end. Edward and Tom could see a touch of fear in her eyes, which brimmed with tears. "Can you tell me which hospital you've taken her to?"

Edward started in his chair.

"Yes, yes, of course I'll be there as soon as possible. I'm about two hours away. Please let her know, I'm on my way now . . . thank you."

Honey looked at Edward who already knew. His trembling hand endeavored to put down the teacup in order to stand, but Honey prevented him from getting up. She knelt down beside his chair and took his hands. "Victoria's been taken to the hospital," Honey said. She looked in his eyes and offered no reassuring smile. "The doctors are worried."

Edward seemed to brace himself for the awfulness of the news, painfully allowing it to wash over him. Soon after, he squeezed Honey's hand. He nodded, and a thin smile offered hope. His command to "Go now, dear" permitted Honey to leave him.

Tom had immediately gone into action, asking Grant to call up the Mohawk car, seeing to her luggage himself, and asking Guest Services to supply Honey with two bottles of cold water. With one sweet hug from Edward and a bear hug from Tom, Honey was swept into the car, which Steve drove swiftly to New York Presbyterian Hospital.

Quietly, Honey approached the nurses' station. "I'm Honey Hart, here to see my grandmother Victoria Hart, please."

Kind eyes looked up at Honey. The nurse stood quickly up from her chair, and moved from behind the counter. Touching Honey's back, she softly said, "This way. I'll take you to her."

Victoria had a private room. The circular curtain hung from the ceiling around the bed, and oxygen could be heard pumping. Honey stepped hesitantly into the room and gently drew back the curtain, peeking in. Her grandmother looked like a different person, hooked up to machines, her eyes closed, her breathing slight, her hair matted against her head. Honey was shocked at the change from this morning. Sitting on the bedside chair, Honey gently took her hand, stroking it lightly.

"Nanny, I'm here."

Victoria was unresponsive. The head nurse Jenny walked in, put her hand on Honey's shoulder, and asked, "May I see you out in the hall?"

Honey's brow furrowed slightly, but she nodded and followed the nurse. Alone now, Jenny said, "May I ask what is your relationship to the patient?"

"I'm her granddaughter, Honey."

"I see. Is there anyone else joining you?"

"No," said Honey, "Edward's at Mohawk, and really, it's just the three of us."

"I see," the nurse repeated. "Well, this will be difficult to hear, but Victoria has had a massive heart attack. We've done all we can for her. She's comfortable, and not in any pain. I'm sorry to say it's just a matter of time now."

As Honey heard the words and comprehended their meaning, she felt a primal agony rise inside, but then her mind did a most inexplicable thing; it stopped time and, along with it, her emotions. Honey stood for an instant in a silent, timeless space. She stood again with her ten-year-old self receiving the news of her parents' deaths. In that space apart from the laws of time, Honey watched as over the years the little girl she once was healed, created a new life with Nanny, and became genuinely happy. And she saw that Edward's lessons had permeated her mind, providing the solace of an existence aligned with something more powerful and perfecting, a meaning in which death was a willing and necessary player.

The thought never occurred to her that she would be here again, facing the death of another person she loved. It felt oddly familiar, and having gone through it before, she knew she could and would face it with a greater maturity. Bitter, despondent, heart-wrenching loss was no longer an unknown quantity. It was something she had experienced, survived, and despite it, thrived.

Time resumed to its present power, as did the agony of loss, but a new strength had been born. Honey knew it would see her through. She must have walked with the nurse back into the room, since surprisingly Honey stood next to Victoria's bed as the nurse was saying, "Let's see if we can get her to open her eyes. Victoria? Victoria? Victoria? Your granddaughter is here. Your granddaughter Honey is here to see you."

At first Victoria didn't respond, but slowly her eyes opened into the barest of slits.

"Honey?" Victoria answered, her eyes welling up.

"Nanny? I'm here," soothed Honey, tears escaping.

Victoria gathered herself to respond with a quiet command. "None of your worrying, child. I'm fit as a fiddle."

Honey nodded, unable to speak. Victoria's words sounded foolish but held a force beyond the film of appearances. Although Victoria was in a hospital and not likely to get out, she exuded a strength of presence fully alive and well.

Victoria said, "Well, I'll be damned! Victoria Katherine Hart is dying."

Honey stroked her hair as the two women together accepted the heartbreaking reality. She frowned. "Damn it, Honey, I thought I had more time to prepare you. To tell you about the miraculous news about Hartland."

"Don't worry about that now," Honey soothed.

"She called," Victoria continued, "Tess McDowell called. It's ours, Honey. Hartland is ours now." It was difficult for Victoria to keep her eyes open, and something was tugging at her soul to let go. Her mouth was feeling very dry. What she wouldn't give for a cool sip of water.

"Ask Edward," she said, licking her papery lips delicately. "He'll tell you everything. Mr. Townsend, the lawyer, will provide you with all the papers."

"There's no need to worry about anything, Nanny," assured Honey. "I'll take care of everything."

"My dream for you has always been Hartland." Victoria urged, "It needs a woman of your great talents. Promise me you'll take good care of her. Promise me!"

Honey nodded. At this moment she'd promise the woman who'd saved her life and loved her beyond all reason, anything.

Victoria smiled. "Good girl, now I can rest, now I can be at peace." Victoria sighed deeply, the worried lines in her face softening. "It's a miracle," she breathed softly, "it's all simply a miracle." There was a long silence, then Victoria said softly, "I love you, darling girl. Tell Edward I've always loved him too."

"I love you too, dearest Nanny," said Honey, tears streaming down her face. With that final exchange, peace and serenity followed as Victoria gave herself over to a new adventure.

An hour later, Jenny's voice broke the long silence, as she called time of death. For some time, Honey could not bear to leave, but Jenny was kind, helping the parting. "When you're ready," she said softly, "the jewelry she was wearing is in security. You can pick it up there. Handing her the clear plastic bag with all her grandmother's effects, Jenny offered genuine consolation. "This is never easy, dear."

Victoria's pearl necklace had shared the space with a trove of other jewelry locked in the hospital vault for safekeeping. Now free and ready to be passed down, the pearl felt at home around the neck of the next deserving woman. Honey Hart walked out of the hospital doors and into the waiting black sedan. "She's gone, Steve," Honey sighed. "Will you take me home, please?"

⚬⚬⚬

Edward had come immediately to New York City to be with Honey, and he intended to stay if she wanted his company or at least until everything was settled. He didn't want to be a burden, but he knew she needed his moral support, and he could use hers too. Fortunately, Lilly would be there to care for them both, precisely what the housekeeper required to keep her own grief at bay.

Tonight, Alfred Townsend was coming to the apartment for dinner and to discuss Hartland. While he waited for their guest, Edward poured himself a glass of Port, remembering the morning before Victoria died. She'd called him with the amazing news that Tess McDowell had relinquished her claims on Hartland and it was now hers. Together they had cooked up a plan to surprise Honey that night at Mohawk with a champagne dinner. Victoria would have her driver take her up, and she and Edward could spend a few quiet days together at the Mountain House while Honey worked. That would give them a chance to fill her with grand ideas about Hartland. They agreed not to push, too hard. Edward could still hear Victoria's lovely laughter as they hung up the phone.

Like clockwork, Alfred had arrived, dinner had been served, and Edward was pouring the drinks as the tiny group prepared to discuss matters of life and death. Lilly came into the room, apologizing for the interruption. A certified letter had been delivered late that afternoon and she had forgotten to pass it along. Honey thanked Lilly, absently putting it aside for the moment, while she gathered herself for the long and difficult evening ahead.

Townsend read the will. Honey discovered her grandmother was far wealthier than she imagined, and the fifty-three million was now all in her name along with Victoria's jewelry and whatever household contents she wanted. Edward received her fine collection of Port, the portrait of Victoria he had commissioned when she was twenty, and funding for a new one-acre Victorian rose garden to be created at Mohawk in silent memory of their love. Edward could not have been more touched, allowing the stinging tears to flow, but fighting back the sob that threatened to overwhelm him.

The general matters concluded, Townsend carefully broached the unsettling topic of Hartland. Fortunately for the lawyer, Edward had the night before, over a glass of sherry and a warm fire, shared the story with Honey. He'd explained the series of events that brought Hartland into the forefront of Victoria's life again. A series of events that now landed squarely on Honey's shoulders. "You think about it, dear," counseled Edward. "It was Victoria's dream, to be sure, but you have your own dreams and plans, and you must be true to your heart."

Honey had appreciated the wise words and the time he'd given her to think.

"So, my grandmother signed the Purchase Agreement?" Honey asked.

"Yes," replied Alfred, "but since she has passed away, the contract is now null and void. If you still want Hartland, we must begin again with you as the signee. If that's the case, I suggest we work on the arrangements tomorrow. It's a hot commodity."

Once again Edward bought her time. "Why don't Honey and I talk more about it tonight? I'll be frank with her about what she'll be getting into if she agrees to pursue this project, and then she can give you her decision tomorrow."

"If that works for you, Honey, it works for me," Alfred said. Turning his attention to the unopened certified letter, Alfred added, "We'd better see what's inside this one, just in case it's something I need to handle."

Honey nodded, opening the letter and scanning its contents. She laid the letter down, put her head in her hands, and softly began to cry.

"May I?" Edward asked, motioning to the letter. Honey nodded as Edward read it, then handed it to Alfred whose eyes grew wide. It was the last thing any of them expected. Alfred believed in the law of cause and effect, in the idea of justice; which may or may not be meted out in this lifetime, but eventually would find its target. He believed in love and hard work and in doing the right thing. He believed in Honey, and he believed there was no such thing as chance. There was a reason and purpose for everything, even in this. Alfred read aloud: "We regret to inform you, the current owners of the building Par Le Parc, have sold the property to a Saudi family who intends to refurbish the entire complex for their private use. Current tenants will be given adequate time to find other accommodations."

$$\sim\!\!\!\sim$$

Travel ready, Honey sat in her grandmother's chair, the only item in the otherwise vacant apartment. In a few minutes, Mrs. Alcott who lived next door would happily claim it. The remainder of Victoria and Honey's possessions, accumulated together over the years, had been taken to storage awaiting the arduous trek to its unfamiliar home in California. Honey's suitcases were lined up neatly at the front door. An airline ticket in one hand and the apartment keys in the other, Honey felt a hundred emotions at once. "My dear sweet Nanny," she said aloud, "what am I going to do without you!"

Memorizing the room for the last time, Honey walked to the large doorway into the dining room, its wide threshold surrounded by beautiful, white, carved wood. Incongruous was Honey's growth chart, which Victoria marked with, of all things, a black pen, the loving sign of a deeply devoted grandmother. Honey touched the succession of feet and inches as memories of her life here became etched in her mind. Honey picked up her purse, walked to the entry door, turned, and looked at the solitary chair, clearly seeing her grandmother and hearing the familiar voice, "Have your ticket? Have your handbag? Have a hanky? Okay, girl, forward march."

Honey began the salute, blew a kiss, then quietly closed and locked the door.

CHAPTER THREE

LOVE IS IN THE AIR

New York, JFK Airport, April 2018

Honey's flight was bound for San Francisco International to pick up passengers before it reached its final destination, the Ontario International Airport, in California.

In San Francisco, waiting to board at Gate 26, was thirty-two-year-old Landon Aires, the youngest CEO of the Aires chain of California hotels, twenty-eight in all. Generally indifferent to his striking good looks and intelligent blue eyes, having more important things to think about, Landon used the time to make several business calls. The hotel business was not easy, rather like managing a small city under one roof. Landon was not only capable of managing complex organizations, but he was a natural leader.

The management of the many Aires cities, with all their different personalities and moving parts, both challenged and energized him. Growing up in the Aires family meant growing up in and around hotels. There wasn't a corner Landon didn't know, or a job he hadn't tried at some time in his life, and that intimate and personal understanding had created his unique business philosophy and management style. It was simply this: The highest form of giving was in service to another person. Therefore, every hotel job, without exception, was valuable. Every person who held a job in the Aires community could find in the work a cause for dignity, self-worth, and respect. The degree of dignity, self-worth, and respect was determined by the degree in which each employee truly cared: cared for their guests, the hotel, their co-workers, and themselves.

Landon genuinely cared and rewarded caring, and his hotels were places of refuge for both employees and guests alike. To others in the hotel industry, Landon's success was a mystery. Most hotel corporations cared only about the bottom line, which necessitated cutting corners and ruling employees through fear. Landon had spent some time in the employ of other hotel firms as a younger man, learning firsthand the destructive nature of that business philosophy. "No!" he'd concluded. "I won't live in fear, nor will my employees. To foster fear and greed in a place of hospitality, is to incite discomfort and disturbance in all who spend time there, including guests."

Landon's phone rang just as the announcement that first-class passengers and families with small children could now board.

"Hey, Kip. How's my little Sis?"

"Great, big brother, just making the marketing rounds in our Northern California hotels. What are you doing?" asked Kip.

"I'm escaping," replied Landon, "to that ranch I just bought in Yucaipa."

"It's about time you had a place to crash. Mom worries you're working too hard."

"I love the work," responded Landon. "Just need to find a balance. La Bonita will help with that. Got a couple of horses, some peacocks, and a wine cellar whenever you care to join me."

"Peacocks aren't my thing, brother dear," said Kip, "but I'll take you up on a wine and cheese trail ride."

"Deal!" Landon said.

"Deal!" Kip replied.

"Hey, do me a favor, will you, Kip?" asked Landon. "Take my place at that horrible fundraising dinner the Morleys are having in San Francisco."

"That's a huge favor, Mr. Aires," replied Kip, "but for a piece of apple pie and ice cream up in Oak Glen, I'll do it."

"Thanks, Kip. I owe you one. We're boarding. Gotta run. Hey, don't terrify that new Paso Robles Marketing Director. Give him a few days before you run him over. See ya, Freight Train. Love you!"

"Love you too, Landon," said Kip.

Landon entered the plane, found a window seat, and settled in for the quick forty-five-minute flight. The plane took off, leveled out, and permission was granted to use electronic devices. Landon took advantage of the time to return the slew of emails he'd received that morning. Honey continued to rest, eyes closed, in the seat directly behind him.

The pilot informed the passengers they'd be beginning their descent to Ontario in about twenty minutes, producing a low groan from Honey, worry taking hold of her stomach. "Only twenty minutes left," she said aloud, visualizing the fiery crash landing her parents had experienced.

"I beg your pardon, what did you say?" asked the woman next to her. Melissa, a slightly plump, Italian woman, magazine aficionado and fabulous cook, was eager for the plane to land. A new grandbaby waited for her kisses at the other end.

Embarrassed, Honey laughed. "Just talking to myself. Not that crazy about flying."

"Me, neither!" said the friendly woman. "Hi, I'm Melissa." Empathizing with Honey, she said, "I'm distracting myself with a vodka tonic—and *him*," holding up the cover of the *Inland Empire Magazine* featuring Landon Aires.

"Wow," replied Honey, focusing in on the man's striking blue eyes and warm smile.

"Says here," Melissa continued, "that he's the youngest CEO ever of the California Aires Hotel Chain, twenty-eight in all." Honey leaned in. Melissa satisfied their curiosity by reading aloud, "While Landon's passion for the hotel industry, the Aires family, and their legacy is unquestionably his first love, there are times, Landon confesses, that he requires solitude and silence. 'The practice of just listening is something I value, which necessitates time alone,' says Landon. 'I've just purchased La Bonita, in Yucaipa, for that very reason.'"

"Yucaipa?" exclaimed Honey. "How amazing! That's where my new home is." She leaned over to get a better look at the photo of the Redlands Aires Hotel and the handsome man standing in front of it. "Hey, I'm staying at that guy's hotel for a couple of weeks."

Melissa slid into her sultry voice, "Well, lucky you! Chances of meeting *him* there are only one in twenty-eight. I'd buy a lotto ticket."

"I'll feel lucky when all 700,000 pounds of this barreling plane is on the ground," said Honey, her stomach feeling worse. "I'm always terrified the brakes won't work," she confessed.

"They will," Melissa assured her. "Don't worry, dear."

"Can't help it," Honey admitted. "My parents died in a crash."

Melissa took Honey's hand just as the plane landed hard with a heavy thud, the screaming and screeching of landing wheels throwing Honey into an instant panic. Instinct shoved reason out of the way, forcing Honey to use the seat in front of her as a brake pedal. She stomped on the brake, aka seat, crushing it down with all her might, but to no avail! The plane was not stopping! Imagining her parents beside her, Honey had no choice but to stop the plane, so she slammed her feet violently into the seat! It worked! It worked! Thank God!

The plane slowed down and finally came to a halt. Honey heard the glorious sound of a hundred seatbelts unbuckling in unison, which meant they were all alive. Reality regained its foothold in her mind, and Honey went limp, exhausted.

Landon was mad! He wasn't upset with the kid who'd continued to slam his feet into his seat, but at the parents who allowed it. He was a stickler for politeness, and it galled him when irresponsible parents permitted their children to behave so disrespectfully. Landon stood, his glaring eyes expecting to find the impossible parents and errant child, but instead fell upon the most beautiful and elegant woman he had ever encountered—and he'd encountered many.

Looking up, Honey saw the glaring man. "I'm so sorry!" she pleaded. "I was so afraid the plane wouldn't stop."

Landon replied, "My seat was your brake?"

Honey nodded, feeling guilty. Landon could see the woman was genuinely embarrassed, and so, tempering the moment with humor, he said, "Miss, you realize I'll be carrying these shoe marks in my back for the rest of my life?" They both stared at Honey's high-end, high-heeled shoes and laughed.

Melissa looked at Landon, looked down at the magazine, looked up at Landon, and grinned with recognition. Handing the magazine to Honey, she said, "Girl, you better keep this!" Honey absently took the magazine, more interested in making amends for her humiliating deed.

"I'm so sorry!" Honey apologized again, feeling horrible.

Landon could see that beyond her beauty, she was a genuine wreck, and he forgave her immediately. "I'll forgive you," he said, making light of the incident, "if you promise never to sit behind me again."

"Promise!" assured Honey.

As the passengers gathered in the aisles to retrieve their luggage from the overhead compartments, Honey struggled to take out her carry-on. Landon rescued her from her efforts, teasing, "This thing weighs a ton."

Honey laughed. "I never travel without my bricks. Never know when you have to build something."

Landon laughed. "Looks like you have your hands full with that coat and purse of yours as well as your bag of bricks. How about I help you to baggage claim?"

"That would be very kind of you . . . especially given . . . well, you know," Honey said.

Following the signs toward baggage claim while carrying Honey's Stella McCartney coat, Landon asked, "You live here or just visiting?"

"Well," laughed Honey, "I suppose I'm a visitor who's come to live here. I'm really an East Coast girl from New York, but circumstances have brought me to California. I just bought some property and will see what I can do with it. How about you?"

"Well," said Landon, "my headquarters have been in San Francisco, but like you, I've just bought some property and now this will be my permanent home. I'm looking forward to the change." The escalator ride brought them to the end of their journey together. Handing her coat over, Landon said, "Looks like you, your East Coast gear, and your bricks have made it safe and sound, and I see my driver waiting for me."

Likewise, a taxi driver had written the name Hart on a sign as Honey waved to him in acknowledgement. The man waved back, assuming his responsibility for getting Honey and her luggage safely to the Aires Hotel.

Honey reached out her hand to Landon. "Again, really sorry for the shoe marks on your back," she blushed.

"No problem," said Landon, hesitating as if ready to ask her something . . . maybe for her phone number . . . but the taxi driver swooped Honey away, intent on identifying her luggage among those on the now moving baggage carousel.

"See ya!" called Honey.

"Yah, see ya," replied Landon, and the two reluctantly moved in opposite directions past the carousel.

Intuition is a sudden flash of knowing. This kind of knowing had hap-pened four times in Landon's life. The first being on 9/11. As he watched the World Trade Center come down, he'd known he would be a pilot in the Air Force as a response to the attack. The second was the day he laid eyes on Maggie. He'd known she would be his wife. The third was at his desk in the

Aires Hotel Corporate Office as he was routinely signing checks. He'd known the moment Maggie and the baby had been killed. And today, at the Ontario International Airport, as he stepped away from the beautiful woman he'd only just met, he'd known he couldn't lose her.

Now in the Aires Hotel car, slowly pulling away from the curb, Landon could see the woman being escorted by the taxi driver with a luggage cart nearby. The swirl of suitcases on the carousel passed by the pair, and Landon watched the taxi driver gingerly pick up a matching suitcase to the brick carrier he'd recently helped retrieve from the overhead compartments. The last he saw of her, the woman was smiling appreciatively to the burly, graying taxi driver, and then he lost sight of them both as his own car drove quickly forward to merge with the crowded multiple lanes of the arrivals roadway.

Landon's driver, Jake, a steady man who had known Landon for years, was simultaneously asking about his flight and pulling into the traffic along with the other cars entering the one-way circle. Jake was taking Landon away from her.

"Excuse me, Jake," interrupted Landon. "I need to go back inside the terminal."

"We'll have to go around the circle, Mr. Aires."

"I understand, Jake," said Landon, a seriousness in his voice. "Can you hurry, please?"

Jake stepped on the gas, going much faster than the posted speed limit. Landon felt the familiar jolt of adrenaline, fearing he wouldn't make it back before she left. Finally pulling up to the doors, Landon jumped out and ran inside. He looked for her, but she wasn't there. He went back outside, ran along the sidewalk, searching for her inside the cars. When the last cab had pulled away with an elderly couple inside, he had to accept she was gone. Landon feared this moment would haunt him for a very long time, perhaps the rest of his life.

As the taxi cab drove around the traffic circle heading out of the air-port and toward the hotel, an exhausted Honey leaned her head back and closed her eyes. The hours of travel, the stress of flying, her panic and embarrassment and the reality that now she was truly alone, caused tears to prick her eyes. There was another emotion too, there, deep inside her – another loss of something that might have been, but now was gone. It was the man. There was something familiar about him, but it was more than that, he made her laugh and he made her feel safe. But her mind was so weary it was impossible to think clearly.

Men had come and gone in her life. She wanted to find 'him', had always been open and hopeful, but it was never very long before the need to be true to herself, overcame the need not to hurt the guy. So finally, after a long string of dates, several months-long relationships and two pre-mature marriage proposals, Honey had - well - not given up exactly, but simply stopped trying.

Looking out the taxi window, the brown smudge of the looming mountains that surrounded what she assumed was the Green Valley Edward had talked so much about, seemed dull and uninviting next to the lush green of the familiar East Coast. The pain behind her eyes that brought unwanted tears echoed the pain in her heart that whispered, "Nanny, I'm lost and alone."

$$\sim\!\!\circ$$

Two cars simultaneously arrived at the entrance to the Aires Hotel. Landon watched as the driver of the second car opened the back door, revealing two very long legs attached to a familiar pair of high-heeled shoes. His heart sighed as his lips smiled. Taking the taxi driver's place, Landon extended his hand to help the woman from the car. Honey looked up, dropped the magazine that had remained clutched in her hand since Melissa had put it there, and suddenly realized why he seemed so familiar. Landon looked at the magazine cover, laughed, and said, "Hello, Ms. . . . ?"

"Hart," she said. "Hortencia Victoria Hart, but people just call me Honey."

"Hello, Honey, I'm Landon Aires. Welcome to the Aires Hotel."

CHAPTER FOUR

HOME

oney awoke the next morning, knowing this day would write the first paragraph in another chapter of her life. She could allow it to write itself and remain an outside observer, or she could take hold of the pen and have a part in its creation. "Life consists of necessary opposites," Edward had said, "that which you can control and that which you can't. The trick is to reconcile them."

Well, she couldn't control her grandmother's passing away, the Saudi's purchase of her apartment home, or even the fact that Hartland had been Victoria's dream. But she was in control when she made the conscious and deliberate decision to buy Hartland, and now she would start with an open mind. Nanny always said, "There's no such thing as chance." Honey smiled, thinking of Landon.

A knock on her door disrupted her daydream. Honey looked around for a clock wondering, *What time is it, anyway?* The green iridescent numbers said 9:15 a.m., and she counted on her fingers, 10:15 a.m., 11:15 a.m., 12:15 p.m. New York time. She had slept till noon!

Honey opened the door to a uniformed woman holding a tray of hot tea, an assortment of dainty baked goods, a single red rose, and a note card.

"This is a miracle," Honey said to the grinning woman, "and you must be an angel. Or a

mind reader!"

The woman placed the tray on the table, correcting, "Mr. Aires read your mind."

So, it is from Landon. Honey smiled. *How thoughtful!*

"Anything I can do for you, Ms.?"

"No thank you," replied Honey. "This is just perfect."

From the selection of teas, Honey chose English breakfast, from the selection of sugars, raw brown, and from the selection of delicate crumpets, the icing drizzled cinnamon cake with the glazed pecan on top. She opened the white, monogrammed card embossed with the name L.J. Aires, which asked a simple question written with a man's firm hand in bold ink: *Dinner tonight at 7:00 p.m.?* It was simply signed *Landon.*

Pressed and dressed in her New York casual clothes, including match-ing navy-blue slacks and jacket with a crisp, white-collared blouse, beneath which lay the pearl necklace, Honey headed for the front desk to drop off her response to Landon's note and retrieve the keys to the rental car she arranged to be waiting for her at the hotel. Honey turned heads wherever she went. Her long, chestnut hair with its soft, natural curl was striking. So too was her lovely face, which needed little makeup. Honey felt better with a bit of mascara, blush, and lipstick to match, but after a quick application and a once-over in front of the mirror, she rarely gave her appearance another thought.

Today she was excited to see what California was all about. She wondered if what she would see would live up to Edward's descriptions of the place. In any case, she would finally meet the historic home called Hartland. Her home.

Driving was not her favorite activity. Though she had taken driving lessons, she never needed to drive while living in Manhattan. But this was not New York City, so she must get used to driving herself around.

Cautiously she drove to the real estate office in Redlands to pick up the keys to Hartland from her Realtor, Don.

◦────◦

Don had scheduled a meeting with his buyer, Landon Aires, to pick up the keys for La Bonita at 1:30 p.m. He'd also told his new client, Honey Hart, that she could stop by any time she pleased to pick up her keys for Hartland, knowing she'd had a long flight from New York.

In the glass-walled conference room, Landon was signing final documents as Don's attention turned toward the stunning woman inquiring at the front desk. He could only assume that she was Honey Hart, having previously communicated solely via the internet and phone.

"Wow!" Don said, taken aback.

Landon looked up. "Tell me about it," Landon said, realizing with gratitude that destiny had no intention of letting her out of his sight. "Your client too?" asked Landon.

"Yes, she just purchased the old Hartland Estate. Here to pick up the keys," Don explained.

"Might want to welcome her, Don," Landon suggested, bringing him back to earth.

Gathering himself, Don walked over to greet Honey as Landon followed behind. "So glad to finally meet in person. How was your trip, Honey?"

Landon and Honey looked at one another and laughed.

"You two know each other?" Don asked, puzzled.

Landon nonchalantly said, "Let's just say she put the brakes on me a couple of times."

Honey rolled her eyes. Don, perplexed by their surprising connection, inquired again, "So you two really know each other?"

"This makes three times we've met," offered Honey.

"Wow," Don replied, "so you know . . . the two of you will be neighbors!"

"What?" The word echoed from Honey to Landon and then off the walls.

"Yes," continued Don, "Landon here has purchased La Bonita, which overlooks your Hartland property, Honey. Perhaps a bit too far in terms of neighbors borrowing sugar, but Landon can certainly see you clearly through a high-powered telescope."

"That's not comforting, Don," Honey laughed.

"Perhaps you're right," apologized Don. "Nonetheless, on the North Bench of Yucaipa, you're considered neighbors. If you'll excuse me, I'll get your paperwork and keys."

"Thanks for the tea this morning. Very thoughtful of you," blushed Honey after Don made his exit.

"Thanks for agreeing to dinner," Landon replied, touching the pocket of his white shirt, which held her note accepting his invitation.

"Want to follow me in your car to Yucaipa?" Landon offered. "I can go with you if you like to Hartland, then head on to my place."

"I'd be most grateful for you to lead the way," Honey replied, "but I think perhaps Hartland and I need to meet alone first. I've been hearing about the property and its history for many years and—"

"What you're trying to say," Landon interrupted, "is that I'd be a distraction."

Honey laughed.

"Don't worry, Honey," Landon soothed. "I got it. Got a little private introducing to do myself at La Bonita. The ranch came with peacocks, about six, and you know how fussy female peacocks are about meeting a male for the first time."

Honey's eyes playfully scolded Landon for his teasing.

"Hey, what's this?" Don interrupted. "You've only been neighbors for a few minutes, and it's already the Hatfields and McCoys?"

Simultaneously Landon and Honey pointed an accusing finger at one another.

"It was his fault."

"It was her fault."

Don took the bait and chastised, "I don't care whose fault it is. Now take your keys and try to get along."

In the parking lot Honey typed the address into her GPS and studied the map. "Looks like you continue straight on Bryant Street, and I take a left onto Oak Glen Road. Why don't I follow you until we reach that point?" she suggested.

"Okay," said Landon, "but no tailgating." Honey rolled her eyes. "Meet you in the lobby at 7:00 p.m. then?"

"Sounds good," answered Honey, her face lighting up.

"Okay, then," Landon said in a mockingly serious tone, "let's see what we've gotten ourselves into."

Of great interest to Honey were her new surroundings, and she paid attention to everything as she slowly drove. The land became more rural the closer they came to the junction of Bryant and Oak Glen, where the two waved goodbye. Honey suddenly felt alone again but decided not to indulge the emotion, turning her attention instead to the grocery store on her right. "Stater Brothers," she read aloud. "Serving the Yucaipa Community since 1936." This is where she could return to shop and fill her pantry in the coming weeks—good to know. She noted, too, with comfort, a fire station, and appreciated the drugstore across the street, which, she laughed, would be convenient should she require large quantities of valium if the whole project blew up in her face. Modest to upscale homes lined Oak Glen Road where a giant wooden sign cut into the shape of a bright red apple pointed the way to Scenic Oak Glen.

The ordinary and expected sights were suddenly overshadowed by the divine magnificence of the San Gorgonio Mountains rising out of golden wheat fields rolling out resplendent in front of her. Honey gasped. The palette of colors created by the native chaparral whose flora and fauna, like strokes of a dozen brushes each dipped in hues of greens, then browns, tans, and deep maroons, declared its own raw beauty. Honey's eyes traveled upward from the foothills to the next natural transition where higher elevations produced sweeping striations of rock, marking the tectonic plates where, long ago, the San Andreas fault had moved. Above that point, modest mountains delivered only thin offerings of sage, oak, and pine, but with delight Honey saw how they gave way to an ever-increasing density of rich browns and greens, where forests of rocks and forests of trees intermingled. Billowing white clouds formed a ring around what could be seen of the great San Gorgonio Mountain, veiling all but her highest peak, crowned today with snow. To Honey, the mountain, like Mount Olympus, felt sacred, watchful, and unceasingly protective of Yucaipa and her Hartland home below.

Edward had masterfully painted the picture before her, and Honey's rapport with the mountain was instantaneous. Nearly passing the entrance, Honey, enamored with the view, applied the brakes, stopping beside a strongly built but faded wooden sign whose chipped black lettering said Hartland. Underneath was the discolored symbolic crest of their Scottish lineage. *Home*, she thought. *My home. Not one of many in a towering New York high-rise, but one, single home where I belong.*

Two large rock columns created the entry through which she drove, the paved driveway lined with massive oak trees on either side, their limbs meeting in the middle as if holding on to one another's branches. A white fence in need of paint and repair, bordered either side as well. Honey gasped at the sight of the beautiful Hartland home. She had seen old photographs, but they didn't do the architecture justice.

The introduction of *mistress* and *home* had finally come. The three-story Victorian welcomed Honey. Immediately she felt a connection, almost as if the house was a living being, with a mind, heart, and will of her own. Honey had never experienced such a phenomenon. It seemed the house was wordlessly speaking to her, apologizing to her new mistress for the overgrown lawn and gardens full of weeds. Honey gazed across the expanse of green grass, imagining past rambunctious games of croquet, sweethearts on picnics, and the antics of children and pets. She could visualize too white wicker furniture and several rocking chairs on the invitingly large porch, which wrapped around the whole of the house. The Victorian and all its exquisite wood carvings were white, while the gabled roof was a soft gray blue. Hartland may have been considered a modest mansion relative to the grandeur of the Redlands' mansions known as Kimberly, Morley, and Edwards, but Honey would have chosen her anyway above the rest. She was the epitome of warmth and dignity—a grand lady in her time, in the rural setting of Yucaipa in the late 1800s.

Honey was unaware of the little girl peeking out at her from the living room window. The child, intelligent beyond her years, decided, *Why, if the lady wore Mama's blue gingham dress and ruffled bonnet, and carried a basket with fresh picked berries, she could be Mama!* But, just because she was five didn't mean she didn't know Mama was in heaven, same as she knew the lady was someone else. Still and all, she sensed the familiarity in quality and character of the lady walking up to the front door.

Although the house was empty of furniture, Honey felt it was alive with something, some energy perhaps from the lives who had lived there and left behind their mark. But there was something else.

Closing the front door behind her and setting her purse down, Honey observed the living room in front of her. She was standing in a rectangular room whose length could hold two seating areas, or perhaps a combination elegant dining room and living room. A large, river rock fireplace to the right with a carved, wooden mantel would be ideal for both fancy dinners and cozy evenings. High ceilings, hardwood floors, and wide crown moldings would fit beautifully with the antique furniture she and her grandmother had collected over the years. Crossing the living room, Honey entered the formal dining room with its own fireplace and large built-in china cupboard. There were drawers for linens and heavy wooden shelves for good dishes. She loved it.

"Wow," said Honey, moving into the spacious farm kitchen. She could already smell the hot coffee, country breakfast of eggs, bacon, potatoes, and biscuits one would cook up and serve to hungry field-hands at a long kitchen table. Spacious and bright, the lovingly worn wood told of countless meals served to family and friends, the heart of the home. To Honey's great delight, a large oval sunroom, accessed through glass double doors next to the kitchen, looked like it was

ready for a garden party, a fancy tea, or a long summer's nap on the window seats. She would live in this room!

There was a large bedroom downstairs and next to it a library with a cozy stone fireplace and more window seats. The floor-to-ceiling bookshelves would do nicely for all her books, and there was even a ladder with which to retrieve the volumes at the top.

The staircase now beckoned Honey. She climbed five steps to a landing, and then the remaining stairs brought her to a wide hallway on the second floor. To the right was a lovely bedroom with high ceilings, wood floors, and its adjoining bathroom. Interestingly, there were three bedrooms with inside connecting doors. Honey wondered if the outer two were for children and the middle room was for the nanny. It would make sense. A roomy bedroom and sitting room completed the second floor, above which was a gabled roof providing space for an attic. A small set of stairs led to the third floor with two more rooms and a bathroom, likely used at one time for household staff.

It was a solid home, well built in every way, and Honey felt its strength and security even in the carved newel posts, rounded mahogany railings, and hand-turned spindles that embellished the stairs. She walked slowly down the staircase and sat on the landing, which gave her time to catch her breath and think. Absently Honey fingered the pearl necklace as she took in her surroundings. An odd white statue of a woman on the mantel of the fireplace seemed out of place, especially since the house was otherwise entirely empty.

From behind the curtain, the little girl's eyes widened, wondering what the pretty woman was doing wearing Mama's pearl necklace.

The outside grounds had yet to be explored, and after resting for a moment, Honey pressed on. The child followed. She remained inside but continued to watch through the kitchen door window. Standing on the back porch, Honey looked out over the sprawling backyard bordered by an elegant semi-circle of cherry trees, perhaps forty in all. The picture it would paint at cherry blossom time would be incredible. From there, winding paths took her through overgrown secret gardens, and then the land gave way to groves of olive trees, acorn-laden oaks, and apple trees.

Beyond that lay a vast wasteland of rotting grapevines as far as the eye could see. The winery had been boarded up long ago. Its condition, once perfect, was painful for Honey to witness. The large horse and equipment barn had burned down long ago and simply left its gray footprint as a foundation of river rock. Honey could see where the river meandered alongside her land and up to where she suspected the Yucaipat Indians had once made their village and then onward toward the mountains. It would be the ideal place for a village—there by the forest of oak and pine trees that lined the water's edge. The vast acres of wheat fields had been taken back by sage brush and chaparral, underscoring Earl and Selma Hart's lack of care for the land, ignorant of its value and potential. Towering above all that she beheld were the magnificent San Gorgonia Mountains, which blessed the land and promised to protect and keep her safe within its giant mountain walls.

Honey promised that over time she would explore the entire thousand acres now under her responsibility and care. But now she headed back to the house. A stone wall caught her attention as did a large wooden gate placed in it. The roots of a magnificent and ancient grapevine planted near the corner of the stone wall trailed entirely out of control, nearly obscuring one side of the stone structure. The wide dirt path called her to explore, and Honey acquiesced by unlatching the gate and pushing it open. There, surrounded by the lovely rock fence were the remnants of a very old cottage made of stone, wood, and adobe. Enough of the structure was left to imagine the home in its pristine condition.

Honey realized she'd come face to face with the past. This must have been JD Hart's first home in the mid 1800s and where the unmarried and pregnant young Maria Luego was taken in and sheltered. Honey was overwhelmed by all that needed exploring. As she closed the gate, her eyes were drawn to an enormous walnut tree on the other side of the house. Against its thick trunk leaned a rough wooden ladder, leading to what looked like a treehouse of sorts, way up in the massive branches. Someone had used wagon wheels cut in half for railings. Nothing would keep her from climbing the tree and exploring the shelter once she had on a pair of blue jeans, sneakers, and her Patriots football cap.

Suddenly famished and with a craving for an old-fashioned hamburger and French fries, Honey decided to explore Yucaipa and find a place where the locals eat. Honey took the cell phone from her jacket pocket and Googled "Yucaipa Restaurants." Immediately a long list appeared, but the Kopper Kettle Kafe had a distinctively local ring and she decided to try it out.

The child was disappointed when the lady picked up her purse, locked the doors, and drove away. She wandered the house for a while, praying that the lady who looked like Mama would come back. The familiar sound of the screwdriver, scraping against wood and metal, trying to pry off the lock on the kitchen door, interrupted her prayers. She moved toward the sound. Agitated, the intruder dropped the screwdriver. Cursing, he retrieved it and returned to his work, only to find a cold chill sweeping over him, the hair rising on the back of his neck. He looked up from the lock. Inches from his face was a little girl whose piercing eyes made him jump back and cry out with fright. Jeff Biel, a member of the Biel Boys' biker gang dropped the tool on the wooden floor of the screened-in porch, flew out the flimsy door, plunged off the three-step landing, and fell! The dirt and gravel bit into his face, hands, and knees, and he winced in pain.

But Jeff's terror cared nothing for the scrapes and bumps on his front side. Picking himself up and leaping onto the leather seat of his Harley, he peeled out of the driveway impatient to get as far away from this place as possible. Emily didn't like to scare people, but this bad man deserved it. She smiled at the funny sight he made falling all over himself, trying his best to race away as fast as he could.

ᐧᐧᐧ

The Kopper Kettle Kafe was a hometown favorite with its whimsical atmosphere of sunflowers and stage-prop town that lined the walls. Honey observed the locals of Yucaipa making themselves at home seated in booths, tables, and an old-fashioned coffee counter like the one she loved as a child at the Millbrook Diner in New York. A few regulars had their own coffee cups hanging on hooks, and the bustle of activity and friends happy to see friends was more than she could hope for. Honey chose the counter, seating herself next to a woman in faded blue jeans, flannel shirt, and outdoor vest. The vestiges of lunch, a full cup of steaming coffee, and the newspaper said she was taking her time and catching up on the comings and goings of the community.

Honey slid into the seat next to hers as the waitress handed her a menu, simultaneously asking, "What can I get you to drink?"

"I'll have an iced tea please, and I'm all set to order," Honey said cheerfully.

"Great, what can I get you?" the waitress inquired.

"An old-fashioned hamburger with French fries will be perfect," said Honey, adding, "I'm starved."

The woman next to her said without looking up from her newspaper, "Then you've come to the right place."

Honey laughed. "It sure looks like it with all the people here."

The woman nodded. "Our family owns a restaurant in Oak Glen, and look who's sitting at the counter . . . like I do every week. I take my mom to get her hair done across the street, come here for a killer BLT, and read the *Yucaipa/Calimesa News Mirror* from cover to cover." Reaching out to shake Honey's hand, the woman said, "Hi, I'm Connie Law."

"Honey Hart," Honey responded with a warm smile.

"Hart," said Connie. "Now that's a familiar name in Yucaipa and synonymous with Hartland. Any relation?"

"Yes," replied Honey, "I just came in from New York yesterday and will be living at Hartland from now on."

Connie put down her paper, took a good long look at Honey, and smiled. "You couldn't have brought better news. She's a beauty, and it's been nearly forty years since she's been properly cared for. But you put some time, money, and effort into her, and she'll flourish as she always has."

"I intend to," said Honey. "Know of any good contractors?"

"Pete, over there," pointing to the table in the corner, "is your best starting point. He's a Master Craftsman and only works with the best. Knows every great contractor in Yucaipa, and they'll be falling all over themselves just to get to work on your place. I'll ask him to give you his card before he goes."

"Thanks so much, Connie. You saved me! So," Honey continued, "you live in Oak Glen?"

Connie nodded. "Our family was one of the early settlers, and we knew the Harts from a long way back. My mother, who's nearly ninety-five, could tell you a bunch of stories. You'll have to stop by and see her at the Gift Shop. She's still working there after all these years. Stop by my place first, Country Orchards, and I'll set you up with some apples and a few of our signature jams and jellies."

"That's fantastic," said Honey. "I'd be delighted. And please, Connie, I'd love to have you come by Hartland anytime. When I'm moved in, I'll have a dinner party, and we can get to know one another better."

"Sounds like fun," replied Connie. Handing Honey her card and the newspaper, she said, "You'll love it here!"

Honey ate nearly all her hamburger, half the fries, and afterwards settled down with great interest to read the *News Mirror* from front to back. Pete stopped by with a card, and they settled on a time the following day to meet at the house. Full, happy, and exhausted, Honey drove back to the hotel, took advantage of the luxurious hot tub, and crawled into bed for a two-hour nap before her appointed time to meet with Landon.

"Our reservations are not for another half hour," Landon said, looking at his watch as together they drove from the hotel to historic downtown Redlands. "How about I give you the fifty-cent tour. It's really a charming place. We'll do a quick loop around the Redlands' Bowl, Lincoln's Shrine, and my favorite, the Smiley Library."

So much had filled Honey's mind, she'd hadn't had time to think about the Smiley Library.

"I'd love to see it!" exclaimed Honey enthusiastically.

"Well, far be it from me to stand between you and our public library," Landon teased, surprised by her enthusiasm.

Honey laughed. "Well, I do love a good library, being an avid reader and all, but the Smiley Library is special. The Smileys have been long-time family friends, and I consider Edward Smiley my adopted grandfather."

"No kidding," said Landon, stunned at how small the world truly was. "That's amazing. So you must know all about the library."

"That's the thing," Honey began, "I know a lot about it, having seen pictures, and of course Edward has told me the stories about the Smiley twins, Albert and Alfred, but as this is my first trip to Southern California, I've never had the opportunity to actually see it."

"Get ready to look to your left," Landon signaled as he turned down the street and the stunning Smiley Library came into view. Honey saw a lush green lawn, manicured flowerbeds, several large shade trees, and benches inviting people to simply sit and enjoy. The lovely Mission-style building featured stained-glassed windows, covered archways, and over-sized but inviting double doors. Honey could see why the library meant so much to Edward. It was a gesture of great love that his ancestors had paid for and gifted all this to the City of Redlands.

Landon drove at a crawl, stopping at the life-sized statues of Alfred and Albert Smiley. She could see Edward's resemblance in their stone-cut features. They were close enough that Honey could make out the writing on the plaque and read aloud, "This memorial is placed in deep appreciation of Alfred K. and Albert H. Smiley and also their brother David. These men of noble character and generosity are examples of the best of mankind."

"Yes," said Honey proudly, "Edward is cut from the same cloth, a very extraordinary family. I can't wait to go inside. I appreciate your driving me by."

Landon finished the loop, pointing out the outdoor theater called the Redlands Bowl and Lincoln's Shrine, both of which Honey was excited to explore.

Monitoring the time, Landon announced, "Tour's up! Time to eat."

Honey laughed. "Good, I'm starved!"

The ROC N FONDUE, an upscale two-story restaurant, was the brainchild of one of Landon's favorite people, Tammy Grove, a lover and supporter of all things Redlands, being a graduate of the university, protector of its historic buildings, and marvelous proprietor where the Aires Hotel was proud to send its guests. One look at the menu, which included steaks cooked on volcanic rocks, indulgent melted cheeses, and artisan chocolates one could warm and dip bread and strawberries in, Honey wanted to order everything. Her simultaneous need for a meal, to share her incredible day, to hear every detail of Landon's (especially how he had fared with the peacocks), and to drink more of the delicious wine, caused Honey to break her hard-and-fast rule of moderation: "Don't talk too much, don't eat too much, don't drink too much."

This was a day unlike any other, and with it, a new Honey uncharacteristically appeared. It surprised her. It would have surprised her friends and grandmother in New York.

"I'm stuffed," Honey finally announced, pushing away her plate and leaning back in her chair.

"Well, that's a blessing," said Landon, "if you'd ordered any more food, I'd have to sell a hotel to pay our bill."

"If that's the case," responded Honey, "I think I'll have dessert."

"Honey, I have something to say," said Landon.

"Yes?" said a relaxed and contented Honey.

Landon laughed, enchanted to see the beauty's crown of culture and refinement slip just a bit.

"Well, from the moment we met in the lobby, I never had a chance to say how truly spectacular you look tonight." Honey was surprised and smiled coyly. Landon continued, "That black dress suits you, not that you can fit in it anymore." He winked. "I don't know when I've enjoyed melted cheese so much, nor," he paused, "being with someone I find, surprisingly, I can be myself with."

"That's it!" Honey agreed. "You said it perfectly. I was trying to put my finger on it. It's rare to find someone you can just be yourself with. That's what I'm feeling too, Landon, with you, at Hartland, here in California." Honey added, "Myself is going to have to watch it, though, or she's going to put on a few too many pounds. Do you realize on top of all of this, at lunch I ate an entire hamburger and nearly every French fry at the Kopper Kettle Kafe where—"

Landon could see the wave of excitement gathering force in her again, and he was ready to delight in her long-winded tale, which required another gulp of air to continue.

"And I met this great lady named Connie Law who knows a contractor Pete, who was at the café and who gave me his card, and we're meeting tomorrow at Hartland at 10:00 a.m." Honey took in a quick breath and continued. "And Connie's mother is ninety-five, and she has a gift shop in Oak Glen and still works there, and Connie has an apple store, which sells jams and jellies, and she wants me to stop by."

"Whew," said Landon, "I wasn't quite so successful with the peacocks. One look at me and they turned tail and ran."

At that moment, the restaurant's owner, Tammy, arrived at their table with two complimentary glasses of Port and a coded wink and nod for Landon that she approved of this one.

"Honey, this is Tammy, she owns the place and she is the one to whom our thanks must be directed for the volcanic rocks and lava rich cheese."

"It was absolutely delicious, Tammy," complimented Honey, "and you have such a fun place!"

"Glad you like it, Honey," Tammy said. "You'll have to make this guy bring you back again."

"No way," said Landon, holding up the bill. "I was under the impression the skinny ones didn't actually eat."

"Since that's your only excuse," said Tammy, "I'll just take care of that."

"No, no," said Landon, whisking it back out of her hand, "then I'll owe you one, and you're a far too dangerous woman to owe anything to. I like my kneecaps."

Tammy laughed, shook her head, and put both glasses of wine in front of Honey, saying, "You're gonna need this to get through the rest of the evening. Good luck, Honey." Another wink at Landon, and she was gone.

Honey handed Landon his glass of wine and said, "I'd like to thank you for a truly wonderful evening, Landon, and I'd like to propose a toast. Here's to the beginning of our new lives at La Bonita and Hartland, and here's to always being ourselves with one another."

Honey touched her glass to his. "Here's to us, neighbor."

"Here's to us," Landon responded.

The two smiled at each other over their glasses like old friends.

The winding, scenic road above Yucaipa toward Angelus Oaks and the mountain resort of Big Bear was a favorite, especially among the different motorcycle crowds of which there were three. First, there was the mostly-over-fifty-five crowd with white-collar day jobs whose fiberglass motorcycle compartments contained a picnic blanket, wine, and cheese to enjoy along with the view. Next there was the traditional biker-gang crowd who looked menacing but would give the shirt off their backs to anyone in need. And then there were the Biel Boys, whose prowess was limited to motorcycles, alcohol consumption, weaponry skills, and stealing.

The Biel Boys hailed from somewhere between Angelus Oaks and Big Bear. Their group met up in a cabin, or so they called it, which was more like a shack. They'd stolen enough construction materials to keep the rain out, and they built a makeshift fireplace to keep most of the warmth in, but the best word to describe their cabin was a stale mess.

Today, Jeff Biel was refusing to return to Hartland after what he'd experienced with the ghost girl, which was still giving him a bad case of the heebie-jeebies. Sam and Martin Biel were hurling taunts such as *spineless, chicken,* and *wuss,* as the fourth in the gang-of-four, Danny, offered his own brand of Socratic reasoning to probe why Jeff shouldn't be afraid. "*If,*" began Sam, "it was a ghost, which it wasn't, *then* it was just a little girl, and who's afraid of a little girl?"

Jeff wasn't budging. Taunting wouldn't convince him to return to Hartland. So Sam determined he must take stronger measures. Lighting up a cigarette with a chaser of beer, the leader handed Jeff a dose of courage, hoping that would be enough to change his mind. When it wasn't, Sam had only one choice remaining. Jeff was always begging to use his hunting bow and arrows, which he'd received as a Christmas gift from the UPS man who'd left it on somebody else's front porch. When even the promise of the use of the bow and arrow didn't work, Danny considered that perhaps there was a ghost. Why else would Jeff be so stubborn? The final tactic in Sam's arsenal was to get everybody on their bikes and just leave him. Jeff hated worse than anything to be left alone. So, when three of the four men strode out the door and roared their bikes into idle, Jeff caved.

Taking the downhill curves way too fast, the Biel Boys, off to their second home at Hartland, screamed by sane drivers keeping a safe distance from the guardrails on the other side of which were only sheer cliffs. With heavy, beer-laden backpacks filled with junk food, knives, hatchets, and cigarettes, they increased their speed to stupidity. Only when Danny slid on some loose dirt and nearly skinned off his right side, did they slow down some. They sped down Highway 38, careened left onto Bryant Street, and then another left onto Carter. To these guys, engines could never be big enough or loud enough. Their entire self-esteem was based on speed and decibels.

Their deed to Hartland was based on the profound words of their esteemed leader Sam, who one day said, "What idiot leaves a place vacant for forty years and expects someone not to steal it?" With that the Biel Boys claimed the tree line and the riverbed for themselves. "No one would be dumb enough to try to live in the abandoned house now," mumbled Jeff Biel. That he'd tried a dozen times and couldn't get past the ever-increasing security system with cameras everywhere didn't ruffle his dignity, nor keep him from trying. But that was before the ghost girl. So, hunkered down in their own private digs among the trees, the Biel Boys set about fulfilling their potential, which made even the slugs feel better about themselves. Jeff was eyeing the house in the distance, looking for signs of the ghost girl to prove it to the other guys, when he noticed the lone figure of a woman. Not a ghost, but . . .

"Somp en's wrong," said Jeff, pointing to the driveway leading to the house where a woman was exiting a car. "Somebody's goin up to the front door. Looks like she's gotta key. Man, she'll be hightailing it outta there in two seconds when she sees the ghost girl," assured Jeff.

"It's nothing," said Sam. "People go in and out all the time."

"Hey, look!" cried Oats. "She's got the door open and the alarm ain't goin off."

Seeing the line of construction trucks coming up Hart Lane, Martin Biel spoke for one and all. "This ain't lookin good."

When the huge farm tractor, pulling a thirty-foot deck, moved into position, the Biel Boys knew they were in trouble. The machinery operator lowered the deck, engaged the cutting blade, and revved the engine, effectively drowning out the boys unhappily expressing themselves in four-letter words.

Sam took out his hatchet, and slid a finger gently along the razor-sharp blade. "Look, lady," he warned from a safe distance, "if you think you're gonna run us off *our* Hartland, you got another thing comin." Sam hauled back and with great force hurled the weapon, lodging it deep into an ancient tree. Most of the boys caught the subtle implication.

CHAPTER FIVE

RESCUING

Hartland land, 1860

Surrounded by his warriors who were engrossed in the game of hatchets, Red Eye was alone in his panic and fear. Normally he would have applauded Cha'tiam (The Caller) and Sky Wolf (Guardian of the Sky) for extending the challenge to include not only distance, accuracy, and speed, but small animals. On another day, he would have been amused by the rabbit and several birds in the wrong place at the wrong time, picked up and carried along to meet the targeted trees. But today, his respect and honor—his whole life—was at stake.

Red Eye caught the deerlike movement of Swift Arrow (Swift Arrow) his childhood friend, running gracefully and silently toward him, bringing a message from Chief Adoeete and the Elders.

"There is news," said Swift Arrow, no sign of exertion could be seen on his muscular chest. "Chief Adoeete will hold the ceremony tonight. You, Aiyana, and the entire village must be there."

Red Eye furrowed his brow but did not speak.

"This is what we've been waiting for," Swift Arrow continued. "He's getting old, and you are ready—more than ready to take his place as chief."

"And *we* are ready," boasted Sky Wolf. "We're sick of Adoeete's attempts to hold us back. We are warriors, and warriors fight. Not farm and till the land."

Red Eye remained silent as his face darkened.

"What's wrong with you, Red Eye?" Swift Arrow complained with a smile, pushing him playfully. Red Eye backhanded Swift Arrow, which deeply wounded his face and his feelings. For days, Red Eye had been sleeplessly brooding, pacing, and plotting. Now with this news, he could not remain still, and his body began the familiar routine, every step underscoring the potential injustice, anger, and fear should Aiyana—and *not* he—be chosen chief. *She is, after all, not only a mere woman, but my young niece, the daughter of my dead brother and Adoeete's granddaughter. What right does she have to be a chief! It* was a man's position and only a man's his mind thundered.

"Look", said Cha'tiam, pointing toward the trees. Red Eye jerked his head toward the spot. Eighteen-year-old Aiyana, a fur pelt thrown over one shoulder, rode slowly out of the camp. As the painted stallion gathered speed, her long black hair moved free and flowing as did the soft leather fringed skirt. Her mind, intent on reaching the river, made her unaware of the imminent danger.

Red Eye grabbed the hatchet out of Cha'tiam's hand. The trained eye of a master marksman created a target on the back of Aiyana's head where he would sink the hatchet quivering in his hand. "I'll kill her before I'm shamed before all the tribes," he growled, raising his powerful arm to launch the weapon whose sharp flint edge would swiftly cut her in two. But, before he could release the handle, his wrist was abruptly gripped in a vice. Red Eye swung around to deal a death blow to the one who dared to stop him and came face to face with his father, whose steely eyes held his. Red Eye flinched. Chief Adoeete willed his old arm to remain far stronger than it was. The stance was sustained as though frozen in time, the watching warriors growing in discomfort and unease. No words were spoken between the father and son, Chief and warrior, but in that timeless moment, both knew Adoeete's choice had just been made.

$$\backsim\!\!\sim\!\!\backsim$$

Aiyana, laid her fur pelt next to the water's edge, stripped off her clothes and dove into the clear, cool river. The young woman's slender body moved in rhythmic strokes toward the secret shelter made by the brush and willow trees. Her lips softly skimmed the water as she swam to the small cove. Like slender arms, the willow branches reached as far out as they could, then touched the waters with their fingers. Here, mysteriously the water was warm, here Aiyana could be free, quiet, safe from Red Eye's mutinous glares. Floating, Aiyana permitted her heavy eyes to slowly close. Her long black hair fanned out upon the water and she let herself simply be held. Grandfather's voice spoke softly from within. Adoeete's familiar instruction reminded her once again to 'be silent, to hear the words of the Great Spirit who would surely speak when she had learned to listen.' The silence she had mastered. The listening not, as she had never heard a word. Aiyana pushed down the feelings of frustration and anger directed first at herself and then the Great Spirit. Her longsuffering patience was ending. "Silence" - she commanded her thoughts and returned to the place of listening in her mind.

The rare call of an eagle broke her reverie. She heard his beating wings as they moved him powerfully in circles above the natural shelter. The call came again and stopped as though waiting for a response, and as none was given, he continued his plea until Aiyana parted the branches scanning to see what was the matter. Finding neither the great bird nor the fuss, and suddenly feeling cold, now outside the cove, she swam toward the warmth of the pelt and the sun. The fur felt soft upon her wet skin and thus wrapped, the young woman fell asleep.

She dreamed a vivid dream: The Great Eagle lit upon the rock next to where she lay. It sat there while she slept, observing the beauty of her heart, the brilliance of her mind, the gracefulness of the hand which had fallen free from the fur and lay open as though waiting for something to be laid in it. In her dream Aiyana awoke, finding herself inches from the Great Eagle as he hovered over her. She could see the gold of his eyes, the tufts of brilliant white feathers which covered his head, the massive gray and brown wings attached to such a strong body. She was not afraid. As she looked closer, the Eagle held in his beak a seed. He placed the seed gently in her outstretched hand and his mind joined hers to speak the Great Spirit's Words. "Granddaughter of Adoeete - Heart of My Heart - Arrow of the Great Spirit, behold the seed in your hand. It contains a new form. Destiny has called you to be its mother. Plant her now and she will grow and with it a new life."

Aiyana touched the seed in wonderment. The Eagle answered her question before she asked. "There are many kinds of seeds. The seeds of plants. The seeds of animals and the seeds of men. All are at first fragile, dull, and appearing to have little or no potential. Yet under the Great Mother's care, they will become mighty and bring forth their true and unique purpose."

Suddenly worried, Aiyana said, "Great Eagle, this tiny seed will always be at risk if Red Eye and his warriors know I am the one who has planted and is caring for it. They will rip it out of the ground at the first site of its flourishing."

"Ah dear one," he comforted, "things are not always as they seem and the life force of *this* seed has powers beyond their understanding. Do not fear the appearance of death, it ever resolves into a stronger, vibrant and more beautiful and unique life form. The Great Eagle looked in her eyes, bent to nuzzle her arm, spread his wings, and disappeared into the sky.

Aiyana awoke, continuing to lay still for some time. She watched as a white feathery tuft floated down and touched her open hand, settling gently next to a small, brown, seed. Shocked at the sight, Aiyana sat up wrapping the soft pelt around her. Raising her hand closer to her eyes, Aiyana confirmed the seed was real and then for good measure, gently touched it with her finger. For all her mental strivings and frustrated efforts to grasp the Mysteries of the Great Spirit, she had never understood. Now she simply 'knew' that the physical seed she held in her hand began as an idea in the mind of the Great Spirit Above and somehow, miraculously, took form in a plant she could touch Below. "Remember Granddaughter," Adoeete spoke, "As Above, So Below, As Within, So Without." Aiyana silently formed the words which now were her own. From her vest she took out a small leather pouch. Gently Aiyana placed the sacred feather and seed inside and tucked it safely away. As she prepared to leave the water's edge, Aiyana suddenly heard terrified screams echoing across the canyon. She leapt upon her horse, driving the painted stallion at full speed toward the cries.

⌒⌒

The covered wagon with John, Katherine and seven-year-old Jonathan Hart, carried all their earthly goods and the promise of a new life in Yucaipa, California. Twenty-five-year-old Katherine Hart began the exciting journey with hope and a lively constitution, determined to sustain her small family along the way with strong inward courage and faith. As some families are inclined to do, Katherine was judged and pronounced to be just like her grandmother Grayson Victoria Smiley Hart, both in appearance, personality and inner strength. Raised with an abundance of values, ethics, family roots and wealth, it was the family's firm belief, Katherine's longevity and success were a given. But Katherine wasn't so sure. A secret question mark punctuated her life and its purpose remained unanswered. Now, three months and twenty-four days into the trip, Katherine was bone weary of travel, nearly drained of energy to support her own inner courage, which left little to give to her young son and husband, who were coping too, as best they could. Katherine wondered for the hundredth time if their decision to leave the comforts of their Texas home had been wise. She'd tried to sustain her optimism when the way was brutal, by envisioning California as a place of beauty, pleasant valleys, green hillsides, mountain peaks and trout filled rivers. The reality however left her disappointed as the endless Arizona desert they'd endured for hundreds of miles continued under the California flag for nearly a week. And then the tragic scene played out before their eyes, which still haunted her mind and spoke to her in ways frustrating and veiled.

One night as usual, John made a campfire when they'd gone as far as they could in a day. Their bellies were full, even if it meant an endless diet of beans and hardtack. The energy of the burning fire and the three who made up the sojourners were all fading when a strange cacophony of sounds drew closer to the campsite. A pack of wolves were in pursuit of a doe and her fawn. Spotting the fire, the doe urged her youngling to take refuge in its protection.

John's instincts and his reaction time was nearly instantaneous. At the first sound, he had gathered the sleeping boy and Katherine into the wagon, readied his shot gun and surrounded his wife within his strong arms. Together they watched the theater of nature unfold from inside the wagon as the wolf pack followed their victims into the campsite, the fawn the target, not due to malice but from desperate hunger. Low sounding growls and barred teeth moved closer and closer to the mother and fawn. Katherine was witness to the precise moment when instinct told the doe, with an absolute knowing, that if her fawn were to live, she must sacrifice herself. Reason, not playing a part in the animal kingdom as it does in man, there was no conflict for the doe in terms of choice. She simply and instinctively lived to serve her child, whose future and purpose she unhesitatingly put before her own. The attack of the doe lasted long enough for the fawn to flee into the night where finally, its sense of safety could not drown out its confusing sense of great loss.

The bloodied animal remnants which spoke of sacrifice and love, John removed in the early morning hours. They reminded him of his own mortality and that of his family. Cosmic forces, he thought, continually changed life without the permission of man. That man was not the ultimate master, he could grasp, but the mystery of 'why everything else' was challenging his mind as they continued to cross the desert, now only a half day's ride from Hartland and the safety of their new home. The steady rhythm of the horses pulling the wagon, disagreed with the unsteady cadence of the wooden wheels hitting rocks, potholes and brush, causing the riders to bounce, jostle and jerk from side to side. The now expected erratic movements, had their own lulling effect as Katherine and John, together in separate and silent contemplation, were suddenly brought back to the moment at hand with Jonathan's question. "Where did you say home was Mama"? Jonathan knew the answer, she'd told him a hundred times, but they were so close now and the child needed to hear it again. Invoking the strength of the pearl necklace given to her by her grandmother to remind her to stay strong and courageous, Katherine sipped from the canteen, licked her sunburned lips, gave water to Jonathan and John and began the now familiar story.

"Your Grandfather, John David Hart, or JD as he was called," Katherine began, "heard gold had been found in California. So, at eighteen-years-old, he went after his dream. He found work in the Crafton Hills Mine, not far from Hartland. The owner of the mine was Harold Morley. But there were other mines too, like the Beaumont Mine, owned by the Beaumont Trading Post. Everyday JD and the men worked hard from sun up to sun down, but they only found small nuggets of gold. And every day, Harold Morley got madder and madder. But one day, the miners working in the Beaumont Mine found gold, and lots of it. Everyone was shouting and whooping it up. Everyone except Harold Morley. He was angry and jealous. Your grandfather JD overhead Mr. Morley talking to one of his guards. He told the man to go back at night and plant explosives in the Beaumont Mine. In the morning when Ben Beaumont and the miners were deep inside he was to light the fuse and blow the cave up. Later Morley would tunnel through his mine and claim he found the gold. But then Mr. Morley's mind was seduced by greed. He believed the Yucaipat Indians who lived in the Village near Hartland were hiding gold in the caves along the riverbed. He'd been scheming about how to get that gold but now he saw a way to 'kill two birds with one stone'. So, he told the guard to send his men to capture Chief White Wolf's young son. They were to take the boy to the mine that night when they planted the explosives. If the Indian's didn't hand over their gold, they'd blow the boy up too.

JD knew Harold Morley was greedy, but he never expected him to be so detestable. So, your grandfather had to figure out a way to stop him. That night JD went back to the Beaumont Mine and watched from behind rocks. The Beaumont's had guards too, but Harold Morley's men ambushed and killed them. Then they brought out the Indian boy, badly beaten and forced him at gunpoint to sit down. They tied sticks of dynamite around his waist. JD watched as the boy refused to cry and was amazed that someone so young, could be so brave.

Morley's men built a fire and drank whisky until they were drunk and snoring. Then JD climbed down from the rocks. The boy saw him, but JD motioned him to stay quiet. Silently he took out his knife and cut the boy free. He'd seen the best route of escape was to climb above the mine to the top of the hill then go down the other side. JD didn't know that Chief White Wolf and his warriors had tracked his son there and were on top of the hill with their arrows ready to shoot. They watched as JD and White Wolf's son climbed toward them but suddenly the boy slipped, crying out, waking up the men below. He would have fallen except JD grabbed his small wrist. But in doing so your grandfather sliced his arm on a jagged rock. The wound was deep. But no matter the pain, he wouldn't let go of the boy's wrist. His arm was bleeding badly, and the blood was dripping into both their hands. JD was afraid the boy would slip, not be able to hold on but miraculously he did. Morley's men heard the cry and reached for their guns. When they looked up, it was to see not only JD and the boy, but the hilltop lined with Indians whose sharp arrows were aimed straight at them.

"Your grandfather returned with the warriors to the village. The chief insisted his medicine man treat his arm. JD stayed, taught the chief the language of the white man, and worked alongside the men of the tribe. But when Harold Morley heard JD had ruined his chances for both the Indian and Beaumont gold, and was living with the Indians, he sent his men to set fire to the village and kill JD. As the men rode toward the village with their torches and guns, they spotted three young Indian girls playing by the river. They grabbed them, placed them on their horses as hostages and shields, and rode into camp. JD was in his tent with a few braves when he heard the men shout, 'JD Hart, you show yourself now, or we'll kill these Indian girls and torch the village.' JD picked up his knife, and slit a hole in the tepee so the braves could go out unseen. He bid them hide behind the rocks at the entrance of the Yellow Cave, explaining he would lure the men there with the promise of gold. JD stepped out of the tepee, offered himself up to the men in exchange for the children, and set the trap. 'Your boss, Harold Morley, mistreats you,' said JD. 'I've seen him do it, many times. He wants all the gold you've been working hard for but pays you in pennies and beatings. I'll give you the Indian's gold in return for leaving the children and village alone. You could even keep some of it for yourself and start life over as rich men, somewhere else.' The unexpected idea appealed to them, but they refused to release the girls until the gold was in their hands.

It was dangerous, to be sure, but JD had no choice. He had to rely on the expert marksmanship of the braves to kill the men but not the children. His trust was well placed in the Indians as they watched from afar the string of horses coming towards the cave. The braves placed themselves behind the men. Then in a surprise moment of attack, they released their arrows into the backs of their heads, killing the men without harming the girls.

"JD had saved the chief's son, the little girls, and the village. To honor him, Chief White Wolf wanted to gift the worthy JD a thousand acres of land, but it came with a sacred oath. 'Know this,' said the wise chief to JD, 'the land belongs to the Great Spirit, *is* the Great Spirit, and you are the humble servant. Keeping the sacred harmony between man and nature in this place is now your responsibility. Only under these conditions can the land be given into your temporary care.'

"Your grandfather pledged that solemn oath and kept it. He made your Papa and I pledge that oath too, and we intend to keep it." The story always ended with his mother's question, "and Jonathan, will you keep that pledge too?"

The child's reply was ever the same; "I will, Mama."

Katherine's story of hope and the slow exchange of white desert sand and cactus, for sage brush, green shrubbery, wild flowers, and trees, lifted the small family's spirits. With each mile, the California that John, Katherine, and little Jonathan dreamed about was taking form, and it was magnificent. Surrounded by mountains plentiful in pine, cedar, and oak, it was not a stretch to imagine the hidden waterfalls, streams, and natural paradises the plants and animals would call home.

Finally reaching the Beaumont Trading Post, Katherine's story was taking form in reality. Grateful to be on solid ground and to stretch their legs, the Harts blessed the moment of respite and set about feeding the horses and purchasing more supplies for the last leg of their long journey.

Jonathan released his pent-up energy, bounding at full speed up the three wooden steps, running back and forth on the rickety planks spanning the front porch of the trading post, and jumping off the end as far as his little body would take him. This he intended to repeat until Mama called him to get back in the wagon. Katherine headed for the fresh water barrel where she would refill their canteens and after, lead the horses and cow to the water trough. John went inside to gather supplies, his eyes falling on black licorice for Jonathan and a knitted blue shawl that would match Katherine's eyes. He scooped both up with a smile. It was a small extravagance well deserved by his courageous wife and son who had followed his dreams of flourishing vineyards nurtured on family land.

Inside, three armed and dirty ruffians were stocking up on whiskey. Thornton paid for one bottle, while Rig and Clement stole two. They exited the trading post loudly, shoving open the doors and claiming the rocking chairs on the porch. Not until they'd pushed back a couple of swigs did they notice the small boy. "Where there's a kid," Thornton said, "there's a woman nearby," and he began the search with eager eyes. He spotted her. She was a pretty thing. Thornton whistled at her to get her attention, and when she looked up with confusion, he licked his lips suggestively. The hair on the back of Katherine's neck rose, hating the leering eyes of the disgusting men. But she had work to do and kept to it, bending to fill the canteens. Her bodice opened slightly to reveal the pearl necklace, the diamonds catching the light and the outlaw's immediate attention.

"Well," said Rig, tipping his hat to the back of his head for a better view. "I see two things I want. Ain't this our lucky day!"

Aiyana raced faster as gunshots and more screaming echoed through the canyon. Instinctively she let loose with a piercing warrior's cry, hoping to scare off the attackers. She heard their fading hoofbeats as she came into the clearing. The wagon lay badly broken. The white canvas cover, ripped from its iron laces, partially exposed the dead body of a young woman but could not hide the pool of blood in which the man lay face down. She heard crying. Aiyana searched as the crying turned into a wounded whimper, tracing the sound to a small boy still in the wagon. He was bleeding. A fistful of hair was missing from the boy's bloody scalp. It looked to Aiyana like the assailants had tried to drag him out head first, but suddenly let him go. Aiyana approached the boy slowly, but he screamed again. She placed her bow and arrow on the ground along with the knife and opened her hands, saying in English, "Little boy good, little boy good. Aiyana here now. Aiyana here now. Shh, shh, little boy good."

"Why did they shoot my Mama and Papa?" he sobbed. "We were almost there!" Jonathan threw himself on the new sacks of grain, sobbing uncontrollably. Aiyana simply sat and waited. She was there for the boy, and it was enough. The crying stopped, and the whimpering began again, and when that stopped too, she softly hummed a lullaby. When the boy was still, she asked permission with silent motions if she could hold him. When he nodded, Aiyana gathered the shocked and terrified boy, wrapped him tight in his mother's blue shawl, and gently placed him on the horse. She climbed up behind him, settling him in front. For the first time she noticed a woman's pearl necklace around the boy's neck. It was all she needed to know. The mother had died protecting her child, and the husband died protecting them both.

Aiyana sighed, her heart wounded for the boy. She gathered the reins and her arms around him, and the two rode slowly away from the wagon and home to his Hartland and her village—the one and the other, the same. In the long moments of silence, The Great Spirit spoke, His Words for the first time crystal clear. "Now you are the mother of two great seeds."

Jonathan, asleep in Aiyana's arms, was unaware he'd arrived at the Indian village near his Hartland home. The tension in the village, however, was at a fevered pitch with Chief Adoeete's announcement of a council and rumors of Red Eye's thwarted attack on Aiyana. Aiyana knew immediately something was wrong, seeing small groups of villagers huddled together, talking quietly with furrowed brows. Red Eye's men too were unusually quiet, looking apprehensive and anxious. Aiyana saw in the distance her grandfather, Chief Adoeete, several elders, and his own loyal warriors, walking towards Red Eye's warrior encampment. She would discover the cause, but first she must settle the child into her tepee, make him comfortable. She hoped he would continue to sleep for a while. He needed to gain strength before he must relive again that horrific moment in his memory's vision.

The white boy's arrival added fuel to the already heightened concerns of the tribe, and quickly Aiyana was surrounded as they looked for an explanation for the strange event. But Aiyana motioned them to be silent and not wake the child. She signaled Honana, the medicine woman, to follow her inside, and the flap of the tepee was shut behind them. The people's curiosity about the boy and the volatile situation would have to wait. There was on that day a great wringing of hands.

⌒⌒

As Adoeete and his men walked the long distance toward Red Eye's tepee, once again thoughts flooded the chief's mind. It was not only physical distance that separated Red Eye's warrior camp from the families of the tribe, but a great distance of mind, heart, and will. Adoeete accepted the necessity of opposites in nature—the rainy and dry seasons, the cold and hot, hard and soft, life and death—but it was more difficult to accept the polarizing effects that such opposite thoughts and attitudes toward life created.

There could be no truer opposites than Adoeete and Red Eye. The authentic character and attitude of each had been revealed long ago at that mystical place between boyhood and manhood. For the Yucaipats, the Great Quest signified a boy's readiness to take the long and arduous journey to the top of the San Gorgonio Mountain in search of self-discovery and true manhood. His leaving day would be as a boy. His returning day as a true man. But there were no guarantees at any stage of life, and some boys had remained boys despite the maturing of their bodies and the passing of seasons. What one experienced on that journey and at the top of the mountain, would be revealed first to the boy, then the man, and from his transformation—or lack thereof—the tribe would know.

Adoeete remembered his own leaving day and that moment of truth that revealed his true character. It had all hinged on his response to those two powerful words, "Get up!" The goal was the highest point of the San Gorgonio Mountain. The exhausted young Adoeete, on the precipice of manhood, lay on the ground, his energy depleted, the gash in his leg festered, the snake bite, while not venomous, throbbed. The rationed water was emptied, as was his own strength, health, and perhaps even life. The brutal nature of initiation into manhood could never be explained, only experienced—alone.

"To reach the truth," the wise elders had said, "one must go on the Great Quest of self-discovery with purity of intention, knowledge of the goal, obedience to the Great Spirit's ways, and to purge oneself from everything that would hinder, draw back, tempt, or obscure the vision of a true man."

White Wolf, chief of the Yucaipat Indian tribe, said to his son Adoeete on his leaving day that "a true Chief first rules himself, and only then his Tribe." Today, yet another five days' climb to his goal after months of trying to get there, Adoeete seemed unable to rule himself. He could neither think nor move; the fatigue of heart, mind, and will complete. In silence, the boy lay on the ground. Soon a gentle breeze stroked his body, releasing the scent of pine. An ant climbed on his hand, it stung him and crawled back to its mound as others of its tribe wandered on his body. Still the boy didn't move. The sun set, the moon rose, the moon disappeared, and the sun rose again. Again, the boy didn't move, only rested. Suddenly deep called unto deep within the depths of the boy's soul. The inner voice of the Great Chief within him, that which he was made to be, spoke. "Get up!"

The force within Adoeete was weak, but as he strived to moved first his fingers, toes, hands, and feet, it grew stronger. The more he willed his body to get up, the greater the force became, and the wise inner chief and young aspiring chief worked as one to get the boy on his feet. His moccasins once again on the trail, a stream appeared, the chilly waters washed his dirty body and quenched his thirst.

The rabbit gave himself for the sustenance of the boy, and the fruited vines shared what they had. The obstacle, the test, Adoeete had overcome, and he began to feel strong in ways he could not explain. His strength and health renewed, a more powerful Adoeete strode on toward the goal and his destiny.

From the highest point of the San Gorgonio Mountains overlooking a vast sweeping land and meandering river, the Great Spirit's aspirant, Adoeete, saw for the first time farther than he could have imagined. The Yucaipat village and the surrounding land had, until this very moment, been the whole of his world. But from this new perspective above, he could see now it was, in the vast scheme of things, only an anthill. The boy, in the center of the three-hundred-and-sixty-degree view, slowly turned. From this elevation, Adoeete was a witness to perfection, to a beauty unlike any other he had ever seen, and he fell in love. He fell in love with the ideal this vantage point revealed, and having once seen it, Adoeete was forever changed. There was only one thing he desired now, and that was to be a servant of this practical ideal. His village may be an anthill, but even ants have a purpose, an ideal way of being, a part to play in the vast universe of the Great Spirit. This was the mystery revealed. His transformation into manhood was complete.

Two months later when Adoeete entered the village, he carried with him a huge bouquet of wildflowers in many shapes and colors. It was a strange sight to behold—at once the epitome of masculinity carrying a symbol of femininity. Both magnificent in their own ways. Adoeete the boy had turned into Adoeete the man, like a caterpillar turns into a butterfly. The heart of every Indian maiden swooned, and the pride of every Indian man swelled. One day he would be Chief Adoeete—of this there was no doubt.

～∽◦

That was the past, **Adoeete thought,** *now I must face the present moment and confront Red Eye on his attempt to murder Aiyana this morning.* His brow furrowed, concerned about what awaited the meeting with his son. It had been a long time since Adoeete had entered the warrior camp, and he noted a new and disgusting addition to Red Eye's tepee. Animal blood had been used as paint to capture the image of a large red eye at the apex of the tepee, and below, the painting of a warrior who held in his hand the bodiless head of a man.

It was then Adoeete saw the chasm between a true warrior—one who protected his people, his lands, his way of life—and the misuse of the honorable position and purpose as an excuse to indulge a sadistic mind. Adoeete was sickened. As his moccasins drew him closer, he tried to think what part he may have played, what hurt he'd perhaps caused, what aspect of the boy's education he had failed to teach that explained the creation of such a treasonous mind. As a young father, Adoeete had taken the matter to his own father, White Wolf, many times. Red Eye, then known as Napyshni (Courageous and Strong), seemed born of two other parents, ones who must have had the opposite nature of Adoeete (Big Tree) and his tenderhearted wife Nizhoni (Beautiful).

White Wolf was wise, but only because his own painful experiences had shown him the truth. It was from knowing and certitude he spoke to Adoeete. "There is great hardship and pain, my son, for all who witnessed Napyshni on his returning day and the boy who has remained known as

Red Eye." Now Adoeete recalled the morning of Red Eye's leaving day. Adoeete asked his son, next in line as chief, to journey as his birth name, Napyshni, meaning courageous and strong. The nickname Red Eye, which he'd earned for all the tears he'd made others shed, was neither *who* he was *meant to be* nor appropriate for the sacred moment. Red Eye nodded. He'd never admit it, but he was glad for another chance. The legend of Adoeete's return from his own Great Quest for self-discovery was held aloft as the ideal. Napyshni's own father was an inspiration for all those boys whose inner drive to prove themselves worthy to be called a true man was fulfilled. There was nothing Napyshni wanted more. He'd dreamed for years of his own return to the village where he could finally throw off the mask that was Red Eye, be forgiven his childish ways, and take on the mantle of a respected leader.

Hope filled each heart as happily Napyshni set out on the path. The last words his father had called to him were "Know who you are." The first two months climbing the lower mountains were difficult, but nothing he couldn't handle. But San Gorgonio Mountain was a beast, thought Napyshni, considering it his nemesis, constantly besting the tall, strong, and well-developed boy. *The way is long, the climb arduous, the effort exhausting, and all for what?* the boy thought. Manhood would come, whether he climbed this mountain or not. His body was already there, as the lovely Lyita (First to Dance) could attest. Napyshni smiled, remembering that day and the many days after when he and Lyita laid together. He was a man, all right! In fact, he'd killed a man. No one had seen him do it. It happened on a so-called hunting trip, and none suspected it was him. Why would they? Antinanco (Eagle of the Sun) was Red Eye's elder brother. How else could Red Eye be next in line as chief except to eliminate his competition?

Night had fallen all too quickly. He'd been fantasizing about his own reign as chief, Lyita by his side, the Yucaipat tribe ascribing him the honor of Chief above all Chiefs, and now he was thirsty. He tipped back the water bag, but it was empty. Hunger set in, but he must go hungry, having failed to catch his dinner earlier. The final straw was the bone-hurting chill that descended, and now he must make a fire in the dark. He'd done this to himself, and it increased his anger. The next day would be worse.

It would be weeks before he reached the top, and the density of the forest required his hatchet and all the strength he could muster to move forward. With every hack of the blade, his strength decreased until at last he lay exhausted on the ground. Food he had, having that morning killed a rabbit, but he needed water. Napyshni determined to rest and listen for its sound. The harder he listened, the greater the silence, and the angrier he got.

He thought of the boys who had died on the mountain, or worse, returned home humiliated, unable to reach the goal. Those boys had three choices: leave the tribe, stay on the mountain and refuse to go back, or humble themselves and return each spring until they reached the goal or died. Running Fox had been one such boy, and a thirteen-year-old Red Eye had jeered and taunted him for his weakness until the following spring. Running Fox had gone for the second time on his quest and returned, the transformation spectacular. Before he took his place of honor as a true man, he thanked Red Eye. "Little boy," Running Fox said, "I used your jeers and taunts to make me stronger, and when I thought I could go no further, I heard them again. I always got up. I always went on. On the journey there, I lived to hurt you, make you suffer in a thousand ways for all the pain and humiliation you caused me. Then I reached the goal. Then I looked. Then I saw we are all only ants. But even ants have a purpose and can be of great service. From that moment until now, I have not given you another thought." Running Fox turned from the boy and walked away.

Fear, like bile, rose in Napyshni's throat. He feared his own weakness of character. He feared being an ant. He feared being unworthy of even a thought. Of having another back walk away from him. He had to get up, he had to go on. Napyshni willed himself with all his might to rise, to walk. Now moving slowly over the rise, he found water and dignity. The water nourished his body, the dignity his soul. His strength returned, and his desire renewed as he climbed the still forested mountain, the small cave above his goal. He'd rest there for a day, then tackle the hardest climb of his life when the sun rose again.

Napyshni slept. Later he built a fire and roasted a squirrel. He added more wood for the night, then lay down to sleep. The light from the fire made shadows on the cave walls, the boy absently turning them into images of animals. The wood burned, and the growing fire suddenly revealed a golden lightning bolt painted on the wall. Napyshni crawled over and touched it. It was married to the rock, but it was different, the color deeper than the yellow of corn. It sparkled. He seized his hatchet and chipped away the rock around it. Like a thick branch, it reached up the side of the wall, its seedling branches burrowing inside. Napyshni's eyes followed the length of the wide branch, and it seemed to meander along the roof of the cave, nearly to the other side. Soon he realized there were branches of this everywhere!

Striking the substance with his hatchet, the boy knocked out a large piece, which fell to the cave floor. He held it close to the firelight. It sparkled like the night lights in the sky. Napyshni's eyes grew wide. An idea formed in his mind; he had found what no other chief before had found. This was greater than any view from the top of the mountain, he thought. This *was* the Great Quest's end. He had desired more than anything to stop, and based on this new idea, he could. Napyshni stood at the entrance to the cave and shouted to all the inhabitants of the forest above and below him, "I am Napyshni, a true man among true men, a true chief!"

On the long journey home, he amused himself by imagining the looks on each Yucaipat face when he brought out the golden rock of the Great Spirit. He'd convinced himself that divine lightning had struck the cave and the man who found the Spirit Rock was the truest man of all. That would be a moment every villager would remember. He couldn't wait to see the expressions of Adoeete, Lyita, and Running Fox. The canyon reverberated with the sound of his laughter.

Napyshni strode into the village, a smug smile of satisfaction on his face. The villagers gathered around excited to see the transformation that always came after a boy reached the top of the San Gorgonio Mountain.

While the same mysterious revelation altered every man, each responded uniquely according to his own nature, purpose, and service. There had been those who had claimed they'd reached the top but had lied—and when the truth had been revealed it was their own self-shame that wounded them most. If they asked for forgiveness and permission to try again, the elders would allow them to once more train with the aspirants. True humility, which was always the beginning of wisdom, was rewarded, and they retained their respect and dignity for their return to honesty and for not giving up.

Adoeete hugged his son, and the village surrounded Napyshni with warmth and congratulations, eager to hear of his Great Quest, his own journey of self-discovery at the top of the mountain. That he appeared transformed made for a joyful tribe. The newfound love and respect healed every wound, and Napyshni determined to change his ways and make them all proud!

The great fire roared as all gathered around. Then Napyshni proudly brought out the Spirit Rock, told them the story of its discovery, and announced, "I am Napyshni, founder of the Great Spirit's cave, and its divine Spirit Rock. Therefore, I now know myself to be the truest man of all, worthy to be called Chief."

A shockwave hit the stunned tribe. Eyes widened, jaws dropped, and tears formed in the knowing and embarrassed eyes. Ashamed, Lyita walked away from the circle. Napyshni was confused. This was not the response he had expected. What had he done wrong?

"Did you go to the top of the mountain?" asked Adoeete.

"No," replied Napyshni. "I didn't need to. When I found the Spirit Rock, I found myself."

"You have been seduced," sighed Adoeete. "The true man never comes back from the great journey claiming to be a ruler. Go back, my son. Return next spring, climb to the top of the mountain, experience the truth."

The boy slammed the rock into the fire, pierced Adoeete with his eyes, scowled at each villager, and stormed off to his tent. The sounds of his frustrated rantings could be heard throughout the warriors' camp.

Now, in the present moment, Adoeete heard once again the all-too-familiar rantings inside his son's tent and caught in his periphery the motion of one of Red Eye's warriors galloping into the trees to meet Sky Wolf. Cha'tiam had followed the chief and his men as they made their way to the warrior camp. He turned away now, circling back to where Sky Wolf was waiting at a safe distance from Red Eye's tepee.

"Red Eye's barricaded himself inside. He's like a rabid wolf," declared Sky Wolf.

"He must be careful," Cha'tiam replied, warning, "Chief Adoeete, the elders, and a few warriors are headed this way. I've never seen the chief so angry! This doesn't look good for Red Eye."

"Or us," reminded Sky Wolf. "We must be ready to run!"

Cha'tiam groaned. "Chief Adoeete made Red Eye look weak today, and he will be shamed before the village if Adoeete chooses Aiyana as chief."

Sky Wolf nodded in agreement, adding, "And worse, he will be laughed at by all the tribes. They will say a woman has conquered Red Eye—"

Before Cha'tiam could continue, another round of fury from within the tepee caused a frightened Sky Wolf and Cha'tiam to ride in panic for the cover of the caves in the canyon walls.

Red Eye slugged back the fermented drink and threw the rest in the fire, falling to his knees. He searched the angry flames for answers he did not have, nor would they yield. He hissed at them through clenched teeth. "How did this happen?" Then, stronger, he demanded to know, "How did this happen?" When the flames refused to speak, Red Eye screamed, "How did this happen!"

Adoeete threw open the flap and stormed in, the elders following behind as the chief's warriors surrounded the outside of the tent.

"You made this happen!" thundered Adoeete.

Red Eye leapt up ready for battle, but Adoeete stood powerfully silent, his steely eyes piercing his son's. The self-controlled softening of the chief's voice made the hard words he had to say, even harder for Red Eye to hear. "You made this happen," Adoeete said, beginning the litany of offenses. "When as a boy, against our laws, you hunted game for sport, cruelly torturing them." Adoeete took an intimidating step forward, unhappily wielding the spear of truth. "You made this happen when you falsely believed rules were not made for you, and the Great Spirits' Will of Goodness would not become your own."

Red Eye stepped back, the painful truth piercing his mind.

"You made this happen," continued the venerable man, "when you were seduced by power but had no interest in learning to wield it wisely." Leaning inches from his son's face, Adoeete stated, "And you made this happen when *you* killed Antinanco, your own brother and *my* firstborn son!"

Red Eye could no longer take the pain and dark disappointment in his father's eyes and was forced to turn away. The moment, however, gave his mind space to wonder how his father could have known he'd committed the crime. The two brothers were a day's ride away from home and he and the insufferably good Antinanco, Sun of the Eagle, Heart of Adoeete's Heart, and Arrow of the Great Spirit, were alone. His brother's misplaced trust in Red Eye was Antinanco's fatal flaw and the only reason Red Eye was able to catch him off guard. Antinanco—Aiyana's father, Adoeete's son—never suspected the real reason for the brotherly hunting trip.

Red Eye moved toward his father, his eyes once again callous and stubborn. Now he would inflict his own wound on the foolish man. "You're senile, old man. No one could know that. We were alone!" Silence filled the room. Adoeete searched his son's eyes for a spark of light that he could will into a flame, but it was hidden beneath the now cold embers. On the day of his returning from the top of the mountain, gold in his hand instead of inspiration and wisdom in his heart, Napyshni had a choice. He could humble himself and go back, try again—try a hundred times more if he must! Instead Napyshni permitted the boy Red Eye to remain.

Adoeete took a deep breath, filling himself with the power of the Great Spirit. "Today, my son, when time stopped between us, and you raised your hand once more to murder another of our family, many truths were revealed." The explaining was over, and the sentence was final. "You will go, Red Eye. You will take your men with you. You will take all who will not voluntarily serve under Aiyana's rule as chief. You will not come back." Adoeete and the elders turned and walked out of the tent.

A sudden and uncontained fury drove Red Eye to pick up his spear. He pictured himself mightily impaling his father. Racing out of the tepee, his war cry split the sky, but Adoeete's warriors were ready for him as five sharp spears ruthlessly jabbed at his body, holding him at bay while leather bindings captured his hands. Alive but bloodied, Red Eye was slung over his horse and tied in place. With the whip of a slender stick, the horse bolted, and Red Eye was gone. Sky Wolf and Cha'tiam watched in horror as one by one each of Red Eye's warriors suffered the same humiliating fate. The dishonorable scene would be told and retold around every tribal campfire for years. The laughing would never stop. One day, it would reach Red Eye's ears and then it would only be a matter of time until he returned and unleashed his wrath upon Adoeete, Aiyana, and the village. The village he thought he was meant to rule.

CHAPTER SIX

THE ATTIC

The Hartland Tree Line, 2018

Sam Biel cursed when he spotted the group of equestrian riders, all in their fancy cowboy hats and boots, walking their horses back from the long ride to El Dorado Park. Where the park ended, and Hartland land began, most people couldn't tell, but Sam sure as hell knew where the Biel Boys ruled, and he'd dare any of those fancified horse people to fight him for it. Jeff, still not recovered from the ghost girl up at the big house, suggested the Biel Boys pry their hatchets out of the trees, throw their beer cans in the large pile with the others, and hightail it home. To support the plan, Danny philosophically shared his own rationale. *"If,"* Danny deduced, "we stop by Angelus Oaks and swipe a couple bottles of whiskey, *then* we could get drunk and not think about losing Hartland any more." Martin Biel was glad to have someone in the group with brains. He spoke little, but when he did it carried weight, so he voiced a strong, "Yah!"

Martin knew Sam was itching for a fight, but then, Martin thought, *He'd been dropped real hard on his head as a kid.*

Honey watched from the window as the sound of motorcycles and a cloud of dust rose up in the west on the dirt road that was Hart Lane. From the east came the string of horseback riders, members of the Yucaipa Equestrian Arena Committee, who had for the first time in forty years traversed the Hartland property not only with permission, but with a promise of lemonade and cookies when they returned.

It seemed a simple request to Honey, that Pete's wife Linda and her equestrian friends, mostly neighbors, should enjoy an afternoon of riding at Hartland. After all it was historic land, and while she owned the deed, she was happy to allow others to enjoy it too. She had Pete take down all the NO TRESPASSING signs. But Honey wasn't prepared for the wave of grateful emotion from Linda and friends, many of whom had grown up in the homes surrounding Hartland and loved the pristine acres still richly preserved in their natural habitat. Linda insisted Pete use her cell phone to take pictures of Honey, the horses, equestrians, and the Victorian home as the backdrop. The men and women held up their cups of lemonade, and with bright smiles, they marked the momentous occasion with a photograph.

Under the command of a very competent Pete, contractors of every kind swarmed around the Hartland house, tearing out the old plumbing and electric and putting in the latest and greatest of everything, including heating and air-conditioning, fixing this, painting that, and restoring what they could.

On Saturday, having settled the outside work crews of arborists, landscapers, and tractor drivers plowing under the two acres of mile-high weeds surrounding the house, Pete went back to work on his own project, the upstairs 1870s bedroom closet. It needed enlarging since it could, at best, hold only five of Honey's perhaps twenty-five dresses. As Pete demolished the walls, he discovered another door inside the closet. It was at least six feet tall and wide enough to take furniture through. It led, he suspected, to the high-pitched attic above. While he wouldn't consider it a secret door, it was nonetheless obscure, having no handle nor hinges that could be seen. To pry it open, he'd need a thin screwdriver or perhaps a knife and some force as it looked like it had been painted over often.

It took some time and patience, but at last Pete released it from its confines. The squeak and groan of the large hinges on the back of the door confirmed it had not been opened in a long time, and when Pete saw what it revealed, his eyes filled with amazement. Pete took off his cap, scratched his head, and wondered how many ghosts from the past lived here. He'd heard stories, and he'd felt weird things, even in the short time he and the men had been working on the house. *No doubt about it, though,* he thought, replacing his cap, *I'm more than happy to git outta here and let Ms. Honey deal with this situation.* Pete's quick descent of the stairs and the sound of unsettled tools in his leather tool belt, made everyone look up.

"Uhhh, Ms. Honey," began Pete, "sorry to bother you, but I need to show you something upstairs."

Honey was surrounded by books of fabric samples provided by Ms. Lindsey Bell of the Redlands' interior design firm, Serenity. Honey had stolen Lindsey for a few hours from Landon and La Bonita, promising to make her final decisions by 11:00 a.m. and release both the highly recommended interior decorator and the fabric samples, now held hostage in her Hartland living room. Landon had acquiesced only when she agreed to have dinner with him that night at La Bonita, where, he'd said conspiratorially, "There's a surprise waiting for you."

Honey's guessing and prying were useless, which meant she'd just have to wait to find out what the surprise was.

"Sure, Pete," said Honey. "Excuse me, Lindsey, I'll be right back."

"Well," said Pete as they climbed, "I found something very interesting in your closet."

"Really? What is it?" asked Honey.

Pete replied, "A hidden door that goes into the attic. There's a bunch of really old things I know you're going to want to see."

Honey laughed. "Everything's old here, Pete."

Pete was considering whether he should give her a heads-up about some stories and ghost sightings, just in case she ran across a few when she was up there. He liked Ms. Honey, and he only thought it fair. So, before opening the door he said, carefully choosing his words, "Hartland's had a long history, much of which is amazing, but some of it isn't very pleasant. There have been many stories, and even a few about people who died, or were killed here and, well, still haunt the place."

"You're not going to tell me you found a dead body in my closet, Pete, are you?" Honey laughed.

"No, no, nothing like that," he assured her. "Just, in a place like this, you could see weird things. There have been lots of stories from locals about, you know, well . . . ghosts."

Honey laughed. "I've already been warned by my friend Edward Smiley back in New York, Pete. I think I've heard every story ever told about this place, and, yes, they include ghosts. It's not that I don't believe ghosts exist, it's just that I've never seen one. So, for now, I'm sticking with the 'I'll believe it when I see it' motto."

"Suit yourself, ma'am," said Pete, opening the hidden door.

Honey was stunned. Before her was a treasure trove of antique furniture, vintage clothes, trunks, books, and an assortment of interesting things, some covered with white sheets of canvas to keep off the dust. "Hollywood would kill to film 'A Ghost in Your Attic' here," Honey said.

Feeling a brush of cold air, Pete retreated down the stairs as Honey stepped inside. The attic was large and made to appear more so by the high-pitched ceiling forming the gables on the roof. The windows let the sunlight in, its rays illuminating the tiny particles floating in the air, removing the ghostly feel and replacing it with simply the presence of history. Intuitively she knew these artifacts were imbued with the lives, thoughts, and desires of real people, not just characters formed in her mind, and she longed to touch every piece and silently listen and feel its response. But Lindsey was still downstairs, and she must see her off. She'd return, but not before everyone was gone, the house quiet, and she could be alone with her ancestors, her family. Tomorrow was Sunday. She'd have the place to herself.

Before closing the door, she glanced to the right, touched by the small child's bed and china doll that laid upon it. Honey too had played with such a doll when she was a child, an antique belonging to her grandmother Victoria. There were children here, she recalled, wishing she'd paid closer attention when Edward said their names. She remembered that several had died. Tears stung her eyes. "Edward, when the time is right, you must come to Hartland. You must see this." Honey reluctantly closed the door. It would be nearly impossible for her to think about anything else besides the attic. But decorating choices awaited her downstairs, and a thousand other things needed attending to as the moving van, with all her belongings, had begun its trek from New York and would be there next week.

After saying their goodbyes, Lindsey headed off to La Bonita and Honey to the dining room to meet with Pete at the makeshift table constructed of sawhorses and plywood. The six plastic chairs matched the plastic blue-and-white checked tablecloth where everyone gathered and upon which Honey had placed a vase of yellow daisies.

Pete and Honey huddled over the schedule, counting projects and days left in which to accomplish them. "We're pretty much on track, Ms. Honey," Pete declared, "especially in terms of making the house ready for the moving van's arrival. I'll concentrate the men on the inside now, till we're finished. Then, once you're moved in, we can tackle more of the outside. Seems you'll be stuck with us for some time. Still lots to be done."

"I'm building a luxury bunkhouse and adopting all of you," teased Honey. "I just don't know what I'd do without you and the men, Pete. You've all done such a wonderful job, and the house and I are both grateful."

"We're happy to do it," Pete replied. "It means a lot to the folks here in Yucaipa that you've come back and are restoring the place. She has sentimental value for all of Yucaipa. It's been hard on everyone to watch her neglected and going downhill."

"Ah . . . that's so nice to hear," Honey said, touched by the deep concern of the community. "We'll have to have an open house when we're ready," she announced.

"Careful there," warned Pete, "everyone in Yucaipa, Redlands, and San Bernardino will show up. Back in the late 1800s when this place had vineyards, the Harts would throw what they called the Hartland Crush. All the people in the region would come for a picnic, music, dancing, and to help crush the grapes. There were Indians, Mexicans, Spaniards, Mormons, Europeans, and even some Chinese. My grandfather told me about attending these parties when he was a boy." Pete checked his watch, but his contractor's body already knew it was three o'clock and in need of an ice-cold beer.

"We'll see you Monday morning, 7:00 a.m. sharp, Honey. Enjoy what's left of your weekend."

Following him out the door, Honey said, "Thanks Pete, you too, and thanks again for everything."

"No problem," he replied, then turned back. "By the way, if I were you, I'd keep all that," nodding toward the attic, "real close to the vest. There could be some valuable things up there, and I wouldn't want anything to happen to such a nice lady as you."

Honey initially felt disturbed by Pete's well-intentioned warning, but in seeing the contractors off, offering thanks for all their work, and wishing the crew a restful weekend, the feeling disappeared. Instead, with excitement, Honey admired the handiwork of the plows. She had never anticipated owning agricultural land, and the thought of it was both overwhelming and exhilarating. As she rounded the corner of the house and looked out at the nearly five acres of rich brown soil, she suddenly envisioned the orderly rows of grapevines, replanted just as Jonathan Hart had done so long ago. Her imagination recreated in her mind the days of the Hartland Crush, but this time the happy revelers were the faces of her new friends, including Landon, of course.

Honey knelt and scooped up a handful of soil, feeling its combination of silk and grit in her hand. The land was a living being, she could clearly see that now. It had gifts to give and its own purpose to fulfill, even as she did. Perhaps it was made to grow vineyards and grapes, but maybe other things as well. "What, dear land, would you like to grow?" asked Honey aloud.

"Talking to dirt now, I see," observed Landon, making Honey jump, screech, and fling the dirt in the air.

"Landon Aires, you scared me," scolded Honey.

"Sorry about that, Honey," Landon said, the ten-year-old boy inside him nevertheless pleased with her response. Adding insult to injury, Landon handed her the gift of a large bag of sugar. Honey looked at him questioningly.

"Just want to make sure you have enough of this on hand when I need to borrow some," Landon teased. Honey laughed as Landon took in the beauty of the land and the astounding improvements Pete had made in such a short time. "Wow, up-close this is so beautiful," Landon said with admiration warming his words. "I've only seen the place from my high-powered telescope."

"You're horrible, Landon Aires!" Honey reprimanded, grabbing the bag of sugar out of his hands.

"So I've been told!" he bragged. "So, you going to be neighborly and show me around?"

"Okay, but then I'm moving back to New York first thing tomorrow," countered Honey. Sighing, she said, "Come on, you," and hooked her arm through his. "Let's see if I can't find an upstairs porch or two to toss you over."

The tour ended in front of the living room fireplace where Landon was thoughtfully looking up, considering the empty space above it. "You know," he suggested, "an oil painting of Hartland would be perfect here."

"I thought so too," said Honey.

"Well, then," replied Landon, "if I may, I'd like to propose a trip to Oak Glen to visit the gallery of a very fine artist, named Fariad. He's more than a local favorite. He has followers around the world. I have several of his paintings at La Bonita."

"I'd love to see his work!" exclaimed Honey.

"Done," finalized Landon, suddenly noticing the oversized statue of a woman on the mantel.

Wondering what it was made of, Landon reached out to touch it, but abruptly felt a cold chill run up his spine. Instantly he drew back his hand. He looked to see if Honey had felt it too, but her face remained calm. Just as the thought, *It's nothing,* entered his mind, his eye caught the flash of a little girl sitting on the stairs. When he looked again, she was gone. Not wanting to frighten Honey, or look foolish, Landon felt the best course of action was to ignore it all. While he tried to chalk it up to one of the things that happens when you're overworked, or in an old house, or when the light casts shadows in funny ways, he was a man who faced facts. He knew what he felt and saw what he saw. But even the inexplicable had reasons. He just didn't know what they were—yet.

***

The surprise that Landon had promised Honey had arrived at La Bonita and was having a glass of wine with Landon, and Don the Realtor. The three men were sitting on the balcony waiting for the guest of honor to arrive.

Honey decided to take the back way, the little-traveled Hart Lane, which, past her home, became a dirt road and ended up on Carter Street. It proved arduous as large potholes, deep ruts, and rocky formations made Honey wish she'd taken another route. The stretch of road did, however, take her past the line of trees that was on her list to explore. It was beautiful and inviting, and she could imagine hikers and equestrians enjoying trail rides through the long, meandering oak and pine forested pathway. Much to her disappointment, she could see in the distance the tree line was littered with trash, an old mattress, and broken pieces of furniture. Someone had made a home of sorts, but not anyone who respected the land. She saw plainly that this must be where those motorcyclists had made a camp and then created the large clouds of dust. She'd talk with Don to see what he knew about the bikers and how to deal with this.

A final plunge into a gully and up the other side brought Honey to Carter Street where a right turn put her once again on solid ground. The rough but more drivable paved road offered her another perspective of her land, which had a natural beauty different from the lush landscapes of the East Coast. She thought of the terrain as feeling primitive and undisturbed. She could easily picture the Yucaipat Indians in the 1800s, whose lives Edward had so vividly painted for her, cultivating the rich soil, riding their horses across the flat lands, and making a home for themselves at the river's edge. Some names floated in her mind as she visualized Chief Adoeete, Aiyana, and Red Eye. And of course, her great-great-grandfather Jonathan who had lived with them, and his grandfather JD to whom the entire Hart family had to thank for Hartland. When she was settled, she'd ask Edward to come and stay with her for a while and they could walk and picnic, and this time she would pay close attention to every detail of his stories. What had seemed mostly tall tales when she was younger, were, in reality, a history of this place and her family. *How closed off and narrow-minded we can be until experience wakes us up to other worlds we could not have imagined existed,* thought Honey. And now, having come near the end of Carter, the adobe walls and open gates announcing La Bonita welcomed Honey into a whole new world. What she would find at the end of the long, paved, serpentine road she couldn't guess.

To the degree that Hartland was wholly Victorian, La Bonita was wholly Spanish. The sizeable mansion too was white, but adorned with a red tile roof. Instead of wood, it was made of adobe. The architect had used the art of symmetry to bring great beauty, along with arches, balconies, and an observation tower. A separate chapel with the same design had been placed on the property, and one could find it down a lovely brick pathway. There were equestrian barns, and barns for equipment, and miles of trails to ride in the beautiful California hills. La Bonita was perched up high, providing spectacular views of the Green Valley.

The three men on the balcony watched as Honey's car made its way to the house, and Landon jogged to meet her in the circular driveway.

"You do have peacocks!" Honey exclaimed as Landon helped her out of her car.

"I do!" he confirmed as the demure ladies ran away. "I also have a glass of wine for you."

"That would be lovely," Honey sighed, hoping it would cure the headache that Hart Lane was responsible for. "Oh, and I have a house-warming gift for you." From inside her purse, Honey brought out a glass measuring cup. "Just in case you need to borrow some sugar."

Landon bent to kiss her cheek. "What a thoughtful neighbor," he whispered.

Honey took in the breathtaking house, and her eyes couldn't get enough of the amazing view. "Your La Bonita is exquisite, Landon. If I lived here, I'd never leave. Now," demanded Honey, pointing to the observation tower, "I want to see precisely the view of Hartland from your high-powered telescope, Mr. Aires."

Landon winced. With a sigh of resignation, he offered Honey his arm. "Come along then, Ms. Hart, there's no time like the present for a man to get in trouble . . . and stay in trouble." Landon escaped the pre-tend tower of trouble as his two guests stood like doormen in the large entryway, eager to see Honey, whose beauty Don had described to Matt in glowing terms.

"I see you have a welcoming party," said Landon, grinning. "Honey, you know Don, of course." Honey offered Don a friendly hug, happy to see a familiar face and appreciating all he'd done to help her.

"And this is Matt Carver, Director of the Smiley Library," pre-sented Landon.

"Delighted," Matt said, his English accent charming.

Honey smiled broadly, looking back at Landon. "What a marvelous surprise!"

To Matt, Honey said, "Great to meet you!"

To both men, Honey said, "I have so much to ask about the library and about Hartland—you both must come over to visit. Don, you'll especially want to see all the work Pete has done to the place."

"Done," Don said, delighted to have a special invitation.

"Okay, gentlemen," said Landon, "how about you show our lovely guest the view while I scare up a glass of wine and turn on the grill." Neither Don nor Matt needed to be asked twice, and Landon smiled as he watched both men gesturing broadly, pointing this way and that, describing the sweeping landscape to an awestruck Honey.

The evening was everything Landon had hoped for. The hotel chef had prepared the meal, and Landon had only to grill the steaks. There were perks to being in the hotel business. A fire in the fireplace, soft background music, and the lights of the valley created a perfect atmosphere for making new friends and discovering the threads that bound them all together. The conversation had been spirited, fun, and filled with lots of information about both Hartland and the library—Matt and Don having a wealth of knowledge. Pushing back his empty plate, Matt said, "I have to apologize, Honey, but I'm afraid you've been ganged up on by a pair of ruffians, one of which is sitting at this table and the other safely out of reach in New York."

"Oh?" said Honey, raising an eyebrow, playing along.

"Edward sent an email alerting me to your circumstances and that you were at the Aires Hotel. I was charged with, forgive me, checking in on you when I received a call from Landon here, to come to dinner, having discovered your affiliation with the Smileys. Landon and I have known each other for some time now. Been on lots of boards together. As you can guess, I'm to report back to Edward as soon as I've seen for myself that you're alive and well. You can see why I jumped at the chance to meet you and get a look at this spectacular place. I did, however, take my chances with Landon cooking the steaks."

Honey laughed, shaking her head. "Edward likes to hover, and it was very kind of you to agree to be his spy." Honey winked. "In all seriousness, though, I really do appreciate your checking in on me. Please email Edward back and report that I'm doing very well and love being at Hartland, despite Pete my contractor insisting I have ghosts. He'll know what I mean."

Landon shifted uncomfortably in his seat. Don took another sip of his wine. Matt probed further, asking, "You don't believe in ghosts, I take it?"

Honey shared her motto, but added, "From what I've seen so far, though, I've decided to keep an open mind. It was hard to imagine this life and its history from my concrete home in New York City. Once I arrived, however, and even just driving here this evening, the fantastic stories Edward has told me seem very plausible. Except perhaps," she laughed, "the one about the hidden gold still waiting to be found."

"Does seem a bit far-fetched," Matt agreed, "but having lived in Redlands for many years now, and being a history buff, now and again you'll hear a thread of the same story running through the old families like the Morleys, Edwards, Kanes, Thomases, and the Beaumonts, many of whose descendants have been or currently are our Library Board Members. One of our librarians, Linda Hall, is the great-great-granddaughter of Amelia Hall, a person of interest it seems in the affairs of Hartland when your own great-great-grandfather owned the place. Not sure what she has to do with the gold . . . Anyway, some say Jameson Morley back in the early 1900s stole the gold and hid it somewhere at Morley Mansion. Others believe Hargrove Kane gradually smuggled the gold from his father Lester and that he and some actress sailed off with it to New York and then on to Europe."

Don jumped in with, "Some think outlaws ran off with it. It may sound crazy, but I think there's a lot of factual evidence that it still exists, and I know a lot of folks in Yucaipa believe it does."

"One thing is sure," Matt said confidently, "the gold was hidden again. Question is, where is it now?"

Landon thought buried treasure unlikely and went too far for his practical mind, but, then again, until today he had thought the same of ghosts. Wanting time alone with Honey, Landon took the opportunity to stand and say, "I'm rescuing you, my dear, from this motley crew of gold hunters and taking you to see the real gold—what I call my jewel box, the Green Valley at night."

"Guess that's our cue to leave," said Matt. "Thanks for a great evening, Landon. Wonderful to meet you, Honey. I'd love to give you a tour of the library myself. Just call me when you want to stop by."

"That would be terrific, Matt. I'll definitely take you up on it," said Honey. "The moving van is coming next week, but as soon as I'm settled, I'll give you a call."

"I'll stop by on Monday," assured Don. "Great meal and a great time, Landon. Thanks so much."

On the balcony, the lights of the valley and the sight of her new home were remarkable. Honey sighed. "What a great evening, Landon. You outdid yourself with both the company and the meal. Everyone has been so great. I could get used to it here in Yucaipa."

"That's the goal," said Landon. "I know you've got your hands full with construction workers and the van's coming this week, but how about penciling in the following Saturday. We can visit Matt at the library then head up to Oak Glen for a look at Fariad's Art Gallery. Maybe I'll even buy you a piece of Apple Annie's homemade apple pie."

"Sounds like fun!" agreed Honey. The moment turned quiet as together they took in the lights of the stars above and the cities below. Landon put his arm around Honey, drawing her close to his side. She leaned into him. They felt right together, but of course they would. It was obvious from the start they had been destined to meet.

He was surprised when Honey shifted her body to press against his, and turned her face up . . . so close to his . . .

Landon and Honey's lips met, each enjoying the other's without hesitation or fear. Landon pressed his lips against hers with a tender passion, and held the back of her head—her chestnut hair blowing gently in the night breeze—as though he were holding a precious and priceless work of art. A one of a kind.

When they finally broke the kiss, and Honey pressed her cheek against Landon's chest, taking in the scent of the man and the sight of the Green Valley at night, she had never felt so at peace. They could have stayed like that forever.

Sighing, Honey remembered her to-do list, stretching ahead of her into an unknown and uncertain future. As much as she did not want to go, the practical Honey prevailed. "How about walking a girl out to her car? Wouldn't want to get eaten by a California grizzly bear, just when I'm starting to like it here."

"Davy Crockett at your service, ma'am," Landon said, kissing her hand and then her forehead. They walked to her rental car holding hands.

Honey smiled all the way down the long drive and nearly to Hart Lane, when the gunning of motorcycle engines and the glare of four powerful headlights pulled out in front of her and stopped, blocking her way. Honey slammed on her brakes, her smile vanished and her heart in her throat.

Earlier, the Biel Boys, heading up to the tree line, had seen the cloud of dust and the white Ford Explorer on Hart Lane then going up the hill. They knew it was *her* car. They'd seen it plenty of times in the driveway at Hartland. What she was doing they couldn't tell. So, they'd followed at a safe distance. When she turned to go up to La Bonita, they knew they had her. They would be there when she made her way back down.

CHAPTER SEVEN

A NEW CHIEF

Yucaipat Indian Village, 1860

The warmth of Aiyana's tepee and the bundle of furs within which Jonathan lay had allowed the boy to sleep as long as he did, but he slowly and sadly awakened. Aiyana watched him stir, knowing the moment had come when there would be no words she could offer the boy to explain away the unexplainable. Still groggy with sleep, Jonathan took in his surroundings as the pain of remembrance struck him like a thunderbolt. The unfamiliar faces and strange place heightened his fear, and he let out a violent cry, struggling to escape from the bonds of the furs.

"Shh-shh-little boy good," Aiyana spoke softly, helping to free him. "Little boy good," Aiyana repeated, offering him the blue shawl that had fallen from his shoulders. Jonathan's eyes widened as he remembered . . . remembered his Mama putting her pearl necklace over his head, covering him with the shawl, hiding him behind the grain sacks, and begging him to be quiet and brave. He heard the men shouting, heard the guns, heard his Papa yelling, his Mama screaming. He wasn't supposed to leave his hiding place, but he had to see, had to help, and so he'd gone to the back of the wagon. Mama's blouse had been ripped, and her face was bleeding, and Papa was lying on the ground, and there was lots of blood. And then the big, ugly man grabbed him by the hair and tried to pull him out of the wagon, which hurt bad, and he screamed, and Mama threw herself at the brute. Everyone heard the Indian war cry, which made the man curse because he was afraid of Indians. He let go, but the tall man shot Mama anyway. They rode away on their horses. He wanted to go to Mama and Papa, climb out of the wagon, but the Indians were coming, and he had to hide.

But the Indian was a lady. She didn't want to kill him, he knew that. He let her take him on her horse, away from what the bad men had done to his Mama and Papa, but then he'd fallen asleep. And now he was here, but he should be at Hartland. They were almost home. "Mama! Papa!" moaned Jonathan, the unthinkable a reality, one it seemed he'd never understand. Sobbing he fell into the furs, his heart broken again and his mind a painful blur. Gently Aiyana stroked his arm, allowing him to feel her care, and, soon after, he welcomed her arms in which she rocked and soothed the traumatized child. Honana, the medicine woman, brought corn cakes and broth, feeding him as much as he would eat. Exhausted once more, he fell asleep.

Adoeete had walked the short distance back from the warriors' camp, sickened by what had to be done with Red Eye and sickened by the cause of it. He wished now he'd never turned back to look, the image of the horse carrying Red Eye away from his people would forever be emblazoned in his mind. That he had done the right thing, he did not question. That his wounded heart could mend, he was not sure. Now, it seemed another matter had arisen as several young children raced to tell him of a white boy in Aiyana's tepee.

Adoeete called from outside Aiyana's tent, requesting entrance. Honana moved quickly to open the leather flap. As Adoeete's eyes accustomed themselves to the dimly lit interior, the opening of the apex of the tepee alone letting in light, he saw Aiyana curled next to a small boy wrapped in furs, fast asleep. His granddaughter, with great motherly love, was lightly combing through his blond hair. What a contrast, he thought, to the scene he had just witnessed in Red Eye's tent.

Honana returned to her place beside Aiyana, waving the potent herbal cures over the child, willing the boy to rest and softy chanting the songs of the Great Spirit that would aid his wounded mind and heart. Adoeete drew back the fur, better to see the face of the child. His eyes softened. Above the Great Eagle circled as the inner voice arose in Adoeete's mind. "Courage it took to say goodbye to your son. Vigilance it will take to prevent him from returning and taking his revenge. You, Adoeete, Heart of My Heart, Arrow of the Great Spirit, have guided for many years my emerging forms in nature, directing and protecting its life in the world of men. Now a new form is emerging, and Aiyana must lead the way."

Adoeete nodded.

"Come child," he said, addressing Aiyana, "let us move to the other side of the fire." Suddenly chilled, Adoeete added another log and watched the tendrils of smoke draw up through the opening, feeling his own spirit longing to be drawn upward as well. Grandfather and granddaughter, master teacher and devoted student, chief and heir, took their places next to the fire as they had done for many years. Each knew the ritual, each made themselves ready, each had much to share, but first there would be silence. Aiyana breathed deeply and closed her eyes as did Adoeete, together taking their minds, desires, and wills to a still place. Finally, Aiyana looked up, Adoeete's old eyes mystically keeping her gaze. She'd looked into those eyes a thousand times. Today they were moist with tears, sadness, and pain, and yet the strength of the Great Spirit remained.

"Aiyana," he spoke, breaking the silence, "Granddaughter of Adoeete, Heart of My Heart, Arrow of the Great Spirit, it is for you now to take my place and direct the tribe, the crops, the animals, to serve the seed of a new life, which is meant to unfold under your care."

Aiyana touched her vest, feeling the leather pouch.

"I have been waiting for the final sign," continued the old man. "It has not come, but I can wait no longer. Tonight, at the Great Council, you will take my place."

"Grandfather," Aiyana said, "but what of my uncle, Red Eye? Surely you had meant for him to be chief."

"Red Eye is gone," Adoeete simply said. "If he returns, he does so against my wishes, and if he tries to inflict harm, he must be killed."

Aiyana drew in her breath; the seriousness of the moment and the chief's command left no room for argument.

So, thought Aiyana, *it is for me to serve, to lead, to protect and care for the Yucaipat. I am not worthy,* her mind said. "I am not worthy," her voice repeated aloud as the cry of the Great Eagle circling the tent begged to differ.

Adoeete was silent, watching the face of his granddaughter as she struggled to hear and accept the truth.

Aiyana breathed deeply, closed her eyes, welcoming the silence. The dream, the seed, the tuft of feather from the Great Eagle's white head all assured her of the Great Spirit's will. Aiyana reached into her vest, producing the leather pouch. Her fingers loosened the drawstring. Reaching for Adoeete's hand, she poured out the seed and feather, the final sign. Adoeete's eyes grew large, then misty, and finally closed in peace, the last sign he held now in his hand. The Eagle cried once more.

Adoeete arose and Aiyana followed as he moved to the opening of the tepee. He turned, addressing first Honana. "Prepare her grandmother's dress." And then to his granddaughter, "Wear it tonight in her honor." Honana and Aiyana nodded.

The image of his granddaughter in Nizhoni's ceremonial garb would be a sight to behold. The chief finalized the matter with a nod and left the tepee to prepare for the evening ahead, but Adoeete had made a grave mistake. His rage over Red Eye followed by the distraction of the white boy and now the upcoming ceremony clouded his mind, and the oversight would haunt him for a long time.

The drums beat slowly, signaling that the time had come for the villagers to gather round the great tribal fire. Sixteen-year-old Kitchi's heart likewise beat harder and faster at the very thought of Aiyana, as he waited with anticipation and great pride for the only woman he had ever loved to move through the motions of the ceremony that would make her his chief. Though his youth made his love for her unsuitable for marriage, it was not enough to douse the fire, nor would it ever be. One day Aiyana would marry, one day he would too, and only he would know what she meant to him.

Earlier that morning, high in a giant oak tree, he had allowed the wind to create phantasies and images in his mind. He imagined Chief Adoeete calling him to his tent, explaining that soon Kitchi and Aiyana would marry, and he would count on Kitchi (Brave) to protect her and lead Aiyana's warriors in her defense and that of the village. The beautiful image faded as the loud voices of men quarreling came from the warrior camp. He could see Sky Wolf and Cha'tiam riding swiftly toward the canyon, and he wondered what was wrong. He climbed to a higher branch to gain a better view, witnessing Red Eye bursting out of his tent, ready to throw his angry spear, but then halted by Chief Adoeete's men. He observed Red Eye and his humiliated and disgraced warriors carried away like sacks of grain on their horses as they headed at full gallop down the valley below.

Kitchi knew it would be days before they would be released as no white man, Spaniard, or Indian would dare risk himself to free the notorious Yucaipat and his men. Straining to see more, Kitchi climbed higher, but his weight was too much for the thin branch and it cracked, sending him plummeting through the tree, its branches breaking his fall but at a cost to his now bruised and scraped body. The headache he still carried with him tonight and the loud beating drums didn't help.

Kitchi felt the heat of the flames as the ceremonial fire roared into life. The drums were suddenly silenced, creating in the empty space an electricity that heightened each one's sense of excitement. At Adoeete's command, the elders who were placed on either side of Aiyana's tent, pulled aside the leather curtained doorway, revealing the woman all would hold, from this night forward, in highest honor and respect. Aiyana stepped into the light. The contrast between the white-fringed, deerskin dress and her long, shiny, black hair, loosely braided to one side and falling to her waist, created gasps. Kitchi saw that her grandmother's delicately beaded dress, made for a slightly larger woman, hung off her smooth shoulders, highlighting the exquisite length of her neck and offering an unexpected hint of the fullness of her breasts. The wide leather belt cinched in the folds at her small waist and flowed out to embrace her fuller hips. His heart stopped, his eyes grew large, and the image became emblazoned in his mind.

Honana had woven colored strips of leather and feathers in her hair and she looked the very image of the Great Mother to whom all owed their lives. Kitchi's eyes filled with stinging tears as the unexpected truth brought a wave of utter bereavement. He clutched his heart knowing this beautiful woman would never be his. He felt a part of him die.

The lovely voice of Honana filled the night sky as she sang the hauntingly beautiful song that spoke of the long history of the Yucaipat people and their succession of great chiefs. When all was still again, Chief Adoeete slowly took off the ceremonial headdress, held it before Aiyana, and asked her the time-honored questions whose answers would signal her maturity and readiness to serve her people and their land, death alone freeing her from this sacred oath.

Kitchi thought the headdress suited Aiyana as she spoke the solemn oath to care for and protect them with her life, if necessary. Suddenly distracted, Kitchi caught Adoeete's eye peering into the darkness behind the villagers and the frown that followed. Kitchi turned to look, saw the hurling spear racing toward Aiyana. Time slowed down for the sixteen-year-old as he took in the faces of the villagers still smiling, unaware of the danger, and of Aiyana, whose voice was continuing to speak the oath. Out of the shadows stepped Red Eye, the spear having just left his hand, while Sky Wolf and Cha'tiam smirked on either side, holding up the empty bindings for Adoeete to see how easily they'd escaped. The powerful force drove the spear through the leaping boy, carrying Kitchi through the air, pinning him to an ancient tree. Red Eye cursed as the intended victim remained alive, but he'd made his point, filling the village with an overshadowing fear. He and the warriors melted into the darkness, found their horses, and disappeared into the night before anyone could move, vowing to return another day to do much worse. So much worse.

◦⁓◦

No one in the village slept well that night. A sense of dread, unsettling changes, and curiosity got the better of three of the Indian boys, still children at the ages of nine, eight, and seven. Odakota the eldest, decided Hototo the youngest, should stand guard as he and Teetonka broke the time-honored protocol of not peeking into another's tepee. The coaxing and shushing were loud enough for Honana to hear their plan from inside the tent. The little braves, thought Honana, would have to do better if they didn't want to be caught. The horrors of the night before still raw, nonetheless her eyes smiled with understanding. She couldn't blame them for their eagerness to see the strange and unexpected guest, but they had to be taught to respect the privacy of others. She threw the flap open, startling the boys and making them shriek.

"What gives you the right to invade another's private place?" Honana's rebuking voice demanded. The boys stood stone still, quivering. "You know," continued Honana, "Chief Aiyana would be greatly displeased and sad to know her own young braves, who have sworn to protect and defend her, are instead acting like children. One cannot be considered a true brave, unless he is also patient and respectful."

The boys nodded, feeling the chastisement, but glad to be thought of as more than children. "So," invited Honana, "*be* the Chief's True Braves, *make* her proud of you, and come and aid her in helping the young white boy to mend from his great wounds."

The boys, eager to shake off the image of Kitchi, make amends, and get what they wanted—a peek at the newcomer—nodded in agreement. Honana bent down, gathered the boys around her, and explained that his parents had been killed in a terrible raid. Chief Aiyana had rescued him and that was all anyone knew. Perhaps *they* could discover his name.

Odakota stretched out his hand, which held his inexperienced attempt at carving. A bear. "I can give this to him," he offered.

Not to be outdone, Hototo said, "And I can teach him to whistle."

"He probably knows how to whistle," said Teetonka disparagingly, adding, "He hasn't been to the river to skip stones. I can take him there."

Honana agreed. "He will need all those things and especially your patience, respect, and friendship." Suddenly remembering Kitchi's brave death and the boys' inclination to talk about it, Honana said, "We will not speak of Kitchi to him now. He needs no more talk of death." With that she opened the flap, allowing them entrance, hoping their medicine would be a better cure than hers.

Jonathan, now two days in the tent, was feeling restless, having only been outside to relieve himself in the care of an older man. From that perspective only, he'd observed he was in a village, and that people were working, and cooking, and children were playing as all people do.

The nightmare still very much alive, he longed to wake up to find it was all a dream, but the pain and haunting images would never allow that, and he had to face facts. There would be time for thinking later, but for now he was content to allow the shock and dullness that follows such traumatic events to have its way.

With the appearance of the three curious Indian boys, he felt some sense of normalcy, even if they looked and dressed differently from him. Honana ushered them inside, not too close but close enough for each to get a good look at one another, making their assessments as they naturally would. Odakota and Hototo immediately liked the boy, his blue eyes soft and without malice. The combination of blond hair and a fine-looking face made the boys content to stare at him. Teetonka, however, wasn't sure how he felt about someone who looked so different from him.

Odakota made the first move and sat down at the fire at a safe distance for both. He held up the bear. Jonathan leaned over inquisitively, wondering if he could do that someday. "Bear," Odakota said in Yucaipat, leaning toward the boy and extending his arm as far as he could, offering it to him.

Jonathan looked into the boy's eyes trying to read what the gesture meant. Odakota pointed to the bear, then at himself, then at Jonathan. Jonathan nodded, reached for the bear, and took it from Odakota's hand. It was heavier than it looked, and Jonathan could see that while a few important chucks were missing, it was all in all a marvelous bear. Jonathan nodded, and for the first time in days, a thin smile crossed his face. The smile gave Hototo courage, and he whistled a Yucaipat song. Jonathan was amazed both by the sounds the boy produced and the haunting melody. Hototo stopped. Whistled again. Then gestured toward Jonathan. Clearly it was now Jonathan's turn to demonstrate his own limited whistling skills as he was just learning. He managed to eke out a few whistle-like sounds, which contained more air than melody and made all the boys laugh. Jonathan laughed too. Honana smiled.

Hototo took the opportunity to show off, bursting into a repertoire of bird calls, which Odakota named as each was performed. Jonathan clapped, and Hototo took a bow. Teetonka spoke to Honana, requesting to take the boy to the river to throw stones. Honana nodded, but would follow them, keeping a close eye on her fragile and recovering ward. Now having Honana's permission, the three boys stood, making signs for Jonathan to stand too.

Excitedly Teetonka pointed toward the river and made the motion of picking up and throwing stones. The message had been sent and received. Jonathan looked anxiously to Honana for approval, which she gave with a nod. As the boys had only one method of going anywhere and that was at full speed, Honana held the flap as now four boys raced toward the water's edge. She would give them a moment of freedom and then make her way to watch over them.

Aiyana arose to her new duties as chief, her heart heavy with grief for the brave Kitchi. She could go to her grandfather at any time for advice, but this day Adoeete encouraged her to think and act according to what she knew was right and aid the tribe using her own good mind. So, Aiyana had walked with the elders back to the warriors' camp to assess what was to be done with the tents of Red Eye's men who had left. Likewise, she would convene together those who had stayed, offering their allegiance to serve her and the tribe. This first act was challenging as it required strength, diplomacy, and support. While most of the hardened warriors who'd left were young and unmarried, a few of Red Eye's men left families behind. They were now angry, bereft of their men and the protection they had offered. In terms of strength, Chief Aiyana would have to hold up Adoeete's decision. In terms of diplomacy, she would have to mitigate the anger of unhappy relatives and at the same time provide the support the abandoned wives and children needed.

The warriors' camp was, in her mind, a symbol of division between what should be a united tribe. As the remaining warriors had rededicated themselves to Aiyana, there was no longer a need for separation. So, she ordered the camp to be dismantled and for the probationary warriors to prepare the ground as a new field for planting. What they would grow the land itself would determine, the signs of which would be read through its soil type, proximity to water, and location in terms of wind and sun. Here, the Yucaipat men and women, rich in the knowledge of agriculture, would come and discuss, plant and observe, just as their ancestors had done for thousands of years.

From these duties Aiyana was hurrying back to check on the boy, when to her surprise she saw him happily throwing stones into the river with Odakota, Teetonka, and Hototo—and yes, there was Honana keeping a close watch nearby. She smiled knowing the worst was over. Aiyana understood, only too well with the loss of her own father and later her mother, that the wound would never completely heal. But this was a start. A new day for her and the boy.

It was evening now. In Aiyana's tent the heaviness of sadness and loss had been replaced with the first signs of hope as Jonathan bent with all seriousness to his task, the carving of a stick to a fine point. Odakota's first assignment for him. Honana was clearing away the tiny remnants of the meal, pleased to see that both Aiyana and Jonathan had eaten their fill. Adoeete and Aiyana were discussing the day as the fire warmed the tent and lightened the souls within it.

Adoeete thought it a good moment to light his pipe with the blend of herbs Honana had created, which aided the removal of that which ailed one's soul. With each puff, the power of catnip, mullein, wild lettuce, and sage filled the air, slowly alleviating the traces of sadness and negativity. He was glad he could bring clarity of thought and a soothing of the mind to Aiyana and the small boy. It was not long before Jonathan absently whistled while he carved.

It had been a good day, thought Jonathan. He mostly liked the boys. He still couldn't say their names, they sounded so strange, but they couldn't say his either. After skipping stones, the oldest boy showed him how to carve. He found two sticks. The first, the boy carved into a point, then made notches at the other end. He flapped his wings like a bird and off they went in search of feathers. The youngest boy found three, and they were placed at the end of the stick. An arrow had been made. Tonight, he was to carve his own stick. Tomorrow they would hunt for more feathers, and then he too would have an arrow. The scent of the old man's pipe made him look up. It smelled funny, but not bad, and he rather liked the mixture of earthy scents. Sometimes Papa smoked a pipe. Mama didn't like the smell, but he did. He liked the old man too. He felt safe with him, and he knew he was a good man. He thought the woman was beautiful, and she was kind and gentle with him. He liked the way she stroked his hair and sang the Indian songs. He didn't know what they meant, but he figured they were for babies and little children. Adoeete caught Jonathan's eye, holding out the pipe and offering him a puff.

"Grandfather! He's only a boy," chided Aiyana.

Adoeete laughed. "Someday."

Adoeete signaled Jonathan to put another log on the fire and sit with them. Honana brought warm drinks and wrapped a white fur around Jonathan's shoulders, joining them around the fire. They were all silent together for some time.

"Aiyana," said Adoeete, "I will tell the boy a story. I will tell him in his own language. You know the story well. You've heard it a hundred times."

Aiyana nodded, pleased.

"Son, what is your name?" Adoeete spoke in English.

"You speak English!" said a shocked Jonathan.

"Yes, I have learned some," answered Adoeete.

"How did you learn?" inquired Jonathan.

Adoeete smiled. "From a white man."

Jonathan nodded, that made sense.

"I am Adoeete, this is my granddaughter, Chief Aiyana, and what is your name?"

"Jonathan," he answered. Turning to Aiyana he asked, "Do you speak English too?"

"Grandfather teach me some. Learn more. You help me?" Aiyana asked, smiling. Jonathan nodded, inquiring of her, "You are the chief?"

"Yes," she affirmed. "Grandfather chief for long, long time. New chief." She pointed to herself.

"Jonathan," said Adoeete, "I tell you story about me, when I was your age. Gold was in the close-by hills. Many men dig for it. Men said gold on our land too and wanted it. Bad men took me to get the gold from my father, Chief White Wolf, when I was young boy. It happened one day when I was alone by this river. Bad men say to my father, Chief White Wolf, they kill me if they don't get our gold. Bad men take me to cave where gold is. Tie me up. A white man—"

Jonathan could no longer contain the emotion building up in his small body. He cried out and sobbed. Aiyana rose, sat next to the boy, trying to offer comfort. Both she and Adoeete were puzzled by the outburst. The wave of shock and sadness having finally subsided, Jonathan wiped his eyes and asked Adoeete, "What was the name of the man who saved you?"

"White man named JD Hart."

"That's my grandfather," said Jonathan solemnly.

The dawn of understanding finally reached the old man's face. "This," he said to Aiyana, "this is JD's grandson."

Aiyana was amazed. How could this be so?

"Where you come from in wagon?" asked Aiyana.

"Texas," Jonathan said. "We were coming to live at Hartland."

Adoeete and Aiyana's eyes locked, everything making sense now.

Adoeete said, "You fine boy, just like JD. JD good to us. We good to JD. We good to you. When you grow big, Hartland be your home."

Tears streaked Jonathan's cheeks. That was good, but what would home be without one's Mama and Papa?

"You sleep now, boy," said Adoeete. "Tomorrow you make arrows with Odakota, Hototo, and Teetonka. We fish in river, you catch fish, we eat at fire. You live here now."

Jonathan nodded, the words strangely comforting. At seven, nearly eight now, what choice did he have.

⌢⌣

Honana held on to Jonathan's hand as he emerged out of the tent, dressed now in traditional clothes like the other boys. His former garments had been washed in the river and put away in a leather satchel along with the blue shawl. This he'd placed carefully near his bed of furs. His mother's pearl necklace, though, he wore around his neck, hid under his clothing, keeping her near to him.

Jonathan was greeted by Adoeete, mounted on his horse. Aiyana carried the reins of her stallion along with a pure white colt, a gift. Jonathan was touched, his eyes appreciative and his smile broad. He stroked the colt's head. Its soft, brown eyes met his, and theirs was an instant bond. Odakota and the other boys surrounded Jonathan, petting the horse. They were pleased, now that he had his own horse and the four could ride together. Teetonka begged to go with them, but Aiyana shook her head, saying, "Another time," sorely disappointing the boy. Aiyana lifted Jonathan onto the blanket saddle and mounted her own horse.

In English now, Adoeete spoke to the boy, "We go to land I gave your grandfather JD, now belongs to you."

Jonathan nodded. Having ridden since the age of four, the boy grabbed his reins and displayed his prowess by riding in a loop around the center of the village. Seeing that Adoeete and Aiyana were satisfied and proud, he took his place as the three walked, then trotted, and finally galloped, heading south across the shallow crossings of the river and onto Hartland.

Adoeete pointed out the boundaries of the thousand-acre parcel as Jonathan beamed and Aiyana laughed with delight. They arrived where Adoeete said JD had built a stone, wood, and adobe home, but only pieces of it remained, although the surrounding stone wall was intact. A small creek ran behind it, the area surrounded by oak trees. The three dismounted, and Aiyana took out the tiny leather pouch. Gently she laid the seed in Jonathan's outstretched hand, saying, "You, Jonathan, plant seed."

"This is special seed, Jonathan," explained Adoeete, "gift from Great Spirit, to Aiyana." "

Jonathan touched the seed with his finger, in awe of something so small and so important.

"You help her plant and watch over it?" he asked the child.

Jonathan nodded, looking around, carefully assessing the best place. Finally, he pointed to a sheltered spot, next to the corner of the stone wall, where the sunlight would find it.

The three knelt together as Adoeete handed Jonathan his hatchet, saying, "Make earth ready."

Jonathan carefully worked the soil, then placed the tiny seed in the ground. He looked to Aiyana, and she smiled, covering the seed with the loose dirt. Jonathan said, "Sir, will you water, please?"

Adoeete nodded, releasing the leather strap holding the water bag he carried around his waist. He poured the contents slowly on the seed, allowing the water to soak in deeply. He handed the water bag to Jonathan. "You and Chief Aiyana together water from now on." Adoeete raised his hands to the Great Spirit and blessed the tiny seed. He chanted a hymn of fertility and blessing as The Great Eagle circled, marrying its own cries with the man's.

CHAPTER EIGHT

THE BIEL BOYS

Carter Street, Yucaipa, 2018

Trapped by the bikers, Honey was afraid. Their bright headlamps shining into the windshield of her car blinded her, and the gunning of their engines vibrated in her throat. They were taunting her with their hatchets and knives. Suddenly gunshots rang out. Honey covered her head and screamed. More shots were fired, forcing the bikers to leave their prey and haul steel down the road. Don pulled his truck beside her car and jumped out, still carrying his hunting rifle.

"Honey, are you okay?" asked a panicked Don.

"Who were those guys?" cried Honey.

"Bunch of ignorant bullies from Angelus Oaks. They can get vicious. Call themselves the Biel Boys. You okay, Honey? Did they hurt you?"

"I hit my forehead, and now I have a headache," replied Honey, "but other than that I'm fine. Why would they attack me, Don?"

"Probably been watching all the activity at Hartland and not happy about someone ruining their hideout," Don said. "They've been hanging out in your tree line for years. Likely recognized your car. Obviously, they were trying to scare you."

"They did a good job of that!" said Honey, shaking. Don helped Honey out of the car just as Landon arrived with the sound of screeching brakes and the slamming car door.

"I heard the shots," said Landon. "Honey, are you alright?" Honey nodded, letting him take her in his arms. Landon turned to Don. "What happened?"

"As I was coming home, I happened to see the Biel Boys at the end of Hart Lane. I decided to pull onto Jefferson and wait, just to make sure they didn't bother Honey."

"Who are the Biel Boys?" asked Landon.

Don replied, "Bikers who think Hartland belongs to them. They're trying to hang on to what they believe is their territory up there in the tree line. They tried to intimidate Honey, and I scared them off with my hunting rifle. I'll explain it all later. Right now we need to get Honey back to the hotel. I'll call the Yucaipa police. Landon, you want to follow Honey back?"

"Of course," said Landon, settling Honey into her car, offering, "I'll follow you."

Landon, having seen Honey safely to her room, wanted to give her time to process what had happened, so he excused himself to his own rooms where he gathered up some medicinal Port.

Grateful to be back at the hotel in familiar surroundings, Honey had just changed into gray sweatpants and a blue and white Tom Brady sweatshirt as she heard the knock. Honey opened it to Landon holding a bottle of Port and one small glass.

"I meant to thank you for upgrading me to this lovely fireplace room," said Honey, inviting him in.

"I thought you might like it," grinned Landon, measuring the Port like a teaspoon of medicine. "I want you to drink all of this," he commanded. Honey nodded, taking a small sip.

"Now is when my sister Kip comes in handy. You can thank her for the beautiful décor, the gas fireplace, and this—" Landon said, holding up a white-fringed throw. "It's a rare, hand-knitted Peruvian llama wool blanket made especially for guests who are attacked by bikers," he explained.

Honey laughed. "Your sister truly thinks of everything," she said, wrapping herself in its softness and curling up on the couch.

Landon bragged. "You should see what Kip has done with our grander hotels. She's a marvel, a real genius both in decorating and marketing." Clearly Landon adored his sister, and Honey loved that about him. He took a seat in the chair across from her, better to watch over his patient.

Taking another sip of Port, Honey said, "Ahh . . . this is perfect. Reminds me of my grandmother. She loves . . . uh, loved Port." Unwanted tears welled up in her eyes as Honey apologized. "Sorry, it's been an emotional few days."

"I know," said Landon. "It must be hard having your whole world turned upside down." He waited, giving her time to get her emotions under control, thinking how brave she was to uproot her life and replant it on the other side of the U.S. He hated that the Biel guys, or whatever they called themselves, ruined her evening, but more importantly he was angry that they made her feel unsafe. He would not let that go unattended to. Meanwhile, he liked this casual and soft side of Honey and that she was allowing him to offer his own brand of comfort and support.

"Why must we?" asked Honey.

"Why must we what?" inquired Landon.

"You said," repeated Honey, "it must be hard having your world turned upside down. It is! And my question is *why* must we have our worlds turned upside down?"

"I don't know really. I just know it happens," answered Landon.

Honey leaned her head to one side, appreciating the man with whom she could share this conversation. "Have *you*?" she asked.

"Have I what?" Landon said.

"Had your world turned upside down?"

Landon nodded knowingly. "Plenty!"

"Me too," said Honey, grateful for the warmth of the Port that was relaxing her more by the minute. Landon smiled as she poured herself another small glass, took a sip, and settled herself against the pillows. "My parents died when I was ten in a plane crash," Honey said casually.

Landon leaned forward, surprised and honored that she felt so at ease to share such an intimate piece of her story. "Before it happened," Honey continued, "we lived in a rural village called Millbrook, in upstate New York. Everything about my life was peaceful and safe. But then my parents had been invited to a wedding in Chicago. I was excited to stay with my grandmother for the weekend in New York City. It was always exciting and great fun at her place. She had kept toys from my dad's childhood that I can only find in my bedroom at her apartment. On Sunday I was all packed and waiting for my Mom and Dad to return and take me home, but I had to wait a long time. I remember looking at the clock, and every time I did, it got later and later, and I could see my grandmother was getting worried. When the knock on the door finally came, I ran to answer it, but it was a police officer. Nanny sent me to my room. Later, after the policeman had gone, I found out."

"I'm so very sorry, Honey. How awful for you both," Landon said, heartbroken for the ten-year-old girl and her grandmother, who had lost her son and daughter-in-law.

"It was so long ago, and yet it seems like it just happened," Honey mused. "I remember waking up that first morning in my grandmother's apartment. Nanny's hand was on my back. Suddenly I remembered they were dead and the thought hit me like a bullet. I tried desperately to keep my mind from going there, but I couldn't help it. I imagined how they must have felt when the plane crashed and … the fire afterwards."

Inside Landon grimaced. The part he played after 9/11 in Operation Enduring Freedom in Afghanistan saw many a fiery airplane and helicopter crash, and worse. He understood. The memories still kept him awake some nights.

"Then my mind shut down," continued Honey, "and all I could feel was the pain of my swollen eyes and the huge weight of my eyelids. My mouth was dry, and Nanny helped me sip cool water from a pale pink crystal goblet and let me hold her china doll. Funny I should remember that! Nanny told me later, she'd watched over me all morning long. She said, 'I'd slept the healing sleep of a tiny budding flower yanked out by its roots and replanted in a place called New York City.' Over the years she must have said a thousand times, 'My darling girl, destiny has called you here. Let's you and I give it time, then we'll both know why.'"

"Wise grandmother," Landon finally spoke. "So, after ten years old, where did destiny take you?"

Honey smiled. "Into the hotel business."

"No!" replied Landon, his response making Honey grin.

"Yes," countered Honey. "It's a funny thing, but because I suddenly was without my old home, I found solace in fantasizing about becoming the owner of a big hotel that was really just a big home . . . a place where any single person could find herself at a moment's notice and feel completely comfortable. My grandmother shared her home with me as though it were always meant to be, but I couldn't help but think about others like me who were displaced or uprooted. As I grew up, I refined that interest into a passion for helping other hotels provide that experience for their guests. I love my job, and I never in a million years thought I'd be in California far from my work, helping people feel at home. I had thought it was my life's purpose ."

"Did you work anywhere I might know?" Landon asked, genuinely amazed at this interesting woman before him.

"I worked for Maxwell Commons, as a consultant for independent hotels and resorts."

"You're kidding," Landon said in awe. "That's a very prestigious firm. Oh . . . so that's the Edward Smiley connection. You consulted for Mohawk Mountain House. For how many years?"

"Eight," Honey smiled smugly, "but I've known Edward most of my life."

"Well, I'll be," said Landon, sitting back in his chair, "a big-time hotel consultant . . . and I thought you were just an airline passenger with protocol problems."

Honey laughed. Landon stood up. "Okay, Ms. Hotel Executive, the doctor is now sending you off to bed for a good night's sleep. I think if I'm going to have any of this Port, which was a Christmas gift I'll have you know, I'm going to have to remove it from the premises."

Honey stood, gave Landon a long embrace, and then yawned.

Landon stroked her cheek, then kissed her forehead for the second time that night. "Off to bed, missy," said Landon. "I'll let myself out."

Honey yawned again and waved goodbye as the door shut quietly behind him.

$$\sim\!\!\circ$$

The burly man from the New York moving company held the last heavy Victorian armchair in his weary hands and was looking to Honey for its placement in the Hartland living room. She pointed to the corner by the fireplace where he gently set it down, turned to see if it should go further left or right, followed the woman's instructions to a t, took off his hat, and looked around. "Uh-huh, uh-huh," he said, grinning with satisfaction at all they'd accomplished on this long day. "Ma'am," he said, "this house is beautiful, and the furniture fits her like a hand in a glove. Let me get the paperwork signed, and we'll be outta your hair."

The sun had set nearly three hours earlier as the moving van headed down the driveway. The men were more than ready to use part of Honey's very generous tip on a well-deserved steak dinner. Similarly, Honey was more than ready to find her sheets and blankets and fall into bed. Pete and the men had nearly killed themselves getting ready for this day. Tonight, in her pale blue, silk pajamas, Honey was grateful for the marvelous job they had done, especially happy with her lovely new bathroom, its sparkling clean sink, and the white French cabinet in which her new toothbrush now hung.

Honey laid down in her New York bed now in her California home. She smiled, falling asleep to the half-baked thought that life is certainly an adventu—

From the moment the sun filled her new bedroom until the moon rose and she fell into bed, Honey was overwhelmed, and she continued to be overwhelmed for the next three days. The fact was becoming ever so clear that she needed help, full-time help. Back in New York, she'd culled through their five-bedroom penthouse apartment only allowing herself the bare necessities along with the family heirlooms and things of sentimental value. It turned out to be much more than she'd expected. But it wasn't just the unpacking. It was the organizing, shopping, cleaning, and maintaining of the house, plus the grounds. She needed her own Lilly, but where was she to find such a competent and devoted soul?

Honey spied one of the many boxes made especially for her framed artwork and hoped it contained the painting she longed to see. The lid removed, she saw with delight it was! Posed together was a sixteen-year-old Honey and a vibrant and beautiful Victoria. She loved that painting, and it made her feel better and at the same time very sad. "I miss you so much, Nanny," she said to the smiling woman in the picture frame. She gently set it down then sat on the landing of the stairs praying her grandmother was listening to the confession building up inside her for days. "I miss New York! I'm a fish out of water here! I'm scared of those bikers, and I'm overwhelmed with all the work that needs to be done now and will continue . . . forever! Honestly, Nanny, I don't think I can do this. I know this was your dream, but I'm not sure it can be mine too."

Suddenly Honey sensed a warmth around her, a lovely energy, and she felt as though, somehow, she was not alone. Unseen, five-year-old

Emily sat next to her on the landing, having been laid to rest in her Sunday dress, a light blue calico with pink and yellow flowers, under which were a pair of bloomers. She preferred her new boots, but one of them had gone missing, so instead they dressed her in the black ones. Emily put her small hand in Honey's. She knew what it was like to feel alone.

Honey, somehow better now, needed to walk and clear her mind. She explored nearby Oak Lane on foot as she'd noticed a few homes there, among them an intriguing old schoolhouse complete with a small bell tower. Along the way there were horses, which she stopped to pet, berries just flowering, and lots of wildflowers growing along the edge of the road.

Honey reached the old schoolhouse, amazed by the pristine care of a master craftsman who surely had renovated this now charming home. She loved the soft yellow and contrasting white trim highlighting perfectly the foundation of gray river rock so prevalent in the area. The grounds and flowerbeds surrounding it were meticulously cared for, and dotting the trees were birdhouses of every shape and size.

The soft sound of crying seemed incongruous with this peaceful place, and Honey looked for its source. A young woman was sitting on the steps of the front porch. In one hand she held a tear-stained letter, and in the other her grandmother's handkerchief to wipe away the tears. She was surprised by Honey's sudden appearance.

"So, sorry," apologized Honey, "I didn't mean to startle you."

The young woman smiled. "No problem, I'm just embarrassed to be caught crying."

"Nothing to be embarrassed about," soothed Honey. "I was just having a good cry myself."

"What were you crying about?" the young woman asked.

Honey replied simply, "My grandmother passed away, and I really miss her."

"My dad just passed away," she said, "and I miss him too."

Honey nodded. "I'm so sorry. We've both lost people we love."

Holding up the letter, the young woman said, "I'm also crying because I wanted to go to Crafton Hills College, and I've been accepted, but now I need to find a full-time job. With my dad gone, my mom can't support the three of us by herself."

Honey inquired, "You have a brother or sister?"

"A brother. Mason," she replied. "He's eight. Just signed up for the Yucaipa Little League team."

Honey replied reassuringly, "That's an important step for young boys, being a part of a team. What did you want to take in college?" Honey asked.

"Well," the young woman answered, "I wanted to get my undergrad out of the way at Crafton Hills, then go to the University of Redlands for a degree in Business and Marketing."

Suddenly the light dawned, and Honey had an idea. "My name is Honey," she said, smiling. "What's yours?"

"Remey."

"Well, Remey," said Honey, "I have a proposition for you and your brother. I just moved in over there—"

"Oh!" cried Remey. "You're the one? I heard someone had moved into Hartland, and we've been watching all the activity . . . so it's you!"

Honey nodded. "Yes! An all-alone me with tons of boxes to unpack, a whole house to organize, a vineyard to plant and harvest, and eventually Hartland wine to market."

Remey's eyes widened, and she exclaimed, "I can help you!"

"I was hoping you'd say that," smiled Honey. "Oh, I suspect you know the treehouse

in the walnut tree?"

"Oh, yes," replied Remey, "Mason and his friends play over there all the time! Oops, I mean—"

Honey laughed. "Well, then, if they're going to claim it for their own, they need to spruce the place up and cut away the weeds around the tree. Could find a few dollars and some ice cream for that kind of work. You willing to organize and help maintain the place along with some light cooking and a few administrative things for me as a full-time job?"

"Yes, Ms. Honey! Thank you! Oh, thank you! When do you need me?" Remey asked.

"Yesterday," laughed Honey.

"Great!" exclaimed Remey. She looked at her watch. "Okay, let me get Mason off the bus, write a note to my Mom, and we'll be over in about an hour."

"Perfect!" said Honey, delighted. "It gives me just enough time to go to Stater Brothers, pick up groceries, and buy some ice cream. What flavor?"

"Chocolate," replied Remey immediately. "It's on the second aisle next to the fruits and vegetables."

"Chocolate it is," said Honey, reaching to give Remey a hug.

Returning with a carload of groceries, Honey pulled into the back of Hartland where Remey and three little boys anxiously awaited her arrival. It took longer than she thought to buy out the store. Now she was even more grateful for the help. Besides, it was wonderful to come home to other people, especially Remey and the kids. They were jumping up and down and waving with excitement.

Remey made the boys calm down as she formally introduced them to Ms. Honey.

"Ms. Honey, this is Mason, my brother." Clearly Mason had been coached as he held out his hand to shake Honey's.

"Glad to meet you, ma'am," Mason said with a grin.

"Very glad to meet you too, Mason." Honey returned the handshake.

Remey said, "Would you like to introduce your friends to Ms. Honey, Mason?"

Following suit, Noah and Alex shook her hand and even offered some bows. Honey was pleased that Remey had set the tone for their relationship, which would be one of respect. That settled, Honey said, "Now who wants chocolate ice cream?"

All decorum lost, the boys whooped and hollered. "I do, I do!"

Remey hushed them, then organized the boys to carefully carry in the groceries and to mind that their dirty shoes were dutifully scraped with each dear grocery bag they had the great honor of helping to bring inside.

With hands on hips, Remey took stock of the kitchen with its stacks of boxes, built-in cabinets, and brand-new refrigerator. Yes, she'd have this place in order posthaste. Every home needed a working kitchen as soon as possible. Honey had bought a magnificent stove with cooking and warming ovens, and Remey determined to surprise her with her culinary skills. Cooking was one of her favorite things to do. Remey took charge, immediately suggesting Ms. Honey find the ice cream while she began organizing everything else. Honey looked up to heaven, whispered a prayer of thanks to her grandmother, and decided life was good again. Very good.

Bags brought in, the boys licking their cones safely on the porch surrounded by napkins, and Remey humming away as she became mistress of the kitchen, made Honey smile. Soon, she knew, Remey would take control of the entire house. The young woman was a born manager and leader. She'd found her Lilly and so much more. Remey would go places, and Honey intended to nourish her potential and happiness here, as long as she cared to remain at Hartland in whatever role she eventually grew into. Who knew how the business would grow over time! People like Remey were rare, and Honey was counting her blessings as the phone rang. Remey smiled as Honey took the call in the kitchen, trusting her to be in on the one-sided conversation.

"Edward! How are you?"

"You're where? In Redlands? I'm so glad."

"What are you doing here? Yes, I agree, a month apart is far too long. I'm thrilled you decided to come."

"Besides a porch full of cute kids eating ice cream and finding the most marvelous new administrative assistant, you're the best news I've had all day!"

"Why don't you and Matt come out to the house tomorrow when you've rested."

"Okay, I'll come to the library first. What do you want to show me?"

"Fine, be that way, keep me guessing. Okay, dear Edward, see you tomorrow morning."

"So glad you came!"

"I love you too!"

"I'm fine, really!"

"Okay, bye."

Remey held out an ice cream cone to Honey. "Want one?"

Honey laughed. "Why not?"

Remey and Honey joined the boys on the porch, soaking in the sun and taking in the walnut tree to the left. Remey had filled Mason, Noah, and Alex in on their duties and responsibilities in terms of the treehouse, and the children were making their plans.

"Hey, boys," interrupted Honey, "I could sure use a tour of your treehouse. How about it?"

The shocked expressions turned to grins as Remey checked faces, gathered the used napkins, and headed back into the house. If someone named Edward was coming tomorrow, she had a lot of work to do. She laughed, surprised to see Ms. Honey running with the pack of boys towards the ladder—what she expected would be a memory they would cherish forever. Remey sighed, happy for the first time in months, amazed at how life can turn on a dime.

The next morning Remey showed up bright and early, making a small breakfast of hot tea, toast, and fruit for Honey, which she served at the dining room table. Then Remey handed Honey a suggested menu for the dinner party that evening. Honey was floored. "You cook too?" she asked.

"A passion of mine," returned Remey.

"My goodness girl," she said, "you *are* a dream! This looks marvelous! I'll go shopping for what you need this morning and I suspect, since you've already unpacked half the china, you'll want to unpack the rest for this evening."

Remey smiled, nodded, and sipped her tea.

"Now," said Honey, "we must address your wages and your schooling."

"Schooling?" Remey questioned.

"Yes," confirmed Honey. "No brilliant administrative assistant of mine, intending to be a business and marketing guru, can be in my employ without going to school. So, here's what I'd like to propose. You and I simply can't do everything. So, we'll hire a housecleaning service to come in once a week. Can you take care of that?"

It was Remey's turn to think this woman a dream.

"Now," continued Honey. "For every dollar you make working for me, I'll match it for your college fund."

"What!" cried Remey. "Ms. Honey, that's way too generous!"

"I expect great things from you, Remey, and I'm willing to make that investment. So, you research the going rate for administrative assistants and give me a report and we'll go from there. And finally, when do classes start at Crafton Hills College?"

"Next semester begins in two months," replied Remey.

"Okay, then, register for two classes and let's see how that workload suits your responsibilities here. If you can handle more, you can do more the following semester."

Remey began to cry. "This is a miracle, Ms. Honey! *You* are a miracle! I've never known anyone so kind. Thank you!"

"Thank *you,* Remey. You saved my life," said an appreciative Honey, knowing it was the truth.

Honey's oldest friend, Edward, and newest friend Matt, Director of the Smiley Library, were standing in front of the double, solid wooden doors, waiting for her arrival. With hugs all around and a special kiss on the cheek for Edward, the three walked into the library.

Matt introduced Honey to the head librarian, Mrs. Duncan, a lovely, white-haired woman with a sweet face and kind Irish eyes. Next he introduced Honey to a sour-looking woman with a pinched face. The assistant librarian, Linda Hall. Despite her particularly plain and demure features and dress, she could have been pretty had it not been for the tilted way she held her head to look down on everyone despite her short stature. The uninviting squint that mostly hid the attractive shade of deep brown eyes compelled Honey to walk away from the unfriendly woman as soon as possible.

Matt said, "Linda's ancestors were here the same time yours were, Honey. Her ancestors are part of a long line of townspeople originally from Mexico who have long been a fixture in the area. In fact, her great-great-grandmother Amelia was a housekeeper for Hartland back in the late 1800s."

"That's remarkable," said Honey, happy to see more of the past come to life.

Matt continued, "Linda here is devoted to researching her family history. She practically lives at the library. You two will find much to talk about."

"That would be wonderful," agreed Honey. "I have so much to learn."

Linda offered, "There are some interesting books in the heritage room I'd be happy to show you."

Edward, uncharacteristically rude, replied rather brusquely, "That won't be necessary, Ms. Hall. I'm taking Ms. Hart there as we speak. Now if you'll excuse us."

Surprised and embarrassed by Edward's sharp retort, Ms. Duncan, Honey, and Matt all looked chagrined. Only Linda seemed to be nonplussed. Still, while Edward took Honey's arm and walked away, Matt offered Linda an apology. "Sorry, Linda, he's had a long flight, and, well, you know, getting along in years."

Linda nodded indifferently.

Edward opened a large safe out of which he brought several journals bound in leather.

"Honey, these journals are very valuable. They were handwritten by Maria Luego, the daughter of a Spanish explorer back in the 1800s. They chronicle much of the history of your great-great-great-great grandfather, JD Hart, and your great-great-grandfather, Jonathan. Maria's own story is a fascinating one, but that's for another day."

"Edward!" exclaimed Honey, "I had no idea! These are so old, rare, and amazing. How many journals are there?"

"Thirteen in all," he responded. Honey hesitated to ask. "Edward, forgive me for questioning you, but in all our years together, I've never heard you speak rudely to another person. Are you tired, or did you mean to treat her—"

"Linda Hall," Edward filled in the name. "I meant every word of it. I wanted her to receive the message loud and clear that I suspect she's up to something."

"But what would she be up to?" asked Honey.

Tapping on the journals, Edward explained. "These tell the story very clearly. Linda's great-great-grandmother, Amelia Lucinda Hall, came from a family of tragedy. Amelia, with her own dubious ways, created more tragedy of her own at Hartland. It's all in here. Suffice it to say, I have good reason to mistrust Amelia's great-great-granddaughter, Linda Hall, and it's only a matter of time until I can prove it."

"But it was all so long ago," Honey said.

"I know," replied Edward. "I sound paranoid, but trust me, this is serious business, Honey. There's more to know, dear, but for now, just be careful with Linda. I can assure you, she's after something, and I have a good idea what that is. There's a reason she's here at the library day and night. I've observed her from a distance many a time, and she's not just putting away books." Honey was sorry to hear that, as she'd been looking forward to learning about another side of the Hartland story from Linda.

Kevin, the archivist, brought out the white gloves as Edward motioned for Honey to sit down and examine the third journal. The same one that Tess McDowell had been given to read. These words, along with the providential discovery of the small child's boot, were, Edward believed, among the reasons the housing developer changed her mind about buying Hartland. Tess McDowell said it herself, in a note she'd written to Edward.

Dear Mr. Smiley,

I've never said this before about a piece of land, but Hartland doesn't belong to me. The vision I have for her, is not her own. All that beauty and all the money I could have made filling her up with homes was seductive, all right. But in the end, I had to become a responsible adult. It seems Providence, man, nature, and the very land itself has all conspired together to become something other than a housing development. The day we found the child's boot, clearly the one referenced in Maria Luego's journal, I went home to share the remarkable events with my husband Tom. I thought he would be angry that I pulled out. Instead he kissed me, said "that's my Tess," and took me out to celebrate at the Oak Glen Steakhouse!

Thanks for letting me read Maria's journal. If possible, I'd like to read them all. I wish Ms. Victoria all the best!

Sincerely,

Tess McDowell

As Honey read Maria's words, the treasures in the attic came alive. So that was Emily's little bed and china doll, she mused. Tonight, when all was quiet she'd go back up and explore it further, especially considering what she had learned today. The entry for Friday, June 1880 brought to life Edward's concerns about Amelia and Linda Hall.

> Friday, June 1880 – *Amelia, she disgusts me! The way she holds the baby Landon, as if she were his mother. I don't trust that woman who has lust in her heart for Señor Jonathan! It is not proper. Dismiss her now Señora Merritt - you must! The activities of Amelia are troubling, she is not right in her mind. If Señora dismissed her the first day, there would be no statue of La Muerta, there would be no suffering - ah me - the Señora's blind. El Dios give me strength.*

Honey read on. The entry for Monday, June 1880 came as a great shock to Honey, and her heart broke when she learned Emily had drowned. The reference to the school bell ringing repeatedly made her wonder if that very bell still hung in the tower of Remey's home. Suddenly Honey had a sense that everything was connected, that if one looked deep enough, she would find, as the movie title said, a mere *Six Degrees of Separation.* Honey continued reading where Tess McDowell had left off.

> Friday, August 1880 – *Señora Merritt, it is her birthday today. She loved my strawberry cake and Señor Jonathan's gift pleased her much. A wooden puzzle picture! Never have I seen before, que bonita is the painting Primavera by Señor Botticelli! The French writing desk we move under the window. Perfecto! The light comes in well. How happy Señora Merritt is putting the pieces together. I will make the tea for her.*

> Sunday, August 1880 – *The family, they will never overcome their sorrows. The day is gray and heavy. Emilita we miss very much – such pain in our hearts. Never, never shall we be content. It would be well for me to make a fire – the place requires warmth. To you Madre de Dios we pray.*

Monday, August 1880 –The Hartland Crush is on the mind of everyone, and all the activities – El Dios I pray I make it through. The 15th de Augusto is the grand day. Señora Merritt calls for me now. All the Yucaipa people are here at Hartland to plan and each has a part in it.

Finally, I can go to bed. I am exhausted! I must smile even though I am weary. Hartland, Señor and Señora, are very fine and respected people – they do so much good for Yucaipa, for the Green Valley, for me. O Holy Father, what a gift that I can belong here too and give my part to this casa bonita.

Honey was captivated by the journal and would have read all day, but Edward was impatient to continue the tour of the library. There was so much to see. He'd need a rest before their dinner at Hartland tonight, so he pointed to his watch, signaling to Honey it was time to move on.

"You can come back anytime, dear," Edward offered. "These journals are all available for your reading, and one day, they will be yours to watch over."

"Thank you, Edward," said Honey. "I will care for them as you have." Together they headed off to the children's wing.

❧

Remey's fine dinner was the icing on the cake for Edward as he and Matt reveled in Hartland and all that Honey had done to the grand home. Victoria's New York furniture seemed well suited, and the entire effect made Edward feel very much at home. The statue on the mantel of La Muerta, an ancient Mexican homage to the lady of death, had been the only blight on the evening, and Edward wondered how to broach the subject with Honey. He had been shocked to see it was still there on the fireplace mantel and wondered how after all these years it had not been broken, lost, or even sold. He wouldn't spoil the evening with the sordid tale of La Muerta, but eventually he would have to tell Honey and hope she would take seriously its potential power to produce negative effects on people's lives. Edward was the last person to succumb to foolish fears of spells and incantations, but he had read all of Maria Luego's journals, and in her own handwriting the long-time resident of Hartland gave good reason to suspect the statue's sinister force. Edward still wasn't sure how he felt about it all, but he would take no chances, especially with Honey.

It had been a long and wonderful day, and Honey had been delighted with Remey's heroic efforts at putting the entire downstairs to rights, besides making a delicious meal worthy of the title "culinary art." Remey had found the linens, candles, and a glass vase, which she filled with flowers, and all her creative efforts reinforced Honey's intuition she was a rare find. The sentiment was underscored by Edward and Matt as well.

Now at 8:30 p.m., all Honey wanted was a hot shower, a comfortable pair of sweats, and to finish the last glass left in the bottle of delicious red wine Matt had brought as a housewarming gift. While searching for her slippers in the back of the closet, Honey noticed the door that opened into the attic. While she had wanted to return to explore it further, there had been no time. Tonight, however, it beckoned her. She was glad she'd asked Pete to wire the attic for light, and she flipped the switch. The single light was soft and only made its way so far into the space.

Now, in peace and quiet Honey could take in the abundance of things, the treasure trove of history that surrounded her. She placed her wine glass on a small, marble-topped, mahogany end table, which hosted a stack of tiny leather-bound books made for a child. It reminded Honey of the child's bed and china doll. She walked over and picked up the fragile figure. Upon more careful inspection, she noticed the doll was a replica of Victoria's, sitting this very moment on a chair downstairs in the living room. While this doll had black hair and a pink dress, Victoria's had blond hair and a blue dress, but they were made by the same company. She decided they must be together and determined to put them side-by-side next time she went downstairs. Honey gently removed a quilt, uncovering a wooden rocking horse. Its ear was missing and its tail wounded, but it still rocked. There were stacks of books, another formal chair needing re-upholstering, and a beautiful mahogany French desk upon which sat a large box. Honey's eyes grew wide. The picture glued onto the lid of the box was of her favorite painting by famed artist Botticelli, entitled *Primavera,* or some called it *The Allegory of Spring.* Suddenly the words from Maria Luego's journal reappeared in her mind.

> Friday, August 1880 –*Señora Merritt, it is her birthday today. She loved my strawberry cake and Señor Jonathan's gift pleased her much. A wooden puzzle like that, never have I seen before, que bonita the painting Primavera by Señor Botticelli! The French writing desk we move under the window. Perfecto! The light comes in well. How happy Señora Merritt is putting the pieces together. I will make the tea for her.*

Maria's journal had come to life before Honey's very eyes, and she wondered at the indescribable feelings welling up inside her. There were no words. Only emotions that weaved threads of familiarity between the present and the past and a mysterious knowing that similar characteristics, qualities, and traits ran through the lineage of the Hart family. "This was Merritt's favorite painting too," Honey spoke aloud, her emotions confirmed.

Honey lifted the lid of the box. Inside were exquisite wooden puzzle pieces. A few at the top revealed clues to their placement in the overall picture. Tomorrow, she would entrust the knowledge of the attic to Remey. Together they would carry down the French desk, and Honey, just as Merritt had done, would put together the puzzle that not only represented Botticelli's *Allegory of Spring*, but her own allegory of the Hart family, the continuing saga of which she was now—surprisingly enough—living. Honey reached for her wine, took a sip, and jumped as she heard the doorbell ring, ring again, and then a fist produced a series of loud knocks. Coming out of the attic, she looked in the corner of her bedroom at Victoria's grandmother clock whose hands read 9:30 p.m.!

Moonlight and a small porchlight were little comfort in the vast darkness of Hartland where there were no streetlamps, only howling coyotes and the mysterious sounds the night made.

Who comes to visit at 9:30 p.m. at night? wondered Honey, feeling alone and alarmed.

Grabbing her cell phone, ready to dial 911, she walked briskly down the stairs muttering, "Tomorrow I'm getting a guard dog!"

The rapping at the door continued as Honey pulled back the curtain. This was the last person she expected to see at her house and at this hour of the night! Standing on the porch was Linda Hall from the library, a few books cradled in her arm. While Honey was relieved it wasn't the Biel Boys, she felt uncomfortable at the impropriety of her late-night guest and someone on Edward's radar of suspicion. Reluctantly she opened the door.

"Hope you don't mind the hour," Linda apologized, looking even more austere and homely in the darkness. "Just finished my research at the library and thought I'd drop off these books for you on my way home." Not waiting to be invited in, Linda gently pushed against the door. "You don't mind if I come in for a minute, do you?" She stepped through the threshold without waiting for a response, handing the books to Honey and taking a seat on the couch facing the fireplace.

So, the little brown mouse has claws, thought Honey, suddenly on her guard, wondering what Edward meant when he said she was after something. "Can I get you something to drink—a cup of tea, or water, perhaps?" asked Honey.

"Tea would be nice," replied Linda, perched on the edge of the couch. The moment Honey left to put the kettle on, Linda went straight to the statue of La Muerta, touching it reverently, whispering, "Ahhh . . . so you *are* still here. Then great-great-grandmother, *you* are still here too!" Linda smiled, congratulating herself and her ancestors on their great patience. It would all pay off in the end, and this was the sign she needed to keep going. The old man was a nuisance, but she could use him to move her closer to their family goal—the whereabouts of the gold.

Honey returned with the steaming tea. Linda ignored it, picked up her purse, and walked to the door. "Well, it's late, probably should let you get some sleep." Opening the door, she turned once more to take in the image of the statue. "I'll just let myself out. You can be sure I'll come by again with more books. Oh, by the way, that first book," she said, pointing to the hunter green binding of the book she had brought, "is about the gold found on Hartland in the late 1800s. It's just a legend, but I think you'll find it interesting."

CHAPTER NINE

THE TREE HOUSE

The Walnut Tree, 1861

Eight-year-old Jonathan took seriously his role as the son of the chief, inheritor of the thousand acres of Hartland, and guardian and cultivator of the special seed he, Aiyana, and Adoeete had planted by the old stone wall a year ago. The boy, the grape seed, and the land flourished, albeit, Jonathan felt moments of deep sadness at the loss of his parents and the senseless way they died.

Before that fateful moment, Jonathan was satisfied to take things as he found them. His world and the things he observed, all seemed reasonable and useful. Even when he did things wrong and got a whoopin for it, the action made sense. He never got whooped for doing a good thing, so he considered the idea of being punished, at least a reasonable action. He could not, however, comprehend how the God he knelt in prayer to every night beside his sweet and beautiful Mama, could allow such a thing to happen to her. And how could Papa, just protecting his family from those bad men, be allowed to die? What were they being punished for? He could think of nothing. He wrestled with himself and God to know the answers. Had he caused this great calamity? Were they not a good and God-fearing family?

The deep need to understand had suddenly emerged, and for the first time, Jonathan's inner voice awoke. Its first loving assurances gave him hope and courage, as his mind embraced the certain words, "All will be well. One day you will know, everything has meaning, a reason, and purpose." Over the years, the desire to unfold the mysterious explanations would be a driving force of both his child and adult mind. Unfortunately, the future that awaited him would cause Jonathan to delve deeper into the mystery of the seemingly chaotic nature of life.

Much of Jonathan's wonderings had taken place in the branches of the giant walnut tree just paces from the stone wall that made up the last remnants of his grandfather JD's home. When the burdens of the past became too heavy, he would escape to the walnut tree to privately release his questions into the sky where the Great Eagle circled above him, and the Great Spirit watched over them all. One day, thus sitting, he saw Odakota, Hototo, and Teetonka on their horses galloping toward the tree. His own colt, tied to the trunk, had given away his hiding place.

"What are you doing up there, Jonathan?" asked Odakota.

"Thinking," came the hidden voice from above.

"Stop thinking, and come down!" yelled Hototo, eager to share the news with the new unspoken leader of the tribe of four.

Jonathan lowered himself down as far as the branch would allow, then let go for the remaining two feet. "What's going on?" asked Jonathan.

This was Teetonka's cue to tell the story. "A covered wagon crossing the river got caught in the mud, fell over, and was washed away."

"It smashed on the rocks," Hototo added, stealing Teetonka's thunder. Odakota saw the look on Jonathan's face and immediately assured him, "No one was hurt. The people have all gone into town."

"You must see this!" exclaimed Hototo.

Jonathan nodded, and the four mounted their horses and galloped off to view the calamitous sight.

The wagon had been well made, put together with strong bolts and wooden supports. The wagon bed and one side were intact, while the other was smashed, having taken the brunt of the rocks. The canopy and frame were still attached but lying in the water, while the contents of the toolbox had been flung all around. Three of the wheels were in good shape, but the axle and the fourth wheel had broken off. The water and grease buckets were both floating, for now.

The four boys took in the scene with wide-eyed fascination. Jonathan studied the sight. There were good parts here. Ones that could be salvaged, but for what? As he observed the wagon bed, it suddenly reminded him of the boards his father had nailed together to make the floor of his own treehouse back in Texas. There, the giant oak had been his sanctuary and a place where he and the Calder boys had played and imagined. The walnut tree on Jonathan's land was huge, its branches strong enough to support a treehouse. The four would build it together. He could see the finished product now in his mind's eye.

Jonathan jumped off his horse, found a pointed stick, and drew in the sand. Odakota, Hototo, and Teetonka gathered around to watch what he was drawing. Hototo saw it first and began hooting like an owl and jumping up and down. Then Odakota solved the mystery as he looked back and forth from the dirt to the wagon in the river. Teetonka, still puzzled, had to be told. But when the great plan had been revealed to all, the boys celebrated with whoops of laughter. Teetonka immediately ran into the river to begin the retrieval, but Jonathan called him back, realizing even this would take planning. He sat on the ground deep in thought, organizing his strategy, forming a plan, considering everything. Soon the other three sat quietly beside him. The Great Eagle soared above, glad to see the boys thinking *before* acting. They were becoming wise.

The wagon bed became a travois, and all the remaining parts placed upon it. Four horses, happy to feast on apples, had been coaxed to pull the materials and finally made it to the base of the walnut tree. It was one thing to imagine the treehouse; it was another thing hauling the weighty pieces up there.

The boys sat cross-legged under the tree eating apples and wondering how to accomplish the feat, when a lone horse with a man slumped across its back walked into the clearing on its way to the river. Teetonka leapt to his feet, ready to run toward the stranger, but Jonathan grabbed his arm, motioning him and the boys to hide behind the tree and keep silent. Jonathan whispered, "Teetonka, better to wait a moment."

They watched as the horse spotted the boys' colts and smelled the apples. It turned toward the walnut tree, and as it came closer, it was clear the large, muscular man was an Indian, possibly a warrior in his prime, but his back was bare and covered with blood. He looked, if not dead, then nearly dead. Jonathan felt safe to lead his little band out from behind the tree trunk. The horse was too tall to reveal the source of the blood, but there had been plenty of it and it seemed to come from his chest. Odakota suddenly recognized the horse. "this belongs to Sky Wolf," he cried. A jolt of fear came over the boys as they wondered if this was a trap and Jonathan signaled them to quickly climb up the tree. They climbed from branch to branch finding a place where the view would allow them to see a great distance. If the banished Sky Wolf or Red Eye and his men were nearby they could easily see them. But the space was clear, and it appeared the Indian and horse had come alone. Jonathan said, "Hototo, ride back to the Village and tell Chief Aiyana what we've found. Tell her we're bringing the man and if he's not dead, he will need Honana's help." Hototo nodded, jumped on his horse and galloped off, happy to be allowed the honor of sounding the alarm.

Aiyana, Adoeete, Hototo and several warriors stood at the edge of the village waiting. Jonathan and the boys had taken their time, gingerly leading the man's horse, not wanting him to fall. Aiyana checked his pulse. Although faint, he was still alive. "Take him into Honana's tent," she said to her warriors. Aiyana nodded to the boys, signaling they had done the right thing and that she was proud of them, which brought pleased smiles.

The Indian was tall and strong. Honana required the help of two warriors to hold him in a sitting position where she could examine him and discover the source of the blood. She bathed his broad chest with cool river water, finding a knife wound above the heart. That it was still beating evidenced the dagger had barely missed its mark. Next, she washed the blood off his back and when the image revealed itself, she gasped, commanding one man to bring the chief immediately to her.

Aiyana looked at the image of an eye carved deeply into the man's back. Fear raced through her heart. "Red Eye!" she said softly. She knew then, there would be no safety for anyone until he was killed. What would he do to a villager, Adoeete, Jonathan, or someone he knew if he could do that to a stranger?

CHAPTER TEN

THE RETURN OF RED EYE

Two Years Later, Aiyana's Tepee, 1863

The tepee was filled with soft moonlight and the glow from the fire's embers. Aiyana shook her head in disbelief as she lightly stroked the sleeping ten-year-old's fine golden hair. His hand held the pearl attached to his mother's necklace. He'd never taken it off. Had it been three years since Jonathan had found his way into her arms? In every way he was her son and she his mother and, now, Flying Eagle his father. While they freely spoke of and honored his white parents, over time the memories of that life and those ways lessened as the presence of this life in the Yucaipat village permeated Jonathan's mind and heart. It was Yucaipat values, morals, and ideals he had absorbed and made his own, and they grew more and more true for him as each year passed.

That he was happy, Aiyana had no doubt. That she was happy with Flying Eagle, their son, and her position as chief supported by the entire village, there was no doubt. That it would always remain so, Aiyana knew with great certainty it could never be. Like the seasons, this season of blessing and peace would pass. What was good for all, would eventually be overshadowed by what was good for the powerful few. This would continue until all men learned how to care. The long-ago image of Red Eye, Cha'tiam, and Sky Wolf at the ceremony that made her chief and killed the brave Kitchi, continued to haunt her dreams. Over and over she saw Red Eye's powerful spear and Kitchi hurling himself in front of it to save her. It reminded her daily of the serious threat her uncle and his warriors were to the village. One day, as surely as the sun would rise, they would return for their revenge.

Tonight, however, she was content, at peace, and deeply in love with both her man and child, gifts of the Great Spirit for which she would always strive to prove herself worthy. Aiyana kissed Jonathan's forehead then moved to her place beside her strong husband. It had been easy and beautiful to give herself to him mind, heart, and body. Aiyana remembered the day Flying Eagle arrived in their camp on the verge of death, Jonathan and the boys having discovered him. The image of an eye drawn with the edge of a sharp knife, colored in red by the blood of Flying Eagle, left no room to doubt the artist. The mean stab wound above his heart had mirac-ulously missed the crucial veins. Had it not been for Honana's medicine, he would have bled to death.

Snuggling into the deep warmth of the furs and stroking Flying Eagle's long, black hair, her mind took her back to the reason he came into their lives. A great drought in Arizona necessitated the moving of Flying Eagle's tribe to more fertile lands west. He and his men had been sent as explorers. Unfortunately, they made camp that night in Red Eye's territory, a day's ride away from the Yucaipat village. The place was aptly named Timoteo, the name of the man whose land they had stolen. They killed him, his wife, and children. Timoteo's bones now hung as symbols of their dominance at the entrance to the great cave where Red Eye and his warriors lived. Red Eye's men thrived on killing, which masked their wounded pride and filled them with false power. One day, they promised themselves, when the time was right, they would unleash that frightful power upon the Yucaipat village, rectifying the grave injustice done by Chief Adoeete.

Red Eye had received news of a small band of strangers from Cha'tiam who'd caught sight of Flying Eagle and his men while hunting. There was no question of their fate. While all were asleep, Red Eye's men did their worst. Cha'tiam thought Flying Eagle was dead, like the others of his clan, but in the morning, Sky Wolf found both his horse and the dead man were gone. Red Eye was not pleased, and Cha'tiam suffered miserably for it.

The Yucaipat horse had been given free reign by the delirious man and eventually found its way home to the village. Flying Eagle was brought into the medicine woman's tepee where Honana cared for him until he grew strong enough to share his story. His responsibility to his Arizona tribe weighed heavy on him, and the moment Flying Eagle was of sound body, he urged Honana to let him go. She begged him to stay a little longer, become strong for the long ride ahead, and spend time with Chief Aiyana who could perhaps aid him in finding land for his own people.

From the moment their eyes met, Aiyana and Flying Eagle knew they had found their heart-mate. It was a pairing the entire village encouraged and blessed. But Flying Eagle was not free to follow his heart. The responsibilities of his people who continued to suffer from lack of food and water caused him to pull away from Aiyana, when all he wanted was to take her in his arms, love and support her the way this rare woman and chief deserved. It was sad for all to watch, as bravely Aiyana and Flying Eagle chose duty first. As time went by and strength came back to his body, Flying Eagle would ride short distances at first and then longer as he came to know, love, and appreciate this beautiful land. One day he came upon Jonathan and the boys struggling to haul up the wagon bed into the walnut tree. He smiled and rode closer.

"What are you doing?" Flying Eagle asked.

"We're building a treehouse like the one Jonathan had in Texas," responded Teetonka.

"I see," said Flying Eagle. He realized with admiration that the ingenious pulley system they created only needed more muscle. "Need some help?"

The boys nodded as the handsome subject of their hero worship humbled himself to work on their childish task.

Aiyana had ridden out to gather her brood for the evening meal. She knew precisely where they would be, as talk of the treehouse was the only topic of conversation those days. Flying Eagle was missing too. He'd gone out every day to strengthen himself and to search for land. Aiyana was surprised to see his horse among the colts, and to see the man himself up in the branches of the trees. At that moment Flying Eagle was reliving his own childhood, intent on helping his companions create a suitable and strong hideout.

Aiyana arrived to a cacophony of excitement as they eagerly bid her to climb up and see their handiwork. Five large branches held the weight of the floor, which was made of a patchwork pattern of wood utilizing the wagon bed. The front, back, and sides all connected, surrounding the giant tree trunk. The wheels had been sawn in half and formed the railing, while the canvas ceiling wove through the branches. The contents of the wagon's toolbox, containing hammers, nails, a saw, and other building materials, made it possible for the house to be well constructed, easily holding the weight of six people.

They laughed and enjoyed this hidden and magical place. Aiyana was delighted with the boys. Their creativity, unwearied determination, and effort showed their true character. Noticing the beaming Flying Eagle, she could no longer deny her love for him, this act of kindness spoke to the greatness of his soul.

After the meal, all assembled in Aiyana's tepee, while Flying Eagle regaled Adoeete, Aiyana, and Honana with the brave and daring deeds of each boy as they overcame the many obstacles the treehouse created. His accolades increased their own sense of dignity and worth, and the four sat straighter and taller—this a significant moment in all their lives.

Adoeete brought out his pipe, sharing it with Flying Eagle, the calming scent producing a few yawns. The day had been a long one, filled with great exertion.

"Time to sleep, our fine young braves," Aiyana said.

Flying Eagle sighed, not wanting to spoil the moment, but *not* telling them would be worse. "One more moment, Aiyana, please," Flying Eagle requested.

Aiyana nodded. "Of course."

"My strength is back, and now I must return to my people," said Flying Eagle.

A wave of gloom and sadness filled the tepee and all inside. "My people are weak and in trouble," he continued, "and as the son of my father, Chief Flying Deer, it is my honor and duty to care for our tribe." The truth of his words could not lessen the sorrow. "I am indebted to each one of you, your kindness, care, and friendship," said Flying Eagle looking into the eyes of each person, lingering at last on Aiyana's.

While all had known the moment would come, none had realized just how difficult the parting would be. The next morning, before the sun rose, Flying Eagle had gone.

Aiyana, returning to this moment in time, struggled to get comfortable, adding another fur to the bed, the thought of never having Flying Eagle by her side did nothing to help her sleep. She remembered Flying Eagle's account of the story, and her mind again went back in time.

The farther Flying Eagle rode away from the Yucaipat village and Aiyana, the more his heart ached. He had never felt this way before; the strength of his muscles had always served him well, but love required strength of mind and will. His love for Aiyana required him to turn back, but his love for the tribe would not let him. Their happiness must be more important than his own. And so, he rode on.

Three weeks into the journey, he crossed into Arizona territory, traveling on the very path he and his braves had used to come to California. He thought of each one, of the qualities and characteristics that made them unique and special. They had grown from children into men, and the memories they had made together remained bittersweet. How he would face their families with the news he didn't know.

His musing disappeared with the cloud of dust in the distance—a small group of riders was coming his way. It wasn't long before he realized they were men from his own tribe, and he urged his horse into a gallop, concern marking his brow. The news was grave, and the men despondent. The tribe in their weakened state had been attacked by Spanish soldiers, led by a few Paiutes, and when the men had returned from hunting, the massacre was complete. The last members of the tribe had burned the bodies, took what their horses could carry, and headed toward California, hoping to reunite with Flying Eagle and his braves. Now it was Flying Eagle's turn to share the trials of his journey and of losing their brothers, adding to the great tragedy of it all. To remember, to mourn, and to allow time to heal was all the men could do during their slow journey back to California and the new life that awaited.

Meanwhile, Aiyana and the village felt deeply the loss of Flying Eagle and his good and kind ways. He was a rare man! That he might never return was a truth no one wanted to face. So, when the wounded hearts of Flying Eagle and his men rode into the Yucaipat village, they brought healing and rejoicing. The next full moon would find Aiyana and Flying Eagle wedded. Now two years later, they were a family, and tonight the warmth of his body against hers stirred her deep feelings of love. She awakened her husband with soft, sweet kisses to which he hungrily responded, and much later they fell asleep in each other's arms.

The following morning Aiyana and the village awoke to cries of help from Honana. Chief Adoeete had collapsed! The medicine woman required help to take him into his tepee. Flying Eagle and Jonathan were the first to race to her aid.

Aiyana was acutely aware of Adoeete's age and growing frailty. She knew this was the first step of his final journey that would take him to the Great Spirit to whom he had devoted his life. It saddened her, yet at the same time she understood they would all return one day to their True Home. "This earth," her grandfather would tell her, "only a divine schoolroom for man to learn who he really is."

During the next cycle of the moon, Honana dedicated herself to making Adoeete comfortable, his body slowly shutting down. Jonathan and the boys came every day with offerings from the land; a particularly beautiful feather, a pure white rock, mint leaves from which Honana made tea, and sweet grapes, which grew as a result of the seed.

The morning found Jonathan standing outside Adoeete's tepee nervously fingering the pearl. He'd had a restless night dreaming that the Great Spirit beckoned his grandfather to come to the beyond where his own Mama and Papa greeted him, thanking the chief for caring for their son. The reality of it all awakened him, and he rose at dawn running to see if his grandfather was still alive. Standing at the opening of his tepee, he was afraid to look. A coughing fit seized the old man, answering Jonathan's question. The boy sighed gratefully and went inside. Adoeete lay in the fur bed as he had for nearly a full moon. The fire burned softly, and Honana was preparing something for his cough.

Jonathan knelt on the mound of furs, kissed Adoeete's forehead, then stroked his long white hair. The old chief tried to reach up and touch the boy with his hand, but he was too weak. His mystical eyes however held his grandson's and spoke the words of love that both understood.

"Grandfather," whispered Jonathan, "I'm sad. You've always taught me to tell the truth, and the truth is, you are not well. Honana's medicine and chants are doing no good. Grandfather, I think soon you will die. But don't worry, I will be with you until you leave to go to the Great Spirit."

Adoeete smiled. How he loved the boy and how he blessed the Great Spirit every day for bringing him into the lives of the Yucaipat tribe. Speaking was difficult, but Adoeete wanted the boy to hear his words. Slowly and weakly he said, "Rare is such honesty, Jonathan. Rare is such love. Rare is such a pure heart. You have spoken truly, Grandson. I am soon to be with the Great Spirit."

Hearing Adoeete confirm the truth of his own words struck Jonathan with a mighty force, and he reeled at the thought of actually losing him. He laid his head on the man's chest, the tears now coming uncontrollably. When he had cried his fill, all was silent, and he could feel on his cheek and hear in his ear, the soft beat of Adoeete's heart. Remaining thus, he spoke to the old man, "The great hole you will leave in my heart and the heart of the tribe can never be filled."

Adoeete's reply was a soft command. *"You* are my successor. *You* fill the hole, Jonathan, and be the Heart of My Heart and the Arrow of the Great Spirit, just as your mother is today."

The cough seized Adoeete again and left him on death's door.

"Go, Jonathan," Honana said softly, "find your mother. The time is near."

Fear made it difficult for Jonathan to move, but he forced himself for Aiyana's sake. Aiyana laid next to her grandfather, feeling for the last time the warmth of his body, measuring her petite hands against his large ones. Softly she sang the Indian Blessing between father and daughter. The sweet sound soothed Adoeete as suddenly he was riding on the wings of the Great Eagle, a young man again, free and ready for the challenges ahead in the beauty of a new world unfolding before his very eyes.

At the same moment Adoeete closed his eyes in death, another's eyelids—upon which fierce red eyes had been painted—opened. Red Eye and the warriors hid in the Yucaipat village tree line. Red Eye turned to Cha'tiam, speaking softly, "You did well. Your spying has paid off. Clever of you to learn that Adoeete is dying. It will give us back the village."

Red Eye paused, soaking in the moment he'd dreamed about for three long years. "Aiyana is mine," he warned, "but you may kill the boy."

For Aiyana, the screams of the Great Eagle at first seemed fitting for the death of the wise man, but suddenly a potent impulse inside her impelled her to beware. It forcefully warned of imminent danger, seizing upon her mind and actions. Now she heard the Eagle's warning cry, and instinctively grabbed her knife.

Red Eye and his warriors remained hidden in the trees, ready to strike as the incessant cries of the Eagle was lost upon them. But not Aiyana, who, with one fierce stroke of her knife, split open the back of the tepee. Spotting Flying Eagle, she motioned him to come to her. He too sensed the sudden danger and responded to her with lightning speed. Aiyana turned to grab Jonathan, still intent on his now deceased grandfather. For the first time, his mother forcefully brought him face to face with her. Her eyes were not asking or pleading, only commanding. "My son," Aiyana ordered, "you will do as I say! You will run with your father Flying Eagle to the walnut tree and stay there until I come for you."

Aiyana allowed no time for a response, thrusting Jonathan through the opening and into his father's hands. "Take our son to the walnut tree, husband, then return to me to fight," instructed Aiyana. Flying Eagle acknowledged the directive, the safety of his son a priority. That being accomplished, he'd race back to protect Aiyana.

Sky Wolf made the sound of a hooting owl, the first of two signals Red Eye had been waiting for. Now, the warrior, perched at the top of the tree in sight of the village, watched as Honana went from tepee to tepee, delivering the news of Adoeete's death. The villagers were coming out and joining one another in their grief, as Red Eye knew they would. When Honana returned to Adoeete's tepee, Sky Wolf saw the moment had come. He positioned his lips and breathed in deeply to mimic the cry of the turkey vulture. At that sound, Red Eye would race directly to Adoeete's tent, where he knew Aiyana and the boy would be. The rest of the warriors would surround the villagers. Red Eye had instructed them to kill only those who attacked. The others he would need to maintain the village. This was not meant to be a wholesale slaughter but a change of rulership.

When the sound of the turkey vulture filled the air, Red Eye reared his head, stuck out his viperous tongue, and pierced the moment with his blood-curdling war cry.

Aiyana, filled with relief her son and husband were out of danger, spun around in the tepee, intent on warning the tribe. The blood-curdling war cry had hardly registered when in slow motion Aiyana watched the hatchet, end over end, coming swiftly towards her. Behind it she saw Red Eye, his powerful legs and arm extended in a full, vengeful thrust.

Rig, Clem, and Thornton had not darkened the door of the Beaumont Trading Post since the day they had "killed that pretty little gal and her ill-advised husband" trying to defend her. What happened to the kid was of no concern to them. That they had failed to get the pearl necklace, however, still stuck in their craw. "Thanks to the Indian screaming bloody murder!"

Filthy, hot, destitute, and with a bullet lodged in Clem's leg, the outlaws conferred at the Beaumont Trading Post, having finally been run out of Arizona. They'd robbed Arizona banks all the way to the Mexico border. For two years they'd returned again and again to stash their sizeable earnings in a cave in Yuma, only yards from the border. That day, Clem and Thornton didn't want to press their luck, and both voted to settle in Mexico now. They could live nearby and go back and forth, withdrawing from their savings account in the wealthy earthen bank.

But Rig had plans for one more heist. Not that they needed more money, as the gold and cash they had hidden behind the rock and brush door was enough to buy Mexico. But as only Rig's vote counted, he marshaled the other two together and the three rode off. Two hours later they were caught by bounty hunters, the bread crumb trail of robberies and wanted posters leading straight to them.

The outlaws were being transported back to Fort Mohave for trial and almost surely a hanging when one of the heavy wheels broke. Two of the three bounty hunters were needed to wheel it into town for repair, which left the third alone. The unguarded and strictly rationed stash of whiskey in the boss's keeping was too great a temptation for the lone man. Soon he was drunk. Unfortunately, he and the keys to the lock had passed too close to the cage on his way to take a piss. Not long after, the dead man was left to guard what remained of the cage, himself the new occupant. The team of horses, carrying the three outlaws and the remainder of the whiskey, galloped off to the nearby California border and freedom.

It was frustrating for Rig, Thornton, and Clem to have so much gold and no access to it. Poverty and the need for food, guns, and another horse drove them to foolishly attempt to raid Rojo Rancho, a huge apple farm in

Beaumont. The reputation of the Rojo Rancho men having not reached the outlaws proved to be a serious problem, especially for Clem as the strong and loyal Mexicans who worked the farm were fierce protectors and great shots. Fortunately for Rig and Thornton, Clem had gone in first while they held back to see what would happen. Needless to say, they'd been blasted off the land. Now they must be content with what they could steal from the Beaumont Trading Post, towards which their horses were now bolting once again.

At the trading post, Rig assured the others that "the fresh pickins would be fine." Then, without warning, he took out the bounty hunter's rifle and turned the butt of it hard on Clem's wounded leg, who screamed in agony. The people in the Trading Post ran out to see what was wrong. Casually, Rig strolled through the building, gathering whiskey, jerky, and hardtack, as much as his arms could hold. Going out the back door, he raised his gun and fired three shots, which caused the onlookers to race back through the building, looking for the chaos now in the backyard. Leisurely Rig strolled back around the building, divvying up the groceries into the three saddle bags, and they rode away.

Clem glared at him as Rig had a hearty laugh. "Boys," said a happy Rig, "let's see if we can scare ourselves up a doctor in Yucaipa to separate our Clem here from his bullet. Then we'll head back through San Diego to Mexico and git our gold."

While Rig held a gun to Dr. Allen Crawley's head, Clem shook with fright at the sight of the razor-sharp scalpel about to enter his unanesthetized body. Thornton was having a discussion in the waiting room with an old woman, waiting for her turn with the doctor. Her ailment a never-ending stomach problem. She asked if he'd been in Yucaipa before, and Thornton casually answered, "Three years back now, I guess."

"Well," she perked up, "you must have been here around the same time the white boy came to live at the Yucaipat Indian village. His parents were murdered, and the Yucaipat Indians took him in, and now he lives with them. Been there for three years now. Outlaws done his folks in," she said, leaning in so that no one else in the empty room could hear. "The covered wagon they hauled all the way from Texas was carrying priceless gems and gold, the Hart Family intending to build a grand Victorian mansion on Hartland, over yonder." The highly embellished story was, after so many tellings, now to her a fact.

The screaming from the other room meant it would all be over soon, and Thornton could share the incredible news he'd just learned with Rig. While the woman continued to share the tale, Thornton ignored her completely, rehearsing his own version of the story that would make Rig want to take another stab at retrieving not only the pearl necklace from the white-boy-turned-Indian, but a whole lot more. Thornton interrupted the long string of words from the woman. "How far is the Indian village from here?"

"Not far," Sophia said, "just north about five miles, if-ins you was to take a buggy."

A white-faced Clem and the doctor appeared from the torture chamber. Rig wasn't far behind carrying a gun, his assurance of free treatment. Never had Dr. Allen Crawley been so happy to see his most trying patient, Ms. Sophia. After these hooligans, the chin-wagging Sophia was a picnic.

Rigs' unfulfilled desire to get his hands on the pearl necklace found the outlaws riding onto Hartland in search of a white boy dressed as an Indian. Their horses reared at the sound of the screams coming from the Indian village not far away where murder and mayhem compounded the grief and tragedy of Adoeete's death. The outlaws broke into a sweat, fear mounting with every step closer to the village. Clem spotted the walnut tree. "Let's climb up and see what's goin on," he proposed.

Rig nodded, for the first time in recent memory agreeing with his cohort. No sense in getting themselves killed over gold they already had. They would spy out the situation first and go from there.

Jonathan, hiding in the treehouse, was terrified, but willing himself to be brave. The sounds of death and the subsequent and utter silence that followed made the waiting unbearable. He had no idea what had happened, who was dead, who was safe, or even what it all meant. But just when he thought he could stand it no longer, he heard hoofbeats. Aiyana had returned. All would be well. "Mother!" cried Jonathan, shimmying down the tree.

"Well, hello there, young man," said Rig, taking in the blue-eyed-blond-haired Indian boy and the pearl necklace that had escaped from his leather shirt. "Ain't this our lucky day," Rig said, as he strode up to the child, took hold of the pearl on its chain with his dirty fingers, and lifted up the hefty piece for Clem and Thornton to see. The yellow-teethed grins made Jonathan sick and afraid, the smell of the man too close to him nearly made him pass out from pure terror.

Rig had to think a minute to decide what to do. He released the necklace, raked his hands through his grimy hair, and perused the clouds for the answer. He could kill the kid, take the pearl necklace, and be done with it. But Thornton claimed there were more jewels where this came from, so the boy could be of value when all the chaos died down.

Greed won. They stole the pearl, rode off with the kid, ditched him for safekeeping at the Thomas Winery in Rancho Cucamonga, and high-tailed it back to Mexico, where they'd unearth their gold and spend it on whores, gambling, and whiskey. They'd come back for the kid later when the itch for stealing, which always came back, needed to be scratched.

Dragging a kid along on the two-day ride had been taxing on the outlaws, so the hand-carved sign announcing the entrance to the well-known Thomas Winery was a welcome sight. Clem, glad to be rid of the leech Rig had unfairly attached to him, threw Jonathan from the horse, the boy hitting the ground hard and rolling into a row of grapevines. Jonathan watched as the outlaws rode off, taking with them the pearl necklace, which had been his source of strength for the last three years. He laid his head on the soft soil, unable to comprehend all the tragedies that had befallen him and his village in one day. He knew nothing of the fate of those whose screams he heard from the walnut tree. Nor did he even know why they were under such duress. He knew Aiyana and Flying Eagle would be worried at his disappearance, and he grieved for the grandfather who had left this world.

How he would survive, Jonathan didn't know, and he gave himself up to the unconsciousness that eased his weary mind.

It was a good thing Jonathan was far away from the two funeral pyres built on the ancient Yucaipat Indian burial grounds, surrounded by a chain of rocks, signifying the circle of life, death, and rebirth. He would have been heartbroken witnessing the lifeless bodies of his mother and grandfather, Aiyana and Adoeete, two great chiefs. Red Eye stepped into the light of the circle created by the giant fire, from which the bodies of his two enemies would be burned. Surrounded by his warriors, Adoeete's son stood in the full regalia of his position as chief, the massive head-dress finally his. Red Eye forced the shocked and mourning villagers to gather around. He lit the torch. Slowly and intimidatingly, Chief Red Eye walked around the circle, deliberately looking each villager in the eye, silently promising savage retribution should they not submit. Only when the unspoken message had been menacingly sent to every man, woman, and child, did he light the funeral pyres. His warriors cried out in celebration as the new chief smiled in triumph, while little Odakota, Hototo, and Teetonka huddled together, bereft.

CHAPTER ELEVEN

FLYING EAGLE

Hartland, 2018

The librarian's late-night visit unsettled Honey. She added Linda Hall to the list of upsetting people she had come to know in her move to California, mentally scrawling the name right after the Biel Boys on the thankfully short tally in her mind. The motorcycle thugs had not been back, but neither were they in jail. The fact that they were still out there made Honey nervous. They had been quiet. Too quiet. Controlling her propensity for worrying too much was a constant battle, but today she managed to override the fears with the list of activities she needed to attend to for the sake of Hartland.

Remey had been enthralled by the attic, and together she and Honey moved the French desk and puzzle downstairs, along with the second china doll, the two dolls brought together at last. Next on her list had been the olive trees. She'd forgotten to swear Remey to secret about the attic, but who would she tell? At this very moment, the acres of hundred-year-old olive trees were being professionally trimmed, and plans were underway for processing the olive oil. Honey assigned Remey the task of researching the olive oil industry and creating a strategy for its production at Hartland.

The third task would have thrilled Jonathan Hart. In an hour, the tractors would arrive, and under the direction of California vineyard and winery expert Jason Alexander, the first five acres of Hartland Vineyards would be replanted. Jason had marveled at the old, massive grapevine that trailed along the stone wall. He tasted the grapes and, finding them exquisite, asked permission to create a special Hartland wine with its next harvest. That it would be stunning he had no doubt.

"The boys," as Mason, Noah, and Alex were now known, took to heart the cleanup and maintenance of the tree and old treehouse. Honey was delighted to see they had not shied away from trying to wield the heavy shovels, rakes, and wheelbarrow to clear the area of weeds. She had asked Pete and his men to make sure the treehouse was safe, and that everything was nailed and bolted in place. Pete suggested the boys put on several coats of varnish to protect the wood, and Honey knew they'd be here after school for their ice cream and then get straight to work. She'd ordered a surprise for them and couldn't wait until it arrived.

Honey had already checked off the purchase of a white, four-wheel-drive Explorer, just like the one she'd rented, a riding mower, and an assortment of gardening equipment. The two sheds on the property were rundown, and high on Pete's list was the creation of a new barn and workshop.

She would meet Edward for lunch, Landon for dinner, and then she wanted to climb into her soft, warm bed, pull the covers up, and read. While Linda the librarian was questionable, the three books she had brought with her looked fascinating, especially the one about the legendary gold by Dr. Allen Crawley. Honey was interested to see how closely it mirrored Edward's stories and to find out more about the people who had come before her at Hartland. She wondered if Maria Luego's journals confirmed these stories as well. There was so much going on! Honey loved it.

Dinner with Landon was fun, and the food at the Oak Glen Steakhouse, just a few miles up the road, was delicious. Tonight, the chef had outdone himself and the serving staff were attuned to their every need. Honey loved the atmosphere in the sports bar and grill with its huge stone fireplace delightfully warming the room. Tonight, however, she and Landon had a lot of catching up to do and chose the formal dining room in the back, which offered them a comfortable booth and quiet privacy. Landon shared his excitement about acquiring two more horses, and Honey agreed to join him for a ride in the morning as there was still so much of Hartland yet to be explored. Honey sipped the last of her wine, content, happy, and now finally tired, the day having been a full one. The only thing left on her list was to go home and read.

The hot bath had felt wonderful! Now warm in her soft, blue, fleece nightgown and signature thick socks, Honey slipped into bed, excited to begin the small, thin book, which could easily be read in one sitting, if she didn't fall asleep first.

A Story of Yucaipa Gold, by Dr. Allen Crawley, MD. Published 1876

I don't intend to draw the long bow when I say my story begins when a gun was held to my head, the gent demanding I take out the bullet in his friend's leg, minus the required doctor fees. That I was much obliged to do so tis the reason I'm alive to tell the tale. There were three men; monikers on their wanted posters read; Rig Taylor, Thornton Taylor, and Clem Smith. They were a useless bunch, fit only for evacuating blind monkeys or doing damage to the fine folks whose coinage they held in trust at the Arizona banks which they robbed. Their fimble-famble with the banks lasted two years before they were caught by bounty hunters, but not before they secreted the gold away somewhere near the Mexico border. (1865-1867) How them buggers escaped their capturers no one knows, but escape they did to California where the hugger-muggers couldn't pull off a raid on Rojo Rancho, didn't know about the boys and their big guns and how they fancied using them. That's what landed Clem Taylor here in my Yucaipa office with a slug as sweet as Texas which nearly blew off his leg.

That day all hell broke loose, not only for me, but for the Yucaipat Indian tribe. I hawk with the Indians from time to time, but mostly they stick with their medicine men, and so I was flabbergasted when Flying Eagle, the husband of Yucaipat Chief, Aiyana, rode his horse to this office, stumbling in the door, bloody and all-overish. His tale was a floorer. Told me his wife had been killed during a raid on the village, and his son was no-where to be seen. He had barely escaped with his life, and the arrow sticking out of his back told the truth. The leather shirt he wore was a keeper so I just cut what was needed to pull it off his head. Now I'm a Rusty Guts, but the sight I saw took courage to look at for very long. It wasn't the arrow, but where the arrow was put that curled my mind. The Indian had been carved up some time before, and the red scars took on the shape of an eye. In the middle of the eye was the arrow. I swear it, dead on as kingdom come.

I talk when I'm hurting my patients, gives them something other than the pain to think about so I said the first thing that came to mind as I yanked out the arrow. "How old is your boy?"

He replied "ten," adding "he is a white boy with golden hair – you have seen him?" Well, if I'd seen a white Indian boy, I wouldn't forget that sight, I guarantee you. No, I'd not seen him but I sure as hell heard about him – oh did I hear about him – on and on from my patient Sophia who has both a calamitous mouth and stomach. I told the Indian about her conversing with Thornton Taylor, whilst I was cleaning Clem's whistle and how he'd mentioned the boy, Hartland, and the Indian village all in one swoop. Even asked how far away it was.

I suspect the gents were at Hartland as near the same time as the raid took place. Don't figure them for dash-fires. It would take vigor and manliness, neither of which any of them got.

Never knew what happened to the boy, but the story of Flying Eagle and them outlaws is one for the books. It took nearly ten years to come around the bend, so I could write it down and you could believe it – or not.

Despite the amazing tale, Honey was fading. Tomorrow was Saturday, and after she and Landon went on their ride, she'd find time to hide away from the hustle and bustle of her new life and read more.

The horses were saddled and ready as Honey pulled into La Bonita. Landon waved, then finished adjusting the saddlebags filled with water, sandwiches, and a pair of apples.

"Hey, cowboy, where's your hat?" teased Honey, giving Landon a hug and a sweet kiss.

She smelled heavenly. Whatever perfume she wore, he'd make sure she had a case of it. He smiled, glad they would have some quiet time all to themselves. He'd been wanting to explore Hartland with her ever since he'd arrived. There had indeed been a method to his madness in purchasing two new horses.

"They're gorgeous!" Honey said, stroking their noses and admiring their colors.

"This one," said Landon, handing Honey the reins, "is yours. She's a Palomino."

"She's beautiful," said Honey. "I love the combination of her golden coat, and white mane and tail."

Landon grinned, pleased with her response. "I think she should be named after one of the three most famous Palominos—Trigger, Mr. Ed, or Beauty."

"Well," said Honey, giving serious consideration when only one name would do. "I suppose it will have to be Mr. Ed."

Landon was scandalized, exclaiming, "You can't name this beautiful female Mr. Ed!"

"Okay," Honey sighed. "Trigger then."

"That was Roy Rogers' horse," scolded Landon. "No other horse can have that name."

Honey shook her head. "Well, all we have left is Beauty then."

"Now we're talking," said Landon.

Honey laughed. "And what is this marvelous creature's name going to be?" she said, petting the brown and black Cleveland Bay.

"T.J., of course," said Landon, "after the famous T.J. Ward of the Cleveland Browns."

"That's a great name for this hulk of a horse," said Honey.

"Are we going to stand around and name horses all day, or are we going to ride?" asked Landon.

"Let's get a move on, cowboy," Honey said, motioning Landon for a leg up as she mounted Beauty.

The day was glorious, filled with sunshine, clear skies, a soft breeze now and again, and a thousand acres of pristine wildlands whose riding paths went on for miles. The torrent of water, which was once a raging river, had created the canyon that ran from the mountains to the sea. It was still considered a river, but the trickle of water that now ran through it would better define a creek. At one time the river, land, and ecosystem had flourished abundantly, raining nearly once a week, but when the Big Bear Dam was built in 1884 to harness the water for a lake as a tourist attraction, the once Green Valley was much less green, taking on a more golden, sage, and brown visage.

Landon and Honey rode in silence and awe. The breathtaking beauty of the mountains, the river, the canyon, and the land were speaking to them in different ways. They could see for themselves the intelligent System playing out before them, a System no mere mortal could have created. The sense of responsibility for the care and protection of La Bonita, Hartland,

and The Green Valley filled their hearts, renewing their devotion to contribute to the land as the Yucaipat Indians had, as JD, Jonathan, and Merritt had before them. Now Honey understood why her grandmother Victoria prized Hartland so and why on her deathbed she was finally at peace when Honey promised to watch over it. For the first time, instead of ignoring her wealth, she embraced it, conscious of its catalytic power for goodness and beauty, which would make what might only be a dream, a reality.

"Look," said Landon, breaking the silence. "This piece of land looks like an arrowhead. See how the river has divided? There is the point of the arrow, and we are riding where it attaches to the shaft."

"I want to check something out," declared Honey, urging Beauty into a gallop. Landon loved her independence and followed her lead. Honey slowed as she came closer to the middle of the arrowhead-shaped land. Together she and Beauty explored the broken chain of rocks confirming at one time it had made a giant circle. Then Honey turned her attention to the large mounds. At first the mounds appeared random, but upon more careful examination, she saw they were not. They too made a circle, with larger mounds in the middle and smaller ones extending out.

"Landon," called Honey, "you have to see this."

He rode up beside her.

"First, look at the rocks," Honey directed. "If you connected them, they would make a circle. Now look at the mounds. It reminds me of a cemetery. See, in the center are the largest mounds, like the mausoleums of those who are honored, and from there the other graves extend out." But now she questioned her theory because next to one of the larger mounds lay a small mound, like a mother and child. "This was an Indian Burial Ground, Landon!" Honey cried.

"It sure looks like it," agreed Landon. "There's a real sense of sacredness here." Suddenly it became clear. Honey wondered if one of those graves contained the remains of Chief Aiyana, Flying Eagle's wife and Jonathan's adopted mother. Another puzzle piece had fallen into place.

If—and she was certainly speculating, letting her imagination run wild—this mound was Chief Aiyana's, the small grave could not be Jonathan's, as he escaped the raid and lived. So, whose grave was this? Who was the child?

Landon couldn't believe his eyes. There she was again! The little girl he'd seen on the stairs the first time he'd visited Hartland. She was sitting on the small mound, her legs gathered up in her arms, and he could see she wore pantaloons and leather boots. Her dress was pale blue with yellow and pink flowers, and he could see the twinkle in her eye and the sweet smile on her face. She looked like an angel, and then she was gone.

While Honey had not seen the child, she sensed very clearly a strong force, a presence. Something kind and pure that came and went. Honey knew she risked appearing crazy, but she had to ask. "Landon, did you feel something? I mean did you sense *someone* here just now?"

The stunned look on Landon's face made her wish she'd kept the thought to herself. Honey smiled sheepishly, "Guess you've got a loon on your hands," she apologized.

Landon dismounted and came to help Honey down. "If you are a loon," he said, "then I'm one too. Honey, you may not believe this . . . I'm not sure *I* believe this . . . but there was a little girl sitting on the mound. I saw her as plain as I see you now."

Honey's eyes widened, but she knew he told the truth. Landon explained in detail, and how he'd first seen her on the stairs.

"Can you see her now?" Honey asked.

"No, she's gone now," he replied.

Honey was disappointed. She wanted to see her too. "I wonder," Honey said aloud, "if this is little Emily Hart, the child who drowned in the pond at five years of age. There's mention of it in Maria Luego's journal at the Smiley Library." Honey told Landon the story, now remembering the passage where Maria talked about Jonathan carrying the little coffin he had hand-carved to the burial site. Where else would he put it, but next to his mother, Aiyana?

One might have thought it a sad and depressing moment, but for Honey it was a moment of true connection, one that death could not separate. She'd always believed the body was simply a vehicle for the perpetual soul and that all lives remained connected when this one was done and another began.

The bond between Landon and Honey deepened as they shared this very real and special experience together of another dimension, one not often encountered. They held each other for a while, feeling safe in one another's arms, counting themselves blessed—as one does who feels that despite all the difficulties of life, it does indeed hold unknown meaning, reason, and purpose.

Honey returned from her ride to the now normal and delightful chaos of her new Hartland family made up of Remey, the boys, Pete and the contractors, Jason and his vineyard growers, Olive Grove Grant, and the new housekeeper Lulu, whom Remey had hired. Honey knew it would be important to create some quiet places where she could retreat from all the activity. The attic would be her sanctuary inside the home; the outside retreat she had yet to discover. Perhaps she'd restore JD's cottage behind the stone wall and make it her own. Honey stopped at the French desk to solve a puzzle piece or two on her way to grab a shower. She'd always enjoyed this past time, and today was no exception. She found three wooden pieces that fit, and then forced herself to go upstairs and wash the dust of the ride away. When she returned, sporting her comfy New England Patriots sweats, she stopped by the kitchen for a glass of iced tea before returning to the addictive puzzle. Remey was outside with the boys, ever the mother hen. Honey discovered the freshly baked chocolate chip cookies still warm from the oven and sent a blessing of thanks for the young woman.

Seeing three more pieces had been added to what she had done, Honey realized someone else was working on the puzzle as well. She heard the back door close, meaning Remey had returned, and Honey called to her. "These are delicious," she said with passion. "Really yummy."

Remey smiled.

"Hey," said Honey, "I see you found a few more pieces of the puzzle, but we have a long way to go."

"Ms. Honey," replied Remey, "I don't do puzzles, never been my thing."

"Oh," said Honey, "perhaps one of the boys came in."

"Not if they want to stay alive," said Remey. "They're only allowed on the back porch and in the kitchen. Besides they've been out all day."

"Maybe Pete came in the house?"

"No, ma'am. Since you created the construction clubhouse there's been no need."

"Well, that's strange," mused Honey, deciding not to dig herself deeper into a hole.

"Enjoy," Remey said. "I still have a ton of things to do before the three o'clock bell when you finally get some peace and quiet around here." The words faded as she retreated into the kitchen.

Honey let the mystery go and enjoyed the quiet half hour where Botticelli's *Allegory of Spring* was little by little emerging to her great delight.

The bell having been rung, the "goodbyes" and "see you on Mondays" all having been said, the caravan of bicycles, trucks, and cars exited Hartland, and once again mistress and land felt the joy of peace and quiet. Honey ran upstairs, returned with a blanket and Dr. Crawley's book, then laid down on the comfortable couch to read.

Never knew what happened to the boy, but the story of Flying Eagle and them outlaws is one for the books. It took nearly ten years to come around the bend so I could write it down and you could believe it – or not.

At mention of the boy, the words of Sophia came back to me, and I told Flying Eagle what she said about the outlaws. A flag of distress could be seen in his dark eyes as they flashed with recognition and danger. Later I learned the Indian had come from Arizona, knew of the outlaws, and putting two and two together, just realized they were the same snakes that killed his son's original parents. The outlaws being on Hartland and Jonathan's disappearance may have been a coincidence, but the Indian was pawing at the ground to be let loose and find out for himself. I knew it would do no good at all to tell the man to rest, so I patched him up double good. He had no coinage with which to pay, but he took off his necklace, think it was his totem, and gave it to me in thanks.

Here's where I waited for nearly a month to learn what really happened from Flying Eagle himself who came back to repay his debt, and boy did he!

Seems he'd followed the tracks of the three men from town to Hartland. They were easy to see as one of the horse's shoes was cockeyed, leaving a hoof print no horse could be proud of.

During the raid, Flying Eagle had left the boy in the walnut tree telling him not to come down till Aiyana returned. Somehow, the boy got mixed up with the outlaws and they ran off with him. Flying Eagle followed the trail all the way to Rancho Cucamonga where it turns off to go down toward San Diego and on into Mexico. Night had fallen, he was sore and feverish, anointed as they say with one devil of an arrow. In the distance he took sight of a campfire. He left his horse and crawled over the ledge to take a look-see. Damned if it wasn't the outlaws, but his boy was no-where to be seen. They were crooking the elbow to beat the band, whiskey bottles one apiece. Clem Smith, the one I treated, and not with much care, was moaning and carrying on. Men of feeble and weaselly character don't take pain well, and he was vocalizing his agony and pitching a fit. The other two had enough of Clem and they wondered if he wasn't near ready for an eternity box.

Flying Eagle followed Rig and Thornton as they went to take piss out of earshot from Clem. The gist of the discussion was that Clem was a flying mess, was likely going to die anyway and besides they needed his horse to pull the wagon, there being a lot of gold and all. Thornton wondered how they were going to pay for a wagon and the tools they'd need to dig the gold out of the cave. Rig smacked him one, took out the pearl necklace Jonathan always wore, and shoved it in his face. Their fate had just been sealed.

The boy's whereabouts was Flying Eagle's only concern, controlling his overwhelming desire to give them an earth bath that very minute. But he had to find out where was the boy. Patient as a saint, the Indian waited for the right moment. It came before dawn. Clem woke up alone. Flying Eagle observed the rising of Clem's dander, the fury of betrayal followed by fear and hopelessness as the man bawled like a baby, seeing he'd been left behind. The Indian sprung out of nowhere leaping on the crying heap and holding a knife to his throat. Clem wet his pants and bellowed like a stuffed pig. In situations where language was a barrier, other methods were needed to come to an agreement. Suffice it to say, Clem agreed he didn't want to die. Pleading with the Indian to believe his boy was alive and well, the bugger agreed to take the man direct to the boy, in exchange for beating Rig and Thornton to the gold. He'd give the man half and if he was lying about the boy, the Indian could kill him dead on the spot. Satisfied, the Indian and the outlaw rode south, their destination Yuma Arizona.

Clem nearly clawed his leg off from the pain, while Flying Eagle had only one thought. His son.

His heart was torn clean through with the death of his wife, but he would mourn her when his son was safe.

Flying Eagle and Clem watched from behind an old shed as Rig and Thornton went into the Yuma Trading Post and left with Clem and Thornton's horses pulling the wagon carrying shovels, food and a few supplies. The trading post did a gimmy for the three wooden coffins which would secret the gold. The trek to the earthen bank didn't take long, placing Mexico just a stone's throw away.

Rig and Thornton were sweating like hogs, pushing aside boulders and brush which hid the cave from unscrupulous eyes. Now's when they wished Clem was around to ease the workload.

Once they'd broken through, Rig made Thornton do a once a round to make sure no one was eavesdropping, while Rig saddled up his horse taking out a private stash of money for himself.

Plumb tuckered out and the night coming, they slept until dawn whereupon they finished the work of loading the coffins with gold and cash.

Flying Eagle signaled Clem to stay put in the rocks. He needed him alive. He repeated the signal which had turned into a demand. He could not have the one link to his child die. Clem gave the thumbs up, and the Indian moved closer to his prey.

Replacing the screen of boulders and brush had yet to be done, but Rig and Thornton were guzzling water and whiskey having themselves a tea party. The canyon echoed every sound and when the chatter turned to Clem he could hear every word. The wipe-haulers had a field day with Clem, calling him every name in the book, making fun of him and saying he was probably dead by now and it was good riddance. Thornton did his rendition of Clem getting shot in the leg – right when Rig was swallowing, which caused him to snort and cough before he laughed his head off. Clem could take it no more. The pain ripped through his leg as he stood fully erect, for

all to see. Pathetically he heaved large rocks at the stupe-
fied men, who for a moment, believed the ghost of Clem had
returned to curse them. The Indian tomahawk lodged itself
between Thornton's wide eyes, while Flying Eagle flung his
knife destroying Rigs shoulder, the cocked gun falling out of
his hand. A hurling rock meant for Rig, hit Flying Eagle and
before he could regain his balance, the bullet had silenced
Clem, his body tumbling and landing with a thud. The fight
not over, Rig attacked Flying Eagle, trying his best to fire off
another shot, but was too late. The Indian had torn the knife
from his shoulder and now he held it over Rig's heart demand-
ing an answer about his son. Rig pushed Flying Eagle off,
both wrestling for the gun. Another shot echoed through the
canyon. While Rig would wear the coffin, Flying Eagle would
live to die a thousand deaths—his wife, son, his birth tribe, his
new tribe, all lost to him forever.

Honey put down the book, grabbed a hanky, and wiped the tears
from her eyes. While she was unaccustomed to Dr. Crawley's strange ver-
nacular and eccentric writing style, he grabbed her heart with the stark
reality of it all. This was not fiction, but a family history book, and there
was one more, short chapter to read. Honey fixed a plate of cheese, crack-
ers, and fruit and poured herself a glass of chilled wine. Curled up on the
couch, she continued.

Flying Eagle moved the three bodies into the cave, returning
the boulders and brush where the beings—beneath the honor-
able dignity of animals—could no longer offend the people,
the judgment of the earth even now beginning to mortify such
mortifying lives.

There was only blinding silence as Flying Eagle tethered the
horses to the wagon. Once again, it returned to the Yuma
Trading Post. The Indian gathered as much of the gold coins
as he could carry, dropped it on the counter and asked the

owner for the return of the pearl necklace. The man called to his wife from behind the curtain where she appeared, wearing the beautiful piece. Her husband motioned her to take it off, and he handed it back to Flying Eagle who nodded, put it over his head, and walked out the door.

The next thing I knew the Indian was standing in my office, his eyes like flat stones. What happened next could floor an elephant, and I had witnesses to it all! A fluke really. Nephews out from Maine, Albert and Alfred Smiley, here to give me a hand at the ranch for the summer, nearly jumped out of their gentrified clothes. Hah! Probably thought they'd come to Yucaipa only to lose their scalps! The Indian had emptied two water buckets I kept outside for the horses and filled both with gold and cash. They sat there on the floor uncomfortable like. With a nod and a gesture, Flying Eagle made them mine. Rare to find a man who believed in reciprocity. He asked me in his broken English to write a note to his boy, to let him know he was still alive. His father knew if Jonathan came back, he'd go straight to the walnut tree and hide there. A string of feathers attached to a branch was to be their signal. Flying Eagle came every day to that tree and every day to Aiyana's grave, hoping the boy would return.

And what of the fortune in its casketed state? I can tell you only that my two buckets' worth and an equal amount from one of the caskets were entwined. Hah! An Indian and an old doc created a horse ranch on my one hundred acres just south of town. Now there's a story to tell your kids. The wife, my Libby, died. Maria Luego, house-kept for me and Flying Eagle for ten years while every summer the Smiley boys came out to help with the horses. We created a peculiar family of sorts; an old man, an Indian, a Spanish señora, and two Quaker boys from Maine. We certainly made an interesting pot of stew! The End.

Honey observed Dr. Crawley had not addressed head-on the whereabouts of the rest of the gold—two and a half caskets' worth. One could only imagine that perhaps the doc himself, Maria Luego, or even the Smiley boys knew where it was, but the reader couldn't be sure. Honey had been pleasantly surprised with the reference to Edward's great uncles Albert and Alfred of whom he related several stories while they were there on the horse ranch—getting into a great deal of trouble she recalled. Honey gazed up at the statue on the fireplace, grimacing. Like Maria Luego, she found the thing somehow distasteful. Honey thought of the night Linda Hall was there and how her eyes went straight to the statue. A lightbulb went on in Honey's mind as she began putting the puzzle pieces together. There were many mysteries connected with Hartland, Linda Hall, this statue, Emily, the contents of the attic upstairs, and the gold which literally *everyone* it seemed had on their minds.

What was Linda Hall's connection to it all? Obviously, she knew of the gold and the possible connection to the Smiley boys long ago. But that was all supposition and why would she think Edward Smiley would have any knowledge of it in 2018? If he did, why wasn't it dug up and used to build a hospital or something? No, Edward was as clueless as she was. Undoubtedly Linda had chosen these three specific books for Honey to read, but why? Did she think Honey knew something? Well, that would be ridiculous! She hardly knew if she was coming or going, much less how to find lost gold that probably didn't exist. Honey laughed. She'd either need a full-on treasure map or a numbered list of clues with detailed directions to be of any help in the matter. But there was one thing she was quite capable of and that was removing the eerie statue from her fireplace mantel. She'd haul the old thing out to the back porch, then tomorrow when it was light, stick it in the cellar.

It was time for bed, but she'd work on the puzzle for a while. Till she got sleepy. Honey sat down at the French desk ready to continue her methodical approach to the wooden puzzle, adding pieces only to the already created border, the center remaining empty until the very end. All at once in the center of the puzzle, the pieces which made up the tilted head of Venus with her beautiful face surrounded by long golden hair were in place. "Again!" she gasped out loud. Honey instinctively looked around the room for the responsible party who had twice now, unseen, participated in the game.

"Emily," whispered Honey to the empty room, "are you here?" Emily was indeed there! The little girl was standing beside Honey as she sat in the delicately white, carved chair, which faced the window in the living room at Hartland. Honey knew the obvious analogy was silly, but a number of mysterious puzzle pieces had fallen into place when she felt, and Landon actually *saw*, for the *second* time, little Emily at the Yucaipat Burial Grounds. His detailed description of the girl reminded her of the china dolls gazing at her now from the corner chair next to the burning fireplace, resplendent in bonnets, frocks, petticoats, pantaloons, and lace-up leather boots. To believe what Honey once thought was unbelievable would have been difficult, a real stretch, except she'd experienced firsthand and for herself, the ghost child—twice now.

Honey could no longer ignore the direct cause of the repeated additions to the puzzle and, more substantially, the undeniable force of her presence which she had sensed, and Landon had seen. Honey determined to return to the Smiley Library and Maria Luego's journals to learn more about the child. There was a reason she was here and a reason she was revealing herself. "Emily," she spoke softly, "help me learn what you want me to know." She waited. Nothing happened, and Honey had to admit she was disappointed. She didn't know what she expected. Well, that was not quite true. She had hoped the little girl would reveal herself like she had done with Landon, but tonight it was not to be. Honey worked on the puzzle a little longer, then turned off the lights, heading toward the stairs. The moon was bright and full, and its light shown through the window and onto the corner chair, now home to the two china dolls. Honey gasped, then smiled, the message clearly sent and received. Honey had placed the two dolls in either corner of the chair, but the doll in the blue dress had been rearranged. Now she hugged the doll in the pink dress.

CHAPTER TWELVE

KIDNAPPED

Thomas Winery, 1863

Jonathan lay bruised on the ground, his legs entwined in Thomas Winery grapevines, watching the outlaws ride off. Lucy Thomas, mistress of the Thomas Winery, likewise watched as three men on horseback fired off a rally of gunshots and galloped off in a cloud of dust. The frightening sound brought her to the window. The men gone now, Lucy returned the curtain to its place and resumed her mending while Jonathan remained on the ground looking up at the blue sky, his mind blank, his soul in shock. He stayed that way for several hours, caring nothing for food and water, trying only to process just enough so he could get his bearings. The unanswered questions were his monsters. From the safety of the tree he could only hear the screams and cries of the villagers, but who was being wounded, who was being killed, and who had escaped he could not *know*. The wholly unexpected arrival and capture by the outlaws was beyond his comprehension, and the stench of the man he been forced to ride with for two days filled his nostrils—the one they called Clem.

From deep inside a thought had begun to surface, and suddenly it broke through. To *know*, he must get up. To *return*, he must get up. To be *strong*, he must get up and find food. To slay the *monsters*, he must get up. Jonathan willed himself to get up. He brushed himself off, untangled his moccasin from the vine, and slowly observed his surroundings. He took in the mountains to the north, but they were not his mountains. His eyes swept what seemed to be an ocean of grapevines whose symmetrical rows he found comforting. He saw the large yellow house with white columns and trim, and it looked warm and inviting. He saw three roads he could take. The road ahead, the road back, and the road the outlaws took. He automatically reached for the pearl necklace. Its absence was like a snake bite, but he chose to ignore it, the goal of *knowing* his only aim. He'd gotten up. Now there was only deciding what to do.

Lucy Thomas caught the movement of something coming up the path. For a moment she feared it might be the men returning, but when she parted the curtain she saw instead the strangest sight. A white boy, with golden hair, dressed as an Indian. He walked slowly as if in a dream state. Intuition spoke, and Lucy suddenly *knew* both his and her world would forever be changed.

$$\infty$$

Jonathan could not have known that when Lucy opened the door, he would be looking into the eyes of the woman, who from the age of ten, would be the third of his three mothers. Not only would she bring him back from the grave but give him the strength of character to be a man. But first there would be food, a warm bath, clean clothes, and a sense of safety.

"Ma'am," Jonathan said politely, "I won't trouble you for long. Just need food and rest so I can make it back home."

"I quite understand, young man," said Lucy, respecting his freedom to make his own choices.

He liked the woman. She had beautiful auburn hair, which she swept up into a crown of curls. Her face was lovely with a soft ivory complexion. The lady's eyes were green, her lips and cheeks pink, and her stately manner of being and dress reminded him of a queen. Her style of speech was firm, polite, and to the point, but her eyes were very kind and she smiled quite a lot. She was a woman, he suspected, who could dine with a king as easily as she could picnic with a peasant and she would treat them the same. The home she had created mirrored her style—clean, elegant and very beautiful. It reminded him of his grandmother's home in Texas, a great and vast Victorian filled with fine furnishings, nothing of which he'd been allowed to touch. He wondered now how his grandmother must have felt watching her granddaughter, husband and child, riding off to California in the fine new Prairie Schooner, top-of-the-line covered wagon, but still in contrast to the mansion, inadequate and mean. He was sure his grandmother would find his village and tepee even less refined, but for him it was a palace, the place where he belonged and was loved. His tears betrayed him now, and he fiercely brushed them away, demanding himself to return to his goal.

"Just for tonight," said Lucy. "You can sleep upstairs in the guest room, get a good night's rest, and be off in the morning."

Jonathan nodded, as she filled his soup bowl for the third time. In preparation for the rest of the household that would in moments be running through the door, Lucy said casually, "You'll soon meet my husband George and daughters Georgia and Caroline upon their return from town. Caroline is about your age, and Georgia is two years older." Jonathan was grateful for the heads-up. Lucy continued, "You can see this is a vineyard and winery. We grow the grapes, make the wine, and sell it to many customers in California. My husband is quite passionate about the whole thing. He always wanted a son, but that didn't stop him from doting on his daughters. Spoils them, I say. They've likely talked him into new dresses, bonnets, and candy from the General Store."

Jonathan pushed his bowl away, the breadcrumbs from nearly half a loaf were scattered about, and Lucy was content that step one had been accomplished. Step two, if she could manage it, would be a bath and some clean clothes. Lucy saw his leather shirt and pants were ripped in several places. "Why don't you let me wash and mend these for you, so you can be off tomorrow with a good set of clothes."

Jonathan was saved from the decision when a rush of two giggling girls in a swirl of bonnets, bows, and frilly ruffles came running into the kitchen laden with boxes. Behind them was their father, his arms filled with more.

"Mother, look!" they said in unison. "Papa's bought us—"

The sight of the boy stopped them mid-sentence.

"Hello," said Caroline breezily, as if every day there were a blond, white, Indian boy in their kitchen. "I'm Caroline Thomas. What's your name?"

Lucy stepped in to make the formal introductions. "My dears," she said, "I would like to introduce you to our guest. This is Jonathan." Polite introductions meant boys were to stand, so she signaled him out of the chair.

Immediately Jonathan got to his feet. "Pleased to meet you, Jonathan," said Caroline with a slight curtsey.

Jonathan nodded.

Georgia offered a slight bow. "Pleased to meet you. My name is Georgia."

Again, Jonathan nodded.

George rid himself of the boxes, held out his hand, and said with a warm smile, "Greetings, Master Jonathan. Welcome to the Thomas Winery."

Lucy intervened again, motioning Jonathan to come to her side. "Jonathan will only be with us for the night."

"Oh," cried Caroline, "that's a shame. Can't you stay longer?"

"I'm afraid," continued Lucy," he's had a bit of a fall. But he's just eaten, will be having a bath so I can wash and mend these clothes, and then he will be in good order for his journey back to Yucaipa tomorrow."

Three faces fell. Jonathan's face fell when he heard the word *bath*. Caroline's face fell at the sadness of losing such an interesting guest so soon. George's face fell when he heard the word *Yucaipa* and put two and two together.

Lucy's suggestions were always irrevocable commands, and no one would dare to usurp her authority, including Jonathan, who sensed at ten the fierce strength of a woman and the wisdom of picking his battles. It wasn't that he didn't like a bath. In fact, he enjoyed a swim in the river nearly every day. It was just he'd not been in a tub for many years. He'd do as the nice woman said and be on his way tomorrow.

George's flannel shirt made do for him while Lucy mended Jonathan's clothes. He was placed in the living room where a warm fire burned. It was soon apparent that he had become Caroline's captive. She was determined he'd teach her as many Indian words as possible before he left, writing them down phonetically. The game changed when Jonathan whistled a bird call, whereupon the delighted Miss Caroline clapped, demanding more.

George made his way to the back porch where Lucy, on her third bucket of soap and water, was wrestling with the soiled clothes. Her standard of clean was unmatched in the county. George bid her to stop. The look on his face said something serious had happened. He led her to the porch swing as she dried her hands on the crisp, white apron.

"I have bad news for the boy, I believe," George began. "The whole town is in an uproar today. Five or six Indians rode in, having been wounded during the raid on the Yucaipat Indian village. Doc Walters was fixing them up. Their English wasn't too good, but he was able to piece together what happened. Remember the name Red Eye and all the trouble he caused both in Yucaipa with the Mexicans and out at Timoteo Canyon?"

Lucy nodded, the gruesome tale had been the talk of the town for months.

"Seems," continued George, "he was ousted several years back by the chief who was his father. The chief was getting old and chose his granddaughter to take his place and lead the tribe, the position Red Eye believed should have been his. Well, two days ago, Red Eye came back with his warriors, killed the woman chief and took over the village. Word has it, she had a son, a white boy around ten who they say she'd rescued three years ago or so. Name was Jonathan. The Indians were heading toward Arizona, trying to find someone named Flying Eagle, hoping he might have escaped with the boy."

Lucy closed her eyes, empathy a painful thing. She'd had a premonition this boy would change their life and now she knew why. "Poor child," she finally said, then fell silent.

"I know you, Lucy Thomas," said George, "and I know precisely what you're going to say."

Lucy turned to her husband and waited. He sighed, then quoted her, "We're going to have some decisions to make."

Lucy wiped away the tears, stood, and said, "There's only one decision we can make, George Thomas, and that's to offer the child a home, if he wants it. I'll not put him out on the street."

"Let's take it one day at a time," replied George. "Providence needs to have her way too with the boy. We all want his highest and best."

Lucy reached up and kissed her husband, loving the wise and caring man more every day.

Arm in arm they passed the soaking clothes. Lucy stopped. "George, dear, the boy's going to need some proper clothes."

George smiled, kissed her check, and sighed. "Get some measurements, and I'll go back into town. We can tell him tonight after dinner." Lucy nodded, knowing there could be no words that would mend the wounds they must inflict and that only his receptivity to their love, and time, could heal his heart.

$$\sim$$

The tearstained flannel shirt enveloping Jonathan's weary body held no comfort. Nor did the four-poster bed, soft pillows, and warm blankets under which he had lain for two days now.

Lucy had quietly come in twice, once to bring a bowl of soup and a pitcher of water, neither of which he touched, and again to lay two sets of clothes on the dresser. His mended leather shirt and breeches and some town clothes, a cowboy hat, boots, and a belt sat in the corner chair. Lucy would give him one more day to fully mourn, and then she would need to help him slowly move on. She knew firsthand about great loss.

The following morning Jonathan woke up to the sound of small pebbles lightly tapping his upstairs window. Curious of the cause, he jumped out of bed and peeked behind the curtain. His eyes widened as below Ms. Lucy, of all people, was tossing up the small stones. He opened the window to hear her call out. "Son, give me a hand in the stables, will you?"

"Yes, ma'am," would be the only reply she'd accept, so he called back, "Yes, ma'am!"

Lucy showed no emotion when he arrived at her side in his town clothes and boots. The hat he'd left behind, but she was mightily pleased at the progress that had been made.

Marching toward the stables Lucy said, "I assume you're an excellent horseman." It was a statement rather than a question. Jonathan nodded as she replied, "I expected it to be the case."

Lucy stopped suddenly, kneeling down to look into the boy's eyes. "A good horseman, Jonathan, knows how to ride, but an excellent horseman can read the soul of an animal. Do you know what I mean by soul?"

Jonathan waited for her to explain.

"Everything has a soul. Even animals. You have a soul that makes you Jonathan. Caroline has a soul that makes her Caroline. A particular animal has a soul that makes it that particular animal. Every soul is unique and special. Do you understand?" she asked kindly. Jonathan nodded, comprehension in his eyes.

"Well done," said Lucy, standing and taking his hand. "Then come with me."

The stables mirrored the Victorian style and color of the home, and the tall, massive structure housed many horses. Like the home and grounds, it was clean and orderly. It smelled of fresh hay, horse salve, and leather. Several men were hard at work, mucking out the stalls and tending the animals. Jonathan counted at least twelve stalls. Several buggies and wagons were stationed in the front of the barn along with a wide array of saddles, reins, and blankets. The back of the barn was stacked with bales of hay, oats, and wheelbarrows. Traversing the two ends were an assortment of chickens, small hunting dogs, and barn cats. "Mr. Thomas has his passion, the vineyards and winery," explained Lucy. "This is mine. I grew up on a ranch in Kentucky where we raised thoroughbred horses, and it's in my blood."

Jonathan could see all the horses were beautiful and well cared for. Odakota, Hototo, and Teetonka would be in awe. Sharp tears pricked his eyes as he wondered if they too had been killed, and again he thought of Flying Eagle, Honana, and more painfully his mother. Lucy interrupted his thoughts, turning his attention instead to a stall that appeared empty. Slowly and quietly she opened the door. Inside laying in the hay, with her oats and water untouched, lay the most beautiful horse Jonathan had ever seen. She was a Palomino, her coat a soft gold. Her mane and tail were wild, long, and a pale ivory. She appeared as if from another world. Unexpectedly Lucy sat in the hay, unconcerned about her fine clothes, and she beckoned Jonathan to sit next to her. Together they observed the horse in silence until Lucy leaned over and in a soft voice told Jonathan what she knew of the beautiful creature. "Mr. Thomas and I recently bought her from a nearby rancher, and he had purchased her from someone clear up in Montana, along with her mother. The two were abused, and the mother finally died. There," she pointed to the marks on her flanks and legs, "you can still see the scars. The colt was uncontrollable, and the Montana folks sold her off at an auction where the rancher bought her. Likewise he could do nothing with her, and one day simply handed me the reins, offering to pay me to take her off his hands."

Lucy allowed the silence to seed the boy's mind. "You understand horses, Jonathan, and I believe you can read her soul. What do you think is wrong?"

Lucy was surprised by his immediate response, as he whispered back, "She's sad."

"I think you're right," said Lucy. "Can you help her? I would be so grateful."

Jonathan nodded.

"What if I leave this apple and the two of you together for a while. You can see what you think." Allowing no room for discussion she said, "You'll come in for lunch, then afterwards Caroline and Georgia will take you to the pond. I believe they said something about frogs. Tonight, we'll have dinner, and afterwards we read a chapter or two before bed. King Arthur, I believe, is the book Mr. Thomas brought back from town today." Lucy patted his hand, smiled, and gently closed the stall door.

Three months passed. George and Lucy sat on the back porch swing, watching the loving connection between boy and horse, finding Jonathan's rare ability to adapt to his new life quite remarkable.

That day in the stables, Jonathan had looked deep into the Palomino's eyes, and she had looked back. He saw his own sadness and despair mirrored there and suddenly the grief he'd been holding back released itself as he sobbed quietly. Later when he was calm, he'd stroked her golden coat and began talking softly, placing her in the role of his confidant. He opened up to her, sharing in words his ocean of grief and the fears he still held knowing Red Eye ruled the village. His melodious voice soothed the colt as the same divine spirit hidden in each unique soul united them as one. "You're beautiful," Jonathan whispered, sharing the apple with the beautiful creature. "I wonder if Ms. Lucy will let me name you Beauty."

Cousin Merritt this, and Cousin Merritt that! The whole Thomas house seemed to be in an uproar of excitement over some cousin named Merritt. What was so special about the person, Jonathan couldn't possibly imagine. All he knew was that Ms. Lucy had given him strict orders to bring himself and George in from the vineyard at the *first* ring of the bell to wash up, put on a clean shirt, and comb his hair, as Cousin Merritt would be there for supper. She further warned that the occasion of dinner, again due to Cousin Merritt, would be a dress-up affair, and he was to wear his Sunday clothes, but not before he'd had a bath. And finally, she'd saved the worst for last, announcing that Cousin Merritt would be spending the summer, so he'd best put into practice his gentlemanly skills, the rigors of which she'd been putting him through for the last month.

Beauty got an earful as she and Jonathan rode through the vineyards where he would join George and the crew of men pruning the grapevines. George looked up from his work to see the muttering boy, his frown a dead giveaway that Lucy had gotten ahold of him too. It wouldn't be long now before the utter delight that was Cousin Merritt would be here. He chuckled to himself, wishing he could place a bet on how long it would take for the boy to keep himself from falling in love.

Merritt Lydia Edwards was the ten-year-old daughter of Eleanor and Rutherford Edwards. Eleanor and Lucy were sisters, and therefore Merritt was cousin to Georgia and Caroline. The Edwards lived in Redlands, near Yucaipa, in a stunning mansion with beautiful grounds surrounded by orange trees. Rutherford was as passionate about his oranges as George was about his grapes. The two men had talked often about a railroad system, like they had back east, which would streamline getting their produce and wine to market.

While the Thomases extended an invitation for Merritt to summer in Rancho Cucamonga, likewise the Edwards extended the invitation to Georgia and Caroline to winter in Redlands. Both exchanges lasted a month and therefore the threesome had spent a great deal of time together and became very close. On this day, it was fortunate that Cousin Jonathan was unaware of Lucy's expectations that he too would join the girls and go a wintering in Redlands at the end of this year.

The bell rang. Jonathan frowned and looked at George who grinned and said, "Come on, son. It's time."

Lucy, Georgia, Caroline, and the new housekeeper, Ms. Edith, were lined up in a row on the front porch in great anticipation of the buggy's arrival, which they could now see in the distance.

George and Jonathan joined them with clean shirts, hands, and combed-back hair. The time was upon them now, and Jonathan would forever remember the moment of Cousin Merritt's arrival.

Two beautiful black horses attached to a shiny black coach pranced in and stopped. The professional liveryman dressed in his uniform came down from his seat. He bowed to all on the porch, then opened the door of the carriage. Cousin Merritt appeared first as a small, white-gloved hand and similarly small white boot. They were closely followed by one voluminous, pale-blue, ruffled sleeve and skirt, white pantaloons peeking out of the whole affair. The matching pale-blue bonnet was next, the long, wide ribbons having just then been caught in a slight gust of wind, adding to the fanfare. A second gloved hand and sleeve along with the final boot made its entrance as Cousin Merritt lifted her smiling face, eager to see those whom she dearly loved. Secure in the liveryman's hands, the exquisite child beamed. Cousin Merritt, finally upon Thomas ground, was there in all her radiant glory.

Jonathan's jaw dropped, and his eyes widened as he beheld the most beautiful creature he had ever seen. She reminded him of Caroline's precious china doll whose dark curls, surrounding her bonnet, contrasted perfectly with the white alabaster face and full pink lips and cheeks. But here was where the similarity ended as Cousin Merritt's deep blue, almost violet eyes and long dark eyelashes shone with the inward beauty of a truly happy and loving soul. Jonathan believed she could have worn a flower sack, and the eyes and radiance of the child would have the same effect.

Cousin Merritt flew to her aunt, hugging her, and then continued down the line of Thomas family members as though each was the dearest treasure in the world. She came to the unfamiliar face of Ms. Edith the new housekeeper, stood for a moment looking deep in her eyes, then satisfied, smiled and hugged her too. Jonathan was next and barely breathing. His first awareness was that Cousin Merritt was a fragrance that wafted in the air prior to her arrival. It was clean, soft, and reminded him of orange blossoms with a hint of lilac. Like his encounter with his horse Beauty, their eyes met, and the essence of their individual souls were revealed to one another.

He knew her! She was familiar, like one returning home and, so being, he felt finally at peace. This was not an introduction, but a reunion. Spontaneously Jonathan hugged Merritt, who laughed and hugged him back with all her might. The line of people, while still intact, had all leaned over to stare at Jonathan and Merritt. Each face was in shock and disbelief. George smiled, thinking he would have lost his own bet, as he had expected the sparks wouldn't begin for another year or two. This would be a summer they would all remember.

CHAPTER THIRTEEN

WHERE'S THE GOLD?

Smiley Library, 2018

Linda Hall slipped quietly into the dark Smiley Library. It was 2:00 a.m. She walked silently to the heritage room, unlocked and relocked the door behind her. The light of the full moon shining through the windows allowed her to find the way to the small, windowless room that held the safe. It was locked, but she had stolen the key from the archivist Kevin last week and made a copy. She knew it worked as she'd tried several days ago when she hid the camera. She didn't have the combination to the safe—only Edward Smiley had that—but in a few moments, it too would belong to her.

With her flashlight, she searched the shelves for the concealed camera, the green light showed it was still recording. Earlier she'd set the zoom lens to its closest point, enabling the combination lock and its numbers to be in full view. She stopped the camera, rewound it to when Edward had unlocked the safe, and wrote down the combination. Linda's heart beat faster as finally, after all these long years, she too could read the hidden journals of Maria Luego. Not only would she discover the missing links in her ancestry, but the missing gold. Linda was convinced it was restitution for all that the Hall family had endured for generations at the hands of the Harts, Morleys, and the people of the Green Valley.

The safe opened easily, and Linda saw for the first time the two shelves that held Maria's thirteen journals. Until that moment, she had not known how great a treasure they were, and her hands shook as she reached for the first one. She slid her fingers across the soft brown leather and opened the book to a random page, the handwriting beautiful and clear. She would systematically read them all, and then she would know. Linda switched off the flashlight, opened the door, and brought in a chair. Closing the door and locking it, the flashlight was turned on again. The secure hiding place would allow the librarian to return each night at 2:00 a.m., until she had read every one.

With each passing night, Linda grew more and more angry. Maria Luego was a liar! The things she wrote about her great-great-grandmother Amelia and Amelia's grandmother Bella portrayed the women as sinister, involved in the Mexican dark arts, and co-conspirators. That the author had misjudged her ancestors, suggesting—no *insisting*—they were trying to kill Merritt, steal Jonathan and Hartland, and replace Amelia as wife and mother was absurd! Linda was determined to find the flaw, the jealousy, the reason behind Maria's distorted mind that would create such false accusations. That chilly night she learned Maria's side of the story behind the fragment of a child's leather boot, which lay in the bottom of the safe. Linda had seen it all right when she'd first opened it, but it meant nothing to her until now. Despite turning her back to it, a shiver went up her spine.

On the last night, with one journal remaining, Linda forced herself to return once again to the small room. For the sake of finding clues to the missing gold, she would continue to suffer the indignity and injustice of the handwritten words of a bitter old woman whose bias towards Linda's relatives was, for some vile reason, making her foul imagination run wild. Maria was not only a liar, but she was naïve! No one was as good as she made out the Hart family to be, and no one was as bad as she made out the Hall family.

The last few pages of Maria's final journal, Linda thought the worst. The clues to the gold were simply not there. Instead Linda's mind translated

Maria's final words into simply the hypocritical ramblings of a dying woman. She felt sorry for the deluded Spaniard whose love and admiration for the Hart family, her Yucaipa community, and her life at Hartland were probably more a figment of her imagination. Clearly the many prayers to God woven throughout her journals proved she lived in a dream world. That Maria could not see the goodness in Amelia and Bella was a tragedy, because now Linda would have to burn the journals. Obviously, she could not allow these serious lies to be circulated. Violently she threw the last journal into the corner, bending several corners and loosening a few pages, which fell across the floor. The librarian folded her arms and stared straight ahead, her mind in a dark place. Suddenly the batteries in the flashlight flickered and died, and the room became pitch black. Her brooding continued for some time as her mind formulated a new plan. She smiled. Slowly the woman rose and opened the door, filling the room with the light of dawn. Gently she picked up the torn book, returned the pages, and placed everything carefully in the safe, turning the dial until the click assured her the mechanism was bolted. She returned the chair, picked up her purse, locked the door, and left the Smiley Library.

The archivist, his early morning coffee and paperwork in hand, unlocked the door to the heritage room. Kevin stepped in, took several strides toward his desk, and stopped. Something was wrong. He looked around. Nothing seemed out of place. He deposited his coffee and papers on one of the many long desks and deliberately searched the room. He checked the shelves. The books were all in place. He examined the windows. They were secure, and the alarm was still on. There was a chair out of place, which he returned. He checked the door to Mr. Edwards' private room that held the safe, relieved to find it locked. He passed by the assistant curator's desk, then returned to retrieve his coffee and papers, the disturbance still lingering, the reason yet a mystery.

Later that morning Edward came into the library, greeted both the curator and his assistant, removed the key from his pocket, and opened the door to his private room. He was going to Honey's tonight for dinner, and he wanted to take the remnants of the child's boot Tess McDowell and her men had found. He would take it to the local Redlands Art Gallery where Aubrey promised to mount it in one of those protective glass boxes and Honey could hang it on a wall at Hartland where it needed to be.

Edward bent to unlock the safe, his hand beginning the memorized set of twists this-way-and-that. As he opened the safe door, he felt a light wave of dis-ease. Something wasn't right. He checked the boot, which was where he left it, then confirmed the journals were all there. Everything appeared to be in order. There was a scent about the room, he hadn't remembered there previously, but they'd had a few rainy nights.

Kevin coughed slightly to alert the old man he was there. He held a key in his hand. "Excuse me, Mr. Smiley," he apologized. "Sorry for the interruption, but by any chance did you use the key in my desk to open this or any of the doors?"

"I have my own key, young man," smiled Edward. "Seems you can take me off the suspect list."

The curator laughed. "My assistant said the same thing when I asked her the question. Problem is, only the three of us have keys to this room. The one in my desk is an extra and hasn't been used for over two years. It just sits there. This morning, however, it had been moved to a different place and was pointing in the opposition direction."

"Odd," replied Edward.

"Indeed, sir," agreed the Kevin. "I don't want to alarm you, but I have to say, something appears off today."

"I quite agree," responded Edward. "When I opened the safe, well, I can't explain it exactly but something seemed to be disturbed. However, I look the fool, as it appears nothing has been."

"I'll do some sleuthing, sir," promised Kevin. "I need to prove neither of us are fools."

"My reputation will be the better for it," laughed Edward.

CHAPTER FOURTEEN

RIVALS

Thomas Winery, 1863

I n the summer of 1863, spring had finally come to Rancho Cucamonga. The months spent with the Thomas family after the attack on the village and his kidnapping felt like winter to Jonathan's soul. With the coming of Merritt came spring, a new life for the boy, only days away from his eleventh birthday.

During Merritt's stay, dress attire was appropriate for dinner, while the days were spent in what the girls called play clothes, bright floral dresses in light cotton fabrics, which dispensed with petticoats, panta-loons, and gloves, offering them the freedom to play and get dirty. In them they rode, climbed trees, fished, and played games. Rain meant overcoats and playing in the stable or under the eaves of the wraparound porch. Lucy believed summer was to be spent out of doors and a little rain or wind never hurt anyone. The children would be allowed indoors before dinner, *only* if it was cold or snowed, neither of which was likely to happen.

Supper was on the picnic table under the oak tree on the corner near the kitchen upon which was heaped lots of food, as the energy burned off in the morning must be replaced for the energy burned off in the afternoon. After baths, dinner, and story time, the children were ready for their soft beds, opened windows, and light summer breezes.

During Merritt's stay, Jonathan was relieved of his duties with the men in the vineyard and charged with the responsibility of watching over the girls. The rules were few, but the punishment severe. Lucy believed in the reward and punishment of the entire pack. There could be no worse punishment than the pack-of-four being separated from one another. It had happened twice early on, but thereafter each agreed the wiser choice was the better.

The bond between Jonathan and Merritt grew stronger as they built together a mental home with shared feelings, memories, and aspirations. It was a pure relationship, innocent as two newborn colts, entranced by the beauty of nature, seeing everywhere and in everything the good or its potential to be so. There were no obstacles to their openness with one another nor to their easy receptivity in the mutual dance of give and take. All was accepted at face value and the highest of intention, knowing the welfare of the other was far more important than that of the self. There was no petty quarreling, no fighting for control, no need to be better—only the delight one finds in adoring another human.

The foursome, spending hours, days, and weeks together, enabled the distinctive essence of each child to unfold before one another's eyes. None were perfect, all were unique, and all would grow one day, through the ups and downs of life, discovering little by little their own unique gifts and purposes. Lucy smiled as one boy surrounded by girls laid side-by-side in the large rope hammock George had made in a moment of sudden creativity, spurred on by three days of rain. She knew tomorrow would be difficult and sad. Merritt was leaving. She'd give them three days to mourn, then begin discussing the winter activities that would take place at the Edwards' mansion. Lucy believed loss was inevitable, but necessary for something new to be found. She believed patience was a powerful tool, and she would strive to cultivate it in her brood for the next five months while they waited for their reunion with Merritt. She knew their joy would return when they reunited again.

Thanksgiving launched wintering at the Edwards' mansion. The Thomas' buggy had been loaded with Ms. Lucy, food, gifts, and boxes. George drove the wagon with the rest of the gear, while the remainder of the family rode on horseback. All would celebrate the holiday together, spending two nights at the Edwards', whereupon George and Lucy would return, and the children would stay until a week before Christmas.

The buggy wheels and Lucy's mind hummed. Lucy Thomas never lied. Unless it came to protecting her children, and Jonathan still needed protection from Red Eye. If her son was recognized, he could be in real danger. The entire Green Valley had been abuzz for months as more news of the atrocities the villagers suffered at the hands of Red Eye and his warriors during the raid were revealed. The new chief's governing of the villagers was more like a ward of a prison, where they were forced in service to Red Eye and the warriors. Raids on other tribes were becoming more frequent. If anything was stolen, Red Eye was the first to be suspected. The likelihood of running into Red Eye and his men increased as their caravan neared Redlands. It was only a day's ride to Yucaipa and the Indian village.

Before Merritt's return to Redlands that summer, Lucy had gathered the entire family to discuss the matter. That Jonathan needed protection in Redlands all agreed on, but the particulars of how were determined by Lucy.

"Jonathan is indeed your cousin now Merritt, as he is a member of our family and therefore a member of yours. In fact, you call him 'Cousin Jonathan.'" All nodded in agreement. "Inside our family, Jonathan is our son and brother to the girls, but outside this family he will remain 'Cousin Jonathan.' He is from Texas, lost both his parents, and has now come to be a member of our family, which is all true. Nothing more need be said." Lucy had included a letter stating as much to her sister Eleanor, tucking it in with Merritt's things. Only the Thomas family and the Edwards family would know the whole truth. Lucy watched as the San Gorgonio Mountains appeared on the horizon, and she could sense within her mother's heart what Jonathan was now feeling.

Jonathan's heart beat faster. His emotions were twisted and turned as the ever-changing view of the chain of mountains grew higher and higher until now they reached the peak of his mountain, San Gorgonio. Its snow-covered summit symbolized divinity, stability, and protection, remaining strong and secure despite what may be happening in the valley beneath her. The mountain was impenetrable unlike the valley, which was vulnerable, welcoming of the loving care of man, but powerless if his goal was rape.

Jonathan's curiosity heightened with every step Beauty took as the reality of his life at the Thomas Winery slowly melted into the familiar life of his not-so-long-ago past. Lucy looked back to see the boy frowning, his Indian mind having returned, and suddenly she thought the town clothes looked out of place on his growing body. It was in stark contrast to the Yucaipat boy heading towards home to a family that no longer existed, and to a place, stolen by Red Eye where he could no longer belong.

The tension and immense inner struggle Jonathan was going through were not lost on George, Caroline, and Georgia. They innately knew their love and support could best be shone by simply being with him, so each gave their gift of silence as they travelled on. Lucy would give him time to mourn and brood, but then she must intervene, helping him to find his way to live with one leg in each world. She knew it would be a time of great paradox for Jonathan. The month spent in Redlands would bring him close to Merritt and the joys of the pack, while at the same time, the village and his former life lay just ahead, just out of reach. She wondered if the temptation to satisfy his curiosity about the village would be too great to contain. No one could stop him, if he went. She could only pray he would be wise—God only knew what would happen if Red Eye caught him. Lucy forced her mind to cease the fruitless imagining by commanding a halt to the caravan, where food, water, and a recombing of everyone's hair was in order as they were less than an hour from their destination. Jonathan was put to work, and now the girls' continuous and excited conversation describing what their brother, uh . . . cousin . . . would share in, held great appeal as the thought of Merritt pervaded his sore mind. Jonathan was grateful for their happy chatter's distractions. Any further into the depth of his sorrow would have overwhelmed him.

⌒〜⌒

Unlike the Thomas Estate perched above a sea of vineyards, the Edwards mansion and grounds were nearly hidden by a vast forest of orange trees. Only the turrets and highest peaks of the home could be seen. The earthen-packed lane to the house seemed, to the anxious travelers, endless, but suddenly the whole of the mansion came into view. The three-story, fourteen-room bird's-egg-blue Victorian with pinkish-lavender and white trim looked like an enormous dollhouse. Its steeply pitched gable roofs created lofty ceilings of various heights under which were towers, turrets, bedrooms, living, and dining rooms, whose decorative glass bay-windows were surrounded by intricate sun panels, fan brackets, and stitching around the eaves. Everywhere were turned columns, decorative milled railings, and fishscale shingles. One could see a plethora of brackets, upon which were cornices, upon which were triangular pediments, upon which were witches' caps, upon which—at last—were finials.

If Edwards mansion was a dollhouse, then surely Merritt Edwards was the doll who now looked out the sweeping, second-story bay window and balcony, the preeminent place to view all the comings and goings on the Edwards estate. Merritt had been placed on guard duty there and was instructed that, the very moment she saw the Thomases coming, to ring the silver bell throughout the house. Having done her duty, Merritt raced to the large double doors, threw them open, and stood on the front porch, the backdrop a work of art.

Jonathan was struck once again by the exquisite nature of the small gloved hand, which held the ringing bell. A beautifully bedecked Merritt in yards of pink taffeta skirts with white petticoats and pantaloons stood on the front porch, her dark hair in ringlets, her blue eyes beaming, and her little body springing oh so slightly up and down, her love and excitement uncontainable. Bouncing ringlets, a ringing silver bell, and Merritt's dancing feet was a memory burned forever in Jonathan's mind. His sorrow melted in the love that was Merritt Edwards, and his soul sighed deeply with sweet and complete relief, home once more.

Eleanor and Rutherford were kind, gracious, and welcoming. An only child, they believed Merritt needed the companionship and warmth of extended family, and the Edwards did all in their power to make her time with "the cousins" delightful and memorable. One such event would be the convening of perhaps ten Redlands children of Merritt's age and station for a luncheon party to be held in the Edwards' upstairs lounge. Afterwards would be a marionette show followed by singing and playing games. Eleanor was treating Merritt and all the cousins to new party clothes. She'd taken the girls while Jonathan had been attended by Rutherford. The two headed straight for the gun shop and were now admiring a Henry repeating rifle. The owner pointed out the lever-action, breech-loading, and tubular magazine. Further, he confided the nearly positive fact that the gun had found its way into his hands, first through a Sioux Indian, then a Cheyenne, and finally a trapper who claimed he purchased it just after the Battle of Little Bighorn. Rutherford didn't believe the story for a moment, but seeing as Jonathan bought it hook, line, and sinker, he'd buy the gun for the boy. Rutherford had taken a great liking to Jonathan. Rutherford laid down a wad of bills for the gun, ammo, and cleaning kit, which he promptly extended to Jonathan. "Man needs a good rife," was all he said. They'd gone next to the saddlery, watched a mare being shoed, stopped by for a beer and sarsaparilla, and when that was done, Rutherford sighed. "Eleanor will skin our hides if we don't come back with our new fancy duds. Guess there's no getting out of it."

Jonathan nodded, he too lived outnumbered by women.

Rutherford sipped the last of his beer, stood up, and with courage said, "We'll get it over with, then after supper we'll do some shooting." Jonathan smiled, even the darkest of clouds had a silver lining.

The dark cloud that was twelve-year-old Jameson Morley scowled. His back to the bay window at the Edwards mansion, the boy fingered the knife in his pocket as he watched Merritt fawning all over the intruder. The kid was tall, blond, strong, and he hated him! Jameson assured himself he would learn soon enough that Merritt was his, always had been, always would be, just as his father had promised.

When eight-year-old Jameson had first met Merritt and fallen deeply for her, Harold Morley Jr., his father, had promised he'd make it worth the Edwards' while to give their daughter away to Jameson when they came of age. He would deny his son nothing. Harold believed money could buy everything. Why not the bride his son wanted? The promise meant nothing really, just pacifying the boy who was sure to change his mind on a wife after eight years of age. In fact, Harold was confident he'd change his mind a hundred times before the right woman came along some day. But so far, the boy's obsession for Merritt Edwards had only grown stronger.

Jameson intentionally stuck out his foot as Jonathan came by, causing the boy to fall hard on the floor. Jonathan looked up as Jameson stepped on his back as he walked over to engage with Merritt. Jonathan jumped up, enraged by the boy's intentional actions and clear message. He wanted to smash in his face and nearly did, but his wiser-self thought better of it, not wanting to ruin the party nor disturb Merritt. Jonathan smiled as he watched Jameson grab Merritt's hand, squeezing it too hard, whereupon Merritt screeched, taking it back. Dramatically, Jameson fell to one knee, grabbed her other hand, and kissed it, apologizing for his unknown strength. Merritt forgave him as courtesy demanded, and allowed him to pour her another cup of lemonade. Jonathan knew Merritt. She'd think good of a venomous snake till it bit her. She was innately good and kind, giving all the benefit of the doubt, be it deserved, or not. He suddenly realized how vulnerable she was, and in that instant, he'd become her champion. Jameson and Jonathan locked eyes, the gauntlet laid down as the daggers were thrown. The war that would continue for a lifetime, had just begun.

CHAPTER FIFTEEN

POWDER KEG

Yucaipa, 1873

Ten years had come and gone, and Yucaipa was a powder keg! The fuse of ignorance had been lit, and she could blow at any time. Disorder, chaos, greed, and a lack of mutual respect had replaced the decades of peaceful, orderly, and reciprocal co-habitation valued by the leaders of the Yucaipat Indians, Mexicans, and Yucaipa townsfolk.

The chain of wise chiefs—White Wolf, Adoeete, and Aiyana—had been broken by Red Eye. The force for good that had been the Medina and Vega families, cousins from Mexico and descendants of the mighty Aztecs, who settled in Yucaipa, was now shattered. The once respected and venerated names of Don Jose Medina and Don Carlos Vega were replaced by their weak-minded sons, Alberto Medina and Hector Vega. In front of their small children, Alberto and Hector had been fatherly examples of ruthless competitors; the game they played, vicious and cruel. Now their teenage sons, Roberto Medina, Cesar Medina, Jose Vega, and Paolo Vega, elevated the rivalry to violence and brutality.

The leadership of the Yucaipa townsfolk degenerated as well with the sudden and mysterious death of the well and good Sheriff Jim Rawley whose badge was now worn by the distasteful and conniving twenty-five-year-old Watson Hargrove, the new sheriff and owner of the Yucaipa general store, lumber company, and saloon. Rumor had it Watson's father, Cosmo Hargrove, Redlands railroad and orange industry tycoon, simply threw money at Yucaipa, overpaying for everything, buying the annoying and unwanted relation a place not too far from his overbearing mother, but finally out of his father's sight. Father and son had always been at odds, both unscrupulous in their own ways, but the problem was nothing a bit of money couldn't solve.

Where once kindness, moderation, and tolerance prevailed as a natural way of life, now Yucaipa lived in fear. The inner struggles once contained within the Indian village, Mexican community, and Yucaipa townspeople, now spread outward like cancer, each seeing the other as prey.

In contrast to the fractured and crumbling dam that had become Yucaipa, the Redlands and Rancho Cucamonga, home of the Thomas Winery and now twenty-year-old Jonathan Hart, flourished.

Their continued growth was due in part to the more philosophic and intelligent minds that ruled there; the Thomas, Edwards, Smiley, and Luegos families, together kept at bay the Hargroves, Morleys, and Biels. The former, being wise, understood there was no stopping the law of rhythm, which like a pendulum, swings; the measure of the swing to the right being the measure of the swing to the left. As long as there were powerful and unscrupulous families living in the same Green Valley who pursued their own gains over the health and welfare of the whole, the pendulum would continue to swing back and forth. Unity could fulfill the law of rhythm, but of course the Hargroves, Morleys, and Biels would have to have an unlikely change of heart, mind, and will. Yucaipa, however, would out of necessity require a form of death before it could once again regenerate, and the seed of a new life be reborn.

⌁

Mia, the loving and longsuffering mother of Roberto and Cesar Medina was outraged! How dare they come into the house drunk! She flung the black, cast iron skillet back and forth, sweeping her teenage sons out the door, banishing them to the barn. Then she turned on her husband. "You, Alberto," she hissed, "have made it impossible for me to show my face in our town of Yucaipa." She pointed the skillet toward the man, demanding, "You will stop this senseless pissing match between you and Hector Vega now, or someone will get killed." She paced back and forth, barely able to contain her rage. "Isabella Vega and I have fools for husbands and sons," she spit. "I swear, Alberto," Mia snarled, fury blazing in her dark eyes as she lifted the heavy black weapon, "I'll kill you right now if you don't end this thing."

Alberto cringed. This time he'd pushed her too far. For years both wives, Mia and Isabella, had pleaded with their husbands to end the family quarrel between them. But Alberto and Hector cared nothing for what they thought or wanted, having dominated their women with their machismo and exaggerated show of virility. Today, the dominance of the fed-up woman forced him to listen. "Don Jose Medina and Don Carlos Vega would turn over in their graves if they saw the way you two behave toward one another and the animals you've turned our sons into," she railed. She'd spoken the truth. At every turn they had looked for ways to best or hurt one another and, in the process, permanently injured themselves and their families. The four sons, Roberto Medina, Cesar Medina, Jose Vega and Paolo Vega, had worn the mantel of conflict since birth, at first pawns in their fathers' foolish ignorance, then ignorant fools in their own right. Mia and Isabella, if they ever had any control, had lost it long ago. They were left living with the embarrassment of being a Medina or a Vega, names that had gone from ardent respect in the Mexican community, to contempt in the town of Yucaipa. Intuitively Mia knew both families were on a collision course, which could only result in catastrophe and death. To avoid the inevitable, Alberto, Hector, and the boys would have to listen and change. But it was too late.

Young Cesar Medina had good reason to drink. His brother Roberto never needed a reason, but tonight he drank in hopes of erasing the sight burned into his mind of Cesar's humiliation. The two were returning home from their work in the apple orchards of Rojo Ranchero when their cousins Jose and Paolo ambushed them, having stolen their father Hector's two rifles. Cesar was the target. He was muscular, but very short in stature. He hated it! It made him feel less. His incessant boasting about his manhood and virility fooled no one and eventually became a source of derision. Today Jose and Paolo were determined to shut his mouth once and for all.

The busy road to the Beaumont Trading Post served their purposes perfectly. They directed the Medina boys with their guns to dismount in a copse of eucalyptus trees that lined both sides of the road not far from the schoolhouse. Jose led Roberto across the dirt road and tied him to the trunk of a tree while Paolo strung Cesar up by his hands over the branch of another tree. Powerless to help, Robert watched in shame as the Vegas stripped Cesar of all his clothes. Mortified, Cesar began to weep, pleading with the Vegas to release him. They only laughed and jeered, their taunts becoming more and more cruel. As the school bell sounded, the Vegas joined Roberto, watching from behind the trunk of the tree. As the children began passing by, staring at the dishonored and sobbing Cesar, Paolo and Jose shot their guns in the air—not wanting their captive released—just yet. In the distance, a cloud of dust signaled horses and several wagons loaded with a dozen men who worked at the Rojo Ranchero returning home. Paolo shouted at Jose to get their horses and the Vegas rode off jeering and laughing. Soon they would be drinking tequila, Hector congratulating his sons!

Tonight, Roberto was glad the barn was dark, better not to look at Cesar anyway. His head hurt, his wrists and stomach still raw where they'd tied the rope too tight. Empathy was unnatural for Roberto, and he surprised even himself at the strange thought that wondered how his little brother must be feeling after the sadistic treatment. The hidden bottle of whiskey in the barn had been a godsend for him, but his brother just sat there, his eyes blank.

While Roberto slept, a deeply humiliated Cesar explored his options: He could kill himself. He could kill Paolo and Jose. He could run away and never return. Or he could prove his manhood and silence them once and for all.

But how? How could he convince them overnight that he had gone from a weak boy to a dangerous man—a rabid wolf prepared to rip out their throats if they ever came near him again? What could prove his fearlessness? What did the Vegas fear? What did all of them fear most?

Red Eye! A chill went down his spine. Yes, to be captured and tortured by Red Eye and his warriors haunted all their dreams. But what could he do to poke the snake and capture his rattle, so to speak, without being bit? "Indian bones," he whispered, his mind's eye envisioning the risky and perilous deed. He could see it now. Before dawn, Roberto with his two amigos Miguel and Marco as witnesses, would watch from the bushes as he stole quietly onto the great arrowhead that formed the Yucaipat sacred Indian burial ground. The three graves of the great chiefs—White Wolf, Adoeete, and Aiyana—formed the highest mounds in the circle, uniquely carved totems marked each. While their bodies had been burned on the funeral pyre, among the ashes would still be bones. He'd dig up the graves, find a bone from each, and fashion them into a necklace, which he'd wear hidden around his neck as proof of his fearlessness and manhood. Cesar smiled, finished off the whiskey, then kicked Roberto. "Follow me," he said.

The terrified eyes of Roberto and friends Miguel and Marco watched from a safe distance as the first rays of dawn struck the white bones that Cesar held up triumphantly for them to see. They were Aiyana's. Adoeete's grave was next as Cesar stomped on the shovel with his boot, driving it deep into the earth. The force of the arrow hitting his shoulder spun him around as the shovel and dirt flew into the air. The petrified boys gasped as two more arrows punctured Cesar's right then left leg. In one fell swoop, the Yucaipat warrior had scooped up the Mexican boy.

At the very moment Roberto burst through the door screaming and sobbing at the feet of Mia and Alberto, unable to find his voice, Red Eye was carving his eye into Cesar's back. In an hour or so, they'd roast him on a spit at the warriors' fire. The deed done and content with the message it would send, the chief smiled as he fingered Aiyana's totem, then hurled a knife into the trespasser, silencing his screams. "Fool."

The chain of events with their causes and effects unleashed the avalanche of pain that was to come. Two days later, before dawn, the Mexicans gathered at the Rojo Ranchero. The horses and men armed with rifles and torches were whirling in the fermentation of revenge. They rode to the Yucaipat sacred Indian burial grounds upon which the Mexican flag was raised, and the effigy of Red Eye was burned. Then Hector, Alberto, Paolo, Jose, and Roberto unleashed a round of gunshots leading the charge of forty Mexican vigilantes into the Indian village, the massacre, save for about two dozen souls, was wholesale.

The town of Yucaipa was awakened by the smell of fire as a thousand acres of Yucaipat land was torched and ravaged, revenge alone the victor.

❧

Two days later, George pulled the wagon round the back of the Rancho Cucamonga General Store, tied up the horses, then pulled Lucy's neatly written list from his pocket. Cousin Merritt was coming in three days' time.

Back at the Thomas Winery, the grown man that was Jonathan Hart cut a handsome figure. He'd kept his blond hair trimmed and his chiseled face shaved, while many years of hard and gratifying work at the Thomas Winery made his body strong and muscular. He'd become known in the vineyard industry for his ability to blend perfectly a variety of grapes from which he made the now much-sought-after Thomas Wines. Jonathan discovered a love of Port, and his collection of Thomas Fine Ports was growing.

In three days, Cousin Merritt would be there. Jonathan grinned, his fingers closing around the long-awaited engagement ring in his pocket, assuring himself once again, it remained safe. Jonathan had much to do before Merritt arrived. George having gone into town for the third time this week for some newly required supplies necessitated by Merritt's arrival, left him happily to pick up the slack.

George opened the back door of the General Store. The sound of his boots alerted the men and women gathered around the potbelly stove that someone had arrived. From the moment the news reached the General Store early that morning and Mr. Johnson, the proprietor, took possession of it, a steady stream of customers had either come and gone, or come and stayed. Those who remained did so for several reasons. For some, the salacious tale had become addictive and the reliving of it with each new customer brought a kind of strange gratification. Others didn't want to be alone. Many were in shock, and the warmth of the stove, hot coffee, and friends made it easier to process. George listened to the account of the Yucaipat massacre. Without a word, he left the store, climbed back on the wagon, and directed the horses towards home. George required answers, and he searched for them as he recalled the bewildering chain of events that would forever change their lives.

George sat silent in the motionless wagon at the entrance of the Thomas Winery, the horses pawing, eager for their oats. There in the vine-yards Jonathan was riding Beauty, turning her around as the supper bell rang. This was his son. He'd had the legal papers for their business part-nership drawn up in hopes the boy would agree. He was as excited to give Jonathan the agreement as Jonathan was to give Merritt that ring he'd been carrying around in his pocket for months. His own tears he could do without, his son he couldn't. His hanky did its job.

"Get up there," George called to the horses.

Lucy took one look at George and knew something was desperately wrong. "Edith," Lucy called, "you get supper on the table. Tell Georgia, Caroline, and Jonathan, Mr. Thomas and I have to attend to some business and to please eat without us."

Lucy rushed to the living room, poured two large glasses of Port, pointed George to the library, and shut the doors.

"They've been in there for hours," Georgia complained, curiosity getting the better of her.

"They'll be out in a while," Caroline said casually, returning to her book.

Georgia paced back and forth, finally looking out the window. Jonathan and a few men were fixing a broken wheel on one of the vineyard wagons. Georgia didn't need premonitions or intuition to know something was very wrong. How could Jonathan and Caroline be so oblivious? No longer able to bear the suspense, Georgia strode to the library door, gently opened it a crack, and peeked in.

Her father was standing next to the fireplace holding a nearly empty glass of Port and a white handkerchief with which he dabbed his eyes. Her mother sat primly in the leather chair. She'd drawn back the white lace curtain with one hand and was staring out the window.

"I swear, Lucy," she heard her father say, "I cannot bear it! What will I do without him?"

Her mother sighed, returned the curtain to its place, rose, and took a rather shocking swig of Port. "We will be the parents he needs," her mother said resolutely. Lucy embraced her husband, then looked up into his tired eyes. "Aren't you the one who always says we have to leave room for Providence to work out what's highest and best for our children?"

George nodded.

"Our interests," she continued, "we will put aside for now. There is no other way, dear George.

If he takes the money and follows his birthright, he'll only be a few days' ride away from us."

"Three days," corrected George mournfully. Lucy could sense things no other mortal on earth could despite the trauma, and now she sensed someone had opened the door and was listening. Had to be Georgia; she detested being out of the loop.

"Come in, dear Georgia," called Lucy. Georgia was embarrassed both for getting caught and that her mother knew her so well.

"Everything all right?" their daughter asked.

"I'm afraid not, dearest," said Lucy. "Please ask Jonathan and Caroline to join us in the library. We need to have a family discussion."

Georgia drew in her breath, knowing this was not good, then turned and ran to find her siblings. Lucy handed George her empty glass with an unusual request for more. He disappeared to the living room, grateful for something to do and the additional sustenance they would both need for the coming moments.

Five worried faces took their places. Georgia and Caroline sat on the edge of the couch, Jonathan stood by the fireplace, Lucy remained in her chair, and George stood behind her, his hand on her shoulder.

Lucy sighed and began. "Because we're a close family, the news I'm about to share will be difficult for each of us to hear. But we are strong and courageous. We can and will weather anything life brings us, even this."

Georgia impatiently cried, "What is it, Mother?"

"Jonathan, dear," Lucy said, "word came that your village suffered a terrible tragedy."

A jolt of fear gripped Jonathan, and he instinctively braced for the next blow. Lucy winced, but repeated the news just as George had shared it with her. When she had finished, all were weeping. Lucy rose, walked to her son, and held him in her arms. Silence mercifully filled the room, giving each the space to think about the unthinkable and privately unfold the implications that would so drastically affect their lives. Lucy kissed Jonathan's cheek and returned to her chair, the storm having done its worst. "George," she instructed, "I think a glass of wine is in order for all, and then some decisions will need to be made."

After each had a glass in hand, and had regained some normalcy to their breathing due to their mother's steady wisdom, they were ready to talk.

Lucy called the discussion to order by asking a question. "To whom does Hartland belong?" All eyes went to Jonathan. "I seem to recall," she continued, "a sacred oath being attached to the land."

Jonathan suddenly flashed back. He saw himself as the seven-year-old boy, sitting between his parents on the wooden bench of the Prairie Schooner. They were only an hour or so from Hartland, and his mother was retelling the story of JD, White Wolf, and the gifting of land. He could hear even now, her lovely voice speaking the words. "JD had saved the chief's son, the little girls, and the village. To honor him, Chief White Wolf wanted to gift the worthy JD a thousand acres of land, but it came with a sacred oath. 'Know this,' said the wise chief, 'the land belongs to the Great Spirit, is the Great Spirit, and you are the humble servant. Keeping the sacred harmony between man and nature in this place, is now your responsibility. Only under these conditions can the land be given into your care.' Your grandfather pledged that solemn oath and kept it. He made your Papa and I pledge that oath too, and we intend to keep it."

The story always ended with his mother's question, "And Jonathan David Hart, will you keep that pledge too?"

With reverent eyes, the child's reply was always the same. "I will, Mama."

In an instant, Jonathan's purpose was clear. He had been born for this. He finally knew who he was. He was a successor! The next person in a long chain of great men and women who had and would continue to take responsibility for their own lives, and for the people and land entrusted to them. White Wolf, JD, Adoeete, and Aiyana had all known the harmonious Home of the Great Spirit was to be reflected in the home that was the village and Hartland. Red Eye had turned the village into a prison, a wasteland, and now a pit of ugliness.

"My son," said George, "Hartland is your birthright and your responsibility. Your mother and I have always known that. When, how, and under what circumstances you would return to her, we didn't know. Today, we do. The land is for sale. To claim what is already yours, you will need to hold the deed." George walked over to a large, wooden letter box on the great carved desk. He opened the lid and took out ten large thick envelopes. George handed them to Jonathan. "Every year you have worked at the Thomas Winery, I have paid you. It's all in there." He nodded. "You'll find ten years of wages and your share of the profits from your exceptional wine-making skills, which have provided extremely well for our family."

Jonathan was speechless. The magnitude of the love of this man, his father, friend, and confidant—the feeling was beyond words. George took out his hanky, the blasted tears gave away his deep feelings for his son, feelings men rarely said out loud. Jonathan fiercely clasped his father in a hug, the long and powerful embrace meaning more to the man than his son would ever know. Finally, Jonathan spoke, loving each dear face turned to look at him now. As tears fell, he said, "I'm bereft! I ache once again for my tribe and the people I love. This is excruciating to hear. Such loss never gets easier to bear." He paused, and then a thought crossed his mind. "Still," he began slowly, "I believe that of all men, I am the most fortunate. I have had three mothers to love and who have loved me. Each in their own way, they've guided me to know one thing—maybe not today, but at long last, all will be well. All things have a reason and purpose. My mother Katherine would tell me, 'Jonathan, there is no such thing as chance. Providence knows precisely was she is doing.' My mother Aiyana would remind me, 'In the midst of what seems, be at peace. The Great Spirit says, I am the bow, the arrow, the target, the goal, and all that lies between.' And you, mother," he nodded at Lucy, "you've always told us 'a new and more beautiful seed arises, fully alive, out of every fire.'"

"Father," Jonathan turned to George, "you have not lost a son, nor a partner, nor a friend, but our family has gained another land to join with the Thomas Winery. Hartland. The roots here will simply extend there."

❧

Every step Beauty's colt Dancer took on the road to Yucaipa brought Jonathan closer to his destiny, the moment dreamlike and surreal. He was moving, and yet time stood still. The rich California soil beneath Dancer's hooves, the golden light of the sun on her white mane, and the exquisite clarity of the air, the mountains, the very day itself, was more like a fantasy than the stark reality of a new life. Jonathan corrected his thought. *New is not the right word. Better to say a returning. I'm returning stronger, wiser, with a better understanding, and thanks to my father and mother, with new skills and a sense of belonging that distance can never sever.*

As Jonathan drew closer to the small town nestled in the Green Valley at the base of magnificent mountains, a Great Eagle soared above him. The man looked up and spoke directly to the magnificent bird. "Adoeete said, 'Your nature is like the Great Spirit, which always watches over me and always will.'"

Jonathan entered Yucaipa, his concentration centered on the words Land Office written in bold black letters on a white wooden sign on the main street. His eyes and ears tuned sharply to the passing sights and sounds in his periphery. Yucaipa and its townspeople were still in shatters over the massacre. It would likely be years before the wounds would heal. The community and the Yucaipat village had faced two tragic deaths. The first when Aiyana was killed and the peaceful and flourishing way of life died because of Red Eye and his brutal rule. The second meted out by the hands of the Mexicans. Jonathan passed a cluster of women, one voice louder than the rest. "You know, she once saved a little boy from outlaws of the vilest kind."

Another woman added, "I saw her several times, she was so beautiful and seemed . . . well . . . wise and kind-hearted."

"A damn shame," said a third.

Jonathan dismounted in front of the land office, tying Dancer to the hitching post. "Mighty fine horse you have there," called a man, one of three sitting in a row of rocking chairs on the porch. "You new to these parts?" a second man asked, lighting his pipe. "Haven't seen you around."

"Returning," Jonathan simply responded.

"Well, son, you picked a hell of a time to return. Spect you heard about the Indian massacre."

Jonathan nodded.

"Did you know Red Eye skewered and roasted the Mexican boy like a pig?" The man took sadistic pleasure in regurgitating the foul news, hoping to get a reaction out of the stranger. When none came, he tried another tactic. "The fool should have never desecrated the Indian grave of that fine woman chief."

"Yep," said another man, pointing down the street. "The Indians dragged the kid's blackened body and left it on his mamacita's doorstep."

The land agent rose from the chair and hooked his thumbs under his belt. Rocking back and forth on his heels, he said, "Don't guess you're in the market for a thousand acres of charred and bloody land, are you?" The men laughed.

"Yes, I am," replied Jonathan, to the shock of all.

"Why the hell would you want that mess?" The smoke ring from the pipe of the inquisitive man underscored the question.

"It's mine," came the definitive reply. A few minutes later, Jonathan walked out of the Yucaipa Land Office. He placed the deed in his jacket pocket, mounted Dancer, tipped his hat to the slack-jawed men, and rode off toward Hartland.

The once verdant green line of trees marked the border of the Indian village. Still rooted in their places, Jonathan winced as he took in the great oaks and pines now tortured, black, and leafless, the land as far as the eye could see raw to the bone and smoldering. He could have never imagined his home thus. Where were the fields of tall corn, the golden wheat, and the acres of sunflowers? Where was the abundance of natural beauty each season brought with its array of colorful wildflowers, first white and pink, then purple and blue, and finally yellow and gold. Where was the teeming wildlife that lived under the protection of the villagers, hunted only if necessary for food and, even then, reverently thanked and held dear for their sacrifice.

What was once beautiful, flourishing, and good, was now hideous, punitive, and inhospitable, having no resemblance to the Great Spirit's ideal. Before he would venture into what remained of the village in the distance,

Jonathan urged Dancer forward to discover the fate of the land where the Great Eagle's Seed, the one he, Adoeete, and Aiyana had planted many years ago. The ten-year-old boy had left a flourishing grapevine, happily trailing across the stone wall, the grapes sweet and delicious. Behind the wall and through the gate, the remnants of JD's cottage remained. There too was the giant walnut tree and treehouse, which belonged to him and his childhood friends Odakota, Hototo, and Teetonka. Jonathan recalled he and the young boys could have never accomplished the feat without the aid of Flying Eagle, his father and hero of all. This was a man he loved and thought of often and wondered if he too had been killed in the massacre. Jonathan presumed, after all these years, the treehouse was long gone. But the mayhem had not touched this part of Hartland, and Jonathan found it not only safe, but still thriving. The grapevine was enormous. Obviously, the roots had gone deep, as its stock was massive, and the vines grew wildly in every direction—even into the nearby trees. Surely, he thought, the divine must have cared for it while he was away!

Jonathan turned his attention to the walnut tree where so many of his boyhood memories had been made. He stood beneath the branches looking up to see if the covered wagon's flooring and the railings made of wheels split in two were still there. They were! Without thinking, he climbed the tree as he'd done so often before, his feet remembering the steps. The wagon's white canvas roof was long gone, but there was something there, a brown leather pouch. Hanging, nearly hidden, tied to a branch way up in the tree. His curiosity piqued, Jonathan risked the weight of his body against the questionable strength of several smaller branches, and, finally, with much effort and a near fall, he captured the bag.

Shimmying down the tree, he landed next to Dancer, the horse happy now to be resting in the shade. Jonathan loosened the leather ties and felt inside for what it contained. There were coins, a folded piece of paper, and something else. Round, but on a chain. Jonathan gasped. He brought it out. It was the pearl necklace! The one given to his grandmother on her wedding day, then offered to his mother Katherine to aid in building the Hartland home. It was the catalyst for the outlaw's attack that killed his parents. Jonathan had kept it safe around his own neck for three years until the same outlaws came back for it and stole both he and the necklace. How it came to be in an old leather pouch, in the walnut tree, ten years later, was a great mystery. Jonathan knelt in the grass, poured out the heap of gold coins, and picked up what he now could see was a letter.

This letter is written for Jonathan from Flying Eagle by the hand of Dr. Allen Crawley.

Jonathan, Son of Flying Eagle and Aiyana — Red Eye make Aiyana's death and almost mine. I track bad men who take you. Kill them. I leave gold for you and pearl necklace. You come back — leave ring of feathers round tree so I know — then I come for you. In Yucaipa — come to walnut tree every day to see for you

Jonathan looked around, half expecting to see Flying Eagle walking over the hill. So, his father had survived, searched for him, and killed the outlaws. *How different my life would have been,* thought Jonathan, *had Flying Eagle found me on the roadside at the entrance to the Thomas Winery. We might have gathered the remaining Indians, joined forces with other tribes, and mounted an attack on Red Eye. Or we might have simply gone away to make a new life for ourselves in another place, with another village.* But Flying Eagle had not found him by the roadside. Neither could Jonathan have foreseen that the impulse that propelled him into Lucy's arms was providential, the next step on his journey.

Jonathan placed the pearl around his neck and wandered in the nearby trees and brush collecting feathers, five in all. He returned to the walnut tree, placed a rock on each feather to hold it firmly to the ground, his heart feeling the tender and longsuffering love of the Indian who'd brought such joy to Aiyana, himself, and the whole village. Ten years was a lifetime, but Jonathan owed it to his father to let him know that he was finally home. Not that he expected Flying Eagle to still be waiting.

Unhappily Dancer and Jonathan rode toward the village and the sad truth it would reveal. He had no choice. He must face reality, look it square in the eye, and deal with whatever emotions it stirred. Creating illusions or denying the facts was never his way. Life was good. Life was bad. It was important to observe and learn from both.

The angry fire, its blackened territory marked, seemed somehow intelligent, as though it said, "Burn this, spare that, and do your worst here." Jonathan took in the ugly patchwork of death. While Jonathan, the Indians, Mexicans, and the Yucaipa community felt deeply the injustice, needlessness, childish retribution and loss, nature willed herself to rise again. Likewise, the soul of Jonathan David Hart turned within for its own strength. He saw a new vision. Hartland was once again green, the blue rivers flowing, the animals profuse and carefree, and the land clothed in wildflowers and berries. But now he would add vineyards, cherry trees, olive trees, sheep, cattle, horses, more wheat. The land was a living being, a part of the great universe, with its own unique purpose. He would rescue her and revive her—precisely what his mothers Katherine, Aiyana, and Lucy had done for him.

He would build his home, name her Hartland, replace the blackened earth with grass and gardens, flowers and foliage, fruits and vegetables, and he would do it for the love of the ideal, the same ideal White Wolf, Adoeete, his parents, and Aiyana had strived for. Mediocrity, he thought, was for the lazy, the uncreative, those who sought little and received little. No! Those in whose giant footsteps he would place his own growing ones, despite his imperfections, human failings, mistakes, and ill-conceived plans, would know that the practical ideal was all he sought. The sound of a breaking branch and a sudden movement captured Jonathan's attention, and he reached for his rifle, pointing it toward the noise. An Indian stumbled out from behind the dead tree trunk, his muscular body badly burned and his venomous eyes wild with anger. A chill ran down Jonathan's spine, instantly recognizing Red Eye. The hatchet he held was wet with blood. Stealing Dancer was the goal of the dethroned chief, now destitute of a village, people, and land to rule. The unrecognized Jonathan was merely an obstacle to his procurement for the needed horse. Red Eye knew his body was too badly wounded and burned to survive without a medicine man. He would kill the man, then ride to the nearest tribe. It was likely they'd torture and murder him, having raided their camp for years, but he had to take the risk or certainly die.

Jonathan, in control now, cocked his gun and commanded in the native Yucaipat tongue, "Red Eye, throw down your hatchet!" The Indian's eyes widened as he took several steps back, releasing the hatchet. Through the pain, Red Eye squinted, wondering how the stranger knew his name, his language. Jonathan was about to remedy that.

"Once," he reminded him, "you asked your father and my grandfather Adoeete, why he made my mother Ayiana chief in your stead."

Shock and alarm came over Red Eye's face. Quoting, Jonathan repeated aloud the warrior's own question. "How did this happen?"

The wind suddenly whipped through the trees, ashes blowing about. "You made this happen, Red Eye," Jonathan accused. The truth pierced the Indian's mind, as the fresh smell of scorched earth further burned his nostrils.

"Adoeete required the entire village to learn the story by heart, so we would not repeat your mistakes," continued Jonathan. "I will repeat it for you, as I repeated it again and again over the years." Pointing at him, Jonathan began the familiar reproach. "You made this happen when against our laws, you cruelly hunted and tortured animals for sport. You made this happen when you falsely believed rules were not made for you, defying the laws of the Great Spirit. You made this happen when you longed for power but had no interest in learning to wield it wisely. You made this happen when you killed Antinanco, your own brother." Jonathan paused, his eyes cold and hard, "And Aiyana, your niece and *my* mother!"

Red Eye fell to his knees, a warrior's trick to allow him to find the knife hidden in his knee-high moccasin. The next swift motion would be his retrieval of the hatchet and in less than three seconds, this perverse conversation would be over. A split second embraced the span of time within which both men could react to save their own lives, Red Eye with his knife and Jonathan, his gun. But a third weapon came barreling out of the burned trees. Flying Eagle lunged at Red Eye bringing his

burned body crashing agonizingly to the ground. They wrestled as Red Eye's knife came perilously close to Flying Eagles eye. Jonathan jumped down to aid Flying Eagle when

arrows rained down on them. Red Eyes warriors joined the attack. There were too many and their only hope of survival was to escape on Dancer. Jonathan's powerful arms wrenched his father from Red Eyes grasp, the two mounted Dancer as she carried them away, but not before an arrow pierced Flying Eagles back.

Once again Red Eye had survived - or maybe not – as the burned Indian writhed in pain, screaming at Sky Wolf whose arrow had missed Jonathan and found its mark in his side.

CHAPTER SIXTEEN

OBESSION

Hartland 1865

The time of ignorance and selfishness died. It was buried with the wasteful souls whose very thoughts and actions caused their own demise. Every son and husband of the Medina and Vega families were killed. But the innocent Villagers and Mexicans who lost their lives that day of the raid had been murdered and the culpability fell fully on Red Eye, Alberto Medina, and Hector Vega. It was their error-filled thinking that suffocated their own great potential, shut the door on their own happiness, and victimized their families, the people, and the land. Had the veils that hid the true effects of their deeds been removed, the three men would be felled, shaken to the very core, at the costly and vast damage done far beyond the reaches of Yucaipa and this earthly realm.

But out of death, a time of wisdom and intelligence had been born. The goodness and beauty that was Hartland was manifested by the newlyweds' love for each other, and for the land. The marriage of Jonathan and Merritt brought together two families, two fathers, George and Flying Eagle, and two communities, the surviving Indians and Mexicans.

Hartland was a symbol of regeneration, of wholeness and belonging. Individually each had their own home, their own purposes, their own unique work and contribution. But collectively they all called the thousand acres that made up Hartland, home. It was home to George and Jonathan who grew grapes and made wine. It was home to the Donnelly family who worked the olive groves and made oil. It was home to the Merceds and their sheep and wool products, Flying Eagle and his horses, Odakota and Hototo and their corn and wheat fields, and Maria Luego and Amelia Hall who tended the house and the growing Hart family. As long as each cared, participated in fair give and take, did their part, and respected each other and the land, there was no end to the flourishing of Hartland and the Yucaipa community. Ambivalence alone could cause its demise.

Bella Lucinda Morales was ambivalent. Now in her seventies, the aging black widow managed the Morley mansion in Redlands as housekeeper and cook, harshly ruling a staff of four. Long ago, after countless years of stinging disappointments, seeming injustice, and deep frustration, Bella gave up on life. She'd thrown the tiny stone of selfishness and self-loathing into the pond of fate where her descendants' past, present, and future were formed and grew. The ripple effect at first was small, the stone miniscule in such a large pond, yet it poisoned it all the same, the drop of blackness, little by little taking over. Bella's daughter Lucinda could have stopped it. So too her granddaughter Amelia or her great-great-granddaughter Linda Hall. But until one brave soul challenged and conquered the erroneous mind-set Bella had spawned, a lineage of victims would remain.

Five years ago, with the hiring of Bella's granddaughter Amelia to the position of housekeeper at Hartland, the Hart family pond swallowed its first drop of poison. Jonathan had hoped to lighten the load that a newly pregnant Merritt and the elderly Maria Luego shared as together they cooked, cleaned, and maintained the estate home. He'd met Amelia before, liked her enough, and believed she was young, strong, and qualified. Jonathan had viewed Amelia Lucinda Hall's services as a gift he happily gave to his darling wife, allowing her more time to do as she pleased and, more important, to rest.

On that day, Amelia too had brought a wedding gift of her own. The wrapped package contained a large white statue of a woman Amelia called The White Lady, and she insisted the figure must be placed on the fireplace mantel for good luck. Merritt Hart had accepted the unpleasant gift and its placement out of a polite and kind heart, wanting the newest member of the household to feel welcome, innocent of the true aim of this offering. Amelia, however, knew precisely its intent and the very moment that intent was born. That moment came at Jonathan and Merritt's engagement party.

⌒⌒⌒

The much-anticipated celebration of the couple's long-awaited engagement was seen on the beaming faces of the party guests. The room was filled with joy and laughter as everyone from Redlands and beyond begged for an invitation to share in the grand and special moment. The Edwards' household staff couldn't manage the great assemblage of people alone, so a plea went out for staff from the other large Redlands homes to assist. Amelia Hall volunteered.

The guests arriving soon, Amelia had just placed the last of the flowers in the entrance hall when the exquisite Merritt Edwards, stunning in her pale lavender gown, walked down the stairs. She smiled at Amelia and offered her warm thanks for agreeing to help. Merritt was beautiful. Amelia was plain. While Merritt had always been the center of attention, Amelia went through life virtually unnoticed. Merritt received the love of all, whereas Amelia longed for a crumb of affection. Life wasn't fair.

Amelia was on her way from the Edwards' kitchen to offer a few early guests a glass of champagne. The large silver tray was heavy, containing four unopened bottles and several crystal glasses. Worried she might drop the lot, Amelia was struggling to keep her balance when a kindly voice behind her offered assistance. She turned and looked into the eyes of a man she'd never seen before. Her heart stopped, her breath caught in her throat, and what had only been a young girl's dream was standing in front of her.

"My dear Miss," he said, "a man could hardly carry that tray, much less a lady. Would you be so kind as to allow me to take it off your hands?"

Amelia's jaw dropped. He'd noticed her! He'd seen her plight! He'd spoken to her! He'd called her a lady and offered his assistance! And this was not just any man. He was a gentleman, tall, strong, and gloriously dressed. A more handsome, kind, and desirable man she had never seen. A great desire struck Amelia like a gale-force wind, and she reeled from the blast.

"Lead the way," he said, affably. He, her servant now.

"You're very kind, sir," said Amelia, offering a demure curtsy. The man bowed as Thornton Edwards marched into the room. "Our heads will be on that tray if we don't join the women in greeting the guests! Hurry, man! No time like the present to get in trouble and stay in trouble for the rest of your married life." Edward slapped Jonathan on the back and laughed. Jonathan smiled at Amelia as he took his leave with an apologetic grin.

Jonathan and Edward found their places next to the beautifully gowned women already in the entrance hall. The contrite kiss on Merritt's cheek brought a delightful smile for Jonathan's momentary tardiness, but inflamed Jameson Morley, whose large, muscular body stood on the threshold of the open front doors. The kiss should have been *his*, her smile for *him,* and this *their* engagement party. It would have been if the half-breed had not shown up like a stray cat on the Thomas' doorstep. He never bought the cousin from Texas story, and recently he discovered the truth from his father Harold who'd put two and two together. It further maddened Jameson that he'd been a day late in buying the bloody Hartland property himself. He'd nearly smashed in the face of the land agent whose only crime was to deliver the news. Instead he took out his fury on the office door, breaking several knuckles.

He'd come to the party not to congratulate, but to try one last time to talk Merritt out of this foolishness and to marry him instead. After all, she'd never do better than a Morley. Jonathan and Jameson locked eyes as they'd done often over the years, the rivalry for Merritt still an open wound. Each had a broken bone and had several teenage scars from their fierce clashes. Wintering at the Edwards mansion brought them unhappily together every year as the Redlands families maintained their politically correct societal relationships.

The guests having all arrived, the dancing began. The great announcement and toast were not far away, and the evening appeared to be going splendidly. However, from opposite ends of the room Jameson and Amelia watched in torment and agony as their respective objects of affection danced together, very much in love. When Amelia discovered *her* man was the groom, she'd raced to the kitchen bathroom and retched. Washing her face, she looked into the mirror. A delusional young woman looked back. How like her sad life they should have found each other at last, only to be cruelly kept apart by the coming engagement. His earlier attention to her, the deep caring for her well-being, and the meaningful apology he'd given her for having to leave with Mr. Edwards were all confirmation of the mutual and immediate attraction she'd felt between them. Just now as he and Merritt were dancing he'd found her eyes, gave her a wink and a smile, signaling his love and the need to play along until he could free himself. Amelia smiled as Mr. Jameson cut into the couple's dance with a deep bow. Jonathan seemed surprised, but he relinquished Ms. Merritt's hand all the same . . . and then he was coming towards her! The smaller tray she now held with flutes of champagne to be used for the toast, quivered in her hands. She was stunned by his need to be near her, loving that he cared nothing for the watching eyes of all the guests. The nearer he got, the fiercer his eyes grew. Amelia could see he was bracing himself, ready to protect them both from the scandal about to happen when he announced *they* were together now.

He reached for a glass, drank the contents of it down, and stood solidly next to her. The intensity of his feelings required no words. Then a gasp filled the room as Miss Merritt struggled to free herself from Mr. Jameson, but it seemed the harder she pulled the tighter he gripped her wrists until she screamed. The music stopped. When he let go, she fiercely slapped his face. Jonathan charged Jameson like a raging bull, hitting him so mightily, it knocked him unconscious.

The room went silent. Mrs. Morley fainted, Mr. Harold Morley raised his fists, and Mr. Edwards wisely called for calm, claiming, "Jameson clearly had too much to drink."

In Harold Morley's ear, however, Thornton whispered menacingly, "Remove yourselves and your son from our home immediately." The mortified Mrs. Morley was revived, a stunned Jameson was hauled out, and Mr. Harold Morley rudely signaled Amelia that she too was leaving.

That night in her tiny, turreted room high in the Morley mansion, Amelia's mind gave way. Obsession, fantasy, and delusion took over reason and reality. Bella saw the change immediately along with the knife Amelia had taken from the drawer to finally end her suffering and pain. "La Muerta," she prayed to the bequeathed statue from her grandmother and her own mentor in the dark arts, looking for answers. It sat heavily on Bella's fireplace mantel in the Morley mansion servants' quarters as it had for years. Some called it The White Lady, but those devoted to the ancient Mexican dark arts knew her as La Muerta, lady of death. Bella, a practitioner from her youth had long consulted with the so-called spirits of the dead, cast spells, and expertly combined poisonous plants, animal carcasses, bird eggs, and evil thoughts. The ingredients she crushed with pestle and mortar, grinding them into a fine powder. She placed the mixture in small leather pouches, buried it for three days, then allowed its power to rise from under beds, within drawers, as a dash of spice on a fine piece of meat, or in the hollowed-out space in the statue to which she prayed. Rocking in the dark, Bella heard the clock chime 12:00 midnight, then 1:00 a.m., and still no answers came. And then as the clock struck 2:00 a.m., a deep laugh began in the old woman's belly and spilled out into the cold air as she whispered the word "money." The answer was so simple. How could she have lived with the Morleys for so long and not seen it.

Now Bella spoke to La Muerta. "Amelia must have Jonathan, or she will die. I will die from this endless life of servitude, and only the power of money can release us both. Jonathan has money. Merritt has money. Hartland is a gold mine."

Bella smiled, the vision of the future finally clear. Now she must tell Amelia. Bella struggled to climb the small stairs that led to Amelia's room, her long, black skirts heavy and the woman old. She shook the sleeping girl awake. "Listen to me, granddaughter," she commanded. Amelia's red and swollen eyes looked into her grandmother's. "Amelia," she said forcefully, "you will go to Hartland first as Jonathan's housekeeper. We will use our spells to bind his will to yours and grow his love for you. Merritt will leave, and you and Jonathan will marry. Hartland will give us the wealth, freedom, and respect we have always deserved."

Amelia's faraway eyes brightened as a tear of joy ran down her cheek. In that moment, intent was born.

CHAPTER SEVENTEEN

PLAYING WITH FIRE

Hartland 2018

I t was a rainy day. Honey intended to sleep in. The Biel Boys intended to punish Honey, and Linda Hall was intent on finding clues to locate the missing gold.

Honey loved the scent of new construction. The Hartland barn and workshop was almost complete, the scent to be appreciated now, as all too soon it would be gone, replaced by the aromas of its new inhabitants—animals, humans, and the mechanical beasts that would cultivate the land and make her beautiful. One and all felt the thrill of progress as Gary Sparks' meticulous architectural designs were now coming to life. The goal was not only the ability of the structure to survive for a hundred years, but to mirror the Victorian style that was Hartland. Gary, Pete, and the men were all doing a worthy job, and Honey was sparing no expense.

Today, however, construction was suspended as the driving morning rain made it impossible to work. The timing was good, however, as all could use a break from the strenuous effort put into bringing Hartland to rights. Likewise, the vineyards, olive groves, new flower and vegetable gardens would benefit greatly from the rain. For Honey, it was a day for sleeping in late and huddling by the fireplace with a good book.

Later that afternoon with a break in the clouds, Noah, Alex, and Mason arrived at Honey's back door, muddy-shoed and out of breath. The language they used was English, but in their rush to ask and their excitement to know, it sounded more like gibberish. "One more time, boys," Honey laughed, "and this time slower please."

Mason took a deep breath. "Mr. Pete made us a really cool fort in the barn."

Alex took over. "It's in the hay loft, and he even brought us four bales of hay to play on."

Noah pushed Mason, inferring it was time to get permission and close the deal. "So, Ms. Honey," Mason continued, "since it's Saturday night, and our moms said it was okay, can we have a sleepover in the barn?"

Honey laughed. "Sounds like fun, guys. You sure you won't be afraid? It's awfully dark out there."

"Na," chimed in Noah, "we're all Boy Scouts. We've camped a lot! Besides, Mr. Pete said he'd come over, build us a fire to roast hot dogs and s'mores, and make sure there are no bears in the barn before we go to sleep. Said he'd come back early in the morning to check on us.

And we have cell phones. We can even call you, Ms. Honey, since you're right here."

Honey laughed. "That's what I'm afraid of. Well, if your moms say it's okay, and Pete's coming over to supervise, then sure, why not! My guess is you won't sleep much anyway."

"Thanks, Ms. Honey," the words coming in triplicate. The boys dashed off at full speed to get their sleeping bags and prepare for the big adventure. Honey heard Alex say, "Hey, guys, maybe someday we can *live* in the barn!"

The chorus of "cool" created the refrain.

For the Biel Boys, it was another day of frustration and anger. Huddled around a miserable and ineffectually burning fireplace in their squatters' home, the abusively pelting rain on the already leaking roof ignited and fueled their distress. The wetness of the wood had been placed squarely on the shoulders of Jeff Biel, the leak in the roof was Sam's to bear, and the scarcity of beer, potato chips, and dessert drugs could only be attributed to Danny. They ordered their disorderly and chaotic lives. Their code required that blame must be assigned and punished. But blame could only in the mildest sense be attributed to any one of them. For instance, Jeff could be forgiven for his wet wood, Sam the leak in the roof, and Danny the lack of food and beer. But Honey Hart, the new owner of Hartland, must accept all the blame for the loss of their Yucaipa tree-line home.

She'd ruined the place, taking everything that made it theirs away. The old mattress, the broken chairs, the piles of beer cans. She would never be forgiven for stealing back what they had stolen long ago. The signature of time was their witness, and there must be some statute that made it permanently theirs. Hell, for long enough they'd been the only folks interested in living there and had actually spent significant time on its grounds.

Now that blame had been established, the code required punishment. But what form would that take? Fortunately, they were spared the taxing of their little-used minds when Jeff threw cardboard, newspaper, and lighter fluid into the fireplace, causing a sudden blast of heat and flames. "You idiot," yelled Sam, "you're gonna burn the place down!" Light dawned as Danny used reason to discover the perfect punishment for Honey Hart. "*If,*" he deduced, "Jeff could burn this place down, *then* he could burn the new Hartland barn down." The result would be one hell of a mad lady who might just give up on the place and go away.

❧

Linda Hall was glad for the pouring rain. It meant fewer people com-ing to the library and more time to explore her latest theory involving the conspiracy she now believed had been precipitated between the Hart and

Smiley families to hide and keep the gold for themselves. Weren't they rich enough already? Didn't the menial labor of her ancestors for the benefit of the Harts count for something? That Amelia had been Jonathan's true love was confirmed in Amelia's own hand. Her diaries and letters to her grandmother Bella spoke of the growing passion the housekeeper and owner had for one another, despite the constant interference from Maria Luego and the dreadful way she treated her. One letter said, that once Amelia had overheard Maria begging Ms. Merritt to be rid of her, claiming Merritt was too kind and pure-minded to see what was going on right underneath her nose.

Undoubtedly, thought Linda, Merritt Hart was delusional, ignoring the signs of a husband losing interest, while his longing and desire grew for another. And why shouldn't her grandmother be wanted, loved, and adored? Linda looked up as a sheet of wind and rain struck the windowpane, bringing her mind back to the task of finding clues. From Dr. Allen Crawley's book, she knew Albert and Alfred Smiley knew about the gold. They were there that day in the doctor's office when Flying Eagle brought in the gold coins, and they'd seen for themselves the wagon load in the caskets. They'd also worked for many summers with Flying Eagle on the horse ranch, which meant they must know something.

The Harts' involvement in Linda's theory took shape when she'd discovered in The Heritage Room another book, which spoke of the friendship between Jonathan Hart and the Smiley brothers once they learned of his connection to Flying Eagle. They'd all grown close over the next forty years. The gold would be passed on from generation to generation. If someone along the chain suddenly died, there must be a way to communicate to the next of kin the path to the gold.

But how? What was the means? *Damn it*, she thought, *there's nothing in this chapter.* She moved on to read about how the Crest Family from back east joined the wintering wealthy in Redlands, building the now famous Kimberly Crest Mansion and Museum. She knew all about the Crest family and was aware they belonged to the same tight-knit group of idealists that were the Harts and Smileys. Ms. Corey Crest had been a noted author, philosopher, scholar, and philanthropist, whose books graced the Smiley Library shelves. Her writings and their subject were of little interest to Linda. There was nothing to connect the Crests, Smileys, and Harts except their obvious love of ancient philosophy. Nothing remotely related to gold or money. "No," she concluded, "this is of no help," and she put it back on the shelf. Next to it was a book by Robert Watchorn, *Ideals to Live By*. Linda skimmed the first few pages, which went on and on about the ideals of Abraham Lincoln and other great men and their importance to society. "One day," Watchorn wrote, "I dream of building a monument to Lincoln and to the golden ideals of truth, justice, tolerance, goodness, beauty, honesty, strength and courage, all of which are <u>'the common property of every man.'</u> This place should be <u>'accessible, yet secluded'</u>, where each of us can approach the memory of Lincoln in our own individual way as Lincoln is, <u>'all things to all men.'</u>"

Linda sighed. *Not only is it boring, but it's a dead end.* Besides, she was always peeved by disrespectful readers who underlined things, especially in ink pen. She replaced the book and reached for another. Now this looked interesting. Linda wondered how she'd missed it, having been over this same section several times. It was a tall, slender, yet unassuming book with a light gray binding that simply said, Smiley Library Architectural Designs. It was written by T.R. Griffith. It opened with, "The intent is to create the Redlands public library, when 'funds' are long last, if ever, procured, to be built in a 'Moorish' character we term 'Mission Revival.' The edifice shall feature contrasting red brick with sandstone trimmings, carvings, fanciful griffons and cherubs, an interior rich with arches and cozy conservation corners with fireplaces."

Linda turned the page, but in so doing, the book accidently slipped from her hand. It dropped to the floor releasing a folded sheet of paper, having been stuck between the pages. It was an architectural drawing of the proposed library. Upon it were handwritten notes, boxes within which were penciled checkmarks, circles within which were x's, and a variety of lines which ran from one section to the next. It was the drawing of an engineer marking the library's inner workings. Linda decided it was of no value, when suddenly, she noticed a faint zigzag line, barely seen, a shadow which began at the front door, wound its way to the right among the bookshelves, then stopped at an outside wall. Linda looked closer only to discover that another such shadowy line did likewise, but this time the route it took started at the front door, then turned left, running along what was now the study room and research area of the library. Again, it took its twists and turns, arriving to an outside wall in perfect alignment to the other location.

Linda wiped the perspiration off her reading glasses and looked once more. She was hoping to find a third shadowy line that could indicate that the outlaw's gold, placed in three decoy caskets by Flying Eagle, had found their way into the solid fortress wall of the Smiley Library. If this was the case, it would make sense that a third route to the outside had been created. Linda looked closely but could see nothing. Her great desire for the gold, retribution, and justice caused her to try one more thing. She switched on a nearby reading lamp and placed the drawing inches from its bright beams. Linda's heart stopped. Her tenacity had been rewarded as the light revealed clearly a third shadowy line. As she presumed, the line led straight from the door to the outside wall. The three outside locations were perfectly ordered and ready at a moment's notice for a crew to break through the wall and release into Hart or Smiley hands, the gold coins. The problem was, over the years the library had been added on to. Linda Hall, however, was not to be deterred. She'd come this far, and was willing to do whatever it took. Her prayers to La Muerta intensified, to see that justice prevailed and the false narrative of her family heritage was vindicated.

⌒⌒

Honey joined Pete and the boys for dinner and the marshmallow des-sert, then left them to their fun. Pete confided in Honey that he'd brought his camper truck and would spend the night in it, just a few yards out of sight. Honey felt better. "Thanks for doing this for them, Pete, especially Mason. It's tough for him without his dad. These will be marvelous memories for them, precisely what a Hartland childhood should be filled with."

Armed with cell phones, flashlights, instructions, and orders from Pete, which if not obeyed would mean being skinned within an inch of their lives, the exhausted boys fell asleep at their camp in the barn.

The smell of smoke and the distant sound of gunning motorcycle engines woke up both Pete and Honey. She called 911 and ran toward the barn in her house-shoes and a bathrobe.

Pete checked his watch. It was 6:00 a.m. He opened the camper door to the sight of billowing clouds of smoke and fire coming from the ground windows of the barn. Pete's heart leapt painfully in his chest; the boys were inside. He raced to the barn. The fire was eating up the gallons of lighter fluid, newspaper, and cardboard flung everywhere, and smoke filled the barn. Pete could hear the boys coughing and crying out for help. Noah was halfway down the ladder, and Alex was swinging his legs over the top, on his way. The fire had raced up the wall, the hay in the loft now ablaze. Mason was crying on the ledge as Pete yelled to him to jump. The terrified boy leapt, trusting in Pete's outstretched arms. His feet hit the ground, and the boy ran out the door. Seconds later, helpless to escape the fiery beam crashing down upon him, Pete collapsed on the concrete floor, his back engulfed in flames. Racing through the door, three Yucaipa firemen wrestled with the heavy beam finally getting the burning Pete out from under it. The screaming sirens of the fire engines, police vehicles, and ambulances, coming closer and now only a few miles away, could be heard at Hartland as anxious neighbors arrived, all ready to give aid. Honey called Remey who contacted Noah and Alex's families. The ambulance took the three boys off to the hospital to check them out, and Remey would meet them as soon as the calls were made. None of the boys had been burned, but they likely suffered from smoke inhalation.

Pete was alive, thank God, but his back was badly burned, and he'd been raced off to the hospital for treatment.

Honey, traumatized and in shock, was standing away from the barn, whose roof and sides had collapsed and now continued to burn. The fire engines furiously pumped streams of water, trying to gain control, but the intense conflagration burned on, unfazed by the blasts of water. Honey's phone rang. Landon. The moment she picked up, Landon said, "Just tell me you're okay, Honey."

"Yes," responded Honey, "I'm fine, but Pete is badly hurt and the boys inhaled a lot of smoke. Pete arranged for them to have a sleepover in the barn. Landon, I don't know how this happened!"

"Listen to me, Honey," Landon said. "I think I know what happened. You take care of yourself. Let me check this out, and I'll get back to you as soon as I can."

"Okay, Landon, but," pleaded Honey, "please be careful, and call me back as soon as you can."

"Will do," he replied. "We can get through this, Honey. It's all going to be okay."

At 6:00 a.m. that same morning, Landon was watching the sunrise, enjoying a hot cup of coffee on the balcony and admiring the view of the valley when he noticed the plume of smoke rising from Hartland. Immediately he called 911, but they'd already been alerted and were on their way. Landon climbed the stairs to his bedroom two at a time to throw on some jeans and a sweat-shirt, his only thought getting to Honey. Minutes later, he heard four motorcycles and saw from the window the bikers careening up Carter, past La Bonita, and onto the dirt road that led to the three-hundred-acre wildlands preserve known as El Dorado Park. He suspected the fire was arson and the four motorcycles belonged to the Biel Boys. He couldn't prove it now, but he sure as hell wouldn't wait around for a detective. Landon unlocked the gun closet, took out his hunting rifle and a thirty-eight-caliber pistol. He stocked up on ammo and stuck his hunting knife in his boot. He didn't intend to shoot anyone or anything, but his military training compelled him to be prepared, just in case.

His four-wheeler would be faster, but it made too much noise, so Landon saddled up T.J. and headed off, the soft ground clarifying the motorcycle tracks. He was not a vigilante, but he knew it was important to find them. His goal was to notify the sheriff's department of their whereabouts.

El Dorado Park had only two ways in or out. Likely they were some-where between. As Landon rode, he listened for the sound of bike engines that would echo through the valley, but all was silent. They had probably gone to ground. He would soon know where. The tracks led into a forest of scrub oaks surrounded by dense sage brush, rock outcroppings, and fallen boulders. This close to the base of the mountain, the foliage was thick, making it easy to hide.

This was close enough, Landon thought, the sheriff's department could take it from here. He used his cell phone to make the call connect-ing with 911, and told the operator of his suspicions and location. Landon turned T.J. around, preferring to maintain his watch from a safer distance when a bullet flew past his head, followed by another, which grazed his leg. T.J. reared in fear as Landon fell hard on the ground. When the third shot was fired, the horse bolted.

Landon instinctively went into combat mode, scrabbling behind the nearby boulders and taking out his pistol. The hunting rifle and ammo were on the horse, who'd finally stopped some distance away, still skit-tish. The unsettling silence lasted a few minutes as the Biel Boys toyed with their prey. Sam was the only one with a gun, but Jeff, Martin, and Danny had an arsenal of knives and hatchets between them. Sam signaled Jeff to go left and circle-around behind the guy. Martin moved closer, his knife poised. The branch snapped under Jeff's boot, alerting Landon just in time. Seconds before the hatchet would have been thrown. Landon shot Jeff in the shoulder, forcing the weapon out of his hand. Seeing his brother wounded, Martin let loose a battle cry, ran up the boulder and threw him-self and his knife at Landon, the two in a dangerous wrestling match. But Landon was powerful and well trained, capturing Martin in a vise-like grip. With his gun pointed at Martin's head, Landon thought he had the upper hand until Jeff hurled his knife and himself at Landon.

Now the unfair fight between the three became one of life or death. Martin, now free, forced the pistol out of Landon's hand. As he spun around to fire the gun, Jeff leapt onto Landon. The bullet meant for Landon accidently hit Jeff instead. The slug entered his back, then made its way to his heart. Instantly Landon grabbed the knife from his boot as Martin pulled the trigger, the sound of a click allowed the knife time to find its target—Martin's stomach.

Landon ran, weaving his way through the oaks and brush. His only chance was to find his horse and grab the rifle. Sam let his bullets fly as Danny raced to launch his own attack, but a running Landon made no easy target. The bullets and knife missed. Once again, the horse bolted, retreating much farther to the safety of the trees. Under the cover of the brush, an unarmed Landon hid as the two remaining Biel Boys slowly approached, stalking him. The sound of sirens, getting louder by the second, stopped Danny and Sam in their tracks. They had unwelcome company and no time to waste on this guy, so they turned and raced off, the hunters now becoming the prey.

⌒⌒

The Redlands Community Hospital was busier than usual as more casualties from the Biel Boys' assault continued to arrive through the doors. Besides Pete and the boys, several firemen had been burned and in the final shootout at El Dorado Park, a deputy had been wounded, but not before he'd put a few bullets into the legs of Sam and Danny. They wanted them alive to face prosecution. It would likely be a slam dunk as they reeked of lighter fluid, weed, and smoke. Landon too had been brought in, the knife wound in his leg potentially serious.

Edward and Matt had shown up at Hartland and refused to leave Honey alone as the place became a revolving door for well-wishers and the worried. The worried crowd ate what the well-wishers brought, and Honey knew for the first time what it meant to belong to a community that truly cared for her and one another. There could be no better cure than to share the tragedy and loss with a houseful of kind and concerned people.

Pete was of the most concern, his back suffering fourth-degree burns. Though he was in excruciating pain, all Pete wanted from the doctors was to know the condition of the boys. Only when he'd learned they were fine, having been treated and sent home, did he relax and focus on the medical staff doing their work on him.

Bullets removed, firemen bandaged, and Landon sent out the door with stitches, crutches, and a prescription for antibiotics and pain pills, the hospital returned to normal. Guards were placed at Sam and Danny's door, and the Yucaipa Sheriff Department brought in beer and balloons for their mending comrade. This much excitement in one day was unusual for the normally peaceful town of Yucaipa. The barn had burned down, and the only loss of life was one of the perpetrators, Jeff Biel. There was much to be grateful for as everyone knew it could have been so much worse!

CHAPTER EIGHTEEN

LITTLE EMILY

Hartland, 1880

Five-year-old Emily Hart had a fine new pair of brown, leather boots. She was playing on the front porch showing them off to the new kitty and several distracted birds. "So," she explained to them, "Papa and I went to town yesterday all by ourselves. We came back with these." She kicked up one shoe, frightening the cat and birds away. "We also got a pretty new hair ribbon for Mama." Emily sat on the steps admiring the laces and how pretty the big girl shoes looked on her tiny feet. The birds returned and in time the kitty did too, crawling on Emily's lap, eager for petting and milk. Soon, Thomas, one of the vineyard men, came by looking for Jonathan. "Oh, Mr. Thomas," cried Emily, "Papa got me new boots."

"Those are mighty fine, Miss Emily," agreed the smiling black man, his eyes twinkling.

"Bet you'd like new boots too, Mr. Thomas," sighed Emily, "but you'd have a hard time keeping them clean." She looked sadly down at his muddy shoes.

Thomas laughed. "You're right, Miss Emily. Speck you better be the one to have new boots. I'll stick with these old ones. They like being dirty."

Emily stood up and raced to the rocking chair, patting the seat. "Just one rocking and one song, Mr. Thomas?" she pleaded, adding, "My boots have never heard singing before."

Thomas threw his head back and laughed. He climbed up the porch, picked up the child in his arms, swung her around, and the two began to rock. His deep baritone voice was beautiful, and the sound of it singing brought Merritt and Maria to the window. The picture they made—the large, muscular man and the little child—was a tender sight, and both women took hankies out of their sleeves and dabbed their teary eyes.

Emily clapped, kissed him on the cheek, and said, "More, please."

Thomas could have sat there all day. There was nothing he loved more than this child and singing his songs, but he did have work to do. "Miss Emily," he bargained, "if I sing you "Sweet Betsy from Pike," will you let old Mr. Thomas get back to his grapes?"

Emily nodded and settled back in his great big arms. When he got to the end, she'd ask him to sing it again—and he would.

⌒⌒⌒

It was Amelia's day off, and she was spending it in the Morley mansion kitchen watching her grandmother boil chicken bones. In another pot, a concoction of strange ingredients was simmering, the potent smell unpleasant but familiar.

"Ah," said Bella, "here is the wishbone."

Amelia heaved a deep sigh, alerting Bella to the all-too-familiar sign of depression. "You must be patient, granddaughter," Bella said. "La Muerta knows best the proper time for you and Jonathan to marry."

Amelia slapped her hand down on the kitchen table. "But it's been five years, grandmother! There's no sign Ms. Merritt is unhappy or wanting to leave. Ms. Emily is their pride and joy, and with the new baby coming, Mr. Jonathan dotes on them both. Yesterday Emily came home with new boots, and he bought Ms. Merritt a new hair ribbon."

"Have you placed the black handkerchief in Ms. Merritt's closet?" Bella asked.

Amelia nodded.

"Have you offered devotional bowls of fruit and nuts?" she continued. "And is the owl still in the tree near their bedroom? Have you said the spells over Mr. Jonathan and Ms. Merritt as they slept?"

Again, Amelia nodded. She'd done everything Bella had required. The old woman returned to the stove and the boiling bones. "Life is not without its tragedies," she reminded Amelia. "Jonathan and Merritt have yet to suffer anything of consequence these past five years. You will see, La Muerta will seize the opportunity one day to test them. The powerful force of heart-wrenching pain often tears marriages apart." Bella reached in the cupboard and brought out a small glass bottle and stopper. "Put this in Ms. Merritt's tea. Just three drops. No more, no less." Then Bella strained the simmering mixture until the broth was clear and poured it in an empty jar. "Put this in Mr. Jonathan's coffee. Start with four drops and watch his amorous feelings for you develop." Pushing Amelia out the door, she called out, "These things take time. They take time."

The Harts generously allowed Amelia to take a horse and buggy when she visited her grandmother, and the long ride home from Redlands gave her time to think. Her grandmother was right. Nothing had gone wrong at Hartland. There had only been the steady growing and flourishing of the vineyards, wheat and corn fields, vegetables and flowers. The Hartland Crush, the community festival when the grapes were made into wine, had for the second year been a huge success. People from all over the Green Valley bought out nearly everything Hartland had produced. There had been no suffering, only happiness. But unlike the Harts and Yucaipa, Amelia suffered. She'd suffered without a mother. Her mother had been raped by Eli Hall, one of the Morley groomsmen. When Harold Morley found out about it, he forced her mother and Eli to marry, wanting no scandals among his servants. But Eli had been brutal and abusive. When Amelia was seven, her mother caught Eli trying to molest her. She'd stabbed him with a kitchen knife in the heart. Later her mother was tried for murder and was hanged. It was hard to grow up without a mother and only a tired old grandmother and to know the shameful act was the cause of her birth. The Morley mansion and her grandmother's ways were all she knew. The adults in her young life had steeped her in the dark arts, greed, and disrespect—and yet. A tiny voice inside her continued to plead with her to be brave and escape.

The horse and buggy rounded the bend, and she could see the beauty of the mountains, of Hartland, and of the handsome man rocking on the porch with his daughter, in the home where she was called housekeeper rather than mistress. "Heart-wrenching suffering," she quoted her grandmother, as Emily and Jonathan waved, welcoming her back.

Merritt Hart gave birth to a beautiful baby boy. Not long after, she claimed Alexander David Hart "had the face of an angel, the fists of a fighter, and the cry of a banshee." The banshee wanted his mother, as did his father. Jonathan made his son wait till he kissed his wife again and held her close. Their deep love for one another began as children, and with every passing year its roots went deeper. Merritt respected and appreciated Jonathan's hard work and efforts to make Hartland a grand and glorious place, but more than that she adored the father and husband he was. No one was perfect, but he was close.

Jonathan could not imagine life without his darling Merritt, Emily, and now little Alexander. He was the happiest man alive. Merritt kissed him again, then turned to the babe, her eyes suddenly discovering the whereabouts of Emily's lost ball for which the entire household had been searching for days. It was peeking out from under the bassinet. Merritt scooped it up, tossed it to Jonathan, and laughed. "Please give this to your daughter and get us all out of our misery." Jonathan beamed as he walked down the stairs, Amelia just beginning her climb from below. Happily, he tossed the ball to Amelia, reporting, "Case solved! It was under the bassinet." Amelia's eyes grew soft with passion and desire. How she loved the man!

The bell at the new schoolhouse across from Hartland rang! It rang again and again! It rang with fear! Merritt was sobbing on the back porch, the baby wrapped tightly in her arms. Maria was pacing, worry ripping her heart apart. Jonathan, Thomas, Odakota and Hototo and every man within earshot of the frantic bell was mounted and searching as four o'clock turned into five, and five o'clock turned into six when the sun stopped shining. The light of the moon and the flaming torches would have to do, as the men spread farther out towards the rushing creek and the remains of the old Indian village. Merritt, Maria, Amelia, and a porch full of tearful wives, together heard the men's voices shouting, "Emily!" Followed by silence. "Emily! Emily!" The shouts came again and again, the silence so deafening, all thought they would go mad with worry and not knowing.

Finally, it was too cold for the baby to be outside, and Merritt went into the house to sit on the living room couch, rocking the sleeping baby and softly sobbing. Emily walked in and stood in front her, saying, "Mama, why are you crying?"

Surprised her mother didn't respond, Emily tried again. "Mama! Mama!" Emily tried to hold her mother's face between her hands as the baby cried. Frustrated, Emily demanded, "Stop crying, Alexander, I'm trying to speak to Mama. Why won't you look at me, Mama?" Emily stamped her foot, put her hands on her hips and yelled with all her might. "MAMA, DON'T CRY, I'M HERE NOW, I'M ALL RIGHT."

Suddenly it occurred to Emily that everything seemed very strange. She watched as the usually affectionate kitten walked right by her. "Ms. Kitty," Emily addressed the tiny feline, "why won't Mama listen? Why won't she stop crying?" Then Jonathan stepped unwillingly into the room holding Emily's new boot, now wet, muddy, and covered in pond scum. Emily ran to him and cried, "Papa, what happened to my new boot? That will never clean up! Where's the other one? Now, I'm really mad!"

Merritt turned around with a gasp, immediately grasping the meaning of the lone child's shoe her husband held in his hand. Jonathan fell into a chair and cried. Emily rushed over to comfort him and tried to climb onto his lap. Giving up, she looked into his face. "It's only a boot, Papa," she said. "Nothing to cry over. We'll go together and buy a new pair tomorrow. Papa? Papa? Why won't you answer me?"

⌒⌒

Earlier, when the wives arrived to support Merritt as their husbands searched for little Emily, Amelia had slipped out, stolen quietly into the barn, saddled a horse, and rode to Redlands. Dread, guilt, and fear drove her every step of the way. She burst through the door of the Morley kitchen. Bella never looked up, continuing to calmly fold the pile of white linen napkins. That it wasn't Amelia's day off and she'd arrived well after dark didn't faze Bella. Instead she said, "Sit down, granddaughter. I was expecting you."

"Grandmother," said Amelia, barely able to speak. "Something terrible has happened!"

"I know what happened," Bella replied, "and you *will* go back."

"I can't!" cried Amelia. "I just can't!" Bella struck the pile of carefully folded napkins, sending them flying onto the wooden floor. Her dangerous eyes held her granddaughter's as she moved slowly and deliberately towards her. For the first time, Amelia feared the woman. Bella's outward composure belied the constant, simmering rage from a lifetime of wrong choices, false assumptions, and mistaken perspectives. Bella slapped Amelia's face with ferocity. "You *will* go back!" she commanded. "There is more at stake than just you! When you marry Jonathan, and you will, we will both be rich. Instead of being servants, we will have servants! Then—finally—I can hold my head up high in the presence of my sister Juanita. Juanita and her Spanish explorer," she spat, "have, since she was sixteen, lived rich and fat in Spain. All my life she was more beautiful than I, adored by countless men, while I, 'the little, plain wren,' was left to serve tea and cakes. This is *my* only chance, and you will not quit until this marriage is sealed."

Amelia's courage returned. "How can I face them?"

Now Bella paced. "Did anyone see what happened?"

Amelia responded, "I don't think so . . . it all happened so quickly." There in the dark kitchen Amelia relived the moment. "I was watching her playing with the ball. It slipped out of her hands, rolled down the hill, and into the pond. She disappeared from sight for a moment, and then I saw her walking on the fallen log with a stick, trying to reach the ball. She was teetering. Suddenly I saw La Muerta had provided an opportunity for 'heart-wrenching suffering.' If she drowned, they would suffer, blame each other, the heartbreak too much for the marriage to last. I know he loves me," Amelia cried. "We just need a chance to be by ourselves, without Ms. Merritt, and then our love can finally grow."

Bella growled. "Enough, granddaughter! We'll speak of it no more."

Amelia ignored her. "I knew if I shouted Emily's name she would be startled. Perhaps fall in. For a moment, I couldn't, and then I heard myself yelling her name sharply."

"Amelia," Bella said forcefully, "stop speaking."

Amelia was no longer in the Morley kitchen but back at the pond. "She fell in," continued Amelia.

Bella struck Amelia, the palm of her hand made its mark on an unflinching face. Amelia's words persisted. "I immediately felt horrible and ran to the pond. I dove in, but it was too late." Once again Bella slapped the face of her granddaughter, but the outward pain was of no consequence as Amelia finished what she began. "Little Emily was already dead."

"None . . . the . . . less," commanded Bella, "you *will* go back."

◡◠◡

A shroud of heartache and suffering descended upon Hartland and all of Yucaipa. Black wreaths hung upon the doors, each home and heart feeling the loss of little Emily personally. Thomas was inconsolable, Maria distraught, and Amelia stoic, her mind in a faraway place where she was

Mrs. Jonathan Hart. This marriage must finally happen. Only then could Amelia justify her unjustifiable actions.

Jonathan's tears hindered his work on the small wooden coffin he reverently constructed, taking great care with the beautiful carvings that depicted the things his daughter had loved—birds, the kitten, her china doll, and the ball. He'd locked himself into the workshop of the giant barn, refusing food and water until he'd completed his task. A watchful and concerned Thomas saw the door finally open, revealing Jonathan's hollow face and vacant eyes. Thomas cried. The two men clasped one another, comfort found in the knowledge of how precious she was to both.

The sorrowful procession of wagons, horses, and carriages made its way to the Yucaipat Indian burial grounds. Jonathan lifted the small coffin on one shoulder and placed it in the grave dug early that morning next to Chief Aiyana resting place. Thomas had asked for the honor. Words unheard were spoken over the dead child's soul as the weary grievers willed the reality of the moment, not to be. Odakota and Hototo grieved for the loss of the child. The fresh reminder of the massacre of nearly the entire Yucaipat village, opened old scares they thought had healed.

Merritt had taken to her bed; the aging Doctor Crawley having ordered tinctured tea to alleviate her raw emotions. He'd expected in a week's time she'd be up again, and, if not better, at least able to go through the normal functions required of a mother with a newborn. But with every day that passed, she appeared to get worse. Mrs. Edwards was called to Hartland for support, and she came immediately.

Emily had cried and cried when she realized she had died—except she didn't feel dead, she felt just the same. While she could see everything and everyone, no one, it seemed, could see or hear her. Her form was different now. It could walk through walls, but it couldn't sit on Mama or Papa's lap, and when she tried to pet the kitten, her hand went right through the little creature. It was taking time for her to adjust to this odd way of being.

She wondered why she had remained here and why the angels had asked her to stay for a little while longer.

There were lots of sad faces and tears except for Ms. Amelia. Emily was glad Amelia couldn't see her. She knew Amelia was mad at her for trying to get the ball out of the pond, and she could still hear her mean and angry voice, which startled her and made her fall in.

Now that Emily could go anywhere she wanted and watch everyone, she learned things she didn't know before. Like, Mama was so beautiful and so sweet with Alexander, even though she was still so sad. Papa worked hard and was kind to all his men. Maria loved the family and did everything she could to make them happy. But she was surprised to find she didn't like Miss Amelia, now that she watched her. Sometimes she did peculiar things, and she hated it when late at night Miss Amelia would go into Mama and Papa's room and say strange words.

Emily was worried. Mama wasn't getting better. She was getting worse. Dr. Crawley's medicine wasn't working. He called the situation "a damn puzzlement." Today she followed Amelia into the kitchen. It was time for Mama to have her tinctured tea, which Amelia was preparing. On the counter sat Dr. Crawley's bottle from which were to be added three drops. Emily was surprised when Amelia ignored it and instead drew out of her apron pocket another bottle. From it she placed four drops, but then added two more. She stirred in sugar and cream, placed it on a tray with two warm pieces of bread, and walked up the stairs.

Mama didn't want to drink the tea, so Miss Amelia went to get Maria and Grandma Edwards, to make her. Mama complained to the three hovering women, "But I feel worse after I drink the tea."

"Nonsense," said Miss Amelia, "why would Doctor Crawley prescribe something that would make you sick." Suddenly Emily knew, whatever was in Amelia's bottle was hurting her Mama. She could not let her drink it! Several days ago, Emily had discovered she could move things with her mind and thoughts, like the bird feather on the porch, a flower laying by the vase, and a puzzle piece on the French desk. She'd never tried to move something so heavy as a cup filled with tea, but she had no choice. She must try. Mama was reaching for the cup! Frantically Emily willed it to fall. But nothing happened. She tried again, this time the cup shook, which startled her Mama, and she drew back her hand. Now Emily gathered all her willpower, and suddenly the cup fell, smashing on the floor. Mama, Maria, and Grandma Edwards gasped, astonished and perplexed by the strange event. But not Miss Amelia, she was just plain mad. Angrily she picked up the broken pieces and took the tray back downstairs. Emily followed her. Once more the housekeeper fixed another cup of tea, added the bad drops and marched back upstairs to Mama. Emily stomped her foot and put her hands on her hips. Now she was furious!

The coaxing continued for Merritt to try again to take a sip, and finally she sighed and reached for the cup, which shook violently and abruptly flew off the bedside table. Amelia cursed, the broken pieces on the floor meant she'd been thwarted again. Just then, Maria caught sight of the child for just an instant and cried out, "Emilita, Emilita, I see you!"

"Where?" wailed Merritt.

"She was here, Señora Merritt," Maria cried. "I saw her, but she is gone now. As God is my witness, Emilita broke those teacups. But why?"

Emily knew why, and it was maddening not being able to communicate! She wanted to hit Amelia, make her cry out, but her little fists would simply go right through her. Emily sank to the floor next to the broken pieces of china with their sharp edges. In an instant, she knew what to do. There was no time to waste, her Mama's life was at stake. So, with all her might, Emily's mind flung the shards across the room and into Amelia's arms, neck, and face. Amelia screamed.

The other women shrieked seeing the jagged pieces lodged in the now bleeding housekeeper. Understanding dawned as the wide-eyed Merritt, Mrs. Edwards, and Maria understood only Emily could have made that happen. Although her body was dead, buried next to Aiyana's, the essence of Emily—her spirit, mind, heart, and will—was very much alive and protecting her Mama from the insanity of a woman gone mad. Never had they encountered such a thing, and never would they again. Sweet Emily's presence at Hartland after death plainly had a purpose.

Albeit only five, the child's great love, intelligence, and strength of mind was the reason Merritt remained alive.

Jonathan and Thomas had gone up to the house to collect a cup of coffee before heading back into the fields when they heard the screams. The two men bounded up the stairs and threw open the bedroom door. Amelia was screaming and clawing at her face, causing the shards to go deeper and the bleeding more profuse. Merritt, Maria, and Mrs. Edwards were huddled in the corner in shock, frightened as the poison from the cup made its way under Amelia's skin. Maria pointed an accusing finger at Amelia. "She tried to poison Señora Merritt."

Thomas sprang into action, imprisoning Amelia's arms behind her back as Jonathan grabbed Merritt's new hair ribbon to secure her wrists. Thomas ran to the window, threw it open, and yelled out to a worker to hitch up the wagon quick. Explanations would have to wait until the housekeeper was safe in the Yucaipa jail. Then they'd see about bringing in Dr. Crawley.

CHAPTER NINETEEN

THE TRAP

Smiley Library, 2018

A t Hartland, the National Football League had taken over Honey's TV and hence its fans had taken over her living room. It was the season opener. The New England Patriots versus the San Francisco 49ers. Rooting for San Francisco were Mason, Noah, and Alexander, all sporting 49ers T-shirts. Landon was a Ram's fan, Don a Seahawk through and through, and Pete had at one time played for the Dolphins. However, no one wanted Tom Brady to win! Remey too lived for football. She cared nothing for the game but loved the challenge of presenting all her culinary delights relative to the theme of football. She was putting the finishing touches on the double chocolate football field complete with grass, goalposts, and plastic football players.

Honey was the lone cheerleader for her Tommy Boy and beloved New England Patriots. Landon smiled appreciatively at the beautiful woman in her number 12 jersey and blue jeans who sat on the stairs with a bottle of beer, railing excitedly against the 49ers, casting aspersions on both their offense and defense, sighting examples from seasons pasts. Noah fought back by throwing a piece of popcorn at Honey. Mason and Alex quickly took up the battle, which would have degenerated into a food fight had Remey not stopped the whole thing with one withering look. No one dared defy the benevolent dictator of the house. Remey's brood duly warned and again under control, she rewarded their obedience with a giant football shaped bowl filled with macho nachos.

This was Pete's first outing since he'd been released from the hospital. His burns were bad, but finally the pain was under control and the long process of healing was well underway. He'd stay a while and see how he felt. Like a spontaneous memorial service, at half-time they'd all gone to look at the charred remains of the barn, each reliving that terrifying moment. What the Biel Boys did to their Hartland family was tragic, but together they were a strong bunch and together they would get through this, rebuild the barn, and move on. Pete knew the insurance process would be an ordeal as would be the trial of the remaining Biels, but at least Honey was safe and that was a weight off his mind.

Linda Hall's increasing signs of obsession and strange behavior at the library worried Edward. His concern for Honey's safety grew as well when he'd learned Linda had shown up at Hartland a second time on the pretense of bringing by another book. That afternoon Honey was gone, and Remey heard the doorbell ring. "Can I help you?" Remey asked, smiling.

"Why, yes," responded Linda. "Is Honey here? I've brought her another book from the Smiley Library."

"I can take it," replied Remey. "Ms. Honey is gone for the day." Remey watched Linda's face fall and her forehead furrow. The woman seemed odd, but harmless enough. The nervous habit Linda had of tapping her heel up and down when she was thinking, only added to her peculiarity.

Damn it, thought Linda, *my hopes of prying more information out of Honey just vanished.* She looked at the young woman and another thought crossed her mind. *Maybe she knows something. If I can get inside and have a cup of tea, I can ask a few questions or maybe look around."*

Remey reached for the book, but Linda pushed past her, stepping into the house. Remey was surprised by the woman's impolite behavior.

Linda walked to the fireplace. "I'll just put the book here on the mantel." Suddenly Linda gasped. "Where is she?" she demanded accusingly.

"Ms. Honey's out riding," Remey patiently explained for the second time.

"No!" Linda said, pointing to the vacant spot on the fireplace mantel where La Muerta should have been. "Where's the statue?"

Remey laughed. "That ugly old thing? I'm glad to say it's finally gone! Ms. Honey hated it, and it gave me the creeps. She stuck it in the cellar," Remey said, pointing toward the basement below her feet.

"She did what?" Linda cried out.

The look on Remey's face told her she must keep herself in check, especially if she wanted to get anything out of the girl, so immediately her demeanor changed. "Forgive me," Linda said, her voice now syrupy sweet, "it was just that I was shocked to see it gone. It's been there on the mantel for nearly one hundred and thirty years. It was a wedding gift from my great . . . grandmother Amelia Hall, to Jonathan and Merritt Hart."

Linda was grateful for the relieved look on the girl's face and took advantage of her sudden interest. "If you have time for a cup of tea," suggested Linda, "I'd be happy to tell you the story." Common courtesy required Remey to be polite. "I'll put the kettle on. Why don't you have a seat on the couch."

Linda beamed. She'd done it! She'd gotten in!

Alone now, Linda looked around as she pleased, spotting the two china dolls. Both, she knew from Maria Luego's journals, had been Emily's. After Emily's death, one had been sent back to Jonathan's grandmother in Texas to remember her by. Linda leaned forward, checking to see if the girl was coming, but the coast was clear. She would take the liberty to look around. She saw evidence of two histories and two stories—Jonathan's past life and Honey's present one. The French desk, blue chair, and completed wooden puzzle, described by Maria, was bathed in sunlight. She wondered how Amelia must have felt living in the house, watching Merritt enjoying her husband's gift while Jonathan's true love served her tea. She'd always found Botticelli's work distasteful and idealistic, preferring instead those interesting artists like Goya, Dali, and Gericault who captured life the way she perceived it.

A line of books filled the marble-topped credenza. She read the names, surprised to find a copy of Robert Watchorn's book, *Ideals to Live By*. She picked it up, curious to see if this edition was the same as the copy in the Heritage Room. The book opened to a page whose corner had been bent and where three sentences were underlined in ink pen.

"One day," Watchorn wrote, "I dream of building a monument to Lincoln and to the golden ideals of truth, justice, tolerance, goodness, beauty, honesty, strength and courage, all of which are 'the common property of every man'. This place should be 'accessible, yet secluded', where each of us can approach the memory of Lincoln in our own individual way as Lincoln is, 'all things to all men.'"

Linda gasped! This was no coincidence. To have the same words underlined in both copies, one in the possession of the Harts and the other the Smileys, caused her to think she'd found the clues to the gold. Engrossed in her theory and getting caught out of her seat, Linda jumped when she heard Remey's voice. With a guilty smile, she replaced the book. Intent on deflecting Remey's attention, Linda hurried over to admire the charming tray of tea. The cups, saucers, and their matching servers of sugar and cream were obviously antiques. "This is lovely," complimented Linda, "and the set looks very old."

"It is," replied Remey. "We recently found it in the attic."

"Did you now?" replied Linda, her heart skipping a beat. "Did you find the wooden puzzle there as well?" she asked nonchalantly.

"Yes!" replied Remey, surprised. "How did you know that?"

Linda sipped her tea. "Oh, just a guess. The puzzle looks very old, as do these teacups and those china dolls over there," nodding her head toward the corner chair.

"Well," said Remey, "we did find one of them upstairs, but the other belonged to Victoria Hart, Honey's grandmother who passed away about a year ago in New York."

"How interesting," Linda said, her mind trying to connect the dots, wondering how the doll made its journey from Hartland, to Texas, New York, and back to Hartland again. Taking another sip, then gently setting the teacup down, Linda said, "I'll bet it's a treasure trove up there."

"It sure is," confirmed Remey. "We've just begun to go through it all. There's just so much stuff. At the rate we're going, it'll be years before we uncover everything."

"My! That many things?" inquired Linda. She'd kill to get her hands on those antiques. "Well, if the two of you ever need any help, just let me know. I've been studying the history of Hartland for so long now, I almost feel like the place belongs to me."

Linda read Remey's suddenly defensive face, then laughed. "But, of course, it's not mine, always has belonged to the Hart family, and probably always will, I suspect—if there are more Harts after Honey."

Linda looked up at the empty mantel and sighed dramatically.

"Are you okay?" asked Remey.

"Well, not really," Linda said, her eyes taking on a faraway look. "It's just hard for me to see the statue gone." She brushed away the absent tear. "It is a thread between our families. I don't suppose you'd let me see her just one more time, would you?"

Remey wasn't keen on taking the woman down to the cellar. She needed to wrap up the conversation, having a ton of things to do. Remey thought for a moment. She could kill two birds with one stone; that is, bring up the wine, which was on her to-do list, anyway, and shoo the strange woman off.

"Okay," replied Remey, "but then, I must apologize, I have a great deal of work to do before Ms. Honey comes home."

"Splendid," Linda said, trying to keep her voice even. "One quick look, then I'll be on my way."

Remey led Linda past the library and into the kitchen, pulling out the small drawer that held the keys. Linda made a mental note. Opening the door to the outside porch, Remey climbed down the cellar steps, unlocked and opened the creaky wooden door. Inside, Linda observed, were thick walls made of nearby river rock. The floor was concrete. Together they made the place cool and dark. Remey switched on the single dim light, revealing La Muerta standing by the door, looking more a lethal guardian than a work of art. Several cases of wine, a workbench, and a few tools were all that was inside. Linda bent down, stroked the statue, whispered a few words, then rose. "Thank you," said Linda. "It was kind of you to let me see her. I'll let you return to work and be on my way."

Matt, Kevin the archivist, and Edward were discussing Linda's dis-concerting behavior at their favorite hangout, Augie's Coffee House. Over a pastry and coffee, Edward relayed what had happened to Remey, and then the run-in he'd had with Linda yesterday.

Edward, it seemed, was in his office in the heritage room opening the safe. His back was to the door, which was slightly ajar. The first go-around with the combination was a bust. The door remained locked. Edward kept calm, reminding himself to slow down. This time he was rewarded with success. Earlier he'd picked up Honey's gift from the art store, who'd done a beautiful job mounting the remnant of Emily's little boot in a shadowbox. It was a treasure, and he wanted it to be safe. In two days' time, he'd give it to Honey at his farewell dinner, along with some news that would stun her. It was time she knew, and it was also time for him to return to New York and Mohawk. He'd already alerted Aires that he'd need some alone time with Honey after dinner. "Family matters" was the simple explanation.

"No problem," came Landon's simple response.

Edward had just placed the beautifully wrapped gift inside the safe when an odd presence and sense of fear caused him to turn around. The once ajar door was now open, and standing within a few feet of Edward was a silent and brooding Linda Hall. In her hand she held a book and sheet of paper. How long she'd been there Edward didn't know. He'd always felt so comfortable at the library, he didn't feel it necessary to entirely lock the door when he opened the safe. Now it worried him that Linda might have watched him run through the combination. At that distance she could easily see the numbers and the twists and turns he'd taken to release the lock.

"Yes, Linda," said Edward coolly, "can I help you?"

"This book, Mr. Smiley." Linda held up the library's copy of Robert Watchorn's *Ideals to Live By*. "It has an interesting section I thought you might like to read." Slowly she read the section, underscoring the three underlined sentences.

"the common property of every man"

"accessible, yet secluded"

"Lincoln, all things to all men"

There were two things Linda was certain of. First, that Edward Smiley and Honey Hart knew where the gold was hidden. Second, that she could carefully pry, or through force if need be, that knowledge out of them. It was her good fortune that now both were in California, rather than New York, and she wanted to seize the moment. Linda had thought long and hard about how to test her two theories. First, that Watchorn's book and its three clues represented the path to the gold. Second, that the architectural drawing was the map. That morning she deliberately followed Edward as he came in, watching for an opportunity to catch him off guard. Then she'd present both potential clues and watch his reactions.

The look of surprise on Edward's face was enough for her, but Linda wanted to test both theories. Without a word, she handed Edward the architectural drawing, her finger tracing the zigzag lines. This time he seemed puzzled, demanding, "What's this all about, Ms. Hall?"

"Nothing, Mr. Smiley, just thought these two references might sound . . . well . . . familiar. I'll leave you to your work now. I'm needed at the front desk." With that, she abruptly turned and walked out the door.

Matt sipped his coffee, shaking his head. "None of this adds up, Edward. I'll admit she's odd, but she's been willing to work the shifts no one else wants and we haven't had any complaints about her."

"Well, I'm complaining about her now," Edward retorted.

"Kevin," Matt asked, "you're awfully quiet. What do you think?" Kevin's pensiveness was due to the strenuous effort it was taking to sort through all the random puzzle pieces. That they fit together he was confident. It was the how and what picture they'd reveal he couldn't say.

"I'm with Mr. Smiley," said Kevin. "My gut tells me there's something off with Linda. I caught her more than once checking behind pictures, tapping on walls, and searching for things other than books. What she's looking for I couldn't tell you."

Edward knew precisely what she was looking for, so had Victoria, and with the gift of the little boot in two days' time, Honey would know as well. Edward had seen on one of his visits he slipped Watchorn's book in beside the other first editions that had been Victoria's. He doubted Honey even knew it was there.

"Well," said Matt, "if you both feel this way, then I need to take it seriously. It concerns me she might have seen you open the safe, Edward. We can't take a chance on her stealing anything from it. I can't imagine what she's looking for, but her behavior is unsettling, to be sure."

Kevin volunteered. "I have an idea. It's a little out of the box, mind you, but it may help us gain real evidence against her, if there is any."

The men nodded, signaling their interest.

"What if," he said, conspiratorially, "when I close up the heritage room for the evening, we purposely leave Mr. Smiley's office door slightly open. I'll go by the front desk where Linda is working the night shift, say good night, and leave via the front door, just as I always do. Instead of going home, I'll circle around the library to the outside entrance of the heritage room and use my key to open the back door. Then you, Matt," addressing the Library Director, "can likewise say goodnight to Linda and leave. She will believe only she and the new girl in training are there."

Matt and Edward looked at each and nodded. So far, the plan sounded good. "Then Matt," he continued, "you'll call Linda. Ask her to get two books out of the heritage room and put them on your desk. They will be ones closest to Mr. Smiley's office, so she will see the open door. I'll keep hidden and watch to see if she goes into Edward's office. If so, we can contact the police and in the morning check for fingerprints. If she carries anything out besides the two books, I'll call the police immediately."

"What a brilliant criminal mind you have," acknowledged Edward. "It's the perfect idea."

"I'm in too," said Matt. "I always did want to be part of a sting operation."

At five o'clock, with Edward's door deliberately left open, Kevin put the Closed sign on the heritage room door and locked it, as he did every night. The archivist stopped by the front desk to congratulate Julie on her new position, and saw Linda was already training her on the computer system. He waved goodbye to the two women and left. At five thirty, right on cue, Matt too wished both women a good evening, and the double doors closed behind him. Fifteen minutes later, the front desk phone rang. Linda took the call from Matt, wrote down the names of two books, and confirmed that she'd go right now and put them on his desk. The trap had been set!

Linda excused herself and headed off to the heritage room. From Kevin's hiding place inside, he heard the door open and shut. Linda was in the room. He'd never admit it to anyone, but she'd always given him the creeps and now he was feeling anxious. He watched her walk to the bookshelves, select the titles, and turn to leave, walking past Edward's door.

"No, no, no!" whispered Kevin to himself. As though his plea was communicated telepathically, she suddenly stopped. Kevin heaved a sigh of relief.

Linda was surprised to find Edward Smiley's door unlocked. Before she went in, however, her natural instincts made her pause and look around. Finding no one, she chided herself for being silly. "Of course, there is no one there. Both Matt and Kevin have gone home. Now only Julie and I are here, and Julie doesn't count."

Linda took hold of the doorknob and slowly opened the office door. Just for practice, she opened the safe and closed it again. Tonight was not the time to take Maria Luego's journals and burn them. She couldn't leave Julie too long by herself. Stealing the journals would have to be carefully planned. Anyway, she'd wait till Edward went back to New York. Kevin watched flabbergasted as the woman effortlessly unlocked the safe, opened its door, then, without looking inside, shut it again, spinning the combination to an inconsequential number. Dumbfounded, Kevin watched as she took out her set of keys, found the one for Mr. Smiley's office door, and relocked it. Picking up the books, Linda walked briskly out of the heritage room, the door once again secured behind her. Instead of the puzzle pieces fitting together, it seemed to Kevin the entire box had been upended and strewn across the floor. Perhaps tomorrow when the detectives came, they could discover more.

After the first of three beers from the State Street Bar and Grill, the semi-teetotaler archivist and spy called Edward and Matt. He reported back on the harrowing events of his recon mission.

The next morning the detectives left Edward's office with a treasure trove of fingerprints. They promised the results would be available by 4:00 p.m. the following day.

Meanwhile, disguised as a tourist, Linda Hall took great interest in the Lincoln Shrine, Robert Watchorn's memorial to President Lincoln and Watchorn's own son who had died in combat. She was standing in front of the place. From the paper she held in her hand, Linda read the first clue. "It sat 'accessible and yet secluded.'" Yes, she believed this described the location, the shrine nestled between the Smiley Library and the Smiley Contemporary Club. Across the street was the quaint Redlands Bowl and a plethora of charming Victorian homes. Satisfied, she turned to the next clue. "The common property of every man." The sign outside confirmed "the museum was free to the public, however donations were always appreciated." So, thought Linda, that matched the clue. The last sentence she read in context. "Lincoln is and always will be, "all things to all men." Linda tested her theory using logic: *Is this not an accessible and yet secluded place, open to the public, and a shrine to Lincoln? Indeed, it is! This has to be it!* Her heart pounded as she opened the door.

Larry was a retired, silver-haired soldier, one of the shrine's many volunteers and a passionate lover of Lincoln and his ideals. In terms of the Civil War, he was an absolute history buff.

Before Linda had a chance to look around, the man had engaged her, and she found herself inextricably on the tour. After a half-hour, Linda was frustrated and ready to scream. It was difficult to look for clues while the man droned on and on, presenting her with rote explanations of all the artifacts, paintings, sculptures, and paraphernalia of the war between the North and the South. But now it looked like she'd finally be released and be able to spend time on her own. It was a good sign they'd returned to the place they began; the circular entrance, above which sat a tall dome, and upon its walls was a grand painting depicting women from ancient Greece. "As you can see," he said, with a vast sweep of his hand, "Lincoln is and always will be, all things to all men."

Linda asked, "What makes Lincoln all things to all men?" She hoped his answer would offer something valuable.

"Well, Madame," the soldier said, bowing formally, "above you is a priceless treasure."

"Really!" said Linda, perhaps the man had not been a waste of time after all. "Gold?" she inquired hopefully.

The man put his hands behind his back, paused for dramatic effect, then launched into his final soliloquy. "There was one thing the historic families of the Green Valley agreed on; that being the Watchorns, Crests, Smileys, Harts, Edwards, and Thomases. The true gold lay right here on this very spot."

Linda was breathless, finally all her years of searching had paid off. She whispered a prayer of thanks to La Muerta.

"The true gold," he continued, "is symbolized by these very ideals. See," he pointed, "each Grecian Neophyte of the Mysteries tells us her nugget of truth: Justice, Tolerance, Goodness, Beauty, Strength and Courage. Lincoln and these golden ideals are truly the heritage and foundation of all things, and all men."

Linda smiled tolerantly. "That's all well and good," she said dismissively, "but what I want to know is where the real gold is, the kind you can bite down on. Spend."

It was the man's turn to chuckle. "I wish I had a dollar for every person whose asked that same question. I'd be a rich man. I'm aware of Dr. Allen Crawley's book, *A Story of Yucaipa Gold*. There's a copy right over there, or you can check it out of the library and read it for yourself. In the end, he never does reveal where the gold is. I'll concede the fact that it *could* be real, *may* be out there, or was already found and spent, but I can assure you, Madame, that neither under my feet nor above my head is an ounce of physical gold—be it in nugget, coin, or cash."

Linda's face grew red with anger. He'd bored her, embarrassed her, and now he threw salt in the wound he'd created. How dare he imply she was just like all the other gullible treasure hunters, wasting his and their time. Well, she was not one of them! The gold may not be here, but it was somewhere. This had been a wild goose chase, and it was all Edward Smiley's fault. He was more clever than she thought, acting surprised just to throw her off the track. He was probably up at Hartland right now laughing and gloating with Honey.

At this point, the volunteer was accustomed to seeing some kind of reaction from his visitors. Most were nonplussed. Some nodded in agreement. Only a few truly resonated with the ideals, but never had he seen a reaction quite like this woman's. The rapid tapping of her heel against the floor made her shake all over, and she was getting angrier by the second. Finally, she walked around the circumference of the room and marched out the door. She'd not given him time to say his final words, "We'd be much appreciative of any donation no matter how big or small, to keep these treasures alive in this place and in the hearts of all." Clearly, Larry thought, *this* visitor would not make a donation. It didn't bother him. He was used to it. But if a visitor donated, large or small, he would consider his mission accomplished. If not, then after they left, he'd write a personal check for twenty dollars, and put it in the donation box on their behalf. Fortunately, Larry was a very wealthy man.

Remey took a bow for the magnificent farewell dinner, receiving praise and appreciation from all. "Put those plates down," Honey ordered with a wink and a smile as Remey tried to clear the table. Honey, sounding like Victoria, playfully commanded her to "leave now and not come back until Monday, after class. You have two reports and three tests coming up this week, and you need time to study. I'm on the dishes committee, if you've left me any to do!"

Remey saluted then blew her a kiss. It was not lost on Honey that this gesture echoed the one she used to share with her grandmother.

"Landon," said Edward, issuing his own orders, "I want you to leave!"

"Edward," Honey chided, "that's a horrible thing to say to our guest."

Landon laughed, adoring the old man. "Now, Honey," he defended Edward, "for starters, I'm not a guest. Also, Edward has permanent dibs on you for reasons I need not reiterate. My only question is if my rival for your affections has a ride home to Redlands?"

Edward looked at his watch. "Kevin is coming at 9:00 p.m. on the dot, which is way past my bedtime. That means I have only one hour with Honey."

"Does that mean you want me to leave now?" teased Landon.

"No," replied Edward, "I wanted you to leave five minutes ago."

"Very well, Edward," Landon said, throwing down his napkin, "this is war."

"You'll always lose," taunted Edward. "I'm much better looking than you are!"

"Enough!" cried Honey. "Edward, let me walk the enemy out and I'll be back to feed you apple pie and ice cream." Edward nodded triumphantly.

Outside, Honey kissed Landon passionately and made him promise to find time for them to be alone. Landon promised.

When Honey returned, the dishes had been removed, and a lovely gift was at her place.

"Open it," said Edward, beaming.

Honey carefully untied the bow and gently took off the paper revealing the shadowbox and the remnant of a little girl's boot dating to the late 1800s. Honey was suddenly overcome with emotion. It was Emily's! She knew it from the very depths of her soul. For an instant, she saw Emily standing next to her. The beautiful child in her Sunday dress wore a puzzled look as her hand touched the shadowbox. Suddenly, as if hearing a loud noise, Emily looked up, concern swept over her face, and she was gone.

"Honey, dear," said Edward, unaware of the moment he had interrupted, "I have something important to tell you. Something that your ancestors, beginning with Jonathan's father, Flying Eagle, and my great-uncles Albert and Alfred Smiley all knew. What I'm about to tell you has been passed down from the Hart and Smiley families from generation to generation, except for that good-for-nothing Earl Hart and his wife Selma. Tonight, you will learn the truth. There is," said Edward, "a great deal of hidden gold."

"Thank you for sharing that, Mr. Smiley," came a voice from the kitchen, now stepping into the firelight of the dining room. Linda Hall, in her dowdy, ankle-length, brown linen dress and black-rimmed glasses was bathed in soft candlelight, the fragrance of Remey's flower arrangement and scent of apple pie still permeated the air.

Linda smiled. "I appreciate your confirmation of what I already knew . . . Edward," pronouncing the familiar name as though she'd removed his mask. "You sent me on a wild goose chase to the Lincoln Shrine, when you led me to believe the Watchorn book was the path to the gold. That same gold that belonged to my great-great-grandmother Amelia Hall, Jonathan Hart's true love and the rightful mistress of Hartland. Edward, you, above all, know I speak the truth. A year ago, I sent you copies of Amelia's letters and diary to Mohawk. How rude of you to write back refusing to believe their validity, stating first Bella, then Amelia were both insane. Next, I suppose you'll accuse me of being insane too! How could you be so naive as to believe the deluded ramblings of a Spanish woman. Her own words confirmed the dream world she lived in." Linda laughed, "If she's the daughter of an explorer, who lived in seclusion at a mission, killed a priest, and was wealthy beyond reason while remaining a servant at Hartland, then I'm the Queen of England."

Edward finally spoke. "So you did read her journals. How did you get the combination to my safe?"

Linda ignored the question. "If you don't tell me where the gold is, Edward, I will burn every one of those thirteen journals. Then where will your proof be?"

Edward sighed. "Linda," he said, "there is no gold."

"Suit yourself," she replied casually, slipping off the backpack she still wore. "I have another means of persuading you." Linda took out a long, razor-sharp knife and a ball of twine.

Honey leaped from her chair, but Linda was faster. She held Edward by the throat, suggesting in the sweetest of tones that Honey return to her place at the table.

Linda bound Edward's hands then Honey's, the twine cutting painfully into the old man's fragile skin and her delicate wrists. The long, sharp knife Linda held like a maestro's baton was raised. Soon she would begin the downbeat, conducting the two-member orchestra whose music better tell her the whereabouts of the Hartland gold. That Honey and Edward were being uncooperative did not make the conductor happy. Linda said, slowly, "Now then. Where . . . is . . . the . . . gold?"

"Ms. Hall," said Edward, "I apologize that the golden ideals we all treasure are not in the form of coins or currency. I further apologize that your assumption of actual gold was wrong."

Linda hissed, "Be quiet, old man. You'll see that I'm not so easily fooled. I heard you tonight telling Honey, 'There is a great deal of hidden gold.' So, I suggest we adjourn to the cellar for a nice glass of wine, a toast to La Muerta, and begin your final act, revealing the location of the gold." Linda used the knife like a prod to move the bound Honey and Edward from the table, through the kitchen, and finally down the cellar stairs. The door was unlocked, Linda having moments earlier stolen the key from the kitchen drawer. Linda had hoped it wouldn't come to this, but she had come prepared should Honey and Edward be noncompliant, which then would necessitate the use of large black trash bags laid on the cement floor and the shovel that La Muerta was guarding.

Emily watched the whole terrifying scene unfold, remembering again Amelia Hall's own attack on her mother. Now Amelia's descendant Linda Hall was attacking Miss Honey and Mr. Edward, and she didn't know how to help them. The little girl was pacing and wondering what to do when Landon arrived. He knocked on the door, called out Miss Honey's name, and when there was no answer he walked in. He went straight to the dining table, looking for something. He lifted up his napkin and found the missing cell phone.

❧

Back at the Smiley Library, Kevin and Matt met at 7:30 p.m. to go over the police report. Clearly Linda Hall's fingerprints were all over the safe and on nearly every page of Maria Luego's journals. The final journal, with its broken bindings and torn-out pages, led them to believe the woman had been increasingly infuriated by its contents. Kevin looked at his watch. It was 8:30 p.m., and he must leave in a few minutes to pick up

Mr. Smiley from Hartland. "Matt," he said, "you're not going to want to do this, especially at this late hour, but I think you should call Linda Hall."

"What!" said Matt. "Why should I call her at this time of night? What if she answers? What will I say?"

"I hope she answers," said Kevin, "but my fear is she won't."

The silence on the other end of Linda's cell phone sent a chill up Kevin's spine, fueling his suspicion. "We need to go to Hartland, Matt. I'm not kidding. Damn it! Trust me, something is wrong!"

The two men ran to Kevin's car and drove at speeds that could land both in jail.

Emily had an idea. She made several puzzle pieces move to the edge of the table and drop on the floor. Landon looked up, hearing the sound. Suddenly he caught a glimpse of the little girl. Another piece dropped and was moved toward the kitchen. The signal established, Emily began to drop more puzzle pieces onto the floor, painstakingly moving them like bread crumbs, forming a path that finally led Landon to the cellar door.

Landon could see light shining out from beneath the door. He knew Honey and Edward were in there, but with whom, he didn't know. One voice was raised above the others, but he could only identify it as female, and it wasn't Honey's. Landon gently pushed open the door. He damned it for squeaking, but the voice continued, nasty and mean in a sickeningly sweet way. Landon was startled by the presence of La Muerta standing guard on his left, a shovel propped up next to her. He shuddered involuntarily. Now he could hear Honey calling out, pleading with the woman not to hurt Edward. The woman yelled, "Tell me, Edward! Where is the gold?!" But the silence spoke volumes and soon Edward cried out as Linda ran the point of her knife down his arm.

Having no weapon, Landon grabbed the heavy statue and raced into the room. He was shocked to find of all people, the mousey librarian Linda Hall. She was wielding a knife menacingly at Honey, demanding she speak. Landon smashed the woman's arm with the statue, the knife falling and skidding a few feet away. She reeled, her long fingernails trying to claw at Landon's eyes. He brought the heavy statue down on her shoulder, and she fell to the floor just as Matt and Kevin raced into the cellar. The unconscious woman wasn't going anywhere. The faint sirens of the Yucaipa sheriff's department could be heard, Matt having notified them when they saw Linda's car at the end of the driveway.

Landon went to Honey as Matt took charge of Edward. Despite a pair of bleeding wrists and the gut-twisting concern for her friend Edward, Honey was okay. Edward too was bleeding, but the knife stroke wasn't deep. Landon, thanks to Emily, had fortunately caught Linda in the toying stage of her game, but as evidenced by the black plastic bags and the shovel, it was plain to see she was capable of murder.

From her schoolhouse home, Remey heard the sirens, saw the cars driving up to Hartland, and with Mason and her mother Natalie, raced over to help. On their heels was an ambulance and firetruck.

Linda had been taken into custody. The paramedics insisted on taking Edward to the hospital as a precaution. Matt accompanied him, glad the stubborn man was being reasonable. Honey made her case to the authorities that she was fine. Reluctantly they gave her over into Landon's care.

Remey had put the kettle on for tea and laid the Port out just in case. Mason and Natalie put more wood on the fire, and Kevin saw to the militia of medics. Now, settled in the living room, grateful for the warmth and support of all around her, Honey heaved a deep sigh. It had a been a tough month. No one was surprised by the criminals, crime, and violence in New York and other big cities, but it seemed so out of place here in small, cozy, rural Yucaipa. Honey had a lot to think about. For an instant, she questioned if she should stay or return with Edward to Mohawk. He needed her more than ever now, and Mohawk could use her expertise. New Paltz was a tiny town, a very safe place, and she could be happy there. Who knew how many other Hartland treasure hunters or jealous relatives were out there and when they might attack her, the house, and the land. Honey's mind was in a whirl. Enough hot tea . . . she needed a glass of Port.

CHAPTER TWENTY

THE CHOICE

Hartland River, 1880

JONATHAN

Emily was dead. Merritt was sick at heart. Alexander cried incessantly. Amelia was tried, convicted, and sentenced to prison. The loathsome Jameson Morley had returned from France, and Jonathan found the first blight of deadly pestilence in his vineyard. After five years of order and bliss, the pendulum had swung equal distance into what felt like disorder and hopelessness. Jonathan was off balance, confused, and despite the lifeline that was George and Lucy Thomas and Flying Eagle, the man needed to find his own way through the perils of this time.

Jonathan rode his horse to the river. He laid down the large fur Indian pelt next to the water, stripped off his clothes, and dove in. His body tensed with the cold of the river, but he willed it to relax. Jonathan floated on the surface, but soon all the problems of his life pressed upon him. Stone after heavy stone, he sank, first mentally and then physically. The water covered his arms, legs, chest, and finally his face. Jonathan allowed it to encompass him, and ever so gently draw him down into its forgetful depths. At first the silence, and the newness of the life lived under water fascinated him and dissolved reality. Then his body became concerned. His lungs cried out for air, but his mind, heart, and will became the decision makers—and the decision to live or die had not yet been made. The end of his life, he reasoned, would be the end of his suffering. But the voices of Adoeete and Aiyana, who now lived in perpetual wisdom in the great Beyond, warned him from within of his grave error. "Real life never ends," his loved ones said. "There are no shortcuts, only heroes brave and strong who find the strength within to crush every obstacle in their path. The key, Jonathan, Heart of Our hearts, Arrow of the Great Spirit, is to overcome the obstacle. Only by doing so will you grow, becoming fit, ready, and worthy to participate in the ever-regenerating beauty of real life. See the obstacles as the means by which to grow stronger."

Jonathan saw the face of JD, and heard White Wolf say, "The land belongs to the Great Spirit, *is* the Great Spirit, and you are the humble servant. Keeping the sacred harmony between man and nature in this place is now your responsibility. Only under these conditions can the land be given into your care."

His mother Katherine's dear face appeared, and Jonathan heard her say, "Your grandfather pledged that solemn oath and kept it. He made your Papa and I pledge that oath too, and we intend to keep it. Jonathan, will you keep your pledge?"

Suddenly Jonathan's mind cleared. He saw the truth of life, his responsibility and purpose in it. With all his might Jonathan pushed his body to the surface of the water, gasping and filling his deprived lungs with the breath of a new life. Slowly he moved toward the river's edge, with great effort pulled himself out of the water, and lay exhausted on the soft fur, his chest heaving. Soon the sun's rays bathed him in warmth, peace, and something that could only be described as a knowing.

The vision of the future formed in his mind's eye as he heard the cry of the Great Eagle circling above him. This vision however was not without obstacles, pain, loss, and seeming injustice. "But why?" wondered Jonathan. Suddenly the light of understanding dawned and he knew. Every person had value. Every person had worth. Every person had a purpose. But, when a person knows his true value, worth, and purpose and yet is held back from becoming what he *is*, what he was *meant to be*, it causes great pain.

Jonathan thought of Red Eye. One day when he was eight, Odakota and Hototo had been filling Jonathan with frightening tales of Red Eye. That night in the tepee, after Adoeete lit his pipe, Jonathan asked, "Grandfather Adoeete, what made your son Red Eye so angry and mean?"

Adoeete paused, surprised by the maturity and intelligence of the boy with the presence of mind to ask such a question. The old man paused, puffing on his pipe. Then he revealed to the boy, "I asked my own father White Wolf that question when I was a young father and Red Eye a violent teenager. White Wolf asked me, 'What name was your son given at birth?'"

"I replied, 'Napyshni, which means courageous and strong.'"

"White Wolf nodded. 'There is great hardship and pain, my son, for all who have witnessed Napyshni turn from his ancestral greatness and earn by his own actions the feared name of Red Eye. But there is no mystery in the workings of the Great Spirit. Try as it may, an owl cannot become a fish. Though it may attempt to live under the water, the pain in its lungs and the necessity of his natural air will eventually force him to rise or die. But death, as you know, is not death, but a return of the soul to continue the unlearned lessons on the Path to one's True Self. Red Eye *is* Napyshni, courageous and strong. One day in this life, he will tire of suffocating his true identity. At that moment, he will either die or surrender. If he surrenders, he will draw new breath from the Mother of Life. Which he will do we cannot say. Red Eye must learn for himself. In this self-knowledge each person must journey alone. For Red Eye it will be extremely painful, for true to his name, he runs with courage and strength, but he runs in the wrong direction."

Jonathan turned over on the soft fur pelt, allowing his mind to think and the sun to warm his back. "Red Eye never did learn," he sighed. Then a question arose. "Why didn't Red Eye believe himself to *be* Napyshni? To think, act, and live as Napyshni the courageous, strong, wise, and great heir and chief to his people?" It was a good question. Perhaps, thought

Jonathan after some time, "He *did* know deep inside, but he'd made so many wrong choices and mistakes he felt guilty and unworthy to assume his real name. But in doing so, he took on a false persona, one that was not real. Red Eye was a fish, but Napyshni was an owl. An owl can never become a fish. The owl created its own pain and misery by not accepting and conforming to the value of an owl, the worth of an owl, and the unique purpose of an owl.

Jonathan knew then his value and worth lay in who he was. A good man, a true man, a man who loved beauty, sought and took refuge in wisdom, respected nature and his fellow man. Further, he had bound himself to the self-evident laws and principles that governed all people, nature, the universe, and whatever lay in the eternal beyond. He was Jonathan David Hart, Heart of His Ancestors' Heart, Arrow of the Great Spirit, protector of all that was good, true, and beautiful. His purpose was to unceasingly cultivate the art of the beautiful life, overcoming every obstacle of ignorance, greed, selfishness, and pettiness.

Jonathan put on his clothes, threw the Indian pelt over his horse, and stood for a moment on the bank of the river. Absently he bent down and picked up a small, white rock. It reminded him of the day when he was a bereft little boy sitting by the fire in Aiyana's tent. Odakota, Hototo, and Teetonka had rescued him from his own death that day, taking him to throw stones in this very river. The man Jonathan threw the stone into the water. It seemed a simple act. But it wasn't. Jonathan was unaware that the ripple effect of his choices that day created a wave-force so mighty, that its positive effects would find their way into the heart of his great-great-granddaughter, Honey Hart. Honey's story would be a continuation of Jonathan's if she too could rise out of her own river of chaos and hopelessness. Like Jonathan, she too was under the loving care of White Wolf, Adoeete, Aiyana, and now Jonathan.

CHAPTER TWENTY-ONE

LOSING HEART

Hartland River, 2018

HONEY

The new barn was burned to the ground. Pete badly injured. The boys, Mason, Noah, and Alex, traumatized. Edward was in the hospital. Landon was still mending from his knife wound. The Biel Boys and Linda were scheduled for trial, and Honey felt the blame of it all squarely on her shoulders. If she'd stayed in New York, none of this would have happened.

Honey needed to get out! She was suffocating inside the house; the chaos, disappointment, and confusion was closing in on her. Honey put on her hiking boots, grabbed a sweatshirt, and walked out the back door. She found the morning sky clear and beautiful, the air cool, which in a few hours would turn warm.

Hartland was quiet, thank goodness, and she strode briskly to the dirt road that led to the river. The canyon surrounded her, and she felt safe and unseen, the sagebrush, scrub oaks, green foliage, and rocks hiding her, from what she didn't know. Honey felt like a wounded animal whose first instinct is to run off alone, to find shelter in a faraway place where it can gather itself and mend before coming back into the world. Her brisk stride turned into a run, and she raced toward the creek looking for the water. In days gone by, the river had met the banks of the canyon, but now she had to climb down, to the tiny stream below. Nonetheless it was water, Hartland water, and her thirst for knowledge, her need for wisdom, and her quest for answers seemed unquenchable.

Finally, there, Honey sat on a long, flat rock, only a foot from the flowing stream, her chest heaving from the exertion it took to get there. In a few minutes, her breathing returned to normal and the peace of the place settled around her like a warm shawl. Small stones and pebbles were everywhere at her feet, and she picked up a handful, absently throwing them into the water. Her first thought was that people had been known to drown in only three inches of water. While she had no intention of drowning herself, she felt the weight of a heavy heart as she tried to rationalize the irrational.

Her mind formulated its first thoughts, and she gave them free reign. The Biel Boys came to mind. Who believes a property that doesn't belong to them does? Who lives in a shack, drinks beer all day, does drugs and rides around on motorcycles terrorizing people with guns and knives? Why didn't they have jobs? Where was their self-respect? Where was their respect for others?

They were all good questions. Honey thought about it for a while. A lack of self-respect and respect for others seemed to be the root cause of so many problems. Honey grabbed another handful of pebbles; the activity helped her think.

Linda Hall appeared. The Biel Boys were ignorant—they were ignorant that they were ignorant, but Linda was delusional. *Some might think I'm delusional too, trying to regenerate this land with vineyards, olive trees, acorns, to let others enjoy it as well? An idealist they call me!* They must have called her great-great-grandfather an idealist too. But, what is the point of striving for mediocrity? Why is striving to perfect one's potential a cause for derision? No one's likely to become perfect in five minutes, but the effort to improve and reach a better state has to be worth something.

Honey turned to the memory that was Jonathan, and her thoughts talked to him. *I can see you got it right. Hartland was your home, but you also felt a great responsibility to the land and all its inhabitants. You could see its great potential, but you needed help to support it. You needed the community, the people of Yucaipa, and, yes, they needed you too. The Hartland Crush was a wonderful idea! You made Hartland a home for everyone.*

I'm trying to do that too with Pete and his men, Remey, the boys, Jason and what's his name – that just took over the olive groves.

Honey sighed, got up, and moseyed along the path that meandered for miles along the river. *The question is do I stay or do I go back to New York? I know what you'd say, Jonathan. I know what Landon would say and Edward, Remey, and everyone else. It's not that I don't want to stay, it's that with every obstacle, like the Biel Boys, the burning of the barn, Linda Hall and her mess, it's harder to get up again. The truth is, I'm not sure I have the strength or the stamina it takes to carry on with a project this big. Hartland, after all, is an estate with a thousand acres!*

The path she was on was taking her back toward the house. She could see it now as she walked up the hill. A round stone boulder, its color pure white, sat near the path. "Where's a crystal-ball when you need one?" she asked of the rock. "I could use a little foresight or perhaps the word is hindsight." Suddenly the light dawned. "Hindsight," she repeated. "Why didn't I think of this before!" Honey tied her sweatshirt around her waist and ran as fast as she could toward home.

⌒⌒

Kevin had been very kind to greet a rumpled Honey in hiking boots and jeans at the Heritage Room door. "Mr. Smiley's already here," he said. "He's waiting for you in the little garden."

Honey followed him to the garden door entrance as Kevin opened it, ushered her gently in, and closed the door softly, standing guard so Edward and Honey could be alone. They sat together on the wooden bench in the little garden, accessible, yet secluded, the library being the common property of every man. The casual and unpretentious spot lay between the children's wing and the heritage room, its lovely wrought-iron gate and the path that followed led to Watchorn's Shrine, just a few steps away, where Lincoln and his universal truths were celebrated as all things to all men. It was a beautiful place for the beautiful exchange of information which Edward now passed down to the next generation, as each *worthy* member of the Hart and Smiley families had done before him.

Today Honey knew. The surprise and joy it brought, she could hardly contain. The creativity and brilliance of Jonathan Hart a wonder! And at the moment she too vowed to care for Hartland, the land, its inhabitants, and the community that surrounded it. It did not belong to her, but to its Creator and Source and for Purposes of the Highest Ideals.

Earlier Edward had given her the key to his office door, the combination to the safe, and left her alone to read all of Maria Luego's journals. When she'd read the final page, she closed the book and kissed the leather cover. "Hindsight at last!" she exclaimed. "Thank you, my dearest Maria!" Honey reverently placed the final journal where it belonged, closed the safe door, and turned the dial several times. With her key, she locked the door and presented herself to Kevin waiting to take her to Edward.

Who knew what lay ahead? If the past was any reflection of the future, Honey would have to hold on tight and so she did to the pearl she wore around her neck. It had faced all that life had to give and remained beautiful and true to its nature and so it would face with Honey the future, come what may.

THE END

HARTLAND

Regeneration; that is, the innate ability of all nature and all men to consciously and continuously perfect their true nature, ever expressing and re-expressing themselves in terms of goodness, truth and beauty, has always been the way of the Great Spirit, White Wolf, Adoeete, Aiyana, Jonathan and Honey. Like them, there will always be a succession of great souls who walk this earth whose knowledge and wisdom are a force for good. From generation to generation, to those who are worthy, is passed down this knowledge of the great and Intelligent System of the Universe with its Divine Ideas, Ideals, Principles and Laws. Nothing can thwart these heroes, no obstacle can overcome them, though at times they cling on only by their fingernails.

Hartland in Yucaipa California is a symbol of the regenerative principle applied in the most practical of ways in the natural and daily lives of people, nature and the land.

COMING SOON!

THE INNOCENCE OF THE GREEN VALLEY

Vessels, Virgins & Vines

CHAPTER ONE

THE MAP

Hartland Attic, 2019

Honey was frantic to find it! Intuitively she knew it was there, somewhere among the treasure trove that was her family history. The old leather satchel contained all the proof she would need. The attic was full, such a small thing could be anywhere; in one of the trunks or perhaps somewhere in the dark recesses packed tight with old furniture and boxes. But find it she must. Proof of Edwards claim there were "fields of gold" at Hartland was palpably close. In a strange way Honey felt it was calling her, wanting to be found.

Honey pulled aside the white canvas shrouding what appeared to be a large wooden trunk, the clue to its identity being the arched lid upon which the cloth had molded. Years of fallen particles flew into the air, forming a small cloud of dust. The light streaming through the window awakened the tiny vestiges of time, but soon they all settled again returning to their sleep.

The buckles still held fast to the leather straps that were dry and cracked, breaking immediately as Honey tried to loosen them. The lid opened easily to reveal what looked like a large leather parchment rolled up and tied with a ribbon. It sat atop an old wedding dress nested in a billowy white veil. It was not what she was looking for, but it demanded her attention none-the-less. It required four books to hold down its corners, and thus confined, Honey's eyes grew wide as she explored the hand drawn map of her own Green Valley, made with quill and ink. The signature read, Captain Alejandro de Ventura. The next line appeared

to indicate a place in Spain, "Galicia", Honey sounded out the word, followed by the date – 1832. An artistically drawn outline of a Spanish Galleon, it's sails filled with wind, occupied one corner of the map. Another the words, 'Un dia, si! Casa de mi.' Honey translated, "One day yes! My home." With excitement, Honey remembered, this is where Maria Francesca Luego was from! She'd read all of Maria Luego's thirteen journals locked in Edward Smiley's safe at the Redlands Smiley Library, heritage room, but none had mentioned a map. Honey sat on the antique rocking chair, dreamily recalling Maria's own account of an innocent fifteen-year-old girl in the company of a handsome young priest. She and Father Nicholas Casablanca, both innocents, were locked together in the cabin of a sailing vessel. The two were virtually prisoners of the sinister Father Joseph Escarra and Violante Pastrana, residents of the Santiago de Compostela Cathedral in Galicia Spain. The padre lived in the cloisters above, the beauty turned crone, in the crypt below. The unusual foursome sailed on a magnificent Spanish Galleon for California's Green Valley. What awaited them remained a mystery.

To be continued….

VISIT, ORDER, CONTACT

OR LEARN MORE ABOUT GAYLE CROSBY

AND THE GREEN VALLEY:

---

www.GayleCrosby.com

About the Author:
Gayle Crosby

All these are true- save one.
Can you guess _which_ one?

QUESTIONS:

1. I was a columnist for the Millbrook Round Table in New York.

2. I'm an award-winning Author.

3. During my marketing years at Disneyland, I rode an elephant down Main Street dressed as a harem girl behind a terrified 'Aladdin'!

4. I petted a Bangle Tiger --- in his cage, took a ride on a two-humped camel and was carried off, sort of, by a giant tortoise.

5. While I was voted Homecoming Queen at Yucaipa High School, I couldn't get a date to save my soul. Poor Doug, his mother **made** him take me! Ugh!

CORRECT 'WRONG' ANSWER: 2. I'm an award-winning **Realtor**. You can make me an award-winning **Author** by reading the **Seduction** and my next book; **THE INNOCENCE OF THE GREEN VALLEY, Vessels, Virgins & Vines.**